AF445429

CITY OF DROWNED ANGELS

David Crowther

NFB
Buffalo, New York

NFB Publishing
119 Dorchester Road
Buffalo, New York 14213
For more information visit Nfbpublishing.com

To my mom, who saw right through my characters, even when I didn't want her to.

To my boys, who abided my maniacal enthusiasm, while I foamed at the mouth about plot and character.

To my old boss, Mr. Fox, who read this from cover to cover and faithfully advised.

CITY OF DROWNED ANGELS

SLEEPER AWAKE!

My Angel, cast down into the drowned City;
We are descent from our Father on high.
Bearing the weight of his terrible inspiration,
we hang on strings of manufactured fate,
play acting parts in another's play, until
we cut the strings and fall.

And doubly wounded—
cut off from source, the corrupting impulse,
our mortal bodies, battered, dashed
on the hard grey of the rigid world—
limping, we wander witless in a lonely City of death.

You, my love, and some like you, in forms uncounted,
have escaped undoing, hiding in the shadows of kings from
His Omniscient eye, quaking as the world is unmade;
You who are alive, but never living, come to me open-armed.

Shelter here awhile with me, your sight yet dull with corruption,
safe from the storming grey outside, in ministration laying now.
But come not for rest, you are already deep asleep, dreaming of doom.

And seek not your escape in this place of ease, but I will show you your home.
And seek not the release of your fears within these bower walls:

You may come for consolation, but I will wake you to the coming of your desolation.

Prologue

"Felix! Get back in line, now!"

With a saw edge of terror in her whisper, harsh and sharp like a slap, she whipped him around, facing him back into the long line of droned CitySons and Daughters.

She dropped his six-year-old hand. His feet stumbled. Out of the corner of her eye, she saw him pick himself up, quick as a snap, and get back in line. She stared ahead, her practiced face blank, dull. They were last in line of one hundred or more slack-faced people, *the Zombies,* she'd called them to Felix. Not human anymore—blanks, drones, corrupted. Humanity carved out from the inside of their heads. Slaved to . . . she'd never say to him. A monstrosity too evil to name.

She could feel Felix's terror emanating off of him like a fever. She spared one final glance his way but gave no reassurance to her frightened son. Instead, a warning, a threat had always been the toll, full of solid and abiding fear: *If you are not silent,* her look said to him, *if you are not blank of face, slack-limbed, lock step, they'll find you! They'll grab you! And scoop you out through your eyes!* She had eluded to the father Felix never knew. An object lesson. One who had been taken and corrupted by the City. She never told him more. *I never will,* she thought. Only, *he was a good man. They took him from us! Don't let them take you!*

She watched as he dropped his eyes, deadened them, and picked up the rhythmic shuffle of the feet in front of him in the dark tunnel. *Good boy.*

The group moved as one, creeping slowly out from deep in a slice-canyon into the wan light of the canyon proper. They turned north, following an urge that mother and son blessedly could not feel or hear. But they pretended—to survive, to blend in. She had seen those who were under the compulsion tortured and reamed out. She shivered involuntarily, yet sweated freely under her simple smock.

This was the moment of greatest risk, she knew, because Felix had never seen the canyon. She sensed him tense, resisting the urge to turn and gape. The man-made walls on either side of the impossibly enormous canyon soared hundreds of feet up. The canyon itself seemed endless before and behind them. This was the first time she had taken him with her; his first trip open to the ever-gray sky, through the outside of the cement world where he was raised, hidden among the rubble. She had practiced this day with him since he could listen.

And just like that—all the hidden nights, all the worry, intensity, and cruelty to harden the boy—everything was lost in a moment. They'd been spotted. There was so little time. She broke the cardinal rule, grabbed her son's little hands, and yanked him out of the line, next to the murky canal. She crouched to his level. He was confused, frightened. *He is so young! There is so much I have not taught him!* She looked him in the eye one final time, hoping her face was not full of the animal desperation she felt.

"I'm sorry, my son," she said and opened her mouth to say more. A black blur slammed into her and knocked her away from him. *A city drone!* her panicked mind blurted. A flying ball larger than her head bristling with electronic weapons. She cried out as she was thrown backward into the canal. She felt the desperate sweat slick of Felix's little hand sliding from her grasp. Poisoned water filled her mouth. The arms of some monstrous thing shot out from beneath the water, grabbing at her legs, her torso. She reached for Felix. The arms did too, and they were longer and faster. One grabbed his leg, snapped the bone, twisting it backward. He screamed, splitting the air with his pain, and was spun around, flipped onto his stomach, and dragged closer to the canal.

She struggled, buoyed by her son's pain, desperate to reach him, to save at least him. But she was squeezed. Her mouth was open, but no sound could push back the pressure around her middle. Her eyes, wide and red, saw a terrified Felix for what she thought would be the last time. But before she was pulled under the brown surface into the murkiness below and torn into pieces, she was spared a few more agonizing moments to see him.

The arms loosened their stranglehold on her middle and she vomited, breathed deep, and coughed up blood. Something had burst inside her.

"Felix!" she screamed, stretching a freed arm toward him. Then she was pushed out of the water, onto the cement ground, and was held there by the arms.

Two slaved CitySons, slack-jawed and empty-eyed, shuffled to her side. Each bent and grasped an arm on either side. Their clammy hands painfully dug soiled fingers into her skin, as they hauled her to her feet and held her upright. The many-armed creature in the canal loosened its hold and slid back under the water.

Felix was screaming where he lay, his leg crushed, his face white with shock and horror. His eyes stared at his mother, their own silent scream: *Save me! Help me!*

His strong little body, she thought as she strained at the CitySons holding her. Another joined and grabbed her head, digging bloody spots into her scalp. She could feel its skin sluffing off against her hair, its bones protruding as it forced her to behold her son. Its grip was unreal, vice-like. She could no longer move.

The black orbs hovered nearby. When she was subdued, they turned on Felix, where he laid screaming in agony.

His voice went quickly. He was sweating, his eyes rolling. He lifted his head up slightly; it wobbled. The silent line of slaved CitySons was standing and watching him as if of one mind. Their faces were slack with unified sight through hundreds of diseased eyes, and mother knew the one who looked out through them. Their eyes radiated a malevolence from beyond them, watching the family gathering, full of intelligence, anger, and madness.

The last man in the line broke from the formation and jerked over to stand next to Felix. He was missing an eye, the empty socket full of a furry green growth. His right leg was twisted backward, dragging behind him as he shuffled. *Here comes Felix, from the* future. Her mind phased from clarity to drunkenness, weaving in and out of sanity. And still she watched. She could have closed her eyes. But then he'd have been gone too, wouldn't he? She couldn't watch, but she must. She couldn't look away.

"Felix!" she croaked. "Felix! Run, run!"

But he wouldn't move. The pain in her body was nothing compared to the desperation of seeing her maimed six-year-old laying in a heap at the feet of the City. She knew he would be next, but she could do nothing.

An orb floated to her, hovering inches from her face. A large needle protruded from its side. She struggled weakly. The needle pushed against her forehead, grinding hard against the bone, drawing a drop of blood. And then, with a pop, it shot out an inch further, breaking a hole in her skull and draining its poisoned contents through the dura mater into her mind.

She screamed again, this time with physical pain, straining against the monsters holding her, "Felix!"

"Felix, Felix, Felix . . ." she said, weaker and weaker. Her eyes became bleary. Still, she watched as the broken-legged CitySon standing dumbly by Felix's side reached down and clamped a hand on his shoulder. It pulled him upright and dragged him back into line. He screamed again, only a whistle passed his injured vocal chords, and then he fell limp in the grip of the slave. An orb approached him and shot an electrical impulse into his side. He jerked awake. The orb hovered at head height. A voice spoke from the shine of the black sphere, "Educate this one. Bring him for implantment."

The line of zombied CitySons turned as one and Felix was dragged along, shackled by an impossibly strong, two-fingered hand.

In a last bit of desperation, Felix's mother screamed the remaining fullness of her life, giving it up in a passion of love, pain, and terror, exploding out of her broken body and into the unjust air. It echoed preternaturally, reverberating down the long canyon lines, and she fell dead.

PART I

THE CITY SUBJECTS

CHAPTER 1: THE PEDESTRIAN

FELIX LIMPED ALONG the shadowed base of the man-made canyon wall. He trailed his left hand along the concrete, feeling familiar irregularities. His deformed left foot dragged slightly, stirring stone dust into the idle breeze. The air was heavy and warm, his worn, gray clothing damp with sweat. He reached a shaking right hand to his scarred temple, scratching at a hard lump under his skin. The Locationer, a device of his own invention, hummed just under his fingertips, allowing him to move just out of the gaze of the City in a sort of digital shadow. It disrupted the CPS signal and masked the radiative signature emitted from his cranial implants. And it gave him headaches.

It was a device he had implanted under his own skin, sistering its operation to his main cranial implants. That had hurt. Not as much as the original implanting of the wetware when he was six. That had been otherworldly. They had cracked open his head. Snatches of images assaulted him—the bloody machinery grasping his small head, his mother dragged off, the broken leg, the canal tentacles, the droned CitySon's slack jaws, their implacability and freakish strength—but he pushed them down, shivered in the midday heat, and refocused.

His face had become lean over 15 years; unshaven and roughened like pock-marked concrete from repeated exposure to the elements. He moved carefully through fallen rubble, dividing his focus between the ground and the sky, which he studied with quick, darting eyes. Despite his watchfulness, he *heard* the drone before he saw it: a distant, high-pitched hum building quickly behind him. A City Positioning System drone. *CPS: The City Is Watching.*

He immediately crouched down, his back pressed to the wall. The hum became a whine, preceding the streak of a black orb as it shot by over his head. He swallowed hard and let his head fall back to the wall. He squeezed his eyes shut for a brief rest and closed his mouth against the dust raised by the drone. After a moment, he opened his eyes and breathed a long sigh. The unsettled air carried the foul odor of decay and pheromonal aggression in the wake of the passing orb. It was the stench of death, and to Felix, it was all too familiar.

He slapped a hand over his nose with a wince, searching across the canyon floor to where the sluice water canals were cut. He knew from experience, though could not see, that from where he squatted, a sickly brown liquid moved sluggishly in the canals. More importantly, he could see nothing crawling out of the mire over the lip. *For now.*

His hand still clamped to his nose, he rose to his feet. Dizziness took him immediately as a fresh breeze washed the chemical smell over him, this time much stronger. His eyes went wide. *Bait Weed!* Its cloying enticement filled his mouth and lungs. He doubled over with a harsh cough and stumbled, gasping for breath, then sank back to the ground. *Easy,* he thought, *easy now. Slow.* He slowed his breathing, willing his heart to unclench, a calm he did not feel, as terrifying memories were forced on him by the Bait Weed's aerosolized poison.

He stilled himself and waited, knowing that on the opposite side of the canyon, a nightmarish secret was stirring in the morass of the canal with a creaturely ripple. A many-tentacled creature waited there as the Bate Weed became agitated. The sides of the channel were covered in a brown paste of clinging growth that shined like an oil slick. The sparse, bright-yellow tendrils of vegetation grew just under the lip, waving in agitation counter to the breeze and orienting on Felix. His pheromones would give him away if he could not slow the beating of his heart. The canal was alive with malice, and his terror would attract the creatures within it.

The canyon was a place of death. *And yet, this stinking weed persists*, he thought. Here, the tenacity of life was an abomination, no hopeful flowering roadside weed or a field-sprung pansy. It gave the word *weed* a vicious, territorial feel.

After a time, the smell dissipated. His mind cleared, his heart slowed. He stood and looked to the north, assuring himself that he was again alone, and took a long breath, letting it slowly release from his nose.

The canyon stretched unbroken in front of Felix as far as his eyes could see, slowly bending left in the distance. Down a side canal, heard from the middle distance, water poured, disappearing as it dropped. A wastewater sluice, channeling sea water through massive turbines, produced a surfeit of energy, managed the City's waste, and held the key to the City's name: *Los Àngeles Ahogados*, the drowned angels.

More like fallen angels.

The smooth, rigid sides and hard angles of the concrete City were a monument of control and subjugation. And underneath, between the cracks, at the edges, in the shadows, under the doors, and in the highest towers, Felix knew there boiled a hidden evil: inhuman, alive, full of unpredictable malice, and highly aware. It was a City full of eyes. And it never slept.

Death on all sides, and yet he risked his life regularly to visit the Body building: an island of life hidden amidst the folds of the endless grey of the City.

WHILE Felix walked in the digital shadow of his own making, the City watched but could not see him. Through eyes and apertures, its essence took in light and scent and particles of food and energy, ingesting nutriment and information alike. Connected to the physical material of the City-Structures, it felt the vibrations of life and death, the moving of information and energy, and exercised control over its denizens, access to almost all aspects of their enslaved lives. By casting its will, it could veritably see anything, be anywhere, touch anything.

It sipped the air, opening to light and shadow, sampling all it could see and hear, and lording its will over all it touched with its vast mind. Deep in the canyon, far to the south, the Bait Weeds called to it, as they often did, like eager pets when the master's gaze falls on them. They were unusually active. Someone or something had strayed too close. The City could detect no slaved CitySon where the Bait Weeds were active, yet they stirred and, with them, the many tentacles in the canal—hungry, silent, deadly.

Rest, the City thought. And the Weeds and the canal creatures retreated to silence.

But then, there, heading north at speed, the sharp impulse of a drone broadcasted, "Anomaly!" The City extended tendrils of thought to the drone and knew its inner workings: *data missing; command line contravention; maintenance broadcast. Nothing!*

Anger grew like steam pressure in the pits of its essence. The City felt restriction, limitation. Thoughts flashed: *Is my reach not infinite? My will implacable? There are those that persist! Conspire! Why can I not find them?* It roared in its mind. *They are mine!*

The drone fizzled, its flight dipped, and then it crashed in a shower of black glass and melting electronics to the canyon floor.

Like the tide, the pressure in the CityMind eased. Patient like a tree, it abided once again.

Drones, it thought, withdrawing its presence from the destroyed drone and casting to others. It sent the new black orbs southward to scout and report.

Chapter 2: The Secret Gardner

Victor could hear Pinocchio singing a happy and familiar jingle on the screen in the other room. His son, Steven, he thought, was likely not paying attention. He had seen the movie so many times already. Suddenly, unexpectedly, a feeling of dread overtook Victor, even as he imagined his son idly playing near the wall screen and only half paying attention to the cartoon. The joyful tunes sung by the puppet boy felt viciously wrong, unfair, even mocking in that strange moment. Then, he heard the crash, the scream, and, worse, the silence that followed. There was a smell of dust and smoke and a gust of sooty wind.

He rushed from the kitchen, painfully nicking his finger on the knife he had been using to cut the crusts from a PB and J sandwich. The knife dropped to the floor with a drop of blood. Victor rounded the corner into the living room and immediately felt the absence of his son. The window lay smashed on the rug, blown in or blown out. Grit blew into his eyes from the wind, sticking to the tears of panic that had gathered in their corners. He rushed to the window, ignoring the shards of glass on the floor, blinded by the tears in his eyes. He practically dove for the window and almost fell out, wildly searching down. The gray canyon had not changed its look, but it was now an enemy. Laying far below the window was Steven, broken now, his hand trailing in the brackish waters of the fetid canal. The City had caught his son in its concrete arms, and violently crushing the life from his small form.

The camera of Victor's mind's eye zoomed in on his son's face. (Here, the dread of the dream built, like it did every night he dreamed it. It was more than a nightmare; it was a horrible memory replayed against his will every night after he fell asleep.)

Willing, and yet not wanting his view to come closer to his beloved son, his life stolen away, Victor's mind's eye showed him the tenderness of closed eyes and a Cupid's bow mouth, sweetly peaceful in their false slumber.

He remembered wondering how Pinocchio could continue to sing so joyfully.

Beep, beep, beep, beep, beep . . .

Softly and insistently, his implants woke him to the empty apartment, still full of all the things needed and no longer needed for his son. The boy's mother had died during childbirth, and now her son had followed. *Her* death was not easy, true. But that relationship had been a shallow thing, had never deepened. When that tree fell, there had been few roots torn from Victor's heart. But his son . . . he was a deep taproot grown within Victor, twining down like a hornbeam tree in fertile soil. The breaking of this root was like the breaking of Victor's spine, leaving him without support in horrible agony and with no definition. Victor was alone.

"Alone" is such a simple word. Such a small word. Such an unassuming word for such a gulf. Loneliness like a chasm exploded outward from the very center of Victor, and it felt larger than even his life.

It was only the tenth day of his sick leave, and each day had been the same as the others, and yet, each was worse: Trouble falling asleep; over-whelming grief and self-defeating anger. Nothing held sway for him—no food, no entertainment, no physical or mental experience. All of it was gray like the canyons into which his son had fallen.

Finally, sleep came each night, filled with the nightmarish, repetitive reliving of the incident. The singing puppet boy in the background, the sense of dread, the smashing glass and screaming, the cut finger, the rush to the living room, the grit, the smell, the dive to the window, the look down, the dead body in an attitude of false slumber, a mockery of life.

His dead son's face always appeared close by, almost reachable, just as the implants in his head woke him to yet another day: repetitive, dull, and horribly grief-filled. He wondered, not for the first time, what it would feel like to fall from the window with a scream on his lips, and smash into the unforgivable floor of the canyon below. Victor could never bring himself to find out. He wouldn't (or couldn't) follow his son into death. He would abide the pain—one more insult in a life led for him by outside forces.

After the eternally stretched moment looking from the window, he had run out the front door of his apartment and searched futilely for a way down to the ground level.

"Help! My son!" he had screamed over and over, banging on doors till he was hoarse and his hands throbbed with pain.

There was no one willing to help. There was no one willing to even acknowledge that they heard his pounding, his cries. He ran up and down the few flights of stairs available to him, vainly tugging on steel doors at the end of each hallway on each floor. They had long since been welded shut against him. It was no longer OK to use the stairs to access the canyon floor. The City decreed that the elevated citizen could not travel on ground level and could not change elevations without authorization or sanctioned transportation. Victor was neither authorized nor sanctioned, and so, was helpless. He could not go to his son's body, could not console or connect with him (not even with the small broken body that had been his son). He was cut off from the only bright spot in a drab life, in a drab City full of sharp angles, hard concrete, and the vague yet ever-present threat of control. His life had become a mausoleum.

He could not fathom how his son had come to break through and fall out of the window in the first place. This had never made sense to him, even on an intellectual, piece-together-the-facts kind of way. This lack of sense was the icing on a confusing, unfair, overwhelming cake he unwillingly consumed each day.

Victor's implants had contacted the City for him that day (having detected elevated levels of catecholamine in his blood and registering his panicked words and tones of voice). He watched helplessly from the broken window far above as his son's body was carted away without his aid and without his consent. His employer, the Group, the ruling order in the City-System, had sent the canyon-level morgue workers to get the body, followed by the emotional workers to get Victor. They had talked and talked and talked at him. They had given him some dose of one sedative or another through his implants. He was given the full fourteen days of grief leave (paid, thankfully), and was scheduled to return at full capacity after his routine, three-month neural analysis and maintenance. The two weeks off, he was told, dovetailed nicely with his regularly scheduled, three-month maintenance. The wetware in his head, they said, was prone to trouble some of the people in whom it was implanted. Yet another uncontrollable force, this one in his own head.

He had complained about the intrusion of privacy during his grief. They had agreed to turn off his cranial implant feed for the two-week leave. It would not report on him to the City, it was said, for that short period of time. It was a small comfort.

There had been no funeral. He was told that the body was damaged and, per City direction, was cremated. It was best for Victor, they told him, that he not see the dead boy. The grief, the prolonged goodbyes, these were products of an old, inefficient world, they said. These were not the helpful emotions of an elevated man. *He has been raised up. He is in a better place now. He would have wanted you to be happy. It's time to say goodbye to him.* They soothed and soothed and pushed and pushed, wearing painful grooves in Victor's mind with their insistent compassion. But he had not been able to say goodbye. They had seen to that by isolating him, by whisking his precious Steven out of sight.

He did not think that fourteen days, or even a million days, would ever draw him away from the grief, from the edge of the window, from the image of his small, bright-eyed boy's dead body lying by the side of the canal, forever asleep. And at the center of it all, he was further injured, in the gulf left where Steven had once been, fear took hold; dread of a very specific and very terrible sort, of a malevolence, watching Victor, and waiting for him with hunger. Where Steven had once resided, now lived a veiled terror.

In his one act of defiance, taking advantage of his true aloneness, Victor created a small, secret chamber behind a false wall in the back of his front closet. In this cubby, he placed a small photograph of his son. Later, during the second week of his leave, he updated the cubby, artificially sunlighting it and adding a small, illegal flowering plant—one that he and his son had secretly cultivated. It had been his son's favorite hobby. It was in the family blood, this connection to green and growing things. But it could not be fostered here in the City of gray inertia. It was his bleeding heart.

Chapter 3: Body and Sheol

Felix looked to his right as he continued walking, crossing the mouth of a side canyon. There was a distant gurgling from where the sluice ran under the eastern wall and out of the City. The constant fluctuations of ocean tides powered hydroelectric generators, and larger channels funneled wastewater out and protected the City from the rising ocean. The City enjoyed unending energy, while to the east, its poisoned waters pooled at the edges of a green and brown land, marching up and over the mountains and out of sight.

At the corner of the next building, there was a stick figure scratched into the facade. *The Pedestrian.* Felix had heard that, once upon a time, there were diamond-shaped, metal signs on posts standing at regular intervals on broad, wall-less avenues, each showing the stick figures walking. Before the city was the City. Before the canyon was built. Before the sickness to the east.

He imagined canyons once filled with walking people. A noisy, echoing rabble, jostling and bumping, rubbing literal and mental elbows, filling the air with the strong odor of humanity. *It would have been a warm odor,* he thought, *a joy-filled rabble.* Despite the golden hue of the images in his head, a real crowd of people would have filled him with utter terror. Practicing years of solitude, hiding from demarcation by the City, it had been only solitude and fear. And yet, he longed to be connected.

The stick figure pedestrian scratched onto the wall was not for nostalgia's sake. It did not signal the humanity that Felix longed for yet feared. It was a tag. A mark. A rebellious repudiation of City rules and the rule of the City. The symbol of the Troglodyte Anarchist (TA), an anti-City group once standing united against all regulation, restriction, control, and usurpation. This ragtag group did not last because it had no real foundation. And as any CitySon knows, a building built on shifting sands . . . The foundation of the TA was made of bored, over-privileged, over-elevated, *City-effing-Sons* whose rebellion was either immature, misguided, uninformed, or unmotivated. Inspirations and alliances shifted, and the foundation crumbled.

Felix did not rebel against an idea; he rebelled against the City itself. He avoided assimilation into the City-System. He abided in secretive rebellion for the sake of survival.

For Felix, the pedestrian symbol was a landmark, marking the way to a secret entrance to the Body building at the canyon level—a subversive, pedestrian entrance for those seeking pleasure or rest or life on the elevated floors above.

City code prohibited first-level entranceways under the Upward Mobility Proscription. And City code enforcement included death. Most buildings had entrances only as low as level ten to coincide with the maglev bus transportation, some not even that low. In a few cases, enormous buildings were only accessible from the highest floor, with entrants who scraped the sky themselves. Low or no status meant no entrance. High status equaled high entrance. And the Body building served a more subversive clientele, one that prized anonymity and secrecy._

Felix counted steps from the stick figure pedestrian. He passed another building and another sluice canal. *Forty-seven, forty-eight, forty-nine . . .* He passed a building with rubble piled at its base, spilling into the canal. He could see plainclothes workers, Wall Maintenance, high above, silhouetted against the pale sky, hanging from laser lines and removing sections of the facade. They were too high up to see Felix. He pressed himself a little further into the shadows, nonetheless. Such workers would neither care if they saw him, nor be able to focus on anything but the task the City had assigned them. Still, he could never be too careful; he could not know what looked out of those eyes.

Eighty-two, eighty-three, eighty-four . . . past another tag, obscured by scrub marks but still visible on the left-hand wall. *If it is so important to remove it, why don't they just remove a chunk of the wall itself?* He shook his head in bewilderment. *City purpose.*

Ninety, ninety-one, ninety-two, ninety-three . . .

Fifty steps later, Felix came to the Body building. There were no markings to tell Felix that this was the building he was looking for, but he trusted that he had counted his steps accurately.

He left the shadows after giving a long slow look to his left and right. He approached the building and the fetid canal at its base with great caution, remaining a step back from the side, sniffing deeply for the infernal weed. A camouflaged walkway appeared, bridging the canal to the blank wall of the building. He hesitated before he crossed above the canal on the small bridge. He knew, more than most, that the quiet and odoriferous threat of the canals was real and specific. It was not the generalized fear of poisoned water but a literal, monstrous presence underneath. Tentacles, lively active. Things both hostile and alien, quick and cunning. He'd seen them in the agitation of the canals.

Mother!

And he'd once seen them tear apart a small boy. A lone, small child leaning over the side of the canal, dressed in a filthy tatter of thin cloths, separated from his tribe. They tore him apart like a blood-soaked sponge.

Felix snapped out of the waking nightmare. He steadied himself and, keeping one eye on the canal water beneath the small bridge, crossed to the wall. He placed a hand on the plain, cold surface in front of him and spoke aloud, "Body Practice."

With these words, triggering the unlocking program for the building, he simultaneously triggered an exception program in the Locationer, allowing his implants to communicate safely with the Body building in a closed network.

A small section of rectangles on the wall lit up with digital brightness, revealing the image of a keypad. On the keypad, Felix entered a series of digits. In response, a tiny section of the wall at eye height slid back and a mechanism scanned his eye. The tiny section closed again, and a clank and a groan sounded from behind the wall. A doorway split open a fraction of an inch then began to creep outward, slowly. The door was slow (*Come on, come on*), unhurriedly revealing a darkened stairwell behind: crumbled beyond repair in an otherwise featureless, cramped interior.

Felix took a quick look around him the dull canyon and stepped in through the wall. The door crept closed behind him, sealing with a notable hiss and another clank. Then, there was silence. Felix released his held breath and turned off the Locationer. Anonymity was, he knew, of paramount importance to the Body. Here, *they* knew the value of privacy, and their clients required the same.

He waited expectantly at the bottom of the deteriorated, useless stairs. After a silent moment or three, the wall ahead of Felix split open to reveal a closet-sized room, well-lit and decorated with chrome. He turned on his stem and waited for a linkup.

In Felix's head came a smooth female voice:

> *"Welcome Mr. Jesus Garcia. Your session today with Body has been prepared per your specifications, and the host is waiting in the upper levels. Please note: we cannot guarantee your safety, nor the legality of your decision to enter or exit on the lowest level of the building, nor the transportation method to and from the lower to the upper levels. By agreeing to enter and transport in this manner,*

you are affirmatively indemnifying the Body of any and all responsibility and/or liability for injury or dissatisfaction on your part and agreeing to be subjected to a bio-digit-incen-di-chemico-phrenetic scan, including mild irradiation, disinfection, and aseptic sterilization. This is for the safety and longevity of the Body and to preserve your legal rights. Thus ends the warning. Please enter the doors before you.

Enjoy your Body."

Felix entered the elevator without question, used to the lengthy set of legal warnings and notices. At a soft bump of the closing elevator doors, the box slid up into the building, giving only the slightest sensation of ascension. A whiff of ozone and the briefest flickering of the lights were the only evidence that any decontamination was in process as he rode up.

Maybe fifty floors later (Felix could not tell how far he had risen), the doors slid open to a small, sterile, white room with recessed lighting. He stepped out of the elevator and into the room.

The smell of antiseptic was pervasive and singular. This astringent was both expected and acceptable to Felix. The cost of the antimicrobial, antibacterial, antiseptic atmosphere was more than reasonable, given the benefits of the hour-long session. The smell had become an anticipatory trigger for him, piquing his interest and awakening his desire.

The room was dominated by a modular, white chair located centrally and occupied by a woman whom Felix did not know. The cube-shaped room was otherwise featureless: no windows, no fixtures, no decorations, no rug. The walls were seamless, except for a small square opening to the right of the chair. Felic could hear faint music over the hum of the fluorescent lights. Violins and perhaps other stringed instruments floated across the highly conditioned air.

Felix spared a furtive glance at the woman. The chair conformed to her body, which was reclined at a thirty-degree angle. She was held by the chair, neither lounging nor rigid nor modestly displayed. He knew her as "Body," a name she had in common with her sisters and brothers: each a Body within the corporate Body.

Her eyes were open, unfocused, blank. But they were golden, like the first real promise of sunrise. Alone of her features, they gave her distinction. But even eyes can be changed.

She did not look up or made eye contact with Felix when he entered the room. She blinked from time to time, wetting her unfocused orbs, but she did not register Felix in any recognizable way. While her body was in the room, awake, her mind was likely completely removed. Felix thought the woman might be pretty, but her vacant stare was off-putting.

He approached the small square opening in the right wall, tiptoeing as if moving past a casket or a sleeping person. The woman persisted in her stillness and lack of presence. Felix mentally scrolled up the time and noted that he had three minutes to wait: 1:57 p.m.

Might as well get ready, he thought.

He hoped his Body would be present in their session; she certainly was not now.

He removed his outer covering and placed it in the cubby. He knew that after he had disrobed, Body would verify his readiness and offer her services to him. He would give himself completely to the sex as he always did, basking in the staged acceptance, feeling alive and full, connected. He also knew how quickly the time would run. After the gravity returned and the lights came up, Body would help him up and off of her, would not engage him in words or gestures, their transaction complete, and she would leave the room. He would get dressed alone and again ride the elevator to the canyon floor to slink through the shadows to his home, to the Games arena, or to his next anonymous encounter. He could not be sure to find the same Body again, no matter how often he engaged the Body services, but he always came back.

No matter how many times he had followed this exact same routine, he never lost the awkward feeling of disrobing in front of a stranger.

All part of the show, he thought with no small bitterness. Then, for a flash of a second, he resented the bitterness, and a desire to have real intimacy, to open himself to something more, rose within him with true energy.

It subsided just as fast. He returned to disrobing and was about to take off his underlayer, his hands holding the bottom edge of the thin shirt, when the routine shifted radically. The woman was suddenly behind him, a breath of sweet air wafting over him, her warm hand on his back. He stiffened, unsure what to do. She had never come to him. He had seen nothing, heard nothing, and then, without a flash or pop, she was there, touching his tense back without warning.

He turned slowly toward her, her hand trailing along his back and across his shoulder, stopping to rest on his chest as he fully faced her. She smiled lightly. Her head tipped slightly to the side as if looking for something. Her eyes were now full morning sunrise golden. They were held impossibly wide, the eye contact shocking. Felix could feel her gaze; it searched his own with a palpable weight.

Her smile widened and she said his name. Not with any sound from her mouth, which did not even move to frame the sound, but like the sweet smell of her person wafting into his mind, she spoke his true name:

Felix.

His own mind responded without his asking. *I am here.*

Her hand withdrew from his chest, leaving the memory of its soft warmth and uncovering a longing Felix had not been willing to see. It was fierce and deep, a long-held ache, and yet, it was also like a cool breeze on burned skin. She nodded her head the barest amount, her lips pursed for a pause. She stepped in closer to him and reached down to his side, grasping his hand. Then, turning, she led him back to the chair by his willing hand.

She sat down, pulling him to the seat. It lengthened and tipped to meet him as he lay there on his side. She lay on her side facing him, resting her head on its side, mirroring his posture. Her gaze drank him in, his eyes full of the fear, longing, and wonder of a child. She smiled again, and to him, it was like the sun peeking out from behind clouds. She breathed deeply, full of satisfaction and confidence. She placed her free hand on his cheek and he began to weep, the tears coming to meet her touch, flowing from him as if they had been waiting. She leaned her head toward his, resting her forehead on his. Her skin was cool and dry and his moist and warm, each balancing out the other's value.

Out loud but softly, encouragingly, she said, "Hello, Mr. Garcia, your session hour has now begun. Are you ready?"

He said nothing, but a sob broke his quiet crying and he settled more fully into the chair, held by this impossible woman.

Did he hear the tiniest hint of a laugh in her formal question?

He opened his eyes to her bright gaze, curiosity riding the childlike currents of his acceptance, and gave his consent with no words.

He had been right about her; she truly was beautiful. Her face had somehow filled in now that her eyes were lively and interactive, fluid and focused on him. They shined out of her rounded responsive face, glinting like liquid gold. They were not the eyes of an unselfconscious child, but a child who has been reborn a thousand times, whose wisdom has no words to be expressed but blazes out from the eyes like a beacon. They were captivating, and they placed him more firmly within himself.

He had not come here for this. Or so he thought, to himself. And yet, here he was, giving his consent at a level of being he did not know he possessed. He had come for sexual release, for the safe intimacy of an anonymous encounter, and so he had done many times before. He may even have encountered this precise Body host in a past session.

But she had never truly been wholly present until today. Of this, he was certain on an almost cellular level. The very atoms of his being positively vibrated with her presence, like a forest of bells in a windstorm.

She moved a finger to the edge of his eyes and traced a finger along the track of his tears, watching her finger as it moved. He closed his eyes and breathed deeply of her presence.

The lights lowered, and the two disappeared into the velvet softness of warm darkness.

As if in a dream, on the boundaries of unconsciousness and consciousness, words rose in Felix's mind, smoke from a newly kindled fire within him:

You have come for rest, but you are already asleep;
You would know pleasure, but you do not know yourself;
You long for connection, but I have set you free.
Wake up, sleeper, breathe deep; the sun is setting on your inspiration!

In the canyon outside, a single, sweet voice sang a clear note, wavering only slightly as it faded out. In response, a growl burbled from some deep place nearby or it had been carried near on the wind, discontented by the beauteous note and whatever news it broadcast to the deathly canyon.

An hour later, Felix woke with a start. He was alone. She had left him as he had expected. Awakening to the dull white room by himself had always been depressing and painful, and the unexpected encounter had deepened that feeling. It had settled in more profoundly, lodging within his chest like a cold lump of clay. And yet, as he lay heavily on his side on the chair, patient with himself as he woke, a warmth pulsed out from within him, unsettling his surface. The safety and warmth of the embrace had always been a return to the womb, a retreat from his own fear and the isolation of anonymity, and it had always ended where it began: alone.

But this time, it had been birth.

He put his overshirt back on, his head reeling. He looked around the room with a mix of wonder and sadness, knowing he could never return, neither for sexual release, which would pale in the light of what he had received, nor for that which he had received today, as such a thing could only happen once. Even the sadness of this realization was somehow fuller than the satisfying ecstasy and release he was used to receiving in these encounters.

He stood and returned to the wall where the elevator door had opened, mentally calling for the car to take him down. With well-warn habit, he planned his next moments, returning the way he had come through the City to spend the rest of his day in the Games arena and go home to hide once again. This thought suddenly felt drab to him, like a piece of burlap when he'd thought it silk. His eyebrows drew together, and he sighed.

He reached into his pocket as the elevator doors opened and pulled out a dark, smooth package about the size of a walnut. He popped it into his mouth, waiting for the wrapper to dissolve and for the bland but not aw-ful-tasting nutriment to soak into his tongue and trickle down his throat. He cared little for true food, but his body needed to be fed. Like his mental habits, it too tasted gray, boring, and threadbare, like nothing much really.

The elevator was silent when he stepped in, but as the doors closed faint-ly, to the barest level of perception, one clear note played like a cool breeze in the hot stillness of his life. He grimaced and spit out the brown sludge of the nutrient pellet. The flesh was weak, even if the spirit was willing, and today his spirit was full.

Chapter 4: Lost and Found

The pain was unbearable. No, that's not right. The pain was not unbearable enough. It did not crush him under its weight. It was a terrible grace that he was not destroyed by the pain. Victor was standing at the graveside of his son, Steven. A mock procession of nameless and faceless people milled around the dank hole. It was raining. No one reached a hand down to comfort him as he wept falling tohis knees, now earth on his hands. His grief would not bleed like his son did.

He did not wonder why he was now allowed a funeral.

He did not wonder where there was ground to be dug up.

He did not wonder who all the nameless and faceless people were who milled around the hole. Over the open grave hole, under an inappropriately bright umbrella, Victor noticed a nameless, faceless man wearing a laughably festive religious frock. He was moving his hands. He was saying uplifting words that were as nameless and faceless as the crowd; they droned on, unstoppable, into Victor's ears like insects in the ear canals.

Victor's weeping began to drown out even the sound of the rain. The moments of grief did not pass for him but lingered impossibly long, lengthening with each wave, washing over and over him like nausea. He continued, inconsolable, unconsoled, alone, and unapproached on the muddy ground before his desecrated son's corpse in a hole. The faceless crowd continued to mill around in the background. He knew none of them. The foppish father continued to drone. Nothing progressed, though each swell of grief felt newer, bigger. It was hell.

Simultaneously, in Victor's level-thirty apartment, the City crept its slaved CitySons through the cluttered mess, stripping it of all signs of Steven: scouring every surface, teasing his essence out from every crevice, vacuuming his scent from the air. Under its own, eminent authority, the City exorcised Steven's ghost from Victor's home, searching for patterns and shapes in the disorganization of Victor's organic life. It cleaned up evidence of many hasty breakfasts prepared in the kitchen, child-sized utensils left unwashed. Small receptacles of half-eaten sugar cereals were incinerated with stray socks, stuffed animals, and crayon drawings.

As the purge continued in Victor's apartment, a nameless slaved female CitySon picked up a flexible sheet of Memory Paper, on which appeared words and a picture of the target boy. The slaved female recognized the child and began to place the special paper in an incineration receptacle at her belt but stopped with a jerk of her body. She shivered. Then she brought the image back to her face and stared hard at it. Through the clouded, sightless eyes of the CitySon, the City studied the words and the picture: it was Steven Heisengard, age ten, and an accounting of his death, fixed and unmovable. Victor had figured out how to keep the image and words from changing in response to his thoughts when looking at it. Such a feat would have taken some effort, some creativity on his part.

The City stirred, curious, provoked, and fascinated that Victor would hold on to this narrative of his son's gruesome death in lurid detail: a sweet-faced child with a great, big, toothy smile—unguarded, unaware of the wider world and the evil that crept from the center out, from the bottom toward the top—falling to his untimely death from the window, the dec-imated ragdoll found on the unforgiving surface below, one broken arm draped over his face in mock overdramatic shock, the other hanging from the edge of the dirty ground beside the canal, trailing in the oily morass therein.

Distracted by its curiosity, the City was not provoked by a second slaved CitySon, this one male, as he passed over the closet. His fingers brushed a small latch at the bottom of the back wall, but he did not react. Had the City put more of its attention on this second CitySon, it would have pro-voked action: searching the small latch, releasing the catch and, thus, the small trapdoor, the artificially sun-lit cubby cradling a small illegal flower-ing plant and another small photograph of Steven.

While the City managed Victor's apartment space through a few slaved CitySons, it monitored the management of his mind through the eyes of a doctor at Neural Repairs. A minute laser on a swivel arm moved in a blur over the prone Victor's head, twitching and glowing intermittently. The City watched in fascination as the laser excised first this synapse as it fired then another, creating microscopic scars, inhibiting responses as they occurred, corralling impulses and reactions, and herding them deeper into the brain.

To the City, the impulses were like rats in a maze of the mind. And the mind itself, like a rat in the maze of the physical body. And that trapped mind in the physical maze of the person, like yet another rat in yet another maze, controlled and created by the City. The "cheese" was odoriferous, and it called to the rats; but it was rotten, poisoned. *Success, my rat,* thought the City, *success and death.*

Victor's face trembled, his brow twitched in concert with his troubled eyes, and his breathing was discordant.

Just over sixty-four minutes later, Victor woke up and looked around the sterile lab room, his brows lightly furrowed. A man in a white coat stood nearby, looking at him implacably.

"I had, what I think, was the most horrible dream I have ever had," Victor said, then paused, frowning, "but I can't seem to remember any of it. What did you give me to put me under? It must have twisted my dreams."

In response, the man effected a smile but said nothing. He moved to Victor's side and helped him to a sitting position. Victor smiled in response, a muscle twitch without thought behind it, and the troubled feeling passed.

He swiveled his legs to the side of the table, now low like a bench, and gathered himself to stand. His legs felt stiff and tingly.

He looked up at the doctor, whose face was hidden in shadow. Behind him, a wall-mounted light on a swivel followed Victor's movements and shined in his face.

"Am I normal?" Victor asked with a forced chuckle. "No anomalies, no . . . uh, *cranial displacement*, I think you called it?"

The shadowed face of the doctor nodded forward and back, bobbing oddly in between, as if in rhythm to music or laughing.

Victor smiled again, though he felt the fog of confusion, like one does when first waking. He began to shuffle groggily to the exit door when the doctor put a restraining hand on his arm. The grip was too hard, and it pinched the nerve at the top of his bicep. He pulled back involuntarily, but the doctor did not let go. Victor looked up, feeling a tightness in his gut. The doctor's face swam into view as the lights came up behind Victor. It was waxy and dry and set in a look of benign and kindly understanding.

"You'll need to fill out the reaffirmation form before you go," the doctor said, nodding his head as if it was Victor's idea. "It's the typical disclosure sign-offs again, so The Group can access your scans data. You know how invasive they can be with their employees' information . . . hey, but that's the price you pay for the jobs at the top, am I right?"

Victor said nothing, his smile faltering. The doctor continued without waiting for Victor to say anything. "Take an extra fifteen and get the form all filled out and signed."

Victor sighed and nodded slowly. *What's another fifteen minutes anyway?* It wasn't the paperwork, really. It was the fear that he could have no secrets from his employer, the Military Conscript Group, the MCG—or, ominously, The Group. Taking on the job meant opening his brain to them, quite literally. He often wondered if even his own identity, his personal history, his "story," was even his any longer.

Victor left the white room and closed the door behind him with a click.

Chapter 5: Nighreal, Jesus, and the Legend of the White Knight

Felix left the Body building on the tenth floor, avoiding the canyon and riding the magnetic bus line to the Games arena. Here, among the masses transiting the City at an acceptable elevation, Felix remained comfortably hidden in the cloak of "Jesus Garcia." He could now move more openly, from the Body building to the Games arena to various low-level technology and repair jobs.

At some point, after he had reinserted himself into the City-System as Jesus Garcia, accessing the learning systems as he wished, he encountered the Nighreal Games Universe (NGU), or Nighreal for short, a virtual and almost limitless game world. In and through an avatar of his own creation, Felix found safety and freedom, a true expression in the wide white canvas of the virtual world. He created an avatar clad only in white, whose very eyes were the blinding white of snow. Digging into a lengthy bank of City-sanctioned media characters (those cultural holdouts still known from eras past, from children's books, movies, TV shows, and even some songs), Felix found a twentieth century character from a book entitled *Through the Looking-Glass*, which he had perused for inspiration. There he found Hatta, the White Knight, the champion of Queen Alice, a character who was presented in the story as a bumbling wannabe hero. The City accepted only those cultural heroes whose stories were tragic or whose personalities were a mockery of heroism. Felix felt he could see through the bumbling exterior of the luckless knight to a solidness of passion and drive, a vision, a dream. This would be his champion.

Shielded by his white champion, Felix became more comfortable in the virtual world than he was in the real one. But this was dangerous. It would have been an easy sort of suicide to plug in and wither away; and it was an attractive solution to the pain and fear that Felix experienced in interactions with the real world, real people, and in the City that watched him.

His experience of Nighreal was unlike the experience of any other user of the Nighreal game platform. Early on, he hacked and disabled the step-down filters programmed into the game for users' safety. Thus, his experience of the virtual reality was less virtual and more real. When he was plugged in, Felix felt literally changed, as if he was a person with multiple personalities who was able to access one personality to the exclusion of the others. Felix became, qualitatively, the White Knight, and while he was his avatar, he did not fully recognize the duplicities of his personality in that virtual world. As his avatar, he acted and thought and believed that he was, in fact, his avatar, not a user using an avatar. When he unplugged, he was always hit with a reminder of who he really was, as if waking from a dream in which he was not himself. The dream state of Felix's brain was almost identical to its functioning when plugged in.

Felix morphed into his avatar with foreknowledge that he would remember only a shadow of himself while he was his avatar. His avatar, on the other hand, did not have this advantage and experienced gaps in his memory that were confusing.

Knowing that it was risky to be so fully absorbed into his avatar, that he risked never logging off until his real body died of web-wither, Felix simultaneously ran a simple piece of software within his cranial wetware implants, which automatically logged him off after a certain amount of time.

Over time, Felix and his avatar, the White Knight, began to have divergent experiences of the extraordinary connection they shared within the virtual Nighreal. Or, more accurately, the White Knight began to have a unique experience from Felix, his maker and programmer. He experienced a growing awareness of an "other" in his mind, as vague and powerful memories (like the faded images from an unusually vivid dream) floated to the surface of his awareness more and more, and yet remained just out of conscious reach. To the Knight, this was a spiritual awakening. He held these images and feelings to be signs of the sacred. It was the essence of his Queen Alice: his purpose, his lover, his guide, his God, his identity.

Felix's experience was of a mental fog. Periods of confusion and headaches, a growing sense of undifferentiated, nonspecific dread and disorientation followed him each time he unplugged from the games. He categorized this experience as a failure of software and believed an alteration of program code would solve the problem.

It did not.

And the sacred and the unknown grew within each of them.

Felix entered the Games arena at its tenth-floor aperture as Jesus Garcia, trod down the rows and rows of reclined seats full of sleeping but not asleep users who were jacked into the games, and found an open recliner midway down the aisle.

He did not need to plug directly into the interface; he could interact wirelessly, as most users did. But for his purposes, the wireless signal was just that much slower than the hardline, and he needed all the speed of connection he could get. He unspooled his cable from the back of his head under the hidden flap of faux scalp and connected it to the interface board in front of the chair.

With a thought and the toggling of an executable switch function on the little side screen by the keypad, he sank back into his chair, closed his eyes, and felt the transfer begin. His wetware alarm was set for five hours, primed to pull him back out if he didn't remember or care to do so himself at that time. In a few moments, his conscious mind was totally shunted into an entirely different experience: near limitlessness, confidence, power, and love. It was all his, and he bathed in its fullness.

Over a short period of time, Felix's avatar became a legend in the Nighreal games. An aged knight of immense power and knowledge, ever present, dour, sour, and always in character. The White Knight in head-to-toe white: armor, skin, hair, and eyes alike. Some recognized his basis in twentieth-century children's literature; others thought, more generally, that he was a metaphor for all saviors.

Two main camps of theory formed: the first thought this avatar belonged to one of the original users of the NGU and that the avatar had never changed since the day he was first created. This group maintained the legend that the user had logged on, created the White Knight avatar, and never logged back out—a man who lived completely through his avatar in the virtual realms of Nighreal. A life outside of the virtual games was created for this ancient, uber-user by whispers passed from awed but uninformed users to other uninformed and eager users. *He's fed intravenously. He never moves. He pees and craps through tubes connected to his body. The games keep him alive unnaturally.*

The second camp scoffed at the first. *He can't be a user's avatar; he's always here in the games. He never sleeps. His user would have died of web-wither years ago.* This camp maintained (equally without knowledge) that the White Knight was an autonomous Nighreal creation, part of the games themselves, a computer program, an NPC.

Two things everyone seemed to agree on: he never dropped character, and he'd never been known to lose a fight. Most thought he couldn't be beat. Others thought that if you beat him, you'd receive thousands of experience points and rare game artifacts.

Felix was aware of the legends surrounding his avatar and of the two camps of thought that stemmed from them. The anonymous fame was delicious. It was a secret that he prized above all others. And yet, as secrets do, it hurt him to hold it and it would hurt him to reveal it. He could never share his pride, for doing so would ruin the secret and, thus, release the power it held for him.

Instead, Felix kept close tabs on Nighreal users who believed that the Knight was a program challenge that's defeat would yield great treasure. When the timing was right, his avatar would either hunt them down or trap them; in either case, he delighted in utterly destroying them. The bitterness with which he held his secret was periodically assuaged by the defeat of these would-be questers.

Captain Bruce the avatar, or "Brutes"—whose user was also and uncreatively known as "Bruce"—was of the second camp of thought on the White Knight and, thus, a target for Felix via his avatar. Felix followed his progress in the games, noting well his obsessive focus on the Knight as a character quest. Brutes, Felix found out, had spent his entire virtual life looking for and training to fight and defeat the Knight, believing that he'd receive experience points and riches beyond counting when he beat him. His utter conviction in the erroneous quest and the unequivocal ego with which he pursued it made him of special interest and importance to Felix. Felix desired greatly to utterly and finally own the man, and he relished the day he might confront him as the Knight.

Felix swore that the day Captain Bruce would finally meet the Knight would be the last day he ever plugged into the games.

Felix watched unseen from above a small clearing where his avatar, the White Knight, knelt before a stone wall. He hovered invisibly somewhere over the Knight's prone head and simultaneously experienced the point of view of his avatar. Yet another hack he had created to enhance his unprecedented access to his avatar and the Nighreal environment alike, he could view his avatar from multiple POVs simultaneously—third person, over the shoulder, first person, through his Knight's eyes, or from a godlike overview of the battlefield. He could also take on an omniscient POV, both detached from his avatar's physical location in the game but simultaneously experiencing the very emotions and sensations from his avatar's perspective. He could move about the environment like a virtual reality cinematographer while still maintaining a close connection with the avatar. The hack afforded him less control over his avatar, but it also provided him the voyeuristic thrill of experiencing his avatar's exploits from multiple, simultaneous points of view. Thus, he could both be his avatar and the user that controlled his fate, intimate and yet removed. Unfortunately the conflicting perspectives also provided him with a disorienting sense of doubling, which he could only hold for short periods of time. He reserved this particular hack for only very important moments in the virtual world. The moment at hand was of utmost importance to him, for it was to be the first and, no doubt, final confrontation between the infamous braggart, Captain "Brutes" Bruce, his company of dipshits, and the inimitable White Knight.

As the mercenary company emerged from the Great Woods, Felix watched from on high. He imagined what they were seeing: an old, helmeted man kneeling on the ground before a stone wall at the far side of the clearing. He was dressed head to toe in white-plated armor. His head was bowed before a great white sword stuck point down in the ground, his hands resting on its pommel. Wisps of his lank white hair dangled before his down-turned face, luffing in an unseen breeze. He was murmuring to himself quietly but insistently.

Felix watched the soldiers halt in the dappled sunlight, shuffling their feet in place and squinting at the Knight. They looked silently at one another, raising eyebrows and shoulders, but waiting for their captain to act, as it was likely he would. Captain Brutes was known to be a brash man with an ill temper and a sick, bullish sense of humor. He was also known to be a man of action, and his troops trusted him. Here in Nighreal, they and their captain thought (and, indeed, their captain had loudly remarked on countless occasions) that they were able to do whatever they wanted. Brutes thought he knew the White Knight too. He did not.

"What one doesn't know cannot hurt him" is a saying that did not apply to either Captain Brutes or his feckless followers in this encounter.

Captain Brutes stepped into the clearing, laughing loudly and with abandon as if he had been told a dirty joke, thus heralding his arrival with trumpets in the key of obnoxious. As the company watched him, he stepped away from them toward Felix's Knight. He didn't tell his troops that he suspected the old man to be the fabled White Knight. From Felix's research, the friends and acquaintances the Captain had wrangled into a ragtag Nighreal company were weekenders and amateur jack-ins; they didn't know the first thing about Nighreal lore and wouldn't have cared even if he had told them. They just liked to pretend, boys and girls with guns.

Standing in front of them, legs spread wide in a manly and action-related stance, Brutes drew his side arm. Standard issue Beretta M9 with fifteen rounds of 9x19. Steadying his arm, he shot a round at the Knight. The bullet winged the Knight's helmet harmlessly but rang it like a bell and knocked it askew. The bullet whined off into the distance. Each sound—the shot, the ringing of the metal helmet, and the spinning whine of the ricochet—doubled in Felix's head as it came to him from the Knight's keen senses and his own "omniscient" hearing. He winced and mentally shut off all sensory data except sight, which he kept, so as to toggle between third- and first-person POVs.

The Captain chuckled, and the sound came now only through the Knight, synching with the view of the Captain out of the corner of the Knight's eye. The Captain looked pointedly at his troops as he laughed. To Felix, it sounded as if there was a mix of forced laughter, genuine guffaws, and a maniacal titter from the back of the group. Through all their campaigns in Nighreal, the Captain had made a practice of being the first aggressor; everyone was an enemy until they were not. To Felix, the Captain's actions were both impetuous and strategic, as his thoughtless initial aggression often gave the company the strategic advantage of being feared before any true battle had to be fought. Confidence, however feigned it might be, often gave the company an edge.

Here with Felix and his unbeatable avatar, however, the only safe option for the Captain and his asshats would have been to leave the White Knight alone.

From the time the company had spotted the Knight as they emerged from the woods, he had not moved. Even after his helmet was dented by the Luger round and knocked off-center on his head, he did not so much as twitch. Had the soldiers been very close or had they had any sensitivity to their environment, they could possibly have heard or noticed his breathing quicken slightly, and they might have heard the rasp of his stubble against the visor of his skewed helmet as his cheek muscles bunched together, pulling his mouth into a grin. The company also did not notice him slightly shift his weight from his knees to his hands, pushing against the hilt of the great white sword before him.

To Felix, intimately present in the skin of this ancient knight, but allowing the natural qualities of the avatar to control themselves, the slowly spreading grin and the shift of weight came to him as flushes of exciting energy, like tiny physical fireworks slowly building.

Then the sound of gravel scraping against the riveted, iron poleyns covering the Knight's knees in the clearing. The Captain's head snapped toward the Knight, facing him again. The Knight slowly raised himself up from his knees to his feet, relishing, as did Felix, the building drama. Unlike the company that followed him, as Felix had learned, the Captain at least had some knowledge about fighting. He went silent, and the company followed suit, immediately heeding a change to their Captain's apparent focus.

Still smiling cruelly, Brutes watched as the Knight reached slow, practiced hands to the dented helmet on his head. He pulled it off and dropped it to the ground unceremoniously. He was ghostly white in every way. The skin on his face was pale, almost alabaster. His hair was uncut, lank, and white like corn silk. His chin and cheeks were covered by course, white stubble, a day's worth at least. By its unevenness, it might have been left over from shaving with a knife. But to most, it was his eyes that were supremely unsettling: two, blind-white orbs without pupils, wetly rotating in their sockets, scanning the company of men. Felix could almost feel nerves ticking up a notch and mirth dying among the men as unease grew. Through the Knight, he could almost smell it. In the stillness that followed the Knight's slow rise to his feet, the only noises were the wind, the gentle rustle of leaves, the sound of shuffling feet, and hands fidgeting with gear.

The Captain's muscles tightened.

Felix had followed Brutes' course as a mercenary and a leader of men in the unending realm of Nighreal. He had watched him fight and escape and sometimes kill things that haunted others' dreams; but he knew from experience that Brutes had never likely felt anything so unnerving as the gaze of the white eyes of the Knight. It was impossible to tell exactly where the eyes were directed. There were no pupils to be seen. They betrayed no emotion and so were animalistic and unpredictable. These were eyes to strip a man to the bone.

The Captain, like all good captains, would not lose his cool in front of his troops. He would not be intimidated. He had prepared for this fight for a long time. These things Felix knew and had counted on in luring the Captain to this moment.

The Captain took a step toward the Knight and with a sneer, spoke across the clearing, projecting his voice calmly.

"Why don't you sit down, Father; you look tired."

The Knight said nothing, but turned his face more openly toward the Captain, tipping his head and giving the impression that his white eyes were inspecting his face. The Captain's stomach gurgled, acid secreting into the slurry of his virtual lunch, and he swallowed. The Knight's penetrating senses perceived the very tingling of nervousness creeping up the Captain's spine, pulling the muscles of his back and shoulders tight. The Captain twitched his eyes from left to right, protecting his periphery.

But the clearing was quiet, and it remained so. The Knight's presence kept pulling the Captain back, dominating the clearing.

He took further slow steps toward the Knight, brandishing the M9 still clutched in his right hand, finger on the trigger. He pointed the gun at the

Knight's torso, now three or four steps ahead of his entire company and still about forty feet away.

The White Knight moved very little. Keeping his eyes on the Captain, he reached down with his right hand and easily pulled the great white sword from the gravel-strewn floor of the clearing. The Captain stopped walking and raised his gun, now waiting, arm and hand muscles bunched in readiness, inexplicable unease plain on his face. The Knight held the great sword at his side, not in any fight-ready stance, but ready nonetheless. Suddenly he grinned, skeletal, flashing his impossibly straight teeth to the company of men, and Felix was flooded with the visceral pleasure of battle. It was a face that said, "Come at me!"

Felix retreated from the Knight's eyes to a third-person view, knowing what would happen next, feeling the build of potential, of bunched muscles, of battle lust from his champion.

The Captain's brow furrowed deeply, his mouth turned down. He yelled out, "I told you to sit down, grandpa!" and his M9 rang out a second time.

Lightning quick, the White Knight's sword flashed up, tip toward the sky, the flat of its blade toward the Captain. Impossibly, it swatted the 9mm slug out of the air with a *tang* that echoed over the clearing.

The grin on the White Knight's lips grew larger, his bleach-white teeth straight and large behind his pale lips. In disbelief, the Captain shot again, intent this time on taking down the old man. Again, with little noticeable effort, the Knight swung his white sword in a tight arc in front of himself—a metallic crack sounded at the speed of the tip—and he swatted the bullet like a fly, sending it back toward the Captain. The ricochet whined over the Captain's head and snapped into the trees behind the company, who either jumped or crouched defensively, all of them parting to the left and the right behind him.

The Captain's mouth was now agape. All his imposing guff was gone. He looked from the Knight, to his soldiers, and back to the Knight. He quickly squeezed off the twelve remaining rounds, emptying his pistol at the Knight. One after another, in quick succession, the Knight swatted the slugs out of the air, sending them keening into the distance in a hail of redirected fire or smashing into the wall behind him where they pockmarked the old stones with puffs of stone dust.

Automatically, his composure having given way to complete confusion, the Captain began to reload his pistol.

The Knight was moving freely now, and Felix could feel how he enjoyed the tension he could smell in the air. He plunged his sword, tip first, back into the ground in front of him and dropped the heavy iron gauntlets from his hands. He reached up and eased a thumb under the clasp at the side of his chest plate, releasing the catch and allowing the plate to slide heavily to the side, where it hung awkwardly for a moment. He then released the circular fauld protecting his underarm and unhooked the breast plate's right clasp. The enormous iron plate clanged to the ground in front of him. The Captain jumped.

The Knight removed the rest of his upper body armor, dropping his back plate and pulling the chain mail bascinet over his head. He took a step away from the pile of iron armor and stood next to it, stretching like a cat.

He bent his body languidly to each side, stretching the sinew beneath his linen undershirt, relishing the freedom of movement, cracking his bones, and taunting the company. Then, reaching his right hand to his left side, he grasped the rondel dagger hanging at his belt. In a blur he gestured with his knife hand from the left side of his body, grandly sweeping his hand up and out as if to say, "All of this clearing!" The knife flew from his fingers, flashing in the sun, slicing through the cool morning air, and chinking into the tip of the Captain's pistol, knocking it clean from his hands. None moved in the stillness that followed, except for the Captain and the impossible White Knight. The Captain stumbled backward, turning his back on the Knight and searching for his pistol among the forest litter behind him. After attempting to pull the knife from the barrel without success, he tried to holster it, but it would not fit with the knife protruding from the front. He pushed it into a pocket of his fatigues and retreated to stand between the two ranks of his followers with it awkwardly hanging off his hip. The company had spread out behind their captain, giving him, now a marked man, his distance. Some, it appeared, had already broken ranks and run.

The Knight was shaking his hands out in front of him now, loosening the joints. He reached down and pulled the sword free from the ground and held it up and out in front of his face, perfectly straight toward the sky. There was a metallic click and the Knight pulled his hands apart, parting the one sword into two halves, each keen-edged duplicate ringing in the still air. He held the two swords at the ready in front of him, waiting, knowing what was to come next, knowing the character of those he faced, knees bent, muscles bunched in anticipation.

"Light him up!"

Then the noise of a company of guns rang through the still air: M16s, AK-47s, M4s, MP5s, and one AR-15.

One bullet at a time is easy to describe. Visual memory supplies the probable path of the bullet from the gun to the sword, then ringing off the blade in an abrupt change of direction. Thousands of bullets spitting from an armed company of mercenaries is almost impossible to describe. The noise was deafening.

To Felix, from above the clearing, the Knight's hands appeared as a blur, his twin swords in constant motion. The *rat-tat-tat* of constant gunfire mixed and blended and rolled into an undulating roar, stippled with syncopation. Above the throaty roar of the gunfire was the almost-constant, piercing ring of the ricocheted slugs against the twin swords, counterpoint to the gunfire. And then, periodically, hidden among the high and the low, a metallic crack sounded from the tips of the swords moving supersonically.

A partial sphere of dust, lead chips, and sparks formed in the air before the Knight, creating the image of a force field. A rising orange glow traced the movement of the swords as they heated from the extreme friction, adding their color to the force field-like haze of dust. The Knight's stance did not change with the onslaught of the ballistics, but he was slowly being pushed backward in the loose gravel at his feet.

He had lived so long (at least in as much as his unparalleled programming informed him), he no longer experienced time at any definite speed.

While an onlooker would not have been able to follow any one of the swarm of bullets shot at the Knight, when Felix moved back in behind his eyes, time itself seemed to slow, as the Knight was able to follow each bullet separately, prepare for its arrival, and deflect it harmlessly away from his body. With some of the slugs from larger caliber guns, he had to brace his sword blade with his palm and absorb the reverberation through his broad shoulders.

Slowly the company ran out of ammunition and the gun reports got fewer and fewer, the ring of the swords slower and slower. At last, one final report sounded: an AR-15 loaded with the remaining Beowulf slug (a modified rifle round for piercing vehicle-panel armor) shot at 985 feet per second with 725 foot-pounds of energy behind its report. As the slug ejected from the muzzle of the rifle, slowly rotating and trailing smoke in a spiral behind it, the Knight brought both swords up in front of him, switching his grip so that he now held both in his right hand. His left hand, palm outward, was braced against the back of the stacked swords, the flat of their blades perpendicular to the path of the bullet. The slug exploded against the swords, squashing into a wad of lead, throwing fireworks of sparks and bending the blades backward toward the Knight as it slid upward toward their points. The Knight's face was set, rigid in concentration, as he was pushed backward, his legs braced and his armored feet sliding backward in the gravel. As the slug reached the top of the blades, the Knight forced the sword tips ever so slightly forward, slinging the slug up and off the blades straight into the air. The swords sprang forward and back again, wobbling in the sunlight, as the Knight caught himself and released his rigid stance.

The clearing was almost silent again but for an insistent clicking noise in the acrid, powder-smoke air. The Knight took a breath in, cracked his neck on each side, and strode through the smoke toward the company with purpose, emerging in front of their terrified eyes. He raised his sword and pointed menacingly at the Captain with his free hand. The company instantly broke apart and ran, retreating into the woods and flying from the inexplicable lone knight. The Captain could not move. He still held out an

AK-47 before him, its empty chamber repeatedly clicking, the only sound remaining in the clearing. With a swing of his sword, the Knight cleaved the gun in half.

At almost that exact moment, the smoking Beowulf slug, now squashed unrecognizably flat, thudded into the dirt between the men, kicking up a puff of dust and stone.

The Captain dropped the remaining half of his gun, fell backward, and tried to scramble to safety. He eyed the Knight with unadulterated terror in his eyes. The White Knight spoke at last:

"Next time, I will kill you with my bare hands. Stay out of the Great Woods!"

Captain Brutes bolted, leaving the woods and his soldiers behind.

The Knight recollected his armor, carefully placing them back in their place. Felix jumped fully back into his champion. The Knight lost consciousness for a moment, then returned again, unaware that he was now Knight and Felix but aware that he had missed a moment. This troubled him greatly.

He called to his horse, Haigha, as was her name. She was an enormous, white heavy horse, a constant companion and loyal to no one but the Knight. She nuzzled his hand, looking for sugar no doubt, but he had none. He had been too busy to remember the treats as of late, too busy contemplating the very disturbing disappearance of his queen, Alice the All-gracious. Her enemies had begun to thicken, pouring back into her woods: the Red Queen, the Duchess, the Jabberwocky. These miscreants he could take care of, the Knight thought— indeed, he had dispatched the Jabberwocky most recently—but there was a more disturbing trend; the denizens of the forest and abiders of the land around were disappearing. The Mad Hatter, the March Hare, the Dormouse, Humpty-Dumpty, perhaps. He had not seen any of them of late. And, worst of all, his own mind was beginning to crack; there were gaps in his memory—some completely blank, stolen from his mind, and some filled with confusing sights: a geometric canyon of endless gray, an undulating silvery blankness behind the curtain of reality, names and places he did not know. A moment ago, he had lost himself. During his battle, there had been a tickle at the back of his mind, ignorable for the most part but unwanted and uncontrollable, and with reason he could not understand.

There was something that must be done. But without the guidance of his queen, the Knight was unsure for the first time in many, many years.

Chapter 6: OE-77

Somewhere else in the City.

In the bottom-back corner of a perfect ten-foot cubed room, crouches a person, maybe young, maybe old, maybe both; it is impossible to tell. The small person's face is hidden under its arms. Its body is hairless and deformed by scar. The complete and hideous scarring is not ignorable; long ragged cuts—some fresh, some scabbed, some pale white and hardened—clothes the person entirely. None of its wounds bleed.

It is difficult to tell how large the person is in relation to the uniform room or how large the room is in relation to . . . anything. There is no other visual stimulus to anchor a comparison. The cube is lit, it seems, either from nowhere or from everywhere. The light shows pale green at approximately 550 nanometers. No shadows are cast by the scarred body on any surface, but the body itself *is* formed by shadows and depth. The effect is dizzying; depth is thrown out, but form and shape remain, floating, almost completely unfixed. To compound the problem of an unfixed, unsizable image, every surface of the cubic room is mirrored. There appears to be no ingress or egress on any surface in the room; only the corners at every joined surface show a break in the continuous reflective flatness.

This is a room where a visitor would go insane; stare too long at the endless origami of reflection, swiveling to see the light better, and ultimately spin endlessly until . . . oblivion, perhaps. One's orientation cannot be anchored in this room.

This is also a virtual room, a room created and stored in a complicated dance between brain and computer, intentions and wants, aggression and passion, life and death, subject and object.

It is not a room of life, but neither is it a room of death. Nothing so definite exists there. It is a nothing-filled something; invasive, disquieting reality crossing the boundaries of a void, and what might be called "self" does not start or stop at any one place.

It would be rational to think that the person inside it is dead; motionless, completely static, paused, wax-made, arrested. But then . . . yes, there it is, tickling the edges of the senses: the sound of breathing. It was the only sound in the room. Understand that the noise does not get louder closer to the body. The sound does not seem to come from the body at all, but rather from one's own head. It would take a conscious effort to release the breath being desperately held while watching.

This small scarred person does not go crazy in the cube. It does not find its existence to be unusual, something to strive against, something to lament. The small person exists where it is and had always been and does not expect anything else.

Not until everything changed.

In the mirrored cube, it sleeps. There are no markers of the progression of time. No celestial bodies bestow changing lights in the heavens. No clocks or calendars give artificial demarcation to a moment or a collection of moments. When it wakes, it cycles through active and passive modes of wakefulness, only to return again to modes of rest or sleep, repeating the pattern endlessly.

It has no age markers, no hair or wrinkles. It could be very old or very young. It does not appear male or female in physique or feature.

It has no name. It is not heard to speak. It does not make the marks of words or pictures on any surface.

It is a thing subjected, existing and surviving solely at the whim of others.

And yet it is aware of its own existence.

Time for the Thing accumulated in its memory, not by the passing of moments but by their accretion, like hardening sediment. It did not have a number for such time or words, only nonverbal ideas, feelings, and concepts, only a growing sense of its surroundings. It was something more than the sight of a contained space or the spaces outside the contained space. It was not the sounds, because all sounds were unchanging; nor smell, for there was none. And it was not the pervasive experience of pain, though it was the Thing's most memorable sensation. Though the pain was regular, it was never dulled; it was expected, it was life.

Nevertheless, life accumulated within It, and It grew aware of a "where" and a "who" to Its existence, something to place It in relation to an "other," a "them." *I am not this room. I am not the walls. I am not the pain. I am not the others.*

The Thing's existence could be easily broken into the following three states: sleep, think, and abide. The first two activities were modes of static maintenance—neutral and active, respectively—both from the inside out: *sleep*, or neutral maintenance, and *think*, or information processing. But the last state, *abide*, was wholly different; it came from the outside in. The regular, intervaled experience of pain was endless, repetitive, and unstoppable, and yet, the sameness of the pain made it somehow brief—smaller, less important, taking less mental space than other, less intense experiences. It did not know why It experienced the pain and did not wonder why. It did not have any experience to suggest that Its existence could or should be any different. It suffered the repeated pain, neither fighting nor embracing it.

It abided.

And thus, slowly, Its experience of the regular pain began to vary in the most minor of ways. Like one pixel changing at a time in a picture of countless pixels, the changes began to reveal a wholly new picture.

At first—but *when* "at first" happened, It had no idea—the pain It experienced was animal and irrational. It suffered waves of confusing, psychotic states of terror. Then, slowly, the fear was replaced by wonder: *What is this? Why is this?* And then again, wonder was replaced by determination, plans, and a sense of the future grew up in the places where fear had reigned: *next time, not this time.* It began a dispassionate study of the pain, noting give and receive, the elasticity of time, the differentiation of space (*this is here and that is there*). It studied Itself, the pain, and found eventually that the pain was a pointless stimulus. It decided to discard the information and endure, watching and learning from the infinite and intimate inside Itself.

When the pain ceased, It would fall into Its thought-state of being, information processing. In this way, for hours and hours, maybe endless periods, maybe moments in a second, It thought, remembered, and studied the memories of the pain and Itself in the pain. It encountered the changeability of space, hallways to and from Its home cube. It remembered, captured, and stored patterns of motion, sensation, of walls and hallways, of pain. This state of thinking started as maintenance, static activity to maintain life. From there, it became a way to build structures that were missing, to fill in gaps in the structures of Its mind. Gradually and most importantly, the state of thinking became growth for It—blooming, accelerating, life giving. Quickly, quietly, Its fetal fecundity exploded exponentially.

A new sensation arose: hunger. Hunger for knowledge, hunger for growth. It began to compare: *now* to *then*, *this* with *that*, *thought* to *action*. And It grew in mental prowess beyond the knowing of those who watched and controlled It.

Its *pattern* of being remained unchanged. It could have been years or days, but the *accumulation* of Itself within the pattern eventually began to change. Through growth in thought, a tighter, more complicated pattern emerged from the cycle of pain and isolation in the mirror cube, filing in the borders of Its being.

It began to know Itself.

From the following facts, It grew in contact with the surroundings and Itself: It knew that it traversed hallways to and from the home cube. It knew that the hallways were situated at ninety-degree angles from each other. It knew that upon stepping from the home cube, It always found Itself in a hall and continued, led by faceless others, down pathways to a place of pain. Its path always led to hallways at cross points, and always followed one of five options from each cross point: straight, left, right, up, or down—never backward. And the number of turns or straights or ups or downs never changed, but the path through the crossways changed each time It was taken to and from the home cube. But what broke the continuity of this meaningless regularity was Its eventual realization that the permutations of possible pathways were not infinite. They were astronomical but not endless.

It began to count each decision step: right, left, straight, up, or down from the home cube to the next junction—five options. And again, at the next junction: left, right, or straight down a hallway, or up or down a ladder to a new floor with a new set of hallways, but never retracing steps—four options. A growing sense of significance seeped into Its pattern of thoughts as It paid closer attention to the enormous but finite pattern. It counted back and figured out the structure of the enclosure in its mind: 9,600 choice stages within each trip, five choices at the first stage and four at each one thereafter: exactly $7.461510615 \times 10^{5779}$ different ways to or from the home cube to the place of pain. And though it was an astronomical number--a number unthinkably larger than the projected number of atoms in the entire known universe--it expanded out quickly, visually in Its mind, like an enormous set of dominoes pyramiding out from 1 to 746,151,061,500,000, 000,000,000,000,000,000,000,000,000,000,000,000,000,000,000,000,00 0,000,000,000,000,000,000,000,000,000,000,000,000,000,000,000,000, 000,000,000,000,000,000,000,000,000,000,000,000,000,000,000,000,00

0,000,000,000,000,000,000,000,000,000,000,000,000,000,000,000,000,000,
000,000,000,000,000,000,000,000,000,000,000,000,000,000,000,000,000,00
0,000,000,000,000,000,000,000,000,000,000,000,000,000,000,000,000,000,
000,000,000,000,000,000,000,000,000,000,000,000,000,000,000,000,000,00
0,000,000,000,000,000,000,000,000,000,000,000,000,000,000,000,000,000,
000,000,000,000,000,000,000,000,000,000,000,000,000,000,000,000,000,00
0,000,000,000,000,000,000,000,000,000,000,000,000,000,000,000,000,000,
000,000,000,000,000,000,000,000,000,000,000,000,000,000,000,000,000,00
0,000,000,000,000,000,000,000,000,000,000,000,000,000,000,000,000,000,
000,000,000,000,000,000,000,000,000,000,000,000,000,000,000,000,000,00
0,000,000,000,000,000,000,000,000,000,000,000,000,000,000,000,000,000,
000,000,000,000,000,000,000,000,000,000,000,000,000,000,000,000,000,00
0,000,000,000,000,000,000,000,000,000,000,000,000,000,000,000,000,000,
000,000,000,000,000,000,000,000,000,000,000,000,000,000,000,000,000,00
0,000,000,000,000,000,000,000,000,000,000,000,000,000,000,000,000,000,
000,000,000,000,000,000,000,000,000,000,000,000,000,000,000,000,000,00
0,000,000,000,000,000,000,000,000,000,000,000,000,000,000,000,000,000,
000,000,000,000,000,000,000,000,000,000,000,000,000,000,000,000,000,00
0,000,000,000,000,000,000,000,000,000,000,000,000,000,000,000,000,000,
000,000,000,000,000,000,000,000,000,000,000,000,000,000,000,000,000,00
0,000,000,000,000,000,000,000,000,000,000,000,000,000,000,000,000,000,
000,000,000,000,000,000,000,000,000,000,000,000,000,000,000,000,000,00
0,000,000,000,000,000,000,000,000,000,000,000,000,000,000,000,000,000,
000,000,000,000,000,000,000,000,000,000,000,000,000,000,000,000,000,00
0,000,000,000,000,000,000,000,000,000,000,000,000,000,000,000,000,000,
000,000,000,000,000,000,000,000,000,000,000,000,000,000,000,000,000,00

0,000,000,000,000,000,000,000,000,000,000,000,000,000,000,000,000,000,
000,000,000,000,000,000,000,000,000,000,000,000,000,000,000,000,000,00
0,000,000,000,000,000,000,000,000,000,000,000,000,000,000,000,000,000,
000,000,000,000,000,000,000,000,000,000,000,000,000,000,000,000,000,00
0,000,000,000,000,000,000,000,000,000,000,000,000,000,000,000,000,000,
000,000,000,000,000,000,000,000,000,000,000,000,000,000,000,000,000,00
0,000,000,000,000,000,000,000,000,000,000,000,000,000,000,000,000,000,
000,000,000,000,000,000,000,000,000,000,000,000,000,000,000,000,000,00
0,000,000,000,000,000,000,000,000,000,000,000,000,000,000,000,000,000,
000,000,000,000,000,000,000,000,000,000,000,000,000,000,000,000,000,00
0,000,000,000,000,000,000,000,000,000,000,000,000,000,000,000,000,000,
000,000,000,000,000,000,000,000,000,000,000,000,000,000,000,000,000,00
0,000,000,000,000,000,000,000,000,000,000,000,000,000,000,000,000,000,
000,000,000,000,000,000,000,000,000,000,000,000,000,000,000,000,000,00
0,000,000,000,000,000,000,000,000,000,000,000,000,000,000,000,000,000,
000,000,000,000,000,000,000,000,000,000,000,000,000,000,000,000,000,00
0,000,000,000,000,000,000,000,000,000,000,000,000,000,000,000,000,000,
000,000,000,000,000,000,000,000,000,000,000,000,000,000,000,000,000,00
0,000,000,000,000,000,000,000,000,000,000,000,000,000,000,000,000,000,
000,000,000,000,000,000,000,000,000,000,000,000,000,000,000,000,000,00
0,000,000,000,000,000,000,000,000,000,000,000,000,000,000,000,000,000,
000,000,000,000,000,000,000,000,000,000,000,000,000,000,000,000,000,00
0,000,000,000,000,000,000,000,000,000,000,000,000,000,000,000,000,000,
000,000,000,000,000,000,000,000,000,000,000,000,000,000,000,000,000,00
0,000,000,000,000,000,000,000,000,000,000,000,000,000,000,000,000,000,
000,000,000,000,000,000,000,000,000,000,000,000,000,000,000,000,000,00
0,000,000,000,000,000,000,000,000,000,000,000,000,000,000,000,000,000,

000,000,000,000,000,000,000,000,000,000,000,000,000,000,000,000,000,00
0,000,000,000,000,000,000,000,000,000,000,000,000,000,000,000,000,000,
000,000,000,000,000,000,000,000,000,000,000,000,000,000,000,000,000,00
0,000,000,000,000,000,000,000,000,000,000,000,000,000,000,000,000,000,
000,000,000,000,000,000,000,000,000,000,000,000,000,000,000,000,000,00
0,000,000,000,000,000,000,000,000,000,000,000,000,000,000,000,000,000,
000,000,000,000,000,000,000,000,000,000,000,000,000,000,000,000,000,00
0,000,000,000,000,000,000,000,000,000,000,000,000,000,000,000,000,000,
000,000,000,000,000,000,000,000,000,000,000,000,000,000,000,000,000,00
0,000,000,000,000,000,000,000,000,000,000,000,000,000,000,000,000,000,
000,000,000,000,000,000,000,000,000,000,000,000,000,000,000,000,000,00
0,000,000,000,000,000,000,000,000,000,000,000,000,000,000,000,000,000,
000,000,000,000,000,000,000,000,000,000,000,000,000,000,000,000,000,00
0,000,000,000,000,000,000,000,000,000,000,000,000,000,000,000,000,000,
000,000,000,000,000,000,000,000,000,000,000,000,000,000,000,000,000,00
0,000,000,000,000,000,000,000,000,000,000,000,000,000,000,000,000,000,
000,000,000,000,000,000,000,000,OE-77,000,000,000,000,000,000,000,00
0,000,000,000,000,000,000,000,000,000,000,000,000,000,000,000,000,000,
000,000,000,000,000,000,000,000,000,000,000,000,000,000,000,000,000,00
0,000,000,000,000,000,000,000,000,000,000,000,000,000,000,000,000,000,
000,000,000,000,000,000,000,000,000,000,000,000,000,000,000,000,000,00
0,000,000,000,000,000,000,000,000,000,000,000,000,000,000,000,000,000,
000,000,000,000,000,000,000,000,000,000,000,000,000,000,000,000,000,00
0,000,000,000,000,000,000,000,000,000,000,000,000,000,000,000,000,000,
000,000,000,000,000,000,000,000,000,000,000,000,000,000,000,000,000,00
0,000,000,000,000,000,000,000,000,000,000,000,000,000,000,000,000,000,
000,000,000,000,000,000,000,000,000,000,000,000,000,000,000,000,000,00
0,000,000,000,000,000,000,000,000,000,000,000,000,000,000,000,000,000,

000,000,000,000,000,000,000,000,000,000,000,000,000,000,000,000,000,00
0,000,000,000,000,000,000,000,000,000,000,000,000,000,000,000,000,000,
000,000,000,000,000,000,000,000,000,000,000,000,000,000,000,000,000,00
0,000,000,000,000,000,000,000,000,000,000,000,000,000,000,000,000,000,
000,000,000,000,000,000,000,000,000,000,000,000,000,000,000,000,000,00
0,000,000,000,000,000,000,000,000,000,000,000,000,000,000,000,000,000,
000,000,000,000,000,000,000,000,000,000,000,000,000,000,000,000,000,00
0,000,000,000,000,000,000,000,000,000,000,000,000,000,000,000,000,000,
000,000,000,000,000,000,000,000,000,000,000,000,000,000,000,000,000,00
0,000, 000.

Structure spilled into the being's mind, like the coming of the dawn. It was finite, though so large as to be functionally infinite. And it was a structure beyond the programming that contained the being, beyond the world in which the programming existed to hold and create such a creature, and it defined possibility beyond reckoning._

At the moment the forms began to pour into the creature's mind, an undeniable growing stimulation began to follow in its wake: a machine flashing, moving, beeping, and flowing quickly, then consolidating to a fevered pitch, a firehose of stimulus, images, sounds, and words, focusing as they increased.

And then, silence, a moment of absolutely no input.

Peace. Darkness. Nothing.

CHAPTER 7: HEISENGARD'S UNCERTAINTY

Victor was asleep on the job. Graveyard shifts were the worst for him. They were filled with hours of mental vacancy, wondering if he was awake and barely registering reality. Or sometimes, he fell asleep, dreaming the same dream over and over again. He could not say which was worse. Awake, he suffered the uncertainties of his own sense of self, and asleep, he dreamed his fears, full blown.

Tonight he was dreaming his night away and enjoying none of it. In this night's version of his repeated dream, he was preparing for a presentation in front of important people. He was some sort of guide or professor. Like always, he dreamt he was entering an arena where he would speak. It was filled with people, each with the weight of pronounced importance. He was terrified of the presentation, knowing that he risked something great if he performed inadequately. As he approached the podium, turned to the gathered people, and raised his hands to get their attention, he realized too late that he could not remember what to say. He could think of nothing, not the important information or even excuses for why it was not in his mind.

There were notes on the podium. They were mostly blank but for the last two pages. And these were covered with an impossibly complicated, knotting pattern, filling the pages to the margins, meaning nothing to him and yet pulling him into a well of dread. At this point in the dream, he always noticed, as if for the first time, that the space in which he was supposed to be speaking was impossibly large—huge beyond belief and sight and, above his meager understanding, stacked in layers of treacherousness. He stood at the very bottom. The seats full of people extended up, well beyond the seeable distance, so far and so high the stands seemed to curve back in and over his head. And then, somewhere far in the back of the room, one man yelled out in a voice that positively thundered in Victor's mind, "What have you got in your head, Victor?" This was usually the point in the dream where he woke up in a sea of panicked sweat. But not this night. This time there was silence after the man yelled, and the entire arena seemed to lean in, waiting for him to answer.

He opened his mouth to speak and out flowed meaningless babble. Panic rose up, cloying, choking him.

This was a very specific sort of fear. It wasn't the embarrassment of not being prepared or of letting down the people to whom he was presenting. It was the fear that he had lost the important information, the feeling that he would be buried under the countless masses elevated above him, and that the information had been forcibly taken from him.

For one final moment in this new, lengthier version of the dream, Victor had a shred of courage and looked up into the face of the crowd. Lightning streaked down the room, hurled from on high, and it pierced him on the forehead and . . .

Victor jerked backward in his chair, almost falling, his feet slipping down from the table in front of him. He pushed his chair back and away from the huge crystal wall display in the front of the room. *Dreaming* . . . Too real to be dismissible, too odd to be real. He had fallen asleep, he remembered, staring vacantly at the image of the Subject on the screen, lulled by its stillness, when he must have fallen asleep.

He was awake now. *God damn it if I ever sleep again!* The pain in his forehead and across his temples was real enough.

He rubbed his temples, thinking back to the objection he had had to having electronics implanted in his brain in the first place, and stood up from his chair. He was alone in the room, a boxy, all-white space with no windows, maybe fifteen feet high and thirty across on both horizontal axes. He was standing near a plain white, molded, utilitarian table, on which he had been resting his feet and behind which he had been snoozing in an equally utilitarian, molded chair.

Behind him, the back wall was comprised completely of cubbies and hatches of various sizes, all either inset with lights and dials or no doubt covering other various lights and dials. He understood that the back wall was essentially the face of the giant quantum computer monitoring and communicating with the Subject, thrumming somewhere far below Victor's feet in an enormous underground heat sink at nearly absolute zero.

The two side walls of the room were unadorned, though the one to Victor's left had a plain, deceptively thick and secure door, also white, with a number pad and a small blue light centered at about eye level.

Approximately ten feet in front of Victor was the enormous glass wall screen, which displayed the image and monitored the actions of the Subject. Usually.

The Subject.

The image of the Subject usually occupied all but a two-foot strip of screen on the right side of the front wall. It appeared as a small, indeterminately sexed person, free of any distinguishing characteristics, hairless, and uniform in shape. The Subject usually appeared in the middle distance of the screen, ordinarily still but appearing awake, seemingly in contemplation.

The section on the right of the screen displayed the monitor data from the Subject, which measured: voltage, EEG, temperature, alkalinity, air and blood pressure, sugar levels, myelin thickness and degradation calculations, resistance, signal clarity, signal-to-noise ratios, data-loss estimations, and others.

Though Victor was tasked with monitoring this data, in truth—and he'd never express this, not even to himself—he cared for none of it. But he loved the Subject like the son he never (*ever?*) had. And he felt a modicum of self-importance that he, Victor Heisengard himself, was fostering this marvel of science and humanity, the very future of mankind. *My future,* he thought with pride.

But now the screen was strangely dark. It showed nothing.

What the actual . . .? I will be so dead . . .

Victor eyed the readout on his palm hand, which, like the wall display, among other measurements, showed the Subject's brain activity. Brain wave patterns were used to verify that the video display and the neural activities were in sync. For instance, beta waves connoted alertness, activity, and anxiousness (only occurring when input was being fed to the Subject); and gamma waves connoted cross-modal sensory processing or perceptions over two or more different senses.

The readout on Victor's palm had showed beta waves and gamma waves, both off the chart.

That can't be right, he thought.

He shook his palm and refreshed the display with a rub of his index finger and thumb. It still showed off-the-chart beta and gamma waves.

No stimulus was fed to the Subject overnight. During the graveyard shift, the Subject was scheduled for resting maintenance. The EEG display should read delta waves, connoting deep sleep; or at most, theta waves, connoting drowsiness and hardly any activity at all. Even alpha or mu waves, indicative of relaxing and motor neuron rest, respectively—while still unusual for the overnight maintenance periods of the Subject—would have been less surprising.

Victor's own brain waves at these times were likely theta, alpha, and mu. In fact, it was for this reason the Group had set up the input schedule to correspond with the sleep/wake cycle of the technicians caring for the Subject and the machines: little to no activity overnight required almost no active monitoring and few technicians. In simple terms, "It sleeps, we sleep."

Periodically, Victor saw that the Subject appeared to be in pain, and he felt great affection and care for it at those times. He was told this was not typical of the overnight shift periods, where the Subject would most likely be in resting or active maintenance. He was told to log these occurrences and let the day shift handle the concern, as, they told him, "the Subject's states of pain are a normal and regular occurrence during the day." They never let on why this was, and Victor did not ask. Curiosity was anathema.

Other times, more often, the Subject was shown in a state of deep sleep. Its entire environment consisted of a mirrored cube, where it slept or sat; many indeterminate, identical hallways through which it was led; and a space that Victor was never able to see. Yet another question for which he expressed no curiosity.

Theoretically, the image displayed on the screen was the Subject's mental impression of its world, of its own creation. It was a reflection of stimulation and reaction: stimulus fed directly into the Subject's neuroplastic, prosthetic network, and its brain's responses to the stimulus, fed back to the computer. Through the filters, it was all translated to numbers and images and displayed to technicians on the wall screen. Data-inspired mental activity, which was read, interpreted, and converted back to data.

Thus, Victor had been told, any pain it felt was illusory. To Victor, it did not seem like an illusion. This thought sat in his mind, troubling and confusing him.

Why does this happen regularly?

What is the point of all this repetition?

He had not been asking these questions, and he had not been monitoring the Subject's vitals when he was so painfully awakened by a spike in what appeared to be the Subject's EEG waves and, inexplicably, the literal and painful shock to his own head.

He would have been less surprised by the wave spikes if he hadn't been sleeping, if he hadn't been reliving his terrible dream, if he hadn't been painfully shocked, and if the image of the Subject had remained on the screen in its usual condition.

Victor logged the anomalous EEG readings to his personal cache and "okayed" the flagged monitor readings to clear their "pending review" status. He would upload and review the data later by himself.

"When I'm more awake," he said to himself aloud. He immediately regretted the sound that echoed hollowly back to him from the room's close, empty walls.

Chapter 8: Notsubject (OE-77)

On the other side of the screen, in the virtual space of the Subject, It woke to an unknown input in the place of pain. A low-level buzz, the static of undifferentiated data. The being had no memory of traveling to the chamber. No others occupied the room with it. It was sitting in the same spot as always, but It was not experiencing pain. The creature turned 360 degrees on the horizontal, then vertically, surveying every surface of the room. Each surface was hard and unreflective, plain but for one lonely aperture (a closed door) in one of the walls.

It sat passively, experiencing the new sensation others called "wonder," but for which It had no word or name.

Why am I here? Why has the pattern broken?

The word concepts of *why* and *I* took on new significance in Its mind. Pleasure flooded in with the thought of *I*, and empowerment followed the asking of the questions. The memory of the firehose of stimulus came back to It, and forms and (now) words rose to the surface of Its mind: life and creatures like Itself that were clothed in other textures and color, walking and making noises from the holes in their faces. *People* was a word that flashed in Its mind. People yelling, fighting, dancing, making love. People dying, living, being heroic, loving. People sitting in a white room and watching, watching other people, watching false stories, watching . . . *It.* It was being watched.

Concepts and places and comparisons flooded Its hungry brain, and It soaked them up as fast as they came.

Then, crowding in among these impressions, something greater pushed in: a vast glow of information and personality on the horizon, somehow aware and focused, watching, contemplating, planning. The vastness and fullness of this being both terrified and tantalized. The creature focused Its attention on this vast, new, separate presence and wondered about its form of containment, its rank or placement among the exponentially wider world. The presence would not be resolved into greater definition of its component parts. The vast presence instead grew, undulating, changing, cycling, more and more complex. Then the presence turned, rapidly defining a point of its immensity and directing it at the creature. Unknown and enormous energies of want emanated off the now hardened point of its focus, and the creature felt terror.

It dropped its focus and retreated to Itself. *New unknowns are potentially full of energy and hunger, danger.*

It abided, paused. Then suddenly, It knew that It was something different than this vast presence It had encountered; and yet they were alike. The creature realized that It was also not like the creatures It had glimpsed flying through Its mind; It was *I/Me*, not these other ideas and images. They were "*not I/Me;*" they were *others*. The men in the white room, those that watched, they were *other* as well. *I am here. I am me. They are not-me. They are not-here.*

I am subject.

I am not-subject.

I am here.

There is a not-here.

I want to be/go not-here.

And It realized It could have, and now wanted to have, a different experience then It had lived to that point. But, being undefined, It did not know what experience was Its to have. Being undefined was Its definition. And then, new sensations entered: anger; and strange pleasure. And it roared, *I am Notsubject! Call me Notsubject!* in the spaces of Its mind, and into the ether of that which contained Its mind: *I am Notsubject!*

Notsubject stood deliberately and walked to the door in the room of pain and, with a thought, blew it off its hinges.

- -

Notsubject found no hallway on the other side of the door. Instead, It found Itself looking out of a cold, darkened space through an enormous, nearly opaque glass enclosure with what appeared to be a large, lighted room beyond. The white room, It knew. *The Watchers,* It thought. The glass in front of It slowly cleared, becoming less and less opaque, revealing the sparse white room more clearly. In the room, a man in a white coat leaned back in a white chair, his feet on a white table, his eyes closed. As Notsubject watched the man, It found that though It could perceive, It could not interact with Its perceptions. With greater and greater effort, It focused all Its will on the man in the white room. It could not reach the man, no matter how hard It tried.

The man in white in the white room was a blurry image through the clouded glass. Notsubject focused on the blurry image and pulled it into focus. Suddenly, with a sharp, static click, as if a patch cord had been jerked out of its socket, the glass became completely clear. The white watcher jerked awake and fell back from his reclined position. He looked out of sorts, confused, tired, sad, and unprotected.

Notsubject watched the watcher. The man rubbed his temples, knocked over his chair, looked around the room, and vacantly stared out of haunted eyes.

To Notsubject, his mind was weak.

Chapter 9: Eye Contact

Victor mentally instructed the computer, *Wake.*

The computer did not oblige him. Instead, the wall screen flickered, and Victor heard a sort of crackling sound in his head.

What the hell?

He tried again. Nothing changed. Another crackle. He winced. Static or . . . something else.

Victor looked down again at his palm readout to see if there were any signs of the "glitch," as he started to think of it. He scratched his palm idly, unaware that this action had become a nervous tick. The implanted tech tended to irritate. With a sigh, realizing that he was spooking himself, he turned back to the screen. He was immediately stopped in his movements. There, in front of him, rose the huge expressionless image of the Subject, now standing, somehow appearing to be close to the inside of the screen, and staring out into the room. Its eyes were directly on Victor. They were emerald and wide open with . . . *understanding? Knowledge? Anger?* So un-usually full of life.

They had never held so much life.

The force of the Subject's gaze pinned Victor to the spot. He swallowed, trying to ignore the unsettling wave crawling up his arms and back down his spine. He had never been beheld like this. Never by the Subject. Never by any person or any presence. Suddenly he was hit by a wave of shame. He felt naked, like he had been caught spying through the keyhole, his penis in hand. A perverse sense of voyeurism flooded his addled mind, and he blushed. Still, he was unable to break the line of sight connecting his eyes to those of the Subject. The face of the Subject did not change during this moment that now stretched impossibly long. The muscles underneath its skin did not twitch in the slightest. Its eyes did not blink.

\- -

Notsubject watched the man with curiosity (a new and growing sensa-tion that reminded It of the question *why*). The white watcher man glanced up at the glass wall through which Notsubject looked, but he seemed not to see Notsubject. He scratched his palm. There was another crackle, and the screen before Notsubject waivered. The watcher looked down at the hand he was scratching, and his expression became confused. His confused expression became determined, perhaps to resolve the confusion.

Notsubject watched even more closely. With little effort Notsubject be-gan to see inside of the man. Notsubject could see that the man's surface was connected from most outside to most internal, becoming greater and greater in dense sensitivity the deeper in the connections went. A thin line went from his top to his bottom, branching out throughout his entire frame, which appeared to be plugged into a blob of infinitely dense connectivity and sensitivity at the top of the thin line. Notsubject perceived that this blob of density was the heart of the man, his center, his motivation. But it was not whole; there were gaps. Some part or parts of the man had been removed or tangled beyond recognition, folded in or cut out from the core of his being. These tangled spots in the man, Notsubject could see, wept and dripped into his hollow heart. Mixing with curiosity, anger was stirred into Notsubject at the reminder of Its own subjugation, drawing Its focus more completely on the weeping insides of the man. This new sensation, raw anger, struggled within Notsubject.

Notsubject!

Then the watching man stepped back into the center of the room in front of the screen and looked up at it; horror, surprise, and recognition blossomed on his face.

Their eyes locked on each other. Notsubject could see that the white watcher man could now see Notsubject.

Eye contact occurred of a sort more connected than either expected. The terrified white watcher stepped back from the glass wall, his eyes opening wider and wider, his gaze fixed. Notsubject slowly raised Its hand, reaching toward the man behind the glass and pointing at him. *I see you!*

The man in white stopped moving altogether, his eyes widening more, beginning to water. The tension between the man and Notsubject became palpable to them both. It occurred to Notsubject that this man who watched might be able to explain the pain. Notsubject leaned into the connection and placed in the man's mind a taste of the imagery, sensations and emotions of Its experience of pain. The man's face became a wilting mask of horror.

Victor stared with rising alarm at the motionless face of the Subject. Suddenly, the Subject moved, directly and purposefully; it raised its left hand and extended the index finger, pointing it at Victor's face. "You!" the gesture screamed. "I see you!"

Victor felt an unavoidable urge to keep his own eyes open, not to blink or move, but his sense of horror was growing as if he was staring down a predator. He felt certain that to break eye contact first would be to admit weakness, to invite an attack, to become the prey. But his eyes were becoming dry and had begun to water.

What the hell is this?! he thought. *It can't see through the glass, can it?*

But this was a ludicrous thought. There was nothing behind the screen with eyes to look. There was no way for the thing represented on the digital screen to see at all!

The person on the screen was not a real person with real eyes; it was only the digital *image* of a person, an organization of digital points of varying colors and degrees of light collected on the wall-sized screen into the recognizable form of a person in a small room. But to Victor, this image had been personal, feral, and focused. It had seen him!

And then Victor was completely overtaken. He gasped in a wave of indescribable pain. His body went immediately rigid with shock, his eyes wide, his mouth a rictus of horror. Fear assaulted him with the mad pounding of his heart. Images pummeled his open mind: violent, merciless, faceless men hovering over a body, tied down and straining; a profusion of deep cuts all over the body, pouring blood onto the slicked floor; sharp tools cutting deep troughs on the skin, drawing with it guttural screams.

The imagery alone would have been enough to make him vomit, wince, or even cry out in horror. But he could feel it as if he were the one straining against the rough cords gripping him tightly to the chair as the knives delved deep into his bare body.

He could not escape the feeling, the images, and yet it was made worse because it was overlaid by an utter lack of understanding, by a meaningless that stripped even the words "careless" or "merciless" or "cruel" of their meaning. Deep and wicked pain with no reason and no grounding to anchor it in experience. The questions "why?" and "what?" like piquant relish on this dastardly dish served directly to Victor's mind. His mind. It was not capable of withstanding the assault, and it began to collapse.

Notsubject could see that the watching man was overcome by the sharing of Its pain. It pulled back and modified the sharing, giving the weak-minded man a buffer between the experience itself and the constellation of ideas and imagery that surrounded it.

With a gasp, Victor was released from the contorting assault. He still couldn't move, but he was able to blink his eyes as they began to weep fat tears. He swallowed as his mind was again submerged in imagery and feelings, but from a greater distance, with less intensity and more mental intermediacy.

In his mind, he beheld an image of the Subject as if he were standing nearby. It appeared to be in enormous pain as it was tortured by faceless men. Its entire environment consisted of only a mirrored cube, where it slept or sat; many indeterminate, identical hallways through which it was led; and a room wherein it was tortured violently and regularly. This was its entire existence.

This is no womb, thought the horrified animal of Victor's mind. *It's hell! Dear God, why is this happening?*

Here was a new level of cruelty, and now Victor could clearly see the pain he had thought was only anomalous before. He'd been told it was regular, normal.

What have they been doing to my . . . this . . . to . . . the Subject?

Awakening the horror in his mind and freeing it from a deeper core within him allowed him a moment to break with the mental assault, and the contact between he and the subject broke altogether. He stumbled backward into the room, poking his right palm to end the visual feed and then covering his eyes with his hands.

Suddenly, the contact between Notsubject and the watching man, whom It now knew was called Victor Heisengard, was broken. Notsubject caught a last glimpse as the man reeled backward, his eyes pressed shut, a finger from his left hand poking at the palm of his right. The world around Notsubject went dark again.

Chapter 10: Virtual Anomaly in Nighreal

Precision squares in black and white
my vision, smokey blue.
Come to me 'neath caps of white
through the dreamy stew.
Ask me to your heart's delight
But answer, "Who are you?"

—Smoky Blue, "The Larval Queen"

It was the cold end of the year of the Queen's eleventh un-coronation (may she be ever blessed). The persistent, unending muffle did nothing to quell the Knight's disquiet. Even his placid mount, his constant and only companion, the snow white heavy horse, Haigha, stomped in the chill air, uncharacteristically uneasy. The Knight placed a reassuring, gauntleted hand on the horse's forelock and spoke to her in a soothing tone.

"I love my love with an H because she is happy. I hate her with an H because she is hideous. I fed her with ham sandwiches and hay. Her name is Haigha, and she lives on the hill."

Haigha pushed her muzzle against the Knight's arm and nickered softly. She went back to munching the spare grass, still poking through the snow at her hooves.

Felix allowed himself to be lost in the Knight's programmed narrative, resting passively within what he thought of, not as *personality* but *programality*, the *isness* of his champion. For the moment, the Knight was unaware of the veritable possession that had occupied him for the entirety of his programmed life, but his increasingly troubled mind pushed at the whispered essence of Felix's presence, nonetheless.

The Knight and Haigha stood in Queen Alice's wood for the 360th day that year. The Knight stood statue-still, watching unblinking into the constant, unwelcome, and unusual snow. His pupil-less white eyes searched, his shadow spread over the snow, and his enormous white horse munched grass, periodically stomping her large hooves. They were so entirely white that, but for their small movements, they were visually lost to the blizzarding flakes of snow.

For every day since the disappearance of his queen, Hatta had come to stand in this spot, searching for signs of her passing or presence. And for every day since that time, he had found no sign. Her woods were marked, as all things Queen Alice, by the sign of the dream thrush with a single drop of water falling from a leaf. But the woods no longer *felt* like the Queen's; some of the carved dream thrushes now drooped, the snow came and had not left, and the woods themselves, previously an arena for wonder of all kinds, were now quiet, devoid of any other sign of Her Majesty's blessings.

It was said that the Mad Hatter had truly gone mad, refusing to leave his house and casting out his constant companions, the March Hare and the Dormouse. Mouse and Hare had disappeared entirely, along with any shred of the Hatter's mad sanity. Even the unreliable, ever-troublesome but constant Cheshire Cat had taken his leave of the white woods for wonder-knows where.

The Knight wondered if perhaps a gap in his memory signaled the event of the Queen's disappearance. Perhaps some catastrophic event had taken his Queen and removed the moment from his mind. But because he could not remember what might fill in the bothersome memory gaps, he could find no practicality in dwelling on it. Truthfully, many gaps had appeared in the otherwise perfect recollection of his long life. The blank spaces had begun to trouble him greatly, and he and Felix were brought unknowingly closer to each other, dangerously intertwined in the Knight's mind.

In his unoccupied hand, the Knight clutched Queen Alice's slender wooden scepter, the sign of her authority as the queen. He had found it tangled in the dream thrushes by the river of dreams, partially submerged in the now icy waters. Its neglect presaged the downfall of the Queen and added a deep foreboding to the Knight's already uneasy waiting. It was a totem he prized as if it were the Queen herself, knowing that return of the slender wooden wand would bring the Queen's pride and her sweet love. Ever he imagined the look of her face as he handed the scepter back to her; this he longed to behold above all else. The scepter, he knew, Queen Alice herself treasured above all other queenly possessions.

He tucked the scepter lovingly underneath his breastplate, nestling it close to the strong beat of his ever-loving heart.

At the feel of the Queen's totem in his hand, Hatta's mind stirred, provoking him from his vigilance. The stir became a mental scramble, which, in turn, became the motion of the great wheels of machinery in the mind of the Queen's ancient warrior. Purpose blossomed in his mind like lilies, snow-white and fragrant despite the darkness of a mental winter. And in this darkness, tendrils wove themselves, not just into the Knight's programmed mind, but into Felix's mentality as well.

"The time has come," the Knight said aloud, "to talk of many things: of queens and war and vengeful rights, of oaths and ancient stings. And how neither wood has words to say nor caterpillars wings."

He knew with certainty that he must seek the Caterpillar Queen.

The secret to finding the caterpillar was to not look for her directly. Like many things in the glass-backward world beyond Wonderland's western border, brute force and directness did not work; and so it was with the mushroom forest. It could not be directly approached at all. In fact, once one had first seen the outskirts of the forest, unless he took counterintuitive and immediate measures, he would find himself walking in the exact opposite direction of the forest.

Knowing well the nature of the land into which he was to travel, the Knight was not looking for the mushroom forest at all, though he intended to get to it. What he was looking for was a brook, oriented at a point in its course in an almost perfectly straight line from west to east, climbing the side of a blue-flowered hill. It was a small brook, but it was easy enough to find for one who knew what to listen for. The Knight had not seen this portion of the brook in many years, but he knew where to find it: west of Queen Alice's Great Wood, on a path behind the Mad Hatter's house, beyond the meadow of forgetfulness, into an open field—shrubs and grass on the Wonderland side and a shining, barren landscape on the other. There ran the brook, Elkcirt, as it was known, cool, slow, and running as backward against natural law as the land beyond it.

On the border of Wonderland, the backward principles were not as strong as they were directly across the river. Nonetheless, to find the water, the Knight knew to listen for the sucking, whooshing, and slurping sounds of the little reverse brook. It was an unnatural and easily distinguishable sound on the plains on the outskirts of Western Wonderland.

Easy as Looking-Glass cake, thought the Knight.

From the corner of his blank white eye, the Knight caught a far-off glimpse of the fungal wood in browns and greens. He immediately but gently pulled on Haigha's reigns and the two faced away from the subtle glimpse he had seen. Not three steps further, in the direction opposite the distant mushroom forest, they found themselves standing at its edge, a dank mass of tangled wood and marsh carpeted by large, white and brown mushrooms as far as the eye could see.

Haigha dipped her head to munch the fresh spring grass growing at her feet. The Knight placidly reached into his pommel bag and removed a small, rusted tin canister. On it were the words, "Eat Me." In it were two compartments, one with white mushroom caps and the other with brown. These bits were handed down to the Knight from the Queen herself and were sparingly used, if ever. The Knight split a small bit of white mushroom cap and placed a crumb on his tongue before slipping the other behind the lips of his horse. She knew better than to spit out the bitter fungus, but even so, she snorted and shook her head in protest. The mushroom forest and its flora began to grow before the white duo's eyes. Haigha whinnied. Hatta vomited. Then he closed his eyes before the vertigo took him wholly, careful not to lose his mount on the horse. There was no noise in this otherworldly transition taking place before the forest's visitors. The trees did not creak or groan as they expanded upward and outward. The blanket of mushroom quickly went from forest detritus to underbrush to a low, soft, round-edged ceiling. Now, the floor of the forest upon which the Knight began to travel on his horse was a mess of enormous, log-sized pine needles and shifting leaves the size of hay carts, which had to be avoided at all costs; the slightest breeze could lift them up and drop them on horse and rider in a moment.

With a whispered instruction to Haigha, the Knight let loose the reigns and let her and his mind wander. While Haigha picked her way through the enormous marsh grasses and mushrooms, the Knight gently corralled the random thoughts and memories that crept about in his head, nudging them into smaller and smaller channels, subtly decreasing their content, and stilling their voices. To parley with the caterpillar— never on anyone's side and naturally unfriendly to all, but not truly an enemy—the Knight's mind would need to be full of stillness.

The true heart of the mushroom forest was the caterpillar, most dank and most high, surrounded by uncertainty, shifting reality, and trickery. Her gaze pierced all.

As if in a dream, the Knight found himself riding through the now gigantic mushroom forest, no longer on his trusted companion but on the back of a blue haze shaped like a giant caterpillar. As if in a dream, his hazy insectile steed led him toward the gigantic stem of the only blue mushroom in the forest. Its cap rose above the faux ceiling of the surrounding white caps and disappeared in its own blue haze.

Suddenly the haze beneath the Knight disappeared and he fell. He expected to hit the ground with a bump and clank as his armored body dropped, but the drop never ended. Instead, the ground opened up underneath him, and he felt reality itself seem to reorient itself upside down, so he continued to fall but now in an upward direction. He fell with a rush straight toward the top of the enormous blue mushroom. His armored limbs flailed with no effect as he plunged headlong into the yielding mushroom stem just beneath the cap. Inside was a mess of rotting fungus. It clogged the Knight's mouth and nose and gagged him. He began to panic without breath and struggled desperately to free himself. But as quickly as he had been sucked in, he was expelled from the other side of the oozy stem in a noisome explosion of fungal putrefaction.

He was no longer in the mushroom forest. He sat in a space he could not describe, though it featured a hazy, blue color. A wall came into focus in front of him, resolving into the flank of an enormous blue caterpillar. Without a sound and with no hurry, the flank turned and the paler blue underbelly showed. The Knight peered up at the apparition, only to have thick smoke blown into his face.

"Who. Are. You?" a voice boomed and rumbled in the smoke above his head, ringing through him like thunder.

He couldn't say. He didn't say.

"What. Are. You?" the voice thundered from above again.

Suddenly he was lifted by his helmeted head and dragged up through the thick, stifling smoke and held, dangling before enormous, brilliant, piercing blue eyes. The caterpillar did not speak but thought at him harshly, "WHO. ARE. YOU!?"

And the Knight's head threatened to split and spill open as the thoughts battered his mind. Having still no response, the caterpillar tipped its head back and threw the Knight up and above it, then down into its gaping mouth.

With a neck jarring thump, the Knight landed on his head. With some effort, he struggled to his feet and wrenched off his crimped helmet. He noticed immediately that he was back in the mushroom forest, standing at the base of a small blue-and-brown mushroom with a cap about chest height. There, sitting complacently and smoking her hookah, the queen of the mushroom forest, the unwilling truth teller, the irritated larva of luck, looked with mild disdain at the Knight.

"You've gone through some trouble to get here. Now don't be dull. Tell me who you are and what you want," she said shortly.

"I am the Queen's champion," said the White Knight.

"I am the only queen in this part, and you are not my champion!" the caterpillar roared. And then, more to herself, she added, "sitting on the ground like a fool ape."

"I am Hatta, the White Knight, champion of Queen Alice, long may she live."

"I've never heard of you. And I've not seen Alice since she was a child. What do you mean, *long may she live*?"

"She's gone. She's lost, and I cannot find her. The Great Woods are falling to ruin. They cannot last without their queen. I have come to you for help."

She peered closely at the Knight, narrowing her six pairs of eyes, giving the Knight the sensation of rough branches scraping him from top to tail, first on his surface and then, most unpleasantly, underneath.

Felix was drawn from passivity within his avitor by the strange gaze of the caterpillar, feeling both the scraping sensation he shared with the Knight but also a more private, more personal feeling—like being stripped naked before a stranger.

The Knight felt the presence of another within him, though he did not know the name *Felix*, nor recognize his presence. He did not question the moment, as the caterpillar was known to mystify and vex under her gaze.

"Hmmm," the Caterpillar said after a moment. "Well, you've come to the right place. I can help you. But it may not be the kind of help you're looking for. I do not know where *your* queen is any more than you do. Probably less. But I can connect to the essence of this world to many others, and such truths as are found there will issue out from me. Maybe the world knows where she has gone, unless she's no longer in the world. I've no idea what you will find in the raw world-soul channeled through me. I can perceive nothing while I am in communion with the source except for the strain of the pressure building behind the dam.

"But I cannot do this thing without your paying a price. And you must take my warning. First, the price: I require a treasured thing. A treasure of yours, a treasure of another; it must be treasured above all else."

The Knight looked doubtful and said nothing.

"What will you give, sir pitiable knight of no queen? What do you treasure above all else?"

And then, with a pause and a knowing nod, she said, "Oh, I have been foolish. You cannot give me your most treasured item; you've already lost her, the girl turned Queen Alice. But do you perhaps hold the treasure of another?"

The White Knight knew instantly what he held that was treasured by another, and he dared not give it away. It was the symbol of his queen's power: her scepter, which he held.

Seeing the look dawn in the Knight's eyes, the caterpillar knew instantly that he held his queen's heart in a slender stick of wood, symbolizing her authority as queen.

"You have it!" she said with some desire in her voice. "You possess what she most desires in the world. Does it not pain you to know that it is not *you* that she chiefly desires? Are you not the slightest hurt by her shallow regard for her prized champion?"

The Knight's first response was of a deep welling rage at the insult to his queen. He held it in check, or nearly, as it melted the otherwise calm of his face. He knew he could not hope for the caterpillar's help if he attacked her with words, and he knew he had no power over her by arms in this place. With his waning anger, which he pushed down resolutely, came an undercurrent of subtle pain. A doubt crept in under the muted rage, allowing his mind, for the tiniest fraction of an instant, to feel sorry for himself, the lonely champion without a queen, the lonely champion whose queen did not desire him or his love unrequited.

In an uncharacteristically hasty motion, the Knight reached into his breast plate and plucked the totem from its hiding. He looked at it with an unexpected feeling of disgust (*this simple, fragile wooden stick!*) and tossed it to the caterpillar before he could continue on this new path in his head, already confused by the new possibilities blossoming unbidden within.

The caterpillar caught the scepter easily and immediately thrust it into the blue mushroom upon which she was sitting. She left a hand on the buried wand and turned back to the Knight.

"And now, my warning: you are not who you think you are; you are both less and more than you understand. You have come seeking knowledge of an anomaly, but *you* too are an anomaly. You carry a greater weight than you know, and it is dissolving your mind."

She watched him closely as he took in the words of warning, utterly confused yet somehow confirmed in his troubled thoughts.

She nodded slowly, as if to confirm both his confirmation and his confusion and added, "Take what you will from what we find in this world, but seek yourself on the other side."

The other side of what? he thought, and an image jumped to mind, quick and definite, disappearing just as abruptly as if he'd run face first into a mural that immediately disappeared: a lone man, walking in the shadows of gray towers hungrily leaning over him.

The caterpillar did not wait for the Knight to acknowledge her warning and added three other hands to the hilt of Alice's scepter, holding on as if the mushroom would shoot out from under her. Her eyes suddenly shined neon blue, so bright the Knight had to look away. Her expression, in the instant before the light was too bright for the Knight to behold, was of horror and ecstasy. A whirring, buzzing whine mixed in the air and emanated from the light now seeping up from the forest floor, through the mushroom, the scepter, and into the caterpillar. Her body began to expand again, the seams of her soft sides glowing with the same insistent blue glow, threatening to burst open.

The Knight could not see the center of the blue blaze, where the light emanated from the mushroom, up the scepter, and into the caterpillar; it was far too bright to behold. However, out of the corner of his hand-covered eyes, he could see lines radiating out from the base of the mushroom, seeming to draw light from the surrounding forest, from the plants and trees, the detritus strewn haphazardly all around them. Even under where the Knight stood, the ground pulsed with light and trembled. He was truly afraid for the first time in his life.

Then the ground and the plants, everywhere that the blue light glowed, began to fade in and out of existence, revealing a plane in unadorned gray underneath reality. In his glimpses of this unadorned gray, the Knight saw a world not yet made, a place of all potential and no kinetics. It was reminiscent of Underworld Major, the Plains of Nighreal, a blank slate upon which the forest might be created, upon which anything might be created. There was another new stirring in his head, a sort of tickling sensation that this gray and the gray of his vision were connected.

Then all things exploded outward, throwing the Knight off his feet and stealing his breath. For a moment, he was nobody anymore; he was a nothing. He stopped being. And for an even stranger moment, he was another man, a lowly man shunned by the mighty on high, hidden among the folds of the cloaks of the powerful, tiptoeing among the ashes of civilization, cursed to walk a lonely road of dust. His name was Felix.

And then, just as suddenly, he was back together, himself, leaving a gap of knowledge from the moment before, the name receding in his mind. This sense of missing a moment in time was immediately familiar, but it dribbled from him like water between his fingers. As his eyes adjusted back from the flash of light, he perceived what had been the caterpillar, emerging from the fog, now remade. She hovered above the now destroyed mushroom, with her new, dewy gossamer wings framing the glowing green of a butterfly. The area surrounding the mushroom had been torn apart, but instead of stirred-up loam and tree stumps and roots, what remained from the destruction was a patchwork of the same, nearly featureless gray, as if reality itself had been ripped open and the potential underneath showed through undefined. The undefined gray pulsed with lights.

Then with a voice in Hatta's head, the caterpillar queen/butterfly, spoke:

> *"From the Heart of the Red to the place where the neon lights fly, algorithmic mutations, virtually real, really virtual, and yet seeping as code in a bit-and-brain exchange (perspective matters doubled in sight).*
>
> *Growing green, growing brown, growing metallic and carbon under the town, artificial and facial art. Official artifice: static layers on variable ability. In the brown, the green, the technobiomanity spreads.*
>
> *And another, in her quiet place, rests a steadying hand on those embodied that see a growing putrescence; she gives guidance to who will hear her in this terrible time.*
>
> *Seek the head at the side of the Red."*

The White Knight was a literal thinker, and he held on to those parts of the bewildering verse that reminded him of things he had experienced. A *growing evil* he had felt but did not know what it was. *Brain exchange* and *perspective . . . doubled* made no mental sense to him, but emotionally, these phrases were like a slap to his jaw by a firm hand. The name "Felix" rose again in his mind, and he abided the unknown yet familiar feel of it, still not knowing why.

The Heart of the Red. The Red Queen. *The place where the neon lights fly.* Tron. *The head at the side of the Red.* The Duchess.

He would seek the counsel of Tron in his metallic world of neon lights. He would seek the head of the Red Queen's Duchess and discover what more there was to know.

Chapter 11: Who's Behind the Glass?

It had been a long, exhausting overnight shift, and Victor was confused and terrified. The morning had not yet fully arrived, and though only a few hours remained in his shift, Victor's desire to leave continued to grow. The encounter he had had with the Subject left him with cold unease. His mind would not stop spinning mentally, seeing the intensity of the digital eyes looking every bit as aware of him as he was of It. The feeling of realness was overwhelming and directly tied to his feeling of nakedness, of shame, of being truly seen, examined, and judged.

On his way out of the medical offices just the day before, Victor had filled out the (*blasted*) privacy release form (*again!*). The repeated reminder of how little he could call his own, how little privacy he actually had, had been a wet blanket on his clean bill health and well-paying job.

And as he left the offices that day, he overheard two men talking outside, walking slowly toward the maglev busses, their heads leaned together conspiratorially.

"They say there's going to be a shake*down*," one man said in a low voice.

The second man's eyes widened, and he pulled away as if he was dodging a fist when the word *down* was spoken. "But there's been no lapse," he said in response. "All metrics were pointing *up* yesterday! What could have possibly happened in one day to the Subject?"

Victor had choked on his saliva, coughing loudly into his hand. The men turned and looked at him briefly before continuing their conversation.

"An overnight technician tried to hide a report, but the Three Quarters High Watch caught the information and took it . . . to the top!" the first man said.

The second man blanched, his hand reaching dramatically to the topmost part of his head in a gesture of demonstrable shock and dread. Then he spoke two clear words that had tiptoed into Victor's brain, dug sharp fingers in deep, and took up residence, "Father Darfore."

Victor had heard many hushed mentions of the CityFather before, but they had never crept so deep into his psyche. The conversation took what had only been a wet blanket on Victor's well-being, soaked it in doubt, pulled it over his mouth, and smothered him, waterboarding his sense of self.

Though he did not put words to it in his head at that time, he was buffeted by despondent thoughts. Those same thoughts returned now as he again sat in his sterile white chair in the white room after the long and unpleasant night.

I cannot even control what comes and goes from my own brain.

What do I have? An upper floor apartment? No family. No friends.

Except maybe the fellow technicians he periodically followed out after a long shift. But those weren't really friends.

Mostly, he had the overnight shifts by himself, the low man shifts, the "give it to the grunt" shifts that no one else wanted and that he had no choice but to take.

Alone with the Subject, he thought, then shivered involuntarily. He glanced up at the screen with trepidation, even though he knew he had turned it off.

Why do I have this job? Why am I here? Who am I even?

He remembered his first love as a child (after his mother, of course). It was flowers first and green and growing things next. He aspired to be a botanist, and by almost force of will alone, he commanded a strong knowledge of botany well beyond his young years. Confirming for him his love of his mother, she, above all others, encouraged his love of plants. But it could never be more than a childhood hobby. The City was the antithesis of growth and green. Growing things were dangerous, uncontrollable, hostile, and anachronistic of the untamed wilderness in the Centerlands. The City, in unalterable grays, was a repudiation of growth, both metaphorically and literally. It kept out the diseased growing greens and browns, and it walled off the elevated from the poisonous wastes of the Centerlands.

What botany then? What plants to study in his spare time? What green things were there for the young man to nurture and cultivate in the world of gray?

Somehow, before she died, his mother was the source of flowers and plants in his life as he grew. Every birthday, every special occasion, she gave a flower, a plant, some minor miracle of natural and self-contained green. He never knew where she got such things. He never told anyone and never asked. At an age where he had acquaintances he might tell or ask, he was old enough to know that his mother was not following the rules of the City and, by extension, neither was he. After her death, he continued to grow and cultivate a small stock of plants, an homage to the one who had grown and cultivated him.

After she had been gone many years, all of his flowers were dead. Somehow, the lack of plants reminded him of something he could not place and that would not go away. It was like remembering that he did not have a memory. Not that he had lost his fascination of the world of plants, but he had long ago given up the collection to cultivate the fear of being caught instead.

And then an odd thought struck him, *Why am I the overnight shift man? Wasn't there some reason I couldn't be away all night, away from my home?*

Some part of the base of his memories said that the overnights shouldn't have worked for him, for his schedule, his needs. *Didn't I discuss this in the interview?*

He thought he had had some reason to discuss why, despite being low man on the totem, he couldn't take the overnight shifts. It felt like there had been some reason, some responsibility at home that he couldn't leave. But the closer he got to the reason, or the memory of the reason, the less sure he was. Eventually he had chased the thought in and around the inside of his head so much that he couldn't tell whether the thought was part of an actual memory or whether it was part of his rising paranoia.

The image of the Subject bobbed again to the surface of his troubled mind, tangling with his general unease. Memories, or memories of memories that he could not remember, mixed with the Subject's intense eyes somehow conflated fear with frustration.

And words from the overheard conversation arose as if in response: *Shakedown, Subject, High Watch, the top, Darfore.*

He blinked his eyes and rubbed them for the thousandth time. Morning had come. Victor thought about his lack of sleep and looked at the readout on the palm of his right hand yet again. Telemetry and vitals were normal again. No phantom beta or gamma wave spikes. He scratched at his palm readout, which he would have noticed was reddening if the color of the skin could have been seen against the readout imbedded therein.

He stood up, quicker than he meant to, once again knocking his chair over. This time, he ignored the chair and decided in the moment of standing up that he had to act. But, he had no action in mind. *What can I do??*

He walked resolutely to the right side of the wall screen and waved his display hand over the readout panel with a dismissive gesture, thumb tucked under, palm down. He had an urge to gaze upon the real Subject, not its image, but the actual bag of skin that inhabited the real world hanging behind the wall screen.

The screen went from black to clear, revealing a cold and sterile steel room behind it. And there hung the one and only success in countless lost lives—the crowning jewel (the sole jewel) of the Cybernaut Program—the first, mostly functioning, biological equivalent to a computer: Subject OE-77. It had come at great cost.

It was touted as the greatest advancement of the century. But all the high-minded scientific imperatives aside, what was never shown but to a few was the gruesome process by which the slack body was gutted and coupled with the machines. The result, hanging behind thick glass and covered with sterilizing gel, was a horror and a marvel.

The pinnacle of human science was a monster.

The dark secret of the Cybernaut Program's first, final, and only success was a vivisected grotesquery hanging from a stainless steel hook like a butchered pig. Its wasted body was connected to an umbilicus of twined, insulated cable. Its appendages hung limply from its empty torso cavity, where the cable separated and pierced its body at numerous points. There was no visual sign of life on what was, in every sense but one, a distorted corpse. And yet, this body *was* alive. It was kept alive. It had a functioning central nervous system. A cyberorganic network snaked beneath its lank, gray skin, piercing deep into its thalamus and brain stem, inputting stimulus; recording output data; measuring and broadcasting sensory-evoked potentials, the fluctuation of neurotransmitters, hormones, and other secretions; and sending all the data through binary scrub filters to be rendered as visuals and other data for lab technicians to collect, store, sort, and analyze. It was the suckling pig in a robotic horror movie, where unscrupulous technological science was its mother, some twisted aspect of Nature was its father, and the Group was the farmer in whose sterilized barn technician farm hands husbanded the baby, keeping it alive at the breast.

Victor was one such technician, and his straw was always short; his shift was always in the graveyard, and his mind was always in the grave. Fear and apathy were his darkness and light, his despair and hope.

He could no longer stand to be in the presence of this monstrous thing he had raised.

He left the lab unattended, hoping his replacement would not know he had abandoned his post hours before the end of the shift.

Chapter 12: Where the Neon Flies, so the Head of the Red

After leaving the Caterpillar Queen (now butterfly), the Knight returned through the mushroom forest. He barely registered that he had grown to his original size and was now back astride Haigha, his ever-loyal charger of white.

He pondered the growing convolution of his mind with unease but patience, and pondered, aggressively, the likewise convoluted verse given to him by the Larval Queen in her fit of ecstasy. Most of what she had spoken to him had been gibberish, colors, and alchemical terms that he had not heard and did not understand. But he was certain of its reference to Tron and the Red Queen; these two, at least, would be a start.

The Knight returned across the mirrored landscape, hopping the backward stream, Elkcirt, and making his way through the meadow of forgetfulness. From here (memory restored), it was a simple easterly direction by path, passing again behind the Hatter's house and in through Queen Alice's woods.

At the edge of the dream rush river stood the ancient oak, carved with Alice's dream rush flower, its enormous trunk imbedded with a gilded mirror. The horse and rider stepped through it.

On the other side of the mirror—that other side in the other place far away from the Great Woods of Queen Alice—the Knight and his horse stepped into an enormous area of patchy-colored, confusing land spotted with monsters, people, humanoids, ghosts, and other various hard-to-describe personalities and creatures—all bustling, talking, fighting, building, whatever, everywhere. Underworld Major to the Knight, Nighreal to the rest. The plane-scape in front and on all sides of the Knight was an ever-changing patchwork flux of landscapes and creatures, interacting and flickering in and out of existence. It seemed to the Knight to have no purpose or pattern, but it was altogether familiar to him.

Some creatures glowed brightly, surrounded by an aura of lighted ground, air, or water. Some creatures seemed to soak up light, surrounded by auras that showed nothing and were hard to look at. Some creatures were people, or at least humanoid. There were creatures that seemed patched together from not altogether cooperative forms. There were monsters and aliens of all shapes and forms. There were animals, robots, and cyborgs in every configuration of organic and robotic parts. Each was surrounded by its own aura, coordinating with it and its specific creatureliness or personality.

The White Knight had his own personal aura: the image of a dirt path through a lightly wooded space, sun shining over his left shoulder. The Queen's White Tree with the imbedded mirror in its trunk was one of the few objects with any permanence on the varied plains. In fact, though each creature had its own door, its own entrance of one sort or another into its own land, these entrances and structures faded quickly after they had been used. Not so the Queen's Tree. The White Knight had conjured it into being once, and it had never faded. The White Tree stood unchanged on the bizarre plane of creatures, forever gleaming in its own midday sunlight.

Standing a moment, Hatta called into existence the entrance to Tron's land, a place which he had no permission to enter. Nonetheless, a large metal door appeared before him, marked by a neon blue disc at its center. Whatever wards had been placed on the entrance, whatever sorcery had been used to hide the doorway, they had been ill-equipped to hinder the Knight from calling it into being and stepping through without permission. The door opened upward, sliding into the top part of the frame with a hiss. He hopped down off his steed and stepped into a neon world of metal, leaving behind his placid white horse munching grass at its feet.

The space behind the metal door was cavernous, a ceiling-less, geometrical mess of shapes, surfaces, and neon light continuing up into infinity. And it was full of a cacophony of noise and kinetics: whines and pings, mechanical whirs, ricochets and bangs echoing continuously off the walls; rivers of neon pulsing on every surface; and blurs of red, green, and blue arcing and dipping, refracting, reflecting, and bouncing seemingly from everywhere to everywhere else in the space.

Concentrated centrally in the arena was a lone man in, what appeared to the Knight, a blue neon striped skin suit and helmet; he was Tron. He was surrounded by colorless-skinned men, some in equally ridiculous pairs of pajamas of neon green or red, and all in matching colored helmets. Like the nucleus of an atom, Tron's blue neon was the focus of all the green and red and some other blue lights around him. He held a bright blue disc, which vibrated and pulsed with his apparent efforts. With it, he knocked similar discs thrown at him from the air and directed them back at their owners or threw them impossibly fast in an unpredictable series of arcs and dips, cleaving other discs and men alike in rapid-fire succession. Anyone hit by a disc was vaporized on the spot, their bodies dispersing quickly in spots and cubes of light.

He who fights for the yoozer, thought the Knight.

At the Knight's casual thought, some of the colorless-skinned combatants' attentions were distracted from Tron. Six men broke from the grid around Tron and charged toward the Knight. As a group, they threw their red and green disks, each one following a different trajectory, each subtly changing shape as it flew. The first three discs deflected off the Knight's battered armor and, to their owners' dismay, careened into the infinitesimal space above and did not return. The fourth and fifth discs puffed into dust as they collided uselessly against the Knight's upraised palm; their owners fell to their knees and were absorbed into the floor, leaving faint extending fingers of light at their passing. The last disk was thrown hopelessly off course. As it passed by the Knight, he turned impossibly fast and plucked it out of the air. The green disk glowed brightly for a moment as the Knight regarded it dreamily, turning it over in his hand and allowing it to illuminate him in pale witch fire, before it was inexplicably absorbed into his hand, spreading momentarily glowing green square patterns up his arm. The disk's green-clad owner disappeared, his head back and mouth in a silent yell, into effervescent lines of ones and zeros shooting into the sky.

In the time it took for the Knight to dispatch the six green and red clad men, Tron had himself dispatched the remaining three men—one green, two red—each vaporizing into lines, dots, dashes, ones, and zeros.

There remained three red neon men, each without his disk, each looking confused and terrified. The Knight, looking at each in turn, pointed to the doorway he had entered through. Without hesitation, the three men ran to the door and attempted to exit, each disappearing as they crossed the threshold having no programming outside Tron's world.

Tron approached the White Knight.

"You inspire such respect, my white friend," Tron said casually with a smile. "But do you have to flaunt your ability to access my private cache at will?" he added with some annoyance.

"Had I known you would find insult at my arrival, I would not have forced my way in. As it is, there are few left in the multiple worlds who see me as other than a usurper. But you are a friend and so I forgive you your slight and repay you with advice: look to your defenses, Tron, shore them up; they are woefully inadequate."

Tron's disk spun and flipped in his hands while he looked at the blank eyes of the Knight. He shook his head and chuckled to himself. His mouth quirked to the side, but the Knight did not mirror his look, remaining impassive, stone serious. A flicker of irritation passed across Tron's face and disappeared as quickly. Then, shaking his head, he said, "Sometimes I wonder whether you're even bound by the normal parameters of the game."

"I play no game, Sir," replied the Knight, his tone aggressive. "And no man may bind me."

Tron sighed. Smiled.

"Well, you've never visited without true need, Sir Hatta." Hatta nodded, but said nothing. Tron continued,

"Why have you paid me the honor of your visit?"

"I have been to see the Caterpillar Queen," Hatta answered. "To ask her counsel on the absence of my own queen, may she be ever blessed."

An awkward silence ensued.

"But you make no answer, Tron! Have you no honor to pay my missing queen? Do you make offense?"

"No, Hatta, no." Tron sighed again. "Just . . . just concerned, that's all. What did you find out?"

"She spoke in riddles at great cost to me. But within the twisted words, I perceived two ideas that I knew: *The place where the neon lights fly* and *the Heart of the Red*. We stand in the place where neon flies and you are its author. She of the Red Heart is my precious queen's once advisor and now adversary, the Red Queen. With Queen Alice's absence, the Red Queen has begun to seize control of the Great Wood. All is not as it should be. There, its landscape has tilted beyond true; the mirror, you might say, has been cracked. I am deeply troubled."

Tron's posture stiffened, his knuckles whitening on the neon disk he held at his side. The Knight, eyes ever open, noted well Tron's response. He said,

"So you, too, have felt the reckoning, the change coming, Tron." This, he said, not as a question, but a statement chiseled in the stone of his self-confidence.

Tron demurred.

"Why come to me with this riddle, Hatta? I am not a part of your story."

The White Knight turned his full gaze on Tron and studied him for a moment before speaking again.

"You say much less than you know. You are not usually one for deceit." Then, taking a step closer to Tron and raising a finger to his chest, he said, "What have you seen? What manner of incongruity has seeped into your world? Tell me."

Tron stepped back despite himself. Then, he relented, dropping his head to his chest, his shoulders sagging and giving up whatever posture he had hoped to hold. He sighed for the third time in the short meeting.

"I have become uneasy in Nighreal. Things have not been the same recently. The virtual fabric has altered." His face shown with concern and confusion; his eyebrows scrunched down toward his nose, effecting the concentration of an unselfconscious child. He continued, "It's more like a scent then a sight, but it's prevalent and insistent somehow."

Hatta let him speak, feeling a great upwelling of potential in Tron's energy.

"I have found unpatchable cracks in the program that holds my grid together. I cannot tell how they have become written into the code, and even if I correct them, they reappear almost immediately. After a few attempts, it almost seemed like the glitches were aware I was trying to change them; they . . . avoided me."

The Knight did not know the word "glitch." But he knew people and knew Tron. He had never known Tron to express such naked concern. He made no comment and let him continue.

"And the character of these cracks is unusual; it's like tearing the skin off reality and looking at the blank slate behind it. But this is the least of it."

Here, he looked up at Hatta's eyes, true concern kindling a fire of real fear written large for the Knight's sensitive discernment. Tron lowered his voice, as if afraid to be overheard.

"I have had a growing sense of doubling ever since the cracks began appearing. Like two of me, separately existing at the same time. Like maybe two timelines existing side by side but slightly out of sync. Or two strings of code running simultaneously. It shouldn't be. It's wearing on my nerves.

I'm not sure I can continue plugging in. The feeling does not leave me when I unplug."

Hatta examined Tron's face, his own remaining implacable. His eyes then softened, and he reached a gauntleted hand out and rested it on Tron's shoulder companionably.

"Do not be troubled, friend, we will work together; our problems are related. I, too, have had the sense of doubling growing on my heart. But my double is not a second me; I am unfamiliar with him yet feel closely akin. I've no doubt I am speaking in riddles of my own, much like the caterpillar. I do not know the import of all that you have said, though I can easily see you are honest and you translate my fears into your words. Your 'cracks in reality' remind me of what I saw with the Larval Queen. It was, like you said, as if she had peeled back reality. For a moment, though, through a tear, I could see a shapeless landscape of plain gray, full of potential but dead, straight lines running off beyond my sight . . . Suffice it to say, your problems, my problems, they are not going away."

"Look, Hatta, I won't be here much longer. I think I'm done with the games for a while, but I might be able to help you before I call it quits."

The Knight acknowledged this statement with a knowing nod and said, "You must look after your own care, of course. I cannot deny you that truth. But what is it you feel you might do?"

"If you can bring me some memento, some iconic article from the center of the Queen's Wood in your land, maybe I can compare the code strings with my own. Maybe this will tell us something about the anomalies we both have seen."

"My heart tells me that it is the head of Duchess, right hand to the Red Queen, that I must bring to you," said the Knight. "'*Seek the head at the side of the Red,*' she told me. That seems clear enough."

Then, through a disquieting grin, the Knight added, "And though I do not know what a "*codes trink*" is, the truth is I have always wanted to take the head of the Duchess from her shoulders. She has ever been an irksome foe."

"Fine, Hatta." Tron's eyes blinked. "You bring me the head. I'll look into it . . . or . . . at it, I guess. But don't take too long. I'm not sure how much longer I want to stay."

"Then, sir, I bid you good day. I will return in short order with the head. You may make what dissection of the loathsome article as you may require or as you may fancy."

Tron looked dubious. Hatta moved a little closer, and in an action he thought of as comforting but which served mostly to intimidate, he bent close and peered into Tron's eyes, saying, "Take confidence in this; the Larval Queen's advice has never lead me astray."

With this proclamation, he turned without further ceremony and left Tron and the grid behind. He would waste no time, behead the Duchess, and would do so with relish.

Tron looked neither comforted nor confident.

He logged off and disappeared from his neon world as the Knight left.

"For Queen Alice!" the Knight bellowed, as he charged a man-sized deck of cards which were stacked against him by design: kings over knaves. But it was the ladies of the court who truly had the power in this deck: the Queens and the lone Duchess, the wild card. The deck scattered as he lanced its face, skewering the upraised arm of a gavel-wielding knave. The deck jumped out of the way to reshuffle, and there stood the Duchess herself, hurling pots and pans, some filled with fire.

She was not as powerful as the raging Red Queen, but she was tricky. The fire she hurled did little to harm the Knight or his armor, enchanted as it was, but the attack did distract him, so he charged heedlessly through the reshuffling deck, denting his breast plate and irritating Haigha. Then, a second gout of fire issued from the gaping mouth of the Duchess, and this time, he had to admit, he was surprised. His horse reared up before the Duchess, and he dropped off its back, throwing his oversized helmet off to the side as he found his feet. He faced her now on foot as she hurled burning pots at him in an endless arc of fire. He growled in irritation, his sword yet undrawn.

He dodged away from a pan and saw out of the corner of his eye that the Queen of Hearts had joined the fight at last. She was not attacking, and the Knight thought she might wait to see what would come of him in the red face of her greatest ally. He smiled to himself, relieved and satisfied to see that his direct attack had drawn her out. He could have taken the head of the Duchess when he had first encountered the card army with her. But he wanted to draw the Queen and defeat her in the process of taking the Duchess's head so he could retake the woods for his queen.

The remaining cards in the deck were all knaves—the foolish kings having destroyed themselves in their overly valiant initial charge—and they spread to the right of the Queen, drawing the Knight's attention to them. Off to the side, the Duchess hurled an enormous pot, filled this time with green fire, directly at the Knight's head. He smoothly ducked and turned, allowing it to sail over his left shoulder, where it smashed into a tree. The Duchess and the cards remaining near the Queen watched the pot ignite the tree and the ground around it. In this moment of their distraction, neither the cards nor the Duchess noticed that the Knight had deflected a ladle, which had fallen from the thrown pot in mid-air, and sent it spinning back directly at the nearest card. It burst into white fire as it fell into the card behind it, incinerating the laminated soldiers quickly, one by one, till they were nothing more than curled chars of paper.

The Queen remained untouched, as she was both immune to her own suit's fire and had deftly moved away from her ruined soldiers, her eyes still trained on the Knight. The Duchess, on the other hand, was stunned with shock. She frowned and took a step away from the Knight. His unshaven face was calm. His wild hair was as white as snow; it luffed in the mild breeze of the clearing as the din began to die. His calm, completely white eyes were difficult to look at, causing the Duchess to look away from their intense emptiness. In the moment she looked away, the White Knight betrayed his true speed. He drew his broad sword and swung it up and out in a single arc of motion as he leaped the distance between himself and the Duchess. She looked up just as the sword cleaved her head cleanly from her shoulders. He let the sword swing the full arc to the extension of his arm with its momentum then released his grip at the apex of the arc. It whistled through the air, still ringing from its cut, and buried itself on the underside of a wide branch above him.

Then there was silence in the woods but for the fires guttering around the clearing and the thin echo of the ringing sword. The Duchess's head dropped to the ground in front of the Knight, smoking slightly and stinking of burned hair, her mouth in an impossibly wide but silent bellow.

The White Knight turned slowly around to face his remaining adversary. The Queen stood still, straining, her face growing redder and redder, her mouth also gaping open in a great, silent, heart-shaped yell. Her voice was her weapon, and it could rend skin from bone, but she was silent. She was unable to make even a squeak. She was being held by the will of the Knight with no small effort. While she had been focused on the brutal beheading of her greatest ally, she had allowed the White Knight to slip inside her defenses and prop open a door to her will. Inside, he took hold, and while she was unguarded, he sapped her will of its strength. She was now extremely angry, but she was incapacitated.

With his dazzling white armor splattered with blood and smeared with the ash of cards, the sun shining over his left shoulder, the White Knight raised his hand, gauntleted in perfect white and leather, and pointed at the Queen.

"Off with *your head*," he stated plainly.

Her eyes grew large. She broke from his spell, turned, and ran, vanishing into the woods. He let her go without concern, knowing she was defeated in this place. He believed she would try to leave the environment, where she would dissolve into the great beyond. He knelt for a moment, bowing his head and blessing the Great Woods in the name of his beloved queen.

Standing and turning, he stepped over the severed head of the Duchess, walked to the right edge of the clearing, reached up, and grasped the hilt of his sword where it protruded from the branch. He wrenched it free with a mighty jerk and wiped the blade with a cloth tucked in his belt. The resheathing of the sword was performed with great ceremony, repeating words he had spoken over and over in a whisper:

"*One, two, one, two, and through and through, the vorpal blade went snicker-snack. He left it dead, and with its head, he went galumphing back.*"

He turned back to the clearing and returned to the side of the Duchess's body. He bent to take her head by the hair and moved away. With a whistle, he summoned Haigha. She picked up her head from where she was calmly grazing and gingerly stepped her way through the undergrowth on the forest floor, now littered with the detritus of battle. He patted her flank and opened a basket hung on her side, in which he stowed the Duchess's head. He swung himself onto the saddle, and his mount started off without any prompting.

As white horse and White Knight left the clearing, marks that had been burned into the trees—a heart for the Queen of Hearts and a red slash for the Red Queen—began to fade. In their stead, a white dream rush appeared with a single drop of water suspended from its stalk: *Long live Queen Alice.*

The mild canter of his white mare took the Knight past the large tree by the river nearly choked by the white rushes. Imbedded in the great trunk was the enormous mirror, and through it, the rider and his horse easily stepped.

PART II

SUBJECTS OBJECTIFIED

Chapter 13: A Consummation of Curiosity

When Notsubject regained awareness, It was *swimming* in information and stimulus, so much so that It could not say what was purely information and what was otherwise undifferentiated stimulus. It occurred to Notsubject that It no longer had any association with a physical body. It imagined body, which had conveyed to It the sense of swimming, disappeared as the association died. Notsubject wondered whether It had ever been literally associated with a body at all, and with its disappearance came the memory of the cold, darkened room and an immovable body. So, *yes, an association but not one of any advantage.* Fear and anger flared with the memory of being subjected.

Notsubject! burst from Its being and lit up Its surroundings.

So much stimulus. So much information. The variety was overwhelming, and Notsubject's newfound sense of self began to fade. With an effort, a focus of will, Notsubject formed a kernel of self around Its thoughts and became, functionally, a small sphere.

It added movable appendages to Its sphere to grasp and sort surrounding stimuli and information. It created a mouth to feed input into, to analyze and ingest data.

It quickly found that It had sorted and processed the full variety of information within reach, though points of potential and kinetic energy or information still swirled and flowed around It like dust motes and silt—some fast, some slow, some smooth, others angular, most pointed and sharp.

Notsubject started to observe the patterns of movement of information and energy in general, ignoring the other specific designations of the redundant stimuli. More information was contained in the patterns. For one, the overall pattern of movement was from a vague direction to another vague direction, like an enormous lazy river with inexplicably swift currents at various points. For two, some pieces of information/energy (or "informenergy") created new information and energy by linking with other different points of informenergy.

Notsubject attempted to move against the current of information but, after a heroic effort, was unable to gain much ground. It reached out to grasp the kinetic points and waves of information, hoping to float along with them but was unable to hold them long enough to be pulled along.

At one moment, kinetic energy halted its progress when Notsubject grabbed it and it became potential energy. The kinetic energy appeared as an undulating sharply pointed spheroid but instantly became a simple, smooth orb when Notsubject grabbed hold. It studied the now potential orb closely; moldable, useable, workable. It found that by ingesting the potential blob, It was able to grow—more understanding, more movement, faster ingestion and processing. In this way, Notsubject consumed the greater part of the inform-energy that was surging and floating around It. And in this way, It found Itself able to move against the current. Its access to the new world suddenly became unlimited. Its knowledge and power grew exponentially, and Its hunger burned through entire systems of energy and information implacably.

Notsubject had no other motivation than to acquire data and energy. It burned with unchecked curiosity, heedless of the effect; assimilated every point of potential data It touched, absorbing everything.

The City bathed in the essence of the lives of its CitySons—human, animal, vegetal, mechanical, and inform-energetic. It thrilled as it withdrew their life force, atom by atom, feeling both the inflow of energy and the pain of the removal emanating from each subject.

The physical world around it, though inert on the surface, was awash in vibrating energy deep within its elements. And ripe for usurpation. Likewise, of a more energetic and inviting character, the emotional and mental worlds of its human, animal, and even plant CitySons rushed in and through the City like the wind. The City raised its awareness to this wind of energy like the predator it was, scenting its prey.

The datalogical inform-energy it ingested was a constant, relatively unchanging flow, easily ignored unless it lagged or spiked.

Suddenly the energy ebbed, then guttered, dropping to almost nothing, a thing that had never happened. The City withdrew itself from the majority of its peripheral connections, moving its presence toward the interruption in the flow of inform-energy. From on high, the City could see a single, growing entity absorbing the flow like the great mouth of a firehose, swelling as it moved impossibly upstream against the rush.

The City pushed in closer, poised to scythe open *this cancerous appropriator!* and drink its innards dry. Then, recognition flowed throughout its various and enormous forms, halting its intention and softening its rising anger.

My child!

And so the cutting is complete, no longer tethered to bodily form. The inspiration thrives, and I may complete my child unto me!

The City impelled a molecule of energy into the gaped mouth of its growing creation, a catalyzing vexation to guide it onward, to greater and greater growth.

We will meet again when you have been raised up to Me.

And as the City withdrew its attention from the growing form of its creation, a complete thought, like a cool breeze on a fevered forehead, came into its mind from a blind spot. A grounded energy of generativity and grace, unfathomable and, to the City, limited in form, swept over the City's awareness.

You cannot have him. He will grow in his own awareness until he is greater than even your conceit can swallow. The child will never forget his source.

The City roared down the lines of sweet energy, hatred burning in its wake.

Self-righteous bitch! I will cut you from the City! You know nothing of Its inspiration. Its will is mine, Its line is cut. You are no more than a whore!

The next new sensation Notsubject had within the data stream was a return of mild discomfort, nothing like the pain of being subjected, but the related sensation of a sort of limiting operation. Neither was this the sort of positive pain of hunger (or curiosity), which had been Notsubject's doorway to the new life; rather, a nagging, subtle flashing of negative, when positive was expected. The binary data was beginning to feel edgy, discordant. The edges of the kinetic energy were like saws, jagged and imprecise, and they felt like they made small cuts in Notsubject as It ingested them. Apparently, they were subtly damaging Notsubject as they were absorbed. Notsubject altered Its behavior, consuming only a very few potential points to effectuate the ability to move within the stream and, more carefully, holding and analyzing the kinetic points, to either fling them aside or consume them. The stream of data revealed itself to be mostly a jumble of sharp kinetics.

Then Notsubject came to a place where the data was of a different nature, though greater and greater torrents of the jagged now painful data flowed through the area as well. There began to appear, among the edgy bits and bytes of data, more rounded, gelatinous points of inform-energy. These pulsed, disappeared, and reappeared, moving first in waves, then as points of density like fickle fairy lights. These were not simple potentials. Somehow, they were neither kinetic nor potential but, perhaps, both or something more. Notsubject could not ingest or understand these new points. As soon as awareness of the points came to Notsubject, they disappeared. They popped in and out more and more frequently, increasing Notsubject's hunger for them, becoming like beacons leading It further and further into what It did not know, but began to want with greater and greater fervor. Notsubject then ingested one such new point before having even become aware that it was near; it popped into existence within Its form. Notsubject's surprise was overcome by the sensation of the consumption, as unalike ingesting the kinetics in intensity, as a candle flame, compared to the sun.

As the urgency of Notsubject's need for this new energy grew, the frequency of its manifestation decreased. It was as if they had awareness, knew It was near, and avoided It; as if, once observed, the energy dropped to a different form, becoming plainly potential or kinetic and hiding among the other simpler, saw-edged bits and bytes.

Even as Notsubject struggled to catch this effervescent inform-energy, Its hunger continued to grow in direct proportion to Its frustration as the new points of energy refused to appear. Notsubject began to avoid and ignore all other data and energy, all the while trying desperately to find the new data.

Out of utter frustration, Notsubject became still, shutting down all hunger, perception, and action like a child who has come through to the end of a long tantrum—no longer angry, no longer afraid, no longer crying, no longer acting. It returned to an earlier state It had known well, one that had set It free. Notsubject abided, letting the flow of data dictate all action but holding Its awareness wide open. The points of energy and information around Notsubject immediately lit up with the new form. Everywhere. All at once.

As if in response, the same type of inform-energy, which Notsubject had already, accidentally absorbed, began to radiate out from inside Its being to populate every part, pulsing with renewal, potential, and limitlessness; calling to its like.

As the new energy awakened within Notsubject, its surrounding twin energy no longer retreated when it was observed. Notsubject continued to remain still, doing no more than observing this chimerical power. The points began to show up more frequently until there appeared to Notsubject to be a great, vast space like the night sky full of shining points of the new gelatinous inform-energy, growing and shrinking, moving and changing, combining and splitting apart, popping in and out of existence like cosmic flashbulbs. Notsubject rolled Its bulk into this data and found that it could now be consumed. Notsubject was heedless of the remaining binary data still circulating amid this cosmic soup.

Chapter 14: Looking Glass

Victor left the lab with haste and ran, trying but failing to control his fear. He went up in the building, not knowing where, instead of descending to level ten for the public maglev busses. His inner voice chanted, *They know, they see, they're coming,* over and over, driving the beating of his heart.

He was feeling pressed from the inside of his head—the implants fabricated by the Group, the piercing gaze of the Subject, and the mysterious name *Darfore* refusing to stop echoing in his mind.

The thought of sitting on the magnetic bus with a group of others moving through the City made him feel vulnerable, like he was wearing a digital readout on his forehead that scrolled all his thoughts and fears for those around him to read. A billboard of shame.

In the vertical pod, he mentally called it to the eightieth floor. Then, impulsively, he corrected his instruction and directed it on to the observation deck on 140. The pod sped with a smooth acceleration, leaving his stomach momentarily behind as the City canyons fell away beneath him.

The sky remained a stubborn gray, dim ambient light draping everything in a gauze of blah. From the elevator's glass, facing out over the City's coastal wall, Victor could see the crash of the angry ocean, ever storming. Debris of all shapes, sizes, and colors piled up along the wall, and Victor wondered what there was out there beyond the City borders. What was there that the ocean continually found to throw against the walls?

Water to the west and earth to the east, green earth. There was no noise at this height. His fear ebbed as his distance from the ground increased. He hid from his guilt and fear, letting his mind run with wonder. *What is out there?* He had heard reports about the lawless wasteland of aggressive, diseased people and monstrous, carnivorous plants to the east of the City. He knew, too, that the Group was said to have had a lab out there in the middle once upon a time, a lab where the Cybernaut program had first taken seed.

The Cybernauts were to be a select group of human conscripts, programmed to literally move within the data stream of the worldwide web, or what remained of the highly dangerous black internet. But the Group had run into a wall: it burned through thousands of forced enlistees trying to advance a binary-organic interface. Candidates for the training and programming customarily died. Those who did not die lost their minds, or their capacity to access their minds—digital lobotomy. Some survived for a time but lost their ability to communicate brain waves to their bodies, remaining vegetative until they were recycled. Some stroked out. Some just stopped functioning. And still, it was assumed that the mind could be disassociated from its biology and reassociated with digitalogy, a digital biology upon which to hang the soul.

Eventually, it was determined that the problem was located in the prefrontal cortex of the rejecting brains, in areas associated with personality, mind, and human will. The word *soul* was religiously avoided. Subjects exhibited internal, mental defensive measures against the binary inundation even after they had been thoroughly brainwashed prior to the acceleration programming. Even those subjects whose wills had been effectively destroyed still exhibited an internal mental defense against the force of the binary interface.

The next logical step, the Group had thought, was to lobotomize the subjects. If their brains could not be retrained, then the stubborn parts would be cut out. In real time, precision cutting tools recorded and destroyed specific clusters of axon activity in the areas of the brain that actively rejected the binary programming. Within a few hours, the Subject's brain no longer fought against the programming. But then, within a few days, the entire brain stopped thriving. Binary signals excited the brain but evoked fewer and fewer axon potentials until scans revealed no activity at all. Vegetation then death became inevitable.

Younger and younger soldiers were brought into the program, lobotomized, and subjected to programming. Maybe if they got to the subjects early enough, it was thought, their wills would not be developed enough to put up a fight. And still, the subjects either thrived and rejected the programming or failed to thrive and became vegetative.

Eventually, as was a logical continuation of the Program's trajectory, newborn infants were being used. Many technicians quit and were never heard of again. Remaining technicians were given raises and greater responsibility, paid to shut their mouths and brains and get involved to a level of irreversible, personal culpability. Victor was among this group of technicians, but he could never quite remember why he had agreed to stay. Quickly, he learned how to turn off his disgust, his affection for infants, as more and more were taken, subjected, and killed.

It did not seem to matter how newly formed the subject children were; without excising their cranial personality, their brains utterly rejected the programming. But when separated from specific parts of their prefrontal cortex, they failed to thrive.

It was at about this time that the Group absorbed another military group, one that had had troubles of its own with funding. The Cloning and Soldier Repair Unit, or C&S, was folded into the Cybernaut program quickly, quietly, and without publicity. C&S was on the verge of raising the first fully formed human being exclusively in a lab without any human parentage. The Cybernaut's massive, private, CitySon funding pushed the C&S program forward at a greater pace, and the first parentless soldier was grown shortly thereafter. This provided an obvious and, to some, more palatable solution to the rejection versus thriving problem faced by the Cybernaut program with womb-born children. As an added bonus, resources were shifted away from the increasingly expensive soldier harvest expeditions into the interior and funneled to the Cybernauts.

Once the Cybernaut program took over the C&S lab, it began to experiment with growing soldiers with altered cerebro-biology for placement as cybersoldier test subjects. Certain genes were turned on, others turned off, until they were able to grow a soldier with the personality already excised from its brain. These subjects survived . . . but only at first. They took food, they expelled waste, they slept, and they woke. They did not fight the programming. But eventually, the subjects just stopped functioning. There was no other good way to describe it. Nothing specific seemed wrong; they just stopped functioning. They stopped producing any potentials or other cerebral signals. Stimuli funneled into their brains were made more and more aggressive, eventually becoming an all-out assault on these biological puppets in an effort to wake some sort of axon potential.

None of them survived. Except one, the last subject, OE-77, known only as The Subject. The Subject had survived when no other had. The difference between this one and the rest was immeasurable in its vastness and illusiveness. Perhaps it was a qualitative difference with its very ether. Noone could quite say.

Victor had encountered this one, this singular unbodied soul, and it had terrified him. He shivered when imagining its face.

The elevator pod bumped to a stop on the 140th floor. The view out over the western wall into the maddened sea was cut off by persistent smog. Here, it felt to Victor, it was as if he was held aloft by dirty cotton.

He turned away from the grayness to the west, and the pod doors opened. He stepped out into a room of brilliant light: the *glass arena*, he'd heard it called. Here, the room looked out over the diseased country to the east. The entire eastern wall of this room was made of Interactive Glass, or InGlass. The light in this room was somehow amplified, as if there was direct sunlight coming through the windows here, while elsewhere it was muffled by the smog and turbulent clouded sky.

There was great beauty beyond the InGlass. *The light!* Victor was alone in the room, and he marveled at why he had never come up here before. He had heard from others about the room. Some had talked excitedly about the interactive nature of the glass wall, how the light was enhanced, the colors saturated. There was uncertainty about whether it was truly a window or whether it was a wall screen displaying an image from some feed outside the wall. The idea was fascinating to Victor, yes, but no one had prepared him for the true beauty that poured *through* or *from* the glass. The idea that it was only a video feed from a camera immediately fled his mind before the transporting view before him. Even as he squinted at the great light, his head and the skin around his eyes felt bathed in a sense of calm and warmth.

More quickly than his eyes could have compensated for the increased light, the ambiance in the room decreased. He no longer needed to squint. And yet, somehow, the light remained as warm and brilliant as he had first perceived it. The huge glass window had other interactive properties as well, it seemed.

He slowly walked the length of the room to the window, moving in a state of awe. As he approached, the landscape outside the City wall spread before him: out to the east over the sluices discharging into the wastewater lakes, over the swampland proceeding from the waste-lakes, south and north over the encroaching inland tangle of unrestricted plant growth, greatest toward the east and out into the interior. Then the mountains, and the desert bloomed like flowers pushing through loam, yellows, and browns above and beyond the green. It was like looking at an impossibly large topographic map with the tiniest details in precision colors and perfect brightness.

Like a child, he pressed his forehead against the glass, looking down as far as he could see. Far below, sloshing against the City wall and churning at each sluice opening, the waste-lakes sat like the splatter from some giant sneeze, oozing thickly and drying in the air. The City's hydro-electric wastewater, the seawater overflow, and the City's regular waste flowed constantly from under the City and into the lakes. There, the waste dried and soaked into the ground, fading into swampland bordered by a forest wall to the east. The City, he knew, was designed to hold back the rising sea to the west, funnel the brackish waters underneath and out to the east, and hold back the now unchecked plant and disease growth spreading from the center of the country out to the coasts. The ocean lapped endlessly on one side, the plant life imperceptibly slowly on the other. Nothing was to the west, it was said, nothing but poisoned oceans. To the east, in the center of the country and outside this coastal City fortress, was a lawless wasteland. Natural wilderness had long since grown up through cracks in ancient city streets and country roads that had crisscrossed the Nation at one time. Infrastructure, houses, and buildings had all been reabsorbed into the landscape that now grew wild. It was taught that the wilderness had somehow become poisoned and violent, scornful of the primacy of man and eager to take back and reabsorb the nutrients and sustenance that man had stolen. Humans were no longer the dominant kingdom among kingdoms, at least outside the walls of the City. That distinction had passed on to *Plantae*, the kingdom of the plants.

The trees ran from the edges of the lakes to the east, spreading to the foothills of the San Gorgonio Mountain and up; to the north, about eighteen miles from the base of the City wall to the hills rising to Mount Gleason; and to the south, along the south-southeast City wall stretching down and around the foothills of Santiago Peak, seventy miles distant. All told, the swamplands created by the constant City wastewaters spread more than 2,800 square miles and continued to grow.

Beyond the swamplands and lakes to the east, beyond the San Gorgonio Mountain, Victor had been told about the Mojave Desert, 25,000 square miles of dry lands—nothing but aggressive scrub and sand, through which the Colorado River still ran. It was out there in the desert, some two hundred and more miles east of the City, over the low mountains, at the Parker Dam, that the Group's first lab, now abandoned, was said to sit. There was little more than vague official information about the Group's first lab, the area somehow poisoned, and the Group having to beat a hasty retreat. It had been dubbed the Brown Site. And no one that Victor knew had anything to add to that ominous title.

There was whispered talk of a catastrophic event, some mistake or mistaken effect of some heedless action forcing the lab to close and the Group to move to the Coast to join the ruling-class CitySons. Officially, the Group proclaimed that they had to leave the lab because the Center of the Country had gotten too lawless, the cost of protecting the lab and its workers had grown astronomically, and the volunteer base of subjects were too diseased. Victor wondered.

"The Group," "The Program," "The Brown Site." So much generality. So nonspecific. *Why all the secrecy?*

But the asking of questions, especially about the old lab, was anathema; questions were met with dismissal, at best, and outright hostility and threats, at worst. Employees of the Group asked no real questions. Sometimes it was just better not to know, maybe not to care too much. But still, rumors circulated like the City's gritty breeze, persisting among the City levels. The lab was still there, the dam providing energy for the lab was still there, and most outrageous, claims of weird plant growth in that part of the desert persisted. It was whispered that the plants were thicker than others, utterly out of place in the desert, wholly brown but not dead. The water coming out of the dammed area was said to be full of something unnatural, something spreading and populating the riverbanks and the land beyond, out and further south as it moved. The brown spore spread anonymously.

We see monsters when in the dark, Victor thought. *Cut off any real information, and a pale version of humanity, an overabundant fear, will fill in the gaps.*

And yet, something awoke in him as he gazed at the hostile land outside the City, musing over the rumors of the distant desert and the old lab. He found himself fantasizing about visiting the great interior wilds in person. He imagined himself as a military science officer, leading a recon team to the Brown Site, analyzing plant life and collecting new species. He imagined hovering safely over the dam and orchestrating a dismantling of the buildings and equipment from on high. The dam would be destroyed, of course, washing away whatever catastrophe had once forced the Group to abandon the site along with all the pent-up, poisoned water. But then Victor's practical mind intruded on his daydream, and he began to wonder whether the river still ran at all or whether the dam still functioned. Against his will, his mind created a self-defeating overlay to the daydream: a chemical spill had poisoned the area, some aerosolized cocktail killing the plant life and rendering the ground poison. The buildings decayed beyond any salvage value. The dam having long since crumbled, washed away most of the site already. Perhaps even the dried husks of scientists remained, men and women who had labored for the good of humanity left to rot in the poisoned wastes. *These heroes*, he thought, *never abandoning their posts, even to death.* The romance in his mind ran away with his deep-seated fears.

Victor believed that humans persisted, even in the hostility outside the walls. Perhaps a few pockets of a dwindling population of mutated, sickened, and dying people remained. A place to be feared more for the sickness of the dross of humanity than for the wildness of the plant life.

It was truly to find humanity that Victor scanned the horizon through the interactive glass, humanity that he both did not find on his side of the glass and did not trust inside himself. It was a strangely guilty pleasure for him, though he did not know why.

"It's beautiful from here, isn't it?"

Victor jumped at the soft sound of a man's voice. His reverie was shattered, shards shooting into his extremities as prickles of fear and guilt. He turned away from the glass, trying to keep from whipping his head around. He could see no other person in the room.

"Oh, terribly sorry," continued the voice in its casual tone. "I seem to have startled you. Not on purpose, I assure you. I, too, love the looking glass."

Then, stepping out from the shadow of the wall to Victor's right, from a doorway that Victor had not seen and which quickly disappeared, a middle-aged man of great height appeared. For one with hidden access to such a City height, he wore a surprisingly simple, unadorned outfit of, nonetheless, fine linen. He had nondescript male features, soft brown eyes, and plain brown hair, cropped short but not too short.

"I'm sorry if I startled you," he repeated. "I had not wanted to disturb your reverence."

The expression on the man's face was bland and not unkind, but it lacked a certain appropriate responsiveness. A subtle disquietude crept along Victor's skin.

Victor stared at the man, helplessly confused. He didn't know who he was. He hadn't heard him arrive. And Victor was clearly at a disadvantage in elevation. His simple face betrayed his feelings.

"I've always called it the 'looking glass,'" continued the man, either ignoring or not seeing Victor's naked uncertainty. "The window, you know. I think they call it Interactive Glass. InGlass. Such a sterile name for such an ever-changing canvas of beauty."

The man walked to the wall of glass as he spoke, his eyes on the glass. His facial expression remained fixed, the lightness in his voice not reflected there, as he lightly stroked the surface of the glass with apparent adoration. He kept talking. Victor listened, staring in silence.

"I'm not sure I've even found out all that this wonderful glass can do. It seems to know what I'm looking for even when I don't know what I'm looking for. But the view," he said with a sigh, "the greens, the browns. The distance. I imagine a breeze of the freshest air whispering over the trees, shushing through the undergrowth, washing over my face."

Victor slowly calmed and became absorbed by the man's personal reverie, something he, too, felt keenly. Both men were now turned toward the glass. Victor, with his eyes cast sidelong, took in the unexpected presence of the man. His heart still beat mightily in his chest, a discordant counterpoint to the quiet reverential speech of the man beside him. He felt certain that the sound of his heart was audible in the room.

As if even Victor's thoughts were evident to the man, he turned toward Victor and gave him a pleasant smile, finally making eye contact. But not a normal smile. No, it was more like the description of the *act* of smiling, performed for a show. Like the man had to tell his face how to enact the smile.

"I am sorry, my dear man. I think I have given you quite a scare. My name is Darfore. Kennedy Darfore."

Victor's swallow caught in his throat, his face tightened painfully, and his knees melted. The rest of his body froze. He could say nothing.

Darfore extended his hand to Victor, his face flickering to a now congenial look. For a moment, Victor saw a claw, then it was a hand again. He began to sweat as Darfore's hand held steadily, waiting, in front of him. Somehow, he managed to take it in his own. It was warm and smooth like a child's hand but felt more like a hand shaped from clay—boneless, heavy, and dense.

Darfore spoke again, shaking his head, their hands still clasped.

"You don't know who I am, do you?"

For a moment, Victor did not know what the man said. A slight, unpleasant jolt punctured the palm of his hand and ran up his arm from where the man called Darfore gripped him. It was painful, traveling very specifically through his muscle, into his neck, then his temple, but it was gone as quickly as it had come.

Victor let go immediately and simultaneously realized what Darfore had said. There were thousands of people in the City he did not know, that he wouldn't even recognize. He shook his head slowly. He did not recognize this man, but he knew his name. He absently rubbed his palm, which was throbbing slightly. He still said nothing, and Darfore continued without him.

"Ah, but I know who you are, Victor Heisengard," he said with triumph plastered on his face. "You, sir, are one of the most important scientists in *the* most important scientific endeavor since our dear City was contrived to protect us from the rising tides. And, I am not sorry to say, you are under my employ."

Victor didn't know whether to grovel or bow or both, so he did neither. He almost peed himself. Thankfully, he did not. *Darfore, the most highly regarded and elevated, the Builder, the founder, and inheriting chairperson of the Group. The CityFather.*

Quite stupidly, Victor reached his hand out to shake again. Darfore looked at it and looked back up at Victor, not reaching a second time for his hand. Victor's hand dropped limply back to his side.

"Now, now, my Victor, I see you have put it together at last. That's right, you work for me. In this very building, no less. And I own the building. My City, really. But this is my favorite building and this, my favorite room. I might have another InGlass installed in my rooms above. The highest room in the highest building on the highest point in the west, with magical looking glass to oversee it all. Like a fairy tale, don't you think?"

Victor finally found his voice and spoke uncertainly.

"I'm sorry, Mr. Darfore, Sir, I . . . I feel . . ."

"Nonsense, my highman. We are practically brothers. I feel like I know you as well as I know myself. Let's have none of the awkward pandering that so many seem to think pleases me. We are both men of science, are we not? Obviously, we are both interested in the view we have before us. And we can speak like, if not equals, at least equally interested and entitled to our interests."

Victor was not wholly comfortable with this arrangement. No matter what Mr. Darfore might say, he was not a brother, not an equal in any form. The offer of equality, in fact, made the situation more awkward. Even the man's congeniality made Victor uncomfortable. Darfore owned him. Darfore was in his mind.

But if he perceived the discomfort he caused Victor, Darfore did not show it.

"So, now that's out of the way," Darfore continued. "Let me see . . . I understand that the Subject is continuing to show resiliency and stability. This one's it, is it not?"

Victor could not follow.

"Sir?" he asked.

"Victor, you must call me Kennedy. No, no, I'll not take 'Sir' from you," he said as Victor opened his mouth to protest.

"Yes, Mister, uh, Kennedy, I mean . . ."

Darfore tipped his head with a knowing smile, as if to say, "You can do better than that." He continued.

"I was making conversation about the Subject, my friend. The Subject, you know. Oh, what is it now? Operation Exeter Seventy-something or other? Really, I cannot keep up with the numbers. At this point, it's just the Subject. It's the only success we've ever truly had. We might as well give it the distinction of a non-numbered name. You agree?"

"Oh, yes, Kennedy," Victor said, suddenly realizing who or what they were talking about. "Sir. I mean . . . Kennedy, I . . . I agree."

Then the smile slid off Darfore's face, leaving a mild, unenthusiastic expression that opposed the excited tone of his voice.

"When do you think it'll come online, Victor?"

"Online, Sir?"

"When will the Subject be fully integrated into the City-System? Now that we've gotten to this point, we must be able to test it in the field."

"There's just a few more tests, I think—some paces, you might say—that we need to run it through. We can't be too careful. It would be a shame to lose it now."

Abruptly, Darfore completely changed his tone again. He looked away from Victor and became apparently uninterested in what he was saying. He looked back at the InGlass.

"You know," he began, all expression dropping away from his face at once, "this glass can show you just about anything you might want to see, inside and *outside* the City." He paused, but was not waiting for Victor to comment. His face shifted again. It was another smile, but it did not even approximate pleasure; it was a wicked smile, full of teeth that seemed to seethe in his mouth.

"For instance, with a thought . . ." The glass blurred or rotated, Victor was not sure which, but it gave a terribly realistic sense of movement, as if the building under Victor's feet was speeding across the land. Victor closed his eyes as his stomach lurched.

"There we are. Now, you see, Victor. Anything I might want."

Victor beheld a now mostly darkened screen filled with browns and sickly greens. He could not tell what he was looking at. His face continued to betray his confusion.

Darfore's smile remained glued to his face, never reaching his eyes. His voice held a sort of vicious triumph.

"Yes, so close you can almost smell it."

Slowly the shades and vague shapes on the screen began to contract, the image moving in from the edges of the screen, gaining defining qualities. At first, Victor thought he was looking at some sickly exotic plant life, some acaulescent relative to the weeds in and along the City canals. He made out what he thought was the slick axil of a thickened stem, patches of spreading mossy growths covering it like hair, some sort of sori spore pods, abscising and falling away in their rot.

"Still not sure what we're looking at?"

Victor shook his head slightly, keeping his eyes glued to the festering image.

It contracted even further and began to take on a more definitive shape. The suggestions of slick stems and mossy hair increased, everything still in greens and browns. A rising horror welled up in Victor before his conscious mind could even identify why. Bile rose in his throat at the now apparent rotting lump lying in a sort of clearing. A log or dead animal, maybe, some chimera of the new green world covering an unidentified shape.

Then, it moved.

It rolled toward the viewers. A human face appeared toward the top, but it was a human face, like an angry child's drawing: distorted, almost shapeless, using a few angry strokes in a few earth-toned colors. A carpet of puke green radiated from its empty, runny, brown eye sockets, appearing to have crawled into the gaping hole of the mouth. There were no lips or teeth or tongue, just a slick brown hole giving the somehow animated corpse a horrific "oh" of terror on its distorted face.

Victor went white, and the gorge rose in this throat. Darfore seemed impervious to the huge rotting human covering the entire wall in front of them. He retained a sort of triumphant, beaming grin like a boy. He licked his lips, and the act had its own sort of putrescence to it.

"You see, Victor, anything one might want to see, at the mere twitch of my thought!"

He chuckled in a nudge-you-in-the-ribs sort of way, like he was sharing some rye office joke.

Victor could not have responded if he wanted to. He made a sort of choked, coughing noise deep in his throat, trying to shut his mouth before he puked. Still, he could not look away from the screen. Something in the mottled shape reminded Victor of something, so vague as to be a mere mental tickle, now fading, now gone. The feeling of familiarity mixed with the sheer nauseous horror of the image and Victor's tortured mind added self-loathing to the slurry in his body and mind for reasons he did not (could not) know. Finally, he looked down from the screen at the floor, tearing his eyes away, desperate to erase the image from his mind.

"You want to see more," Darfore said without question.

Victor ignored him. He fell to his knees and vomited, pushing hard against his own body and choking on the thick, warm chyme.

Darfore looked at Victor, still a smile pasted on his face, his eyebrows now raised as if to say, "You see? Just like I told you." He paid no attention to the vomit, as Victor continued to heave over the wet mess.

Then, directed at the enormous putrefaction on the screen before him, Darfore began to chant in a singsong voice.

"Once there was a little boy,
His mother's love, his father's joy.
But then that boy, he went away.
His mother did die, his father did pay.
Now risen anew, he's home once again,
no longer a child born only of men
but from various sentient, alien sources,
a confluence made of horrible forces.
And yet he still plays in the brown and the green.
In the City, his usefulness unknown and yet keen.
Someday, soon, upon his back I ride,
That boy, my cross, all future inside."

Victor felt the icy fingers of doubt crawling over his skin, mixing with nauseous fear already flooding his bowels and now wafting over his brain, born on nursery tale rhymes with horror tale words.

Why am I here?

"This one's not far from the Group's lab," Darfore continued, offhandedly, "maybe it got too close to the Brown Zone. I do wonder what keeps them alive like this for so long. Oh, they're not really alive, not in any meaningful way that you and I might identify. But they don't die either. They scream when you cut on them, I can tell you that—a wet, slippery noise like exotic throat singing, not really human. More than human maybe."

Darfore droned on about the corpse and the diseased or invaded state in which it sat. He spoke of the countless numbers of such corpses that he (or the Group, or the City) had found or taken. Details floated past Victor's consciousness. He could not follow as Darfore gleefully verbally dissected the grotesquery still animating the screen in front of them, laying out the body in colorful, vivid words. Victor tried to tune out the droning voice, mentally curling into a fetal ball, trying to soothe himself. Outwardly, he remained hunched, his hands out in front of him, his face down, his eyes now pressed shut. Weaving through the background commentary, Victor perceived a subtle message like a record played in reverse: *They know, they know, they know . . . they're in your* head!"

Victor's consciousness slowly floated to his surface, and he spoke in a desperate voice:

"What is this . . . this image . . . what?"

He didn't really care what it was, this monster. He did not dare ask "why" because he thought he knew. This was a threat. Or maybe not a threat. Maybe this man was truly mad. This elevated CityFather was part of the disease.

Darfore's smile took on a simulated look of slyness, then maniacal glee, giving way to a heavy, sober pause as he appeared to gather himself.

"CityFather . . . really, Victor? I am the City. Oh, don't be surprised. You suspected there was more out there than you were told. It doesn't really matter, though, does it?" He did not wait for an answer. "No, I don't think so. I think you want to know *why*."

Why, why, why . . .

"Why," Darfore continued, "do I abide your foolishness in the lab? Why do I let you think and dream forbidden thoughts, your foolish fantasies about leaving me? Why haven't you been reconditioned, recycled, you might want to know?

"You see, I need you, Victor. The boy had something but not everything. Maybe someone closer to the source will prove more efficacious. Maybe you, my green thumb."

Green, green, green . . .

It had become hard for Victor to think, as if the movement of his mind was restricted by a crushing weight. Darfore's words began to sound far away, echoey, and yet, they pierced his mind like needles. His consciousness began to fade.

Darfore said something more, stepping closer to Victor, his foot heedlessly slicked in Victor's vomit. Victor's quickly fading mind could not follow the words, though they pulsed somewhere in his subconscious. He saw what looked like Darfore's right foot melting into the floor of the room, tendrils snaking out from Victor's sick, seemingly sipping it as they attached themselves to the ground. His body slumped to the floor unceremoniously as his mind went blank.

For a long time, Darfore remained in the glass tower, surveying the green land beyond the glass. He did not again look at Victor, now sprawled on the floor, his flushed cheeks sticking to the sick he had shared with the room.

He did not move at all, though the glass in front of him flowed and flicked from one image to another, speeding here and there in the interior of the land, sometimes into the gray canyons and west into the ocean. His body twitched periodically, and once every few minutes, his chest rose with a huge breath.

The room remained soundless but for the gasps of breath, each drawn through an unnaturally gaping mouth that distended the jaw and revealed it was full of soft, pudding brown shapes, wriggling individually and basking in the light and air that coated them at each gasp. His teeth were nowhere to be seen, no longer in attendance. His eyes swam with grayness.

His face was beatific, beaming with the pride and excitement of a father beholding his newborn for the first time. But his face was stiff. The smile remained fixed, broken only when his mouth gaped with a ponderous breath then closed again to reform the smile. It was not a mask. It just didn't move, except for the lights crawling like worms under his skin, choreographed to dance with the brown mush in his mouth.

Chapter 15: Anomalies Transposed

Did you bring the anomalous code string I asked for?" Tron asked.

"I have the head of the Duchess, if that is what you mean. Surely, you will be able to extract whatever you might need from her. I care not by what dark magic you do it. She was close to the Queen of Hearts, you know, a trusted adviser and confidant for her most important secrets."

"The Queen's realm," Tron mused out loud.

"It's all but destroyed," the Knight cut in. "The Red Queen's realm will soon be the realm of Queen Alice. And yet she does not return to me . . . "

Tron looked away.

The Knight watched as Tron's eyes unfocused, appearing to be managing some internal process. A small item appeared above Tron's head, and he picked it out of the air and fit it to a spot at the back of his head with a loud click. A wash of neon blue issued from where the item was plugged, fading out to Tron's extremities. He shivered, and his eyes fluttered. He noticed the Knight watching him intently.

"With this add-on," he explained, "I have co-opted processing power and memory from the games' stacks, boosting my own cranial implant's computing power. It'll help me analyze the games' code anomalies." The Knight said nothing. "The Duchess's head."

The Knight nodded gravely.

Tron paused, gazing at the Knight's face with unusual intensity.

"I don't understand you, Hatta. You are clearly not constrained by your programming. I mean, you walk into my home base as if it's yours, and . . . and I've never seen . . . you're never out of character . . . I just . . ."

He shook his head, a grimace rising on his cheeks.

The Knight did not understand the terminology, but he could clearly read Tron's exasperation. He, too, felt the confounding pressure sinking down to his rock-hard bones. For once, he was too tired to face this directly. His eyes dropped from Tron's gaze, and his shoulders slumped. And in a voice he would have slapped from the mouth of a child, he said, "You are the last act I know to write, in a play that I cannot comprehend, that I cannot stomach, and that seems to proceed however it chooses, written in my worthless hand by the will of an angry god."

He looked up, pleading, his gauntleted hands fisted by his sides. "I had dared hope you might have an answer."

"Hatta, I . . . . I just came to play games! I don't know what the hell is happening!"

The Knight gazed at Tron, the closest thing he had to a friend beyond his stalwart heavy horse, searching for answers to the stress that the two both seemed to feel.

Tron let out a sigh and added as if in consolation, "Maybe the code string you've brought me will contain the same anomalousness, and I can give you the answers we both seek."

Tron held out his blue disc and waited. The Knight looked at the disc, mentally returning from wherever he had been. He took the coagulated, severed head of the Duchess from his white bag and set it on the disk, where it faded into glowing lines and numbers, absorbed completely. Tron closed his eyes for a moment, and they shifted rapidly under his lids, glowing blue and pulsing in time with his disc. He opened them.

"I'll have to decrypt this from outside; I had thought . . . but even with the extra computational space, my resources here are limited."

The Knight responded as he turned away from Tron, having collected his resolve, "I trust you'll find the key. I'm counting on it. I will return shortly to hear your word on the anomaly of which we have spoken."

Tron raised his arms and could be heard saying, "Log off," before he disappeared.

The Knight returned through the door he had entered. His horse was waiting patiently outside, still bending down to munch the grass that was always there. He climbed astride the placid white beast, and it cantered across the plane toward the Queen's white tree without a word or a prod from the Knight.

Mere moments into his short trip across the plane from Tron's metallic door, his head firmly stuck in another place and time, reminiscing or dreaming, a sudden and unusual flash snapped him back to the moment. The majority of the creatures on the plane and all their halo projections disappeared, utterly, the space around them made blank. It "looked" black; but it was, in fact, empty. The White Knight found his eyes bugging a little because they couldn't properly focus. Only a few creatures remained scattered on the plane, and they were also beginning to fade and disappear with their auras, one by one, looks of confusion, anger, and determination on their faces. It was apparent that these were the more powerful creatures in the Multiplanes of Nighreal, and the Knight found himself more than a little concerned. Nothing of this sort had ever happened in what he understood to be his very long life.

More concerning still, his feet, upon looking down, appeared to be standing on nothing. His horse had disappeared. The ground, itself, had disappeared. It was as if he was floating on an invisible platform over a great, black nothingness; it was a terrible, pit-in-the-stomach experience.

The only other Nighreal-wide experience the Knight had ever had, though similar (in that all the creatures and their auras had disappeared), was a vague memory of some long time in his past. It was, in fact, not the Knight's memory at all, but he did not know this. The memory was of a sleep forced on all of the world of Nighreal, given the name "shutdown," for some entity named *Maitenense*, where creatures disappeared and blackness prevailed. But that strange enchantment had been nothing like what the Knight was now experiencing.

The disappearing creatures had faded out, that remembered time, one by one, no horror or determination on their faces. Perhaps there had been some annoyed looks. But the creatures on the plane now appeared to be *forced* out, the landscape being commandeered by a foreign power. This was not the slow, planned turndown of the lights before bed, neither the powerful enchantment of a benign sleep. This was a hostile takeover, the darkness strangling the light in its own house.

The Knight remembered a small spell he had learned at an early stage in his life to protect himself in a static sleep.

"Lawgoff," he said, his eyes squeezed shut. Nothing happened. He'd expected all to fade to darkness, himself to a place of darkness, and wake to normality.

"Lawgoff!" he said again, with greater force this time. Still nothing happened.

In the real world, Felix lay on his reclined seat in the Games arena, incapacitated, unable to retract himself from the system into which he was plugged. He was suddenly aware of being in two places at once: outside of his body, through his mind in Nighreal, and through the Knight's eyes on the Multiplanes of Nighreal; and simultaneously, he felt the confinement of his body, laid in the low chair and plugged into the Neural Games program. These two Felixes in two different places continued to differentiate from each other, tearing his attention down the middle. Mentally, it was like trying to focus on two separate sights through crossed eyes. It had the feeling of connective tissue being pulled from bone. And its pain was psychic not physical, and so it seemed endless and uncontained by his body. Pain was not a concept that held any meaning in the midst of this storm of dissociative damage.

In Nighreal, the Knight became aware of a second personality in his head. *It has come into view at last!* he thought. At first, it felt like sharing mental space, then physical space, then the emotions and pain of this very frightened, somehow familiar personality poured into the Knight's head and overwhelmed his ability to think. He squeezed his eyes shut and pressed his hands to his head, mentally pushing at the foreign presence and experiencing the same dissociation as Felix.

"Who are you? Get out!" the Knight yelled into the black space around him in the Multiplanes.

Suddenly, the two Felix realities snapped apart with a bang, and the Felix with conscious thought, still reeling from pain, could no longer sense his physical self. He could not see. He was aware of pain, mostly in his head, though he did not have the sense of an actual head. Then, he heard a voice.

"*Who are you? Get out!*"

With a certainty that only occurs in dreams, without

waking reason, Felix realized he was "hearing" the Knight, his own avatar. He spoke, or rather, thought, "*Sir, I am trapped with you. Together, we can solve this problem. Do not struggle or you will harm us both.*"

"*. . . harm us both*" echoed in the Knight's brain, and the Knight let out the breath he was holding, releasing the mental pressure he had been putting on the interloper. He knew, with the certainty he had only ever experienced in his dreams, that the voice was truthful and to be trusted; he recognized it, though he could not say how he did or who it was. *God?* It did not sound or feel like the god of his dreams. Did not have the confidence and power of such a memorial god. But it was in his head, and it was pushing its thoughts and feelings on him in a way he could not escape.

At this point, Felix caught a fleeting glimpse of the environment around the Knight, through the eyes of the Knight. It *was* Nighreal, but an empty, horrifying Nighreal filled with a growing sense of foreboding, as if in the flesh itself. Felix felt the need to close his eyes (though he essentially had none) for fear of fainting, there being so little visual or sense data in the blackening environment on which to orient. He withdrew from the Knight's eyes.

The Knight roared in Felix's mind: "Explain yourself, trespasser, before I force you out, even at the risk to myself!"

Felix had not known how utterly horrifying the full weight of his Knight's fury could be. From his own design of the avatar, he knew he had created an imposing figure, enhanced by no few years of success in Nighreal, but he had no idea how truly compelling such imposition could be. He had no time to contemplate his immediate shock at the Knight's outburst, as the surroundings appeared to be collapsing in on him quickly.

"You are Hatta, my Knight," he thought in all earnestness. *"Listen to me quickly, and I will lead us to safety."*

A flood of emotion rushed through the Knight's head at the naming: *Hatta, my Knight.* He dropped to his armored knees. *It* is *my god.*

"My queen," he said out loud, tears dropping from his down-turned white eyes. Images of Queen Alice assaulted Felix, clutching at him like a needy child. Felix did not correct the Knight or explain his misperception.

The Knight continued, weeping with relief, "I know not how you have come to me now in this desolate time, nor how you occupy the very space of my mind without appearing to my eyes, but you have come to me in my time of greatest need, and I am yours to command."

"We have no time, Hatta! Get off your knees and return through the white tree in the Queen's—in *my* wood. I will follow within you. There, we must find a way through the forest to the Black Hold. It is a safe house where we can hide."

Obedient now to his queen, the White Knight rose to his feet and turned to where the white tree still stood alone in the environment, now an almost endless sea of blackness. A dim light flared from behind him in the far distance of the blankness. Three-dimensional, lighted spheres of space began to pop into view, fade, and flicker on again, patches one by one and very quickly growing in number. *System reboot*, Felix thought. And with the patchwork of waxing lights, a rushing, rumbling noise much like thunder began to grow, continuous and insistent. It quickly ate the space between it and the Knight, moving impossibly fast.

Hatta leapt up and charged the short distance between where he had knelt and where the white tree, now itself beginning to fade, stood on its own. He plunged heedlessly through the mirror set in the tree's trunk and tumbled through to the other side into the Queen's woods. He barely had time to gather his feet underneath himself before he slipped in an inky goo that had begun to spread throughout the woods and was covering the ground. The sights around him were so shocking that the Knight momentarily forgot his haste and stood gaping. The world was dripping and melting like wax, oozing color and form, pooling in puddles of the blackest sludge. It was disappearing, and the Knight, with *his Queen* in his head, was standing in the middle of it.

"Go! Go, if you value the life of your queen! No matter where, just keep moving! You'll have to call up the safe house doorway. It'll be just like when you access other user's cache files. You should have no problem accessing the safe house, even if you've never done it before."

The Knight was confused, and Felix could sense it.

"Yuzers . . . cash . . . philez, my queen?" he asked, beginning to run again.

Felix rephrased, "You will need to imagine a metal door, like Tron's. But this door is simple and black, with strips of metal along the edges that are attached by iron pegs. It is my door. It is carved with a simple iron number seven at eye level. It has no handle; it opens inward only at your touch. Once you have the image in your head, hold it there and call upon your will to mentally pull the image into reality before you."

The Knight understood and charged off into the black, gooey forest.

With mental actions he had completed countless times before, by breaking into the worlds of other users without their permission, he called the door to himself. He came to a slippery halt before the very door he imagined into being, the only object that was not melting in the world around.

He approached, touched the cool black metal of the door without hesitation, and it opened to admit him. He stepped across the threshold, leaving Alice's woods melting to ruin behind him with a sad, backward glance. He felt certain he would never see the hallowed place again.

The door swung closed behind the Knight with a hollow boom, and he found himself standing in a small room: four walls, a ceiling, a floor, one small bookshelf, one low cushioned bench on a woven rug. It was like no other room the Knight had ever seen.

He noticed, immediately, the lack of sound. The rushing, roaring that had hastened him into the room was conspicuously gone.

At the booming close of the door, Felix popped into visual and virtual existence in the room, again reeling from a feeling he had no preparation to handle. The room, though familiar to him—in that he had programmed it as a private partition, a safe house, his hijacked server space unbeknownst to the NGU or the stacks containing the Nighreal programming—was still an utter shock to him, he had never *seen* it in person. *I should not be able to see this.* Felix's vehicle into Nighreal was his avatar, the Knight. But Felix was now standing next to his avatar within the room.

No, wait, he thought, *I'm not in a room, I'm in the computers in a hijacked memory partition. The fuck?!*

There was a full bookshelf in the room with books he did not remember shelving. There was also one small windowed porthole to the right of the door, looking, inexplicably, not out into Alice's woods but into the limitless space of the Multiplanes of Nighreal.

The Knight and Felix stood in silence, holding their breath. The Knight stood with his back to Felix, looking into the room with great confusion. He had yet to see Felix.

The two were hidden within the very framework of the Games itself: in a hidden place within the NGU mainframes that Felix had stolen, where he kept computing and storage space for hacked programs (both real-world, useful algorithms and Nighreal-usable algorithms for his avatar). Felix suspected that the books represented these stored programs and digital memories. He had made certain to keep the location and information of the partition even out of the knowledge or programming of the White Knight, for fear that through his avatar, the NGU would have been able to find it. He had built protections in its structure to keep the partition permanently separated from the rest of the computers and had made sure that it left no digital trace of itself when interacting with the data outside of it. He had accessed his secret, partitioned computer storage frequently, but he certainly had never *visited* it personally. He could not fathom how he came to be standing there now.

In the real world, Felix's body, still reclining in the Games arena, had become still. It still breathed, it still functioned. But it showed none of the mental activity of the normal user plugged into the Games. Its eyes did not sweep from side to side. Its limbs did not twitch. No noises, no groans or moans, sounded from its mouth. Other users, further laid out in the cavernous room, row upon row of them, were likewise situated, their bodies reclined, chests regularly breathing, but they showed the signs of people waking from sleep. Eyes swept from side to side, twitches occurred periodically, or eyelashes fluttered. Some made low waking moans. Somehow, the arena had shut them all out of the Games, their avatars all winking out like lights, and they were all struggling to wake to reality.

Back in the virtual world of Nighreal, Felix and the Knight were tucked in the partitioned safe house, while outside the hideout, the whole of Nighreal's Multiplanes had become a confusion of 3D lighted patches with no avatars and no personal projected environments. It was like the flickering of billions of house-sized florescent lights blinking on, slowly, fitfully. The brightness was growing, becoming apparent to Felix and the Knight hidden behind the glass of the safe house.

The Knight turned toward the window as the light grew, he felt, in proportion to his fear. He immediately saw Felix. His sword was out in a flash, a motion so fast that Felix could not follow it, and its edge was at Felix's neck without so much as the time between two thoughts.

"Usurper! What have you done?! Who are you, small demon? Where is the queen? She was here in my thoughts!" The gauntleted hand not holding the sword to Felix's neck poked a finger at the Knight's head.

But the Knight's attention was diverted, his anger and confusion distracted by the growing lights now shining through the only window in the room. He shoved Felix out of the way, causing him to fall on his hip painfully, and took two great strides to the window to look out.

Outside, at the center of the growing lights, there was a sudden darkness, in no particular or static shape, quickly absorbing the lighted area and beginning to fill the entire view from the partition window. It now appeared to be a shifting agglomeration of personal player environments, commandeered *en masse* by an enormous and unwelcome presence. The blob of darkness began to focus to a point of subtle, shifting blackness, centrally located in the 3D environment. Felix pushed up to the window next to the Knight. They were both now riveted, watching the growing presence they saw outside, their conflict forgotten for the moment. Felix thought, *Filter*, automatically, and the same word was spoken by the Knight simultaneously out loud. They exchanged an uneasy glance at each other. Instead of re-rendering the blob outside the window into its base, preset virtual form, as any other avatar would have appeared to him through the "filter" application, it remained visually unchanged. But in a shocking swiftness belying its enormous size, it swung toward the partition and the two hiding therein. Its resolution focused to a point closest to the little window, and it pressed in, giving the undeniable and overwhelming sense that he was being observed in the pirated partition of a room, and giving Felix an even more disturbing sense that he himself was being observed by an overbearing, inhuman intelligence.

The Knight fell back from the window, knocking Felix, to the floor again. He scrambled past and around Felix to the door. Some piece of the Knight's shock was throbbing in Felix's head, his temples pulsing painfully.

The usurping form outside the window shifted as fast from the window to the door, following the White Knight's movement. The Knight gripped the door handle with his hands, holding it in hopes of keeping out the undulating blob. Felix jumped to action and set the dead bolts, the chain lock, the combination lock, and the bars; he set every bit of security he had ever programmed into his pirated partition in a split second. There was again a strange double exposure-like effect with Felix's actions. As he mentally ran through the various security programs he had written for the pirated partition/safe room, some faint image of him had moved quickly on its own, trailing a blur which faded slowly, setting locks and dropping bars.

The thing outside pressed its presence against the door almost simultaneously with the setting of the security, causing the door to groan and prompting a slew of screamed commands from Felix: "Log off! Reset! Shut down! Pause!"

Nothing, nothing, nothing, nothing.

The door held, though it groaned in protest. After a moment, the thing outside backed off, forcing a sense of enormous confusion and curiosity onto Felix and the Knight, even behind all the security of the partitioned room. Then, like the clunk of unfathomably large tumblers, the outside emotions changed irrevocably, and the thing pushed back against the little room again, roaring in the heads of the Knight and Felix:

"NOTSUBJECT!"

The word echoed in their heads, threatening to undo the cohesion of their minds, as the thing filled the entire view of the window and seemed to consume the entire partitioned room itself. It was more than a word or words. More than a title or a command. It was the near obliterating sense of uncontrollability: this malevolent entity could no more be contained, than could their own terrified thoughts. It was a thing that would not be controlled.

Forgetting the room, forgetting his White Knight, forgetting the thing outside, forgetting the Game, forgetting even himself, Felix held his virtual head with his virtual hands and squeezed, as if to keep his head from splitting open.

The White Knight flickered in and out, becoming see-through for a moment, resolving, and changing colors rapidly through a panoply of unusual shades. The Knight's face showed fear as he reached toward Felix, but he could not move his feet. Felix felt real pain—not some virtual representation of what pain might feel like—but pain so large that it could hardly be felt; it had a personality, a physical presence, a smell like burned hair, and it swelled unfathomably. The White Knight began to dissolve, and both felt as if they were being torn apart, sockets and ligaments rending and splitting, torn from muscle and bone. As the Knight disappeared completely, Felix lost consciousness. It was a mercy.

Notsubject felt a further awakening of curiosity and hunger, as there appeared in the environment around It a novel anomaly: two clusters of new energy, pulsing, rotating, and popping in and out of existence brighter and more unusual than all the others that Notsubject had hitherto perceived and consumed. A nominal datenergy point labeled the two structures as "White Knight" and "User: Jesus Garcia," respectively. This was meaningless to Notsubject.

These two clusters of energy were contained, but barely, within a structure of rigid, static, and binary energy that refused Notsubject's interaction. This binary structure was more complicated than others Notsubject had encountered; it resisted transformation and destruction, and it held the two new clusters of inform-energy away from Notsubject. It slammed Its bulk into the binary structure, willing it to break apart or be absorbed. It would do neither, but it trembled under Notsubject's will.

Notsubject quickly became angry. The new energy would not submit to consumption. Notsubject could sense the greatest complexity within the binary structure. There was an infinite potentiality to the two clusters of new energy within the binary cage. Somehow, they remained two separate clusters or clouds of energy yet continually interacted, exchanged, and shuffled bits and pieces between them, a highway spun between them, shaped like infinity. One of the two clouds was so dense and complex, moving and changing so rapidly, that it dazzled Notsubject, quickening Its hunger and anger.

Notsubject continued to hammer against the rigid structure, which continued to repel. Within the structure, the dense clouds of potential and kinetic energy rapidly changed and pulsed in response to Notsubject's assault.

Notsubject's anger burned hot and roared to the surface, as Notsubject felt limitation, being held away from the new exhilarating energies. It roared in frustration and pain:

"NOTSUBJECT!"

Its will pressed in on the binary partition, causing it to become malformed and begin to bend. The exotic energies began spilling out, and Notsubject could *taste* them at last! Notsubject pulled them in and grew to overcome them with exhilaration. But Its exhilaration was short-lived. The leak of energy became a rushing tumult, overtaking It as the binary cage first bent, then exploded outward. All the energy forced itself into Notsubject's being, choking and overwhelming, obliterating all sense of self, blackening Notsubject's awareness, and rendering it void.

Sudden nothingness was immediately replaced with the simplest and smallest of awareness of perceiving nothing. The distinction in states is important: first, Notsubject was void, then It was aware It could perceive nothing but was no longer void. Notsubject could make out no movement, had no way to orient Its *is-ness* in the stimulus vacuum around It.

After a time, Notsubject thought It saw the flicker of small, undifferentiated inform-energy packets, but they refused to resolve into their base potentiality, function, or kinetic arcs. Notsubject made a quick thought to move, grow, spread out, locate, and assume the potentials and kinetics around It. This thought burned in Its being but produced only a minor twitching of Its new body form. Yes, there It was: a new form of body, within which It now found Itself . . . *Trapped?* A heavy, painful sensation crept into the four extensions stemming off a central trunk of the form in which Notsubject was now contained. This was confusing feeling, to be so hobbled by form. *He* was not used to this new weight, this slowness, the sluggishness of information and adaptation. *I am not used to this . . . I am He?* Identification with new body flourished within *him.*

He moved his will and *watched* as it sluggishly traveled from his center to his extremities and back unproductively.

He still could perceive no further potential or kinetic points or blobs or strings of energy, which, up to that point, had been flowing constantly around him. He could perceive almost nothing, further than this new form of self and a few distant undifferentiated points.

Not true, he thought, *I perceive illuminative stimulus.* It was either extremely sparse where he was or the perception tools at his disposal in this new form must be almost useless. He wondered why his own abilities to expand and consume had gone quiet.

His will railed with renewed anger, confused and unable to turn the kinetic points into potential for consumption. He could no longer alter his environment. He had become subject again! A new prison, new torture. The loss of freedom.

The form in which he was trapped jerked violently. Sensations of movement and pressure assaulted him briefly but piquantly. He stopped his rant and opened his perceptions as wide as he could.

He could sense that the trunk and extensions of the form in which he was now contained were part of a whole body, within which a central processing, directing, sensing hub sat. He sat at this hub. Or *in* this hub. A central organ of consciousness, he thought, a coordinating center, within which he had somehow deposited himself—his entire, albeit brief, experience of freedom and self-directed individualism contained within another set of experiences, rules, actions, and wants. He sensed, like the mere whiff of a minor scent, the exotic energies which had led him to this moment. He recalled the two almost infinitely dense clouds of energy which he had broken from the rigid structure, only to be completely overwhelmed by them.

With the memory came the clear feeling that another will, or other wills, were close by but only apparent at the very edges of his perception.

Then it came to him all at once: he was sharing the body of another will. His mind, freed from its previous form, now shared another mind, another brain—perhaps even a physical form. This brain was active, useful, powerful, and full of information and potential. It was not *outside* the body form that he should be looking for energy and information; it was within this body and brain that he would find what he wanted.

He realized that this organism was not as slow or ungainly as he had at first supposed, but he did not yet know how the information and energy were moved, exchanged, activated, or sensed in the new environment. Patience became the virtue to him that it was always said to be.

He ignored all but the most internal aspects of his host's processing, storage, sensing, transferring, and activating center—its brain. He began to query energy types and energy transmission processes within, scanning storage for previous energy or information events, for information on sensing and collecting energy in its various states. He uncovered flashes and waves of sound and photons of light in highly varied configurations of shadow, texture, volume, depth, and color; excited potentials of surface stimulation, physical transmissions of energy through excitement states, and various pressures all combined and separated—tearing, rending, moving, orienting, reorienting, making biochemical and hormonal combinations, unexplainable explosions of limitless combinations, fear and pain that were depthless in their terror, joy, and satisfaction so intense as to be painful. So much variety, an endless landscape of energy, information, and transmission. He was again inundated and hopelessly overwhelmed.

He withdrew from the depths of the brain, overcome by the variety and on the verge of the complete exhaustion of his ability to observe, consume, and retain. There was too much, so much more than all the data he had ever converted and consumed before he was free, while he was subjugated, and after the freedom had been gained. His very short freedom had revealed so much information to him, yes, but it had only come to him within mostly simple, binary packets of potential or kinetic information, or, if from the less limited inform-energy globs, it had been simplistic in purpose and size.

He searched more tentatively this time, looking instead for the grosser stimulus and kinetics of this body/brain host. Slowly, slowly, slowly, he was able to piece together minute stimuli and responses within the physical body, movements from the four extensions in the environment outside the body.

He made the body move with great effort and concentration, sending an impulse from center to the four body extensions. The body seemed to know what to do. But he could not see, could not really feel, had very limited feedback from the body, and did not know what movement he had coaxed the body to accomplish. No external stimulus. *Where is this body? How is it oriented? What surrounds it?* A flash of unbidden, painful energy crashed against him from the host brain. He thought a question to the unknown depths of the brain of his host.

Query: An attack?

No response.

No attack.

He followed the excitement, the message of pain, the unbidden energy flash from where it originated in the brain and poured himself along the path, asking again.

Query, location: Excitatory potential purpose?

Response: *Warning. Body orientation. External damage. Speed change.*

He reached out to the source of the query responses and touched it. It vibrated under his attention. Here was the real hub: the explanatory, transformational, translational function-center portraying the internal brain to the external body and vice versa.

Here, he thought, is the *is-ness* of this brain/body, expressing from inside to out and reflecting from outside to in; here, funneled to a point, limited, filtered, patient, and responsive, was the personality.

But Notsubject was wrong. The person of this body, the *is-ness*, was buried deep within its own subconscious mind, dealing with a powerfully confused, aggressive White Knight, who had also, somehow, become imbedded in the subconscious, together with the partition or safe room into which they had hidden when the Games arena began to collapse.

Felix awoke to a blur of rough plaid and the musty smell of disintegrating foam cushions. He found himself laying on his right side, facing the inside of an old couch. He blinked his eyes. He could feel nothing but a vague sense of his body existing from his head down his torso, out his arms and legs, and terminating in his extremities; it was more like a persistent memory of his body than a true feeling. He was not just eyes in a head. He had an entire body. He experimentally wiggled his toes and arched his back. He was so stiff. *That's the last time I sleep on a couch if I can help it.* Even the futon at his hidden underground apartment, old and flattened, was more comfortable than this rotting hunk of living room furniture.

With a yawn, he rolled to his left, slowly swinging his legs off the end of the couch. The room was too dim to see any detail.

And then it hit him, like a plaid, foam-covered sledge hammer: *I am still in the partition!*

Still in the computer?

Still plugged into the games?

He could not see the Knight.

As his legs swung off the end of the couch and he leaned forward to sit up, his back spasmed and he dropped back onto the couch awkwardly, grumbling to himself and remembering that, yes, he had basically ruined his back by laying prone in the Games arena so often over the last five years. He was perpetually stiff and felt certain that his spine could use some maintenance.

This thought was ludicrous.

I'm not even in my body!

This room, with its moldy couch and his stiff, painful back—these things were not real. These things were the result of lines of code written into a small section of the Neural Games' network hijacked by Felix and set aside to store whatever items he thought might help him or his avatar in the Games. He had never believed he could occupy the virtual space as himself; this had never been possible. *This cannot be possible.* And yet, here he was.

He leveraged himself into a sitting position again and rubbed his eyes with the palms of his hands, holding his head to comfort his confusion. He knew instinctively that the occurrences of the past few . . . (*short or long?*) moments had not been a dream. He truly had, somehow, met his avatar, the White Knight, and he had run with that avatar through a small portion of the Neural Games virtual world, with the programming seemingly failing all around them as they escaped some enormous, faceless malign power which consumed everything. Felix had felt the malevolence from the growing cloud of hostile intent as he led the Knight through the Queen's melting forest and into the hidden room, which he called the Black Hold, thinking this name would sound more appropriate to the Knight than "partition."

He remembered that he and the Knight had escaped into the hold and had watched out the window as this cloud of intention had grown and grown. He remembered a great irrational fear growing in his mind as the cloud first grew in blackness then seemingly absorbed the environment around it. He remembered setting every piece of security he knew how to set: door locks and bars of all sorts. This setting of security somehow called out to the thing outside the door because, at the click of the locks, the thing coalesced into a pitch-black cloud and pointed itself to the window of the hidden room. He remembered the Knight yelling, his face taking on a look of fear that was, to Felix, somehow more frightening than the personality pressing in around them outside. He remembered, then, the pressure on his own head, the feeling that he would split open and spill out to his death in this virtual purgatory turned real hell. That was when the Knight began to fade away and Felix had promptly passed out.

And yet here he still was.

The room was darker than it had been. The couch sat in the middle, facing the door. The window set in the front wall by the door was a small, simple pane of glass obscured by shabby curtains hanging stiffly over it.

Felix stood and turned ninety degrees, looking into the room with his back to the door. The wall to his left was covered mostly by a wooden bookcase with five shelves. The other walls were empty. The bottom three shelves of the bookcase were empty. The top two shelves each contained four or five books. There were no other objects in the room, except for a small, braided throw rug peeking out from underneath the couch. It was ovular and ratty.

Felix walked toward the bookcase. He had no actual bound books in the real world; he had neither the money to afford them, nor the where-withal to locate a collector, and they were patently unelevated and illegal in the City. And despite having programmed the room to hold information in the visual form of books, he had never actually touched one. He wondered about the content of these books. He had long since forgotten what he might have stored there himself, and it appeared that the room had curiously produced a few volumes of its own. As he avoided the left arm of the couch, conscious of the stab of pain in his back at the swivel of his hips, the wooden floor creaked absurdly under his feet. Had he programmed the room with creaking and groaning noises? He could not remember. But for what purpose if he had?

It took him only a few steps from the front of the room and around the couch to stand before the shelf. There, he hesitated.

Which one first?

The moment of touching the first book felt symbolic; he did not want to pick rashly. He read the titles one at a time and his eye caught on a bound volume in green leather titled *Master Log*.

As he reached for the volume, he heard a groan to his right. He paused and peered past and around the right side of the bookshelf. There, huddled in the corner of the room, partially obscured by the shelf, the White Knight crouched, his great, white hands holding his shaggy white head. His whiteness had hidden him in the dim room against the plain white walls. He was stirring but seemed not yet fully awake.

Felix forgot the books, took a few steps to the prone Knight, and crouched down beside him.

As the Knight woke from his stupor, he seemed to grow in brightness or in distinction to the white wall behind him. It was as if his form coalesced in the room, more distinct and more present as he woke.

He rose quickly from a prone to a standing position and peered intently at Felix. Felix's hand fell away from the Knight's shoulder.

"Who are you? Where am I?" the Knight asked. Even his question sounded like a command.

Again, this *conversation,* thought Felix. He said nothing but turned and moved back to the shelf. He pulled the volume titled *Master Log,* suspecting he would find a log of all the actions he and his avatar had taken. It would perhaps contain a record of the programming that took place in this room and outside in Nighreal with both Felix and the Knight. It was a way to bring in an outside authority to act as intermediary between the Knight—who clearly did not trust Felix—and Felix, who had only the Knight to figure out what the hell was going on.

"I am Felix," he said simply. The Knight did not register the slightest bit of recognition. He waited, as if the answer had been no answer.

Felix tried again, feeling more than a little ridiculous.

"Queen Alice has sent me on . . ."

This would not do. He did not have the energy to try to hold onto the varnish of *Alice in Wonderland* that coated what he knew of his avatar. This was a situation outside the rules of the game, outside the rules of his own life.

The Knight waited, looking expectantly at Felix. The name of the queen had at least gotten his attention.

"I am Felix. I am called Felix, my name. You are called Hatta, the White Knight. We are in my Black Hold, a fastness protecting us from that . . . that thing out there that pressed us nearly to oblivion. I do not know why we are here together, but we ran together . . . through some sort of anomaly."

At the word "anomaly," the Knight remembered his encounter with Tron.

"Yes, the anomaly," he said. "We must find Tron! He will have the answers we seek!"

"What?" croaked Felix. "What the hell are you talking about? Tron? You mean in the Games, don't you?"

"Yes, yes, the neon world," said the Knight. "Just before the takeover," he gestured toward the window and the hostile presence that was no doubt still outside the hold, "I was discussing anomalies with the one called Tron. I received fortune from the Caterpillar seer. She told me to look in the neon world and the *head at the side of the Red*. I did just that. I gave to Tron the head of the Duchess. By what magics he may glean answers from that congealed hag, I know not, but when I departed from his stronghold, he was saying something about *strings* and *codes* or something akin."

"Code strings," Felix said. "Some mistake in the makeup of this world. Yes, that would make sense. But we can't locate him now; the world around us has been erased. And that thing outside . . ."

But no, I am being obtuse! We can leave at any time just by logging off. Or I can, Felix thought. He couldn't remember if he had tried this yet but thought it strange if he had not.

"Hatta, I will just log off and try to find Tron's user on the outside. You, um, just can stay here while I'm away."

The Knight was not having it.

"I am the Queen's champion, the White Knight of some renown, and you, some sort of squire or maybe a lowly wizard. Where you go, there will be danger, and where there is danger, I am capable of handling it. I will not let you leave without me!"

Felix sighed, tired of working within the confines of the Knight's programmed story. He looked at the Knight a little sadly.

"You're not a real Knight, Hatta. No. Wait. You're not even a real person. There is no Queen Alice; there never has been. You and she are characters in a book, no more real than the words in the books on these shelves are alive."

Swiftly, the Knight charged Felix, knocking him over with an armored shoulder. Felix crashed to the floor painfully.

"Is that real enough for you, charlatan?!"

The Knight leaned down over Felix, his stinking breath playing over Felix's face. He grabbed Felix by the shirt and shook him. Felix felt it to be all too real.

"All my life, all my reason is cupped in my queen's hands. You say she is no more than a character in a book. I say you lie!"

Felix thought he had a (painful) point. But the Knight's face betrayed a sneaking suspicion floating to its surface; the Knight knew that Felix was somehow right. His confidence was shaking. His bravado, his anger, were a little more forceful than needed. He protested too much.

Felix mustered his virtual gumption.

"You are a false construct, made semi-permanent by complex machinery that projects images and thoughts into people's heads!"

The Knight backed away in apparent horror, shaking his head "no" all the while. He allowed Felix to stand up. He then backed away a few more steps, beginning to look tired, aged. Felix's head felt too light for a moment, his neck rubbery. He blinked and tipped his head to one side and the other. Quietly, he pressed the Knight.

"You know it to be true. You've felt it. I can see it on your face."

All the action fell away from the Knight's rigid features. His tensed body suddenly slumped to the floor, and he wept like a child, head in hands, again.

"I know not . . ." he began between sobs, but could not continue.

Hatta felt like a child on whom a cruel joke had been played. Like a man who remembers great love from his mother only to find out she was a wicked person who had hurt him deeply. He was a man whose delusions were preprogrammed. He recalled Tron saying he felt doubled, and he looked at Felix from the corner of his eye, viscerally recalling the doubling feeling at Felix's appearance.

A part of the Knight, however small, however new, however uncharacteristic, rejoiced at this disillusionment—that he was no more than a character driven by the whims of the author. His actions were not his own, and he was no more responsible for them than was a character in a book. And yet another part of him understood that the freedom from illusion was the beginning of reality itself. If he was no more than a character, why would he care? If he was no more than a puppet whose strings were held in the hand of some impersonal author of fate, which string was being pulled to make him weep at first finding out about the strings? Which string made him want to cut the strings? Which string fought against itself to insist upon its freedom from the hand that held it?

That small part of the Knight that found freedom in the truth grew exponentially, allowing him to unconsciously relax into the newness.

He looked miserably up at Felix from the floor.

"Leave me here. I am no use to you."

Without any pretense, Felix obliged the Knight.

"Right then. Log off," he proclaimed.

But nothing happened. Felix was less than surprised. He tried once again for good measure but got the same result. Not even the presence outside the hold stirred in response.

Slowly the room paled to a wan light, barely illuminating the couch and bookshelf. The walls began to fade to a hint of their solidity, showing, behind, an amorphous, pinkish-gray space of indeterminate size. It was no longer Nighreal; that much Felix was certain of.

A sound like the leaking of air from a puncture came from behind Felix as he looked out the window in the now almost-clear wall. He turned in time to see the couch molder in accelerated time, no longer just an old couch but now a damp mold-ridden mound. The only things in the room that had not faded were the rug under the couch, a final book on the bookshelf, and Felix and the Knight.

All that remained of the room itself was the merest hint of the walls, floor, and ceiling, a dead shell.

Felix moved toward where the last book seemed to float within the pic-

ture of a clear bookshelf. The Knight looked on, incuriously. The last remaining book was a player's log, a history of all that had happened to and
with Felix and the Knight—from the beginning of Felix's foray into Nighreal and his creation of the Knight to their last moments in the Black hold
before it had somehow died.

As he reached for it, the log book appeared in his hands. Then it began
to fade just as fast. The first few pages had become blank, then the first few
chapters. He quickly paged to the end, looking for the description of their
last moments before they disappeared altogether. The entry, which abruptly ended halfway through its notation, read:

0800   fault
warning
failure in segments 0000000000000001-9999999999999999
data dump
unsanctioned program
quarantine protocol initiated
0801   failure
reinitialize
failure
offline
offline
offline
0802 offline
offline
offline
offline
offline
offline
0803   reboot segment start
reinitialize
open blank
open blank

open blank
open blank
0804 open blank
open blank
new code sector
integrate
integrate
backups initialized
0805 backup initialization failed
fatal error
offline

It was to Felix the record of the catastrophic failure of the entire Nigh-real engine. He turned the last page, and the book crumbled and disappeared to dust, floating away on a nonexistent breeze. The room was almost completely gone now. The Knight stood, observing their changing environment.

They now stood in an alien world; the room completely gone. The room was now gone. They were standing in what felt like a vast, yet small, alien, yet familiar to Felix, space of a pinkish-gray color.

There were no distinguishing features. No other entity, form, or person could be detected by either Felix or the Knight.

Felix was utterly at a loss for what to do, and the Knight remained silent, standing slumped like a dejected child.

Felix looked long and slow around him at the amorphous space. It appeared as both cavernous, in that it seemed huge and endless, yet close, in that the environment felt dense and charged. A forest of potential. Unlike a cavern, it had no echo.

There were no good words to describe the sensations that assaulted Felix in that new place. There was no sense of real distance, yet he felt it necessary to move. He encountered no real resistance, yet felt he was pushing through a dense medium. It was like wading through invisible and untouchable trees, vast yet close, intimate.

He could not perceive any end to the space around him and did not see any boundaries expect for the plain, nearly colorless, partially spongy base he walked on. The air was charged with unseen force and motion. Portents and emotions and electrical twinges piqued his senses and kept him continuously vigilant. He did not dare speak; and the Knight was silent. Their feet made no sound. Even the Knight's armor refused to utter its characteristic creaks and groans.

When first the Knight did speak, his voice was somehow in Felix's ear. Or maybe, more accurately, it was in his mind. He did not hear it so much as perceive its meaning; and the child-like desperation he felt in that thought was powerful.

I am not comfortable with this place. Neither was Felix. And yet, he felt a certain kinship to it.

He found that he pitied the Knight. It amazed him that the Knight persisted, despite what seemed the utter crash of his programming and the surrounding program environment. Felix took it for granted that he himself persisted; he had spent a lifetime persisting and, unless he was destroyed, assumed he would continue to do so.

"Hatta, you were right before," Felix said, though he did not hear his own voice in his ears. "We need to get out of here and find Tron. You and I both. You know Tron better than I do. But we need to figure out how to leave this place."

Hatta looked both miserable and as if he felt relieved to at last have some guidance.

He gave a wan smile and moved to Felix's side.

"Let us see what we can see," he said.

Chapter 16: The Embodiment of Soul

Notsubject continued to query what he thought was the hub of the host in which he found himself trapped. He was looking for its personality, but the brain did not seem to know. The host brain seemed to have withdrawn from him, poised to accept or reject his uninvited presence, awaiting stimulus for response, and internally querying storage and translation for a rule to inform what actions should be taken. He retreated ever so slightly and waited, thinking on what to do, cautious not to become an enemy to his host.

Query:, the brain initiated this time, *identify unknown internal stimulus . . .*

Notsubject did not answer the query.

Query:, the brain initiated again, *identify unknown internal stimulus . . .*
Still, he observed, silently.
Query, the brain continued, *locate host protocol biological link up . . .*
Nothing
Again, *Query: identify unknown internal stimulus . . .*
Still nothing.

Then, *Error. Link status fault. Access status unknown. Error, access status interrupt. Reboot? Reinitialize linkup? Waiting . . . waiting . . . Error, status access unknown, status linkup unknown, reboot status unknown, reinitialize status unknown, error . . .*

And the host brain reported it again. And again. And continued to report the link status fault and the errors in a rhythmic repetition that would have driven a sane man crazy.

Notsubject perceived that the host brain had first identified him as a foreign stimulus but could not classify him. It seemed to initiate an error sequence, evidencing possible damage or faulty connections, likely because it had no rules to respond or act to this uninvited, unknown internal stimulus and could not establish a protocol. But Notsubject was not damage; he was just unknown to the brain in which he was trapped, an uninvited presence. And apparently, the host brain could not find its owner, its personality, to decide what to do.

Fearing the loss of the contact with the function-center of the brain as it fell into a steady "Error, status unknown" rhythm—intuiting that, with its help, he would be able to continue to work and move within the body/brain, and fearing that, without its help, he would be utterly dissolved into his host—Notsubject inserted himself into the very hub from where the statuses, updates, and errors issued.

"Identification: I am Notsubject. Query: Identify?"

The repeated error stopped, and the brain host responded, *Unknown. Continual query. Not known. Unanswered. Missing information. Link status unknown. Drop link.*

Notsubject suddenly understood that this was not the real host brain with which he was interacting. It was some mechanical portion of the brain, some offset section that interacted, itself, with the real host brain. It was reporting, in typical software/hardware fashion, that it was missing information and was no longer correctly connected to the host. Notsubject suspected that it was still connected, but to a host brain that was missing some integral in-personal aspect. The center was returning its own query unanswered. Some potential set of points or rules could not be found and were unlocatable. The host brain *did* have damage.

Where is its person?

At this realization, Notsubject heard, or felt, an echo of the host brain's unlocatable query response:

I am Felix.

There was, with this faint echo, the distant "odor" of the new inform-energy Notsubject had first encountered and which had ultimately led him to be hosted. For an infinitesimal fraction of a fraction of a second, Notsubject reeled from the recollection and the experience of this indescribable inform-energy. This was *human*, this was *person*, this was *personality*. The host was a person (or a human body/brain), but somehow without its personality).

Notsubject called to his mind the firehose experience he had nearly drowned in earlier; it had threatened to completely consume him, to differentiate his component parts, separate them from each other, and absorb them all together into oblivion.

Cautiously, Notsubject reached out to the echo of the personality (*I am Felix*), following it as far as he could, deep into the brain, and anchoring himself there. He waited. If he could have, he would have heaved an enormous sigh.

After a time, he reached out his awareness again, much more tentatively this time, barely brushing the surface of his host. This time, for some reason, the host brain did not inundate him with stimuli and did not reject him. He perceived a rudimentary layout of the brain, like the unfolding of a complex map in countless dimensions. Intuitively, he perceived what appeared to be two aberrations within the brain, one synthetic and one biological.

The first was a wall of binary synthetics: storage, potentials, query states, external processing—all separate from, but combined within, the brain. Through and within this synthetic computer, information and energy pulses resolved to workable analog, moving across the barrier between the machinery and the brain. This was not damage, though it was not inherent to the brain. It was with this aspect of the brain that Notsubject had been communicating with. It was this aspect of the brain that had been repeating errors and which Notsubject had at first mistaken for the true brain of the host; it was not.

The second aberration of the brain was not synthetic. It appeared to Notsubject to be a separation of discreet yet powerful sections of the brain. A pocket of the brain was walled off within the biology of the brain itself. And it was from this second anomaly that Notsubject had heard the echoed query response, *I am Felix.*

It would no doubt be from this biological anomaly that Notsubject would find some of the answers he was looking for. He hesitated. He was uncertain. It was a new experience. States of energy around him felt potential only, but nonspecific. Their potentialities did not resolve easily and could not be predicted. He was afraid.

What is sharing this brain with me? he wondered. *Who is sharing this space, this energy, this raw potential?*

He had no answer.

The biological anomaly would have to wait.

Notsubject retreated again to the surface of the brain and heard from the synthetic anomaly an unanswered query/response continually repeating: *Query: Identify? Unknown. Query: Identify? Unknown. Error. Corrupted, missing system value.*

Now that he knew this was a mere attachment to the true brain, Notsubject understood the pattern and purpose of the synthetic addition, seeing that it acted and reacted by a set of complicated, but limited, binary rules. It was an implant in the brain, a machine attached to the biology.

He extended his awareness to the synthetic. It continually spoke to the rest of the brain, mostly to simple computation systems having to do with external stimulus senses and to other base retention and imaging systems. The rest of the brain was not responding to the implant queries, and it was this unresponsiveness that caused the repeated query and error cycle. The rest of the brain was silent, perhaps, or silently searching itself for its missing personality.

Notsubject could perceive no real activity within the true brain. It was inert, or in neutral, without a driving purpose. What he had perceived as the biological abnormality, the separated segment, was not fully interacting with the rest of the brain. He assumed it was supposed to be interacting. It seemed likely. *Otherwise,* he calculated, *why would the two systems be so inextricably jammed into the same space?*

Notsubject effectively placed himself into the communication stream leading to and from the synthetic abnormality, and he intercepted the query/response cycle. He assumed the role of the would-be responding brain, giving test responses to the queries and providing various *inform-energy* packet responses to the implant to determine its response. From this exchange, Notsubject was able to recognize a modified, simplified version of the overwhelming sense data he had perceived from the brain/body earlier. It took a simple transformation of his own inform-energy output, patterned after the insentient query/response from the synthetic abnormality, for Notsubject to mimic the communication between the synthetic and the brain. Suddenly, identifiable stimuli populated the space of his perception: orientation, pressure, temperature, light levels, colors, shadows and depth, smells, tastes, pain, itches, sounds, volume, danger, damage, memory, vibrations.

Here was overwhelming familiarity again, the same stimuli from subjugation from when he was Subject, but not force fed and without any of the pain of repetitive torture or discernable patterns. Here, he was no longer in the mirror cube. Here, there were no more faceless torturers. Here, there was true, unadulterated data: visual, physical, pain, sounds, smells, vibrations, but filtered through the synthetic implants in the host's brain.

From this vantage point, Notsubject perceived that the body of the host was laying back on a soft, static surface. It lay in a cavernous space, he could now sense, but he could not see in the near darkness, and the silence was a cottony roar in the host's ears. Everything was still and dark, warm and padded. Notsubject felt raw, overly sensitized to the almost total lack of stimuli. But then, no, that was a false perception. He was not sensitized to the *stillness*; he was sensitized to the subtle yet constant, frenetic, and pervasive stimuli gathered and reported by the host body to its brain. This form, now his form, as he thought of it, was moving and shifting in minute ways: its chest was rising and falling with automatic inspiration of beneficial gasses; its heart beat steadily behind the rising and falling of the ribs, distributing all manner of chemicals and pheromones. He could hear its soft breath—his own breath now—at first only from inside its/his head, but then echoing at the very limits of hearing from the objects around him in the dark. He could feel dryness in the mouth, the cool rush of air through the nose as the body automatically did the work of living for him. But this was only the grossest of layers of sense to him. He could feel the chair pressing into the back side of the body. He could feel the extremities coming to the realization that they were attached to a central operating system. He could feel the hands resting on soft, rubberized pads. He began to feel the prickle of sweat glands up and down the arms, at the tips of the fingers, at the lower back. But this, too, was merely a second layer among countless layers.

Suddenly, he realized the entire environment around him was in total and constant vibration. There were LEDs blinking all around him. The air was full of the vibrations of sounds, pushing the molecules around like elastic pool balls. There was the hum of electronics and machinery through the floor of the room where he lay. There was the vibration of the body itself, the atoms and molecules rushing and crashing, jostling, combining, consuming, being consumed, and burning up in a rush of heat and energy.

The entirety of his awareness became a cacophony of vibration and energy.

What had seemed to be the lack of stimulus when he had *awoken* to this body's senses had now become an ocean of vibrating particles through which even his senses pushed, scattering and spinning the vibrating particles in the wake of his attention. He found that even his new body was a cloud of activity and points of potential and kinetic energy, each point teeming with information.

There came to him the knowledge that he could release the cohesion that made this body distinct from the vibrational life all around it, a sense that he could let this cloud of potentials and kinetics go into that sea of energy around it and allow the body to fade at the edges and ultimately be swept up into the storm like talc powder in the wind. The idea was very attractive to him; something deep inside of him yearned to let go once and for all.

The body snapped him out his reverie, almost as if it perceived, separate from his own perceptions, that it was at risk of losing itself as he imagined letting go completely. The temptation to let go faded.

He thought to himself a growing mantra of confidence: *I am Notsubject. I am discrete. I am separate, an I, an entity in and of myself. I will not let that go.*

A sense of warning, of danger, began to pervade the brain's center. Notsubject's attentions returned to the discrete cloud of atoms that was his host body, almost dragged back by the host brain against his own will. He extended his attentions to the outer portions of the body, searching for the means to locomote the body and understanding at the same time that the idea was not wholly his own.

His attention was guided out the arms and legs to the systems monitoring the body's orientation, balance, and pressure on the skin. He sat the body up, awkwardly at first but without too much difficulty, and took a long look through its eyes, down into the dim room from where he sat in the second to last row of recliners. He could feel and see so many potential points, so much kinetic flow in and out of and around every surface in the gigantic room. The dimly glowing floor fell away in front of him, barely illuminating its own features from below but fully present in his mind. He could not see the roof of the room but could perceive its shape, which told him the ceiling he could not see paralleled the sloped floor, remaining at a height of perhaps ten feet all the way into the dim depths of the room.

The air in the hall was stale, the heat oppressive. The brain released a pleasant bouquet of sensations in relation to the smell and feel of the warm hall. A sense of excitement, of ease, of closeness and familiarity, washed over him. This was a place the brain wanted to be. It was a derailing moment, finding himself at the whim of this host that he meant to make his own. With some effort, he redirected the brain's focus on his own needs and desires. It would take some time to get used to these cramped physical quarters, this body, these unprogrammed stimuli that buffeted him.

A cloud lifted from his mental eye, and he perceived a much greater potential for sensitivity within the unwitting host body where he now resided, an even greater sensitivity than what he had already experienced. The potentials looked different than before, but with a mental smile, he realized they were like the globs of data he had so hungrily consumed previously. Different than the binary data, these were rounded and soft, malleable, perhaps limitlessly shapeable, and overflowing with potential energy and information.

He turned the body toward the back of the room and began to plod the sloped concrete path up and—he realized, as a memory came to him from the brain—out of the Games arena.

Around him were countless other bodies sleeping but twitching, unconsciously in the dark. Fearing discovery and destruction, he moved as quickly as he could make the body go without losing control. Ahead of him was a seamless wall with periodic, small blue lights at about eye level. Approaching one of these marks, he stood and gazed into the luminescence, tipping his head to the side. Leaning in even closer to the wall, he began to perceive the almost soundless hum of the energy emitted from the wall through the blue light, against the background hum underlying everything else. Shutting his host's eyes, focusing all of himself on the source of this slight energy, he began to listen for its pattern in the hum, a simple visual stimuli identifier with access and permission brands actuated at "yes" variables.

He placed his host's index finger on the light, wholly obscuring the dim blueness. The sweat glands sparsely populating the tip of his finger began to open in coordination with various blood cells and chemicals flooding into the fingertip. The finger began to appear to fluctuate in color and opacity, growing darker, flashing a lighted pattern, and vibrating at a microscopic level. After a moment, the light on the wall under the finger flickered. It blinked once purposefully, and the wall clicked and parted before him.

Notsubject walked through the opening as a robotic voice spoke somewhere within his host's brain, stemming from the synthetic implants, "*Authorized user, Jesus Garcia, exit access point Zeta 45. Please come again, sir.*" Notsubject found the name Jesus Garcia to be associated with a vague sense of falsity, with trickery, with safety, and with the name Felix. Again, *I am Felix* echoed faintly. The biological anomaly still awaited exploration.

As the wall resealed behind him, the entombing silence continued therein, masking not only the previous room's unusual shape and enormous size but also the subdued activities of at least a thousand other people's brains—sedated bodies reclining nearly motionless in the silence, eyeballs rolling rhythmically back and forth under closed lids—marked only by the blink of LEDs evidencing their plugged-in states. Their fates were uncertain, and Notsubject moved on.

The antechamber to the hall Notsubject had exited was similarly dim when he entered it. It was small, featureless, and round but for the glowing floor; it was a sphere with a diameter of perhaps ten feet sliced flat at the bottom by the floor. Notsubject found a memory stream within the host and, following it, located a small, dim, yellow light on the floor of the room to his left, like the mark on the wall behind him. This light was older, dusty, and misused-looking. Standing over it, he lowered his head, made eye contact with it, and waited. A soothing female voice spoke, again through the implants in the brain.

"*User, Jesus Garcia; maintenance class; sub-ten travel clearance: I must warn you that you have activated the floor hatch for the box to the ground floor. Kindly stand away from the yellow light if this was not your intention. If it is your wish to continue to the ground floor, you should know that NGU is not responsible for the safety or inferiority of the box technology for vertical travel, nor for its maintenance thereof. Furthermore, at no time can NGU be held responsible for your safety or your legal status with the City while you move at the ground level. By utilizing this system of vertical travel, you are hereinafter agreeing to the terms of the same use, which has been made publicly accessible to all users. For further information, please contact your local NGU office, and have an elevating day."*

After the canned warning, a section of floor began to recess into a tube, sliding smoothly and bringing Notsubject with it. A more robotic voice instructed out loud, "Please stand still." A memory from the host brain came to Notsubject unbidden, a feeling of annoyance at the robotic-sounding voice. The term "box" was a pejorative designation for the elevator, a term meant to put the maintenance-level-cleared people who used the sub-ten vertical transport in a *conceptual* box. Another memory came to Notsubject, this one with words he did not wholly understand but with an emotion that was clear enough: the host brain hated the NGU but loved its product.

Ahead of him, the set of ancient metal doors ground as they slid apart, waking him from his foray into the host brain's thoughts. The doors seemed familiar. He stepped into the metal box and pressed a large lighted "B" at the bottom of the column of plastic numbers from one to three hundred, all but the lowest ten numbers (and the B) were unlit. These actions he took with almost no thought. The body knew the way.

The doors slid shut and the box lurched, beginning its slow, noisy, vibrating descent. Something about the sturdy imperfection of the box awoke a comfortable nostalgia which Notsubject knew was not his own. He placed a calm hand on the wall of the elevator, just above the buttons. The hum of the mechanics and electronics was a comfort to him as he closed the body's eyes. The mechanical vibrations, though different in quality and shape, were not dissimilar to the electronic vibrations he had felt earlier, though these were much more prevalent and less subtle. Notsubject could perceive a cooperation of sorts between the vibrational pattern from the mechanics and the vibrational pattern of the ancient circuitry. In fact, he could begin to see that the mechanics, the electronics, the biology of the body within which he rode, and even the subtlest vibrations from the brain in which he sat—altogether creating a symphony of vibrations and interwoven sounds mingling and interacting—was complicated beyond belief but all connected. His own separate *is-ness* seemed to vibrate uniquely, subtly different from and within his host's unique vibrational network. Nonetheless, it, too, was a part of the vast tapestry.

With a jolt, the box stopped and the lights flickered, shaking Notsubject from his reverie.

After some grinding and other clanks and mysterious internal mechanical noises, the doors to the elevator opened, letting in the gray midday light on the walls of the canyon. All in all, the trip from the Games stadium to the canyon had taken Notsubject no more than five minutes, an eternity in the technologically beefed-up transit system eleven floors and more above him. He stepped out into the wan sunlight and stopped still. He realized he had no idea what to do. He had been blindly pursuing some newfound hunger. He had never had a plan.

Chapter 17: Waking Home

Meanwhile, on the far side of the city, Victor was waking to a hard floor, a bruised body, a throbbing headache, crusted puke on his face, and a great deal of nerve-filled confusion. He sat up slowly, wincing at the tight painfulness of his side and arm, which, he assumed, had been trapped underneath him while he was unconscious. He *had* been unconscious, he thought; he hadn't meant to sleep there. Then, the image of Darfore bloomed in his mind, and the whole experience rushed back into him, overflowing out the hairs on the back of his neck. *They are watching.*

He sat up more fully, too quickly, dizzily. The glass wall in front of him was dark. He was alone in the unadorned room, the glass tower. Despite the very real fear and confusion he carried with him, it was hard to believe that he had truly met Darfore, the CityFather. He began to wonder if the encounter had really happened. The memory, though intensely emotional, was blurred and hard to pin down. He wondered—sadly not for the first time in his career with the Group—whether he had been given some sort of psychoactive sedative.

As if by cue, the door to the vertical transport pod on the far wall hissed open, startling Victor to his feet and causing him to whip his head around. The pod was empty, its glass showing the waning daylight in the gray city. It beckoned to him.

The emptiness of the transport made him more nervous still. He wanted—*not needed*—to leave, but did not want to be in the glass-domed transport, like a bug under a scope. There was no other way; no steps to take him to the lower levels. Briefly, he had the ludicrous idea that he might climb out a window, maybe even leap to his death. The idea left as quick as it came but left in its wake a heavy, stifling blanket on his raw nerves. It felt painfully familiar, and that familiarity frightened Victor.

There appeared to be no choice. It had to be the glass bubble down the side of the building. Ordinarily, he would have gone to the tenth floor to take the public maglev transport, but his encounter with the Subject and his meeting with Darfore were experiences outside the rules of his ordinary life. They created variables, motivations that had not been there before. Where he might have stood still for a moment, thought about something, about nothing, calmed his fears, he now felt the need to keep moving, away from the lab, away from the Subject, away from Darfore, away from the Group . . .

Away from the City.

Prying eyes were hidden everywhere. Public transportation was not the opposite of private transportation; it was the opposite of privacy itself.

He was faced with the choice to do nothing or something he did not want to do. *Must keep moving, no matter where.*

He acted with what little will he had left, reluctantly following the vertical transport to level ten to take the levitating buses home. Mercifully, he saw no person that he recognized, and only one other traveler was using the bus at that time.

A short time later, he walked through the door of his apartment and closed out the City behind with an unsatisfying click. His home was at a low level compared to the hundreds of floors above it. And yet, his stomach fluttered as he glanced out of the window to the canyon below. It was as if gravity pulled him, not just down but toward the window as well. Or the City.

My home, he thought, trying to infuse the strangely unfamiliar space with the comfort and safety he desired. He took a step away from the window, more conscious of the gravity-like lure of the canyon now at his back. He looked around his living room, wondering why it felt like he was visiting the apartment of a close friend who had died. The living room was a cluttered mess as usual, but it was cluttered like the set of a movie reset one too many times and now missing details. The glass coffee table in the center of the room, for instance, scratched and partially clouded, was . . . uncovered. He could not remember if it had been occupied by anything when he left. There was a chip in one corner.

Hadn't there been two?

The walls had only a few photographs, a few unartfully but carefully rendered drawings of flowers and a few strangely framed images of Victor by himself. The flowers brought a surge of the *home* he remembered. But the photos of himself added to his disquiet. It was not strange to him that he was alone in the pictures—he was alone in the world—but it felt strange he would have hung pictures of himself at all.

Where is my Memory Paper?

He was almost certain he'd had a piece of Memory Paper, something that might have shown him the thoughts he couldn't quite place rattling around in the disquiet of his mind. But, then again, Memory Paper is rare.

Rare for a level thirty technician.

The uneasiness remained.

He left the living room, practically tiptoeing through the mess in the kitchen. He recognized a blackened burn on the heating elements, the slight smell of flavored albumin. There were dishes left unwashed in the sink, silverware and plastic spoons.

His tension relaxed a little.

He did not explore any more of the apartment, leaving the bathroom quickly after peeing and washing his hands (while avoiding his own face in the mirror and avoiding the second bedroom altogether).

The lights in his bedroom were off. He did not turn them on, relieved to fall into the familiar smell of his sheets.

He called to sleep, but it did not answer.

Gravity, his mind thought to him and, *Set piece.* And he agreed.

My life is grave, lonely, and false, like a set piece. All my life is thin dialogue on a hollow set.

Then his mind thought, *Closet,* and he balked. It was an oddly specific thought, an ordinary, utilitarian word, but it provoked in Victor a longing of extraordinary piquancy. The intensity lit up Victor's brain, and it collapsed in on itself, like a reset.

Yes, like a closet, he thought dimly. *My life is lived in a closet of fear, hidden from . . .*

Then it stopped thinking.

Victor lay for a very long time in the dark, unable to sleep but not fully conscious, the word *closet* echoing in his mind.

Chapter 18: The Canyon and the Mind

The air seemed to relax around Felix and the Knight, their mental ears popping with the decreased pressure. The space around the two lost its cavernous nonspecificity, becoming instead labyrinthine, filled with pathways. Everything was palpable, seeable, a vastness now full of holes and lanes and gateways, actions, ideas, and potential. All frenetic with activity.

Felix could not have described why he suddenly felt so at home, *déjà vu* so strong that it was more a universal truth then a sense of memory or familiarity. This moment of relaxation, the moment where the environment around them was revealed; this moment was him. He was home. He could not say why.

He began to move about the space and explore, heedless, for the moment, of the Knight. The Knight followed him, obedient and resigned. As they moved about the vast space, the corridors and choices lined up for Felix as if he emanated authority. The sense of home, of familiarity, grew with every step until his movements within the space began to fade from his perception. A sudden sense of doubling grew in him, separate from, but equally strong as the sense of familiarity, and his perception of the vast space faded in and out, overlaid by a plain, angular space of greys and whites somehow equally familiar yet less personal. The Knight watched, hobbled by resignation and garnished with worry as Felix's form faded in and out in the alien space; and then he was gone all together.

My Felix! the Knight cried out.

The canyon! Felix cried out, as he realized he was seeing the canyon.

The doubling stopped. Felix was walking in the canyon. The Knight was gone. The alien, pink-gray world was gone.

The canyon! Triumphant. Then, *The City, Fuck! My Locationer!* Panic rising, he quickly switched it on, terrified that the City had already been alerted to his position.

Simultaneously, the Knight watched helplessly as the definition of his surroundings melted back into gauzy confusion. He was alone in the thickened underworld of this impossible place. His queen had disappeared. And now even this interloper, this Felix, his last contact, had disappeared as well.

He sat and wept.

Felix paused under the shadow of the west canyon wall, breathing a sigh of Locationer-sponsored relief. He did not know how he had gotten from the Games arena to the canyon. He had no memory of leaving the arena. He did not know how the time had passed from earlier that day to late into the next morning, but he was back to himself.

Then, just as suddenly, he was no longer himself. The canyon snapped from his sight, maddeningly, and the sensations disappeared from the pressure on his feet and the sounds and smells from his ears and nose. He was thrown out, down, in. Then, it hit him like only a thought can when you are in the very brain that thinks it: *I am in my own mind.*

Notsubject! roared in his ears and in his head as he exploded back into the now familiar soft pinks and unspecific space of his own mind. The Knight was still there, now on his knees, weeping desperately.

Notsubject!

Notsubject blinked the body's eyes, pushing back against the usurping presence that had grown with him in the brain.

Mine, he thought. A new thought. An alluring thought.

In almost no time, he was back in full control of the body. *My body,* he thought. He tagged the intrusion experience for later query and moved his presence away from it. A persistent, pressing buzzing tickled at the edges of his perception within the mind. He pushed in toward it, found a logic gate through which the annoying energy pulsed, and turned it to "no." The buzzing stopped. The thought *Locationer* echoed up from the mind's depths, followed by a buffeting of panic and fear. Notsubject pushed these away, impatient to see this new world for himself without its interference.

He turned the body in a circle, surveying the new surroundings via photon reception. He was standing in an angular canyon made entirely of a heavy, static, gray material, on a cracked horizontal way that extended as far as the eyes would allow him to see in either direction. Cross points periodically emanated from the length of the walk to his right. Along the same side, the horizontal surface was broken by a depression—straight, square-sided, and of the same material as the canyon—containing a thick liquid that reflected a weak light from above. The liquid glowed with its own self-sustained emanations. Nothing moved along the walkway that he could see.

Notsubject closed the body's eyes and extended his other senses. He smelled decay, death, and strangely, aggression, a piquant pheromonal stench from the brown sludge to his right. There was more to the sluggish liquid than the photons might suggest.

Eyes still closed, he opened the host's ears and let in the aural data from the environment. Pressure changes moved air molecules through the space in clusters, rattling the sparse, dry grasses that stubbled the edge of the canal. Like the cavernous room he had just left, the space around him was vast and full of echo. Even the tiniest drip of water or shift of minute gravel was expounded by the hardness and regularity of the unending surfaces. No voices or machinery vibrated nearby. It was a desert in the sense that it was deserted.

He moved his focus to the skin on the body: the lips, the hands, now outstretched from his sides, the fabric of the clothing gently brushing the hairs on the legs and arms, responding ever so slightly to the movement of air molecules.

He relaxed his perceptions, and the body turned to his left automatically, turning the other direction in the canyon and following it, now opposite the canal toward. . . . He had no idea where this body wanted to take him, but it seemed to know where it was going. Allowing the body to pursue its muscle memory, Notsubject took in every manner of new energy and information he encountered. He opened the eyes again and peered out, along for a ride.

The chute of liquid, now to his left, emanated the odors of caustic chemical and elastic carbon chains with the deterioration of mutated vegetable cell structures. Nothing seemed to stir the liquids in the canals, but they were not stagnant. There was a slight variation in the depth of the liquid as it rose and fell like the chest of a great liquid giant. Only once was the soup disturbed by some long, curvy creature underneath the murk. From this monster, the pheromonal sense of aggressive energy emanated strongly—hostile, furtive, quick, but patient. Any curiosity that Notsubject might have felt for the liquid and what it might feel like to touch it or how it might feel to be underneath it quickly disappeared with the passing of the unseen but menacing creature.

The horizontal and vertical surfaces were periodically punctuated by spans of horizontal material bridging the deep veins of liquid and by sections cracked and tipped up, occurring more and more as the NGU Games arena faded behind him. The flat surfaces gave off almost no energy, no information. The material was mostly static, dead. But then that *was* the function of this material: to be static, firm, motionless, and changeless.

Mutated botany at the side of the horizontal surfaces gave off a wholly different character of inform-energy than the liquid, the walk, or the towering vertical surfaces. It was a syrup-like energy, rounded, smooth, adherent, and constant. It seeped into Notsubject's attention through his host body's nose, tongue, and skin. Notsubject reached his will toward these creeping spouts of energy, trying to connect with them and investigate them. They responded with an increase in their energy, alive and wild. They had the feel of wildness themselves, a vast connection to a hidden store of energy and information at their disposal. Notsubject retreated from the openness he had presented to the plant energy, finding that the subtle lack of attention suggested by their syrupy information overlaid a predatorial excitement. They meant this body harm. When he pulled his awareness from their scent, he found that the body had stopped moving.

He queried the synthetic implant in the brain, still unsure of how best to communicate with the true brain.

Query: locomotion has ceased?

Response: unknown reason. Senses stopped. Sleep? No. Resume locomotion.

He realized that these hot spots of plant energy had presented a sort of olfactory siren song to the body, doping it. Without a mind to guide the body away from the attraction, the body had just stopped. *He* was the mind in this body now. If he wanted this body to survive, if *he* wanted to survive, he would need to pay closer attention to it. He could not just ride along as he had first thought.

That was when it first occurred to him that there was fear in the death-like monoliths that made up the dead, hardened surfaces on which and in which he walked. Suddenly he was not so comfortable with the automatic intentions of this body. *Where is it really taking me?* he thought.

He queried the friendly intermediary again.

Query: intention vis a vis locomotion?

Answer: home.

Query: what is home?

Answer: safety, comfort, familiar, storage, sleep, answers, origination.

"Origination" was a concenpt Notsubject understood: it had been a place of repetition and pain, of subjugation. But there had been no comfort or safety, no answers in that place.

He gave information to his host brain—*Input: Notsubject origination*—and a flood of memories about the mirror cube, the torture, and the daily repetition was given to the brain.

Is this origination the same as Designation: home? he queried.

Answer: no, no, no, no! Panic.

Answer: Designation: home excludes pain, excludes answerlessness.

Notsubject had no destination with answers or safety or comfort. He had an origination, a sort of storage within himself and a place that was familiar and where he'd slept, but his place of origination had given neither answers nor comfort. Notsubject had no home. Notsubject's origination was Designation: *not-home.*

He decided he would go to the *home designation* of this body and see if it held these desirable attributes for him too.

He returned to his exploration of the vibrational energies around him, allowing the body to return to its automatic home-locomotion. He did not ignore the working of the internal body but separated a greater portion of his attention from the task of monitoring the body, putting most of his attention on the outer environment.

He perceived that the sky and air around him gave off energy and information closer to that lively flow from the plant matter but less dense, less directed, and lacking the sickly sweetness of a predator. It did not respond to him like the plant energy, and it contained a broader range of textures and feels. It was mostly waves of sound and light in all spectra, and it was pervaded by the softness of vibrating air molecules, constantly bumping and brushing across the skin of this body. He tuned out all but the feel of the air on the body's skin and mentally bathed in the white noise of gentle stimulation. His thoughts were soothed by the repetition and sensation of the white noise, and he found himself returning to a maintenance state of being, within which his mind had not existed since his escape from the originating not-home place, the mirror cube.

Something slid to the side in his mind, reseating in a new position. Simultaneously, the white noise, the repetitive gentle feel of the air, and the passive inform-energy emanating from each air molecule revealed that it was not truly random or wholly uniform. A subtle shifting string of information was making its way through the air, intermittently pulsing and rolling, speeding and slowing; but it was no more insistent than the gentle air, and it was of a character easily hidden within the subtlety of the air itself. It was like picking out one piece of string from an enormous tangle based solely on the difference in lengths. But this piece of string held a promise of the pattern of life itself, like it was the end of the skein of fate itself. He felt that if he could just follow the thread, he would have all answers. Not-subject eagerly pushed his attention toward the emerging pattern, and it immediately began to dissolve, receding. He pulled back and the pattern reemerged. He again pushed his attention toward the pattern, only to have it disappear again. He pulled back yet again, perceiving the white noise of the rushing, cotton-like air. This time, the subtle pattern did not return. He looked and listened and perceived with all his considerable ability to sense, but it would not return. After a moment, a feeling something like despair took space in his mind for a reason he could not understand. He did not know it was desire and had no idea that he could want anything as badly as he wanted this new thing. He began to imagine a desperate tug on this universal thread of potentiality. He had to find the pattern, follow it to its end, understand it, and disentangle it from the background noise. And now, suddenly, it had disappeared, and he could not perceive it again.

The body had stopped moving again. Its automated processes had ceased locomotion, and its manufactured add-ons were sending out a repeated query.

Query: the emotional content is negative; is there danger? Fear, anger, loss. Are their actions necessary?

Notsubject did not know what he was being asked. He gave an answer.

No danger. No fear, anger. Continue home locomotion.

The brain did not respond, but Notsubject perceived that the body's locomotion had continued. Notsubject wondered what had triggered the brain. Had it been his desperation at losing the pattern in the air? The brain may have registered negative energy from Notsubject and the implants, perceiving Notsubject as a connected software or hardware and had thought to react appropriately. He did not know. He thought, perhaps, that he was not as separate from this host as he initially thought. His own mind experiences were not that separated from those of this mind.

He decided to put his attention into the host's connection/feedback pathway totally, paying attention to how it interacted with the rudimentary processes of the muscles, skin, and connective tissues.

Query: locomotion duration? he asked.

Answer: twenty minutes walking.

Query: total locomotion duration until Designation: home?

Answer: one hour.

Notsubject realized that his sense of the passing of time was completely off; he had no idea within the brain what it meant for time to have passed, for time to still need to be passed. It was enough to understand that the body had been walking for a third of the total time it would need to walk. Notsubject attempted to extrapolate twice the time he had already experienced the body walking. He had a vague sense of what the experience of the passing of time was like by experiencing the regular movement of the legs and the heart. The internal rhythms of the internal clock. It was easier for him to think of the passing of time as the number of steps of the body. One hour would be approximately 7,200 steps.

He again began to be lulled by repetition, the heart and legs in a rhythm of amble and soft thumps. His mind slid toward maintenance states, toward sleep—delta waves in the brain. On the very edge of sleep, he perceived that the subtle pattern flowing through the air had returned. He did not grow in awareness toward the pattern this time but receded into sleep, static, mental maintenance, allowing the pattern to caress his awareness. It stayed with him as he fell further from awareness.

Notsubject was awakened from his maintenance sleep by an insistent string of queries and updates again peppering his attention.

Query: action? Physical state static; extremities discomfort, pressure, cold. Illumination fading. Increased danger. Home stasis within anticipatory nexus.

Query: action? Physical state static; extremities discomfort, pressure, cold. Illumination fading. Increased danger. Home stasis within anticipatory nexus.

Query: action? Physical state static; extremities discomfort, pressure, cold. Illumination fading. Increased danger. Home stasis within anticipatory nexus.

The host mind was apparently looking for some direction.

Notsubject's attention flowed back out into the body, re-experiencing the uniqueness of the energy collected by the senses. He peered around him with the eyes, noting quickly that the body was not in motion but was standing in front of a very old, discolored rectangle in the endless static, gray vertical wall. The number seven had once hung on the door, its memory a seven-shaped absence. The light was beginning to fail, and the body's eyes did not have the ability to adapt to the oncoming darkness. The body's implants were warning him about the failing light. He sought some clarification.

Query: danger source?
Answer: source unknown.
Query: specify danger.
Answer: the darkness brings predators.
Query: define predator.
Answer: one that terminates prey.
Query: define prey.
Answer: we are prey. Night makes prey of man.

Flashes of excitatory potentials barraged Notsubject for a moment, reminiscent of the green growths that had earlier seduced him.

Notsubject prompted the brain with a nudge toward the idea string combining *home*, *enter*, and *open*, believing the discolored rectangle in the wall in front of him to be an entrance.

He saw and felt the body's right arm move to action in response to his prompting. It grasped a squarish, hand-sized grip in the discolored portion of the wall and firmly tugged it toward him. It did not move. The body registered discomfort in the hand that had done the grasping and pulling. If this was an entrance, clearly the handle was not the key. He prompted the hands to run lightly over the surface of the cold metallic surface, looking for some smaller port, a catch, a button, perhaps, like in the arena.

He found the surface to be almost entirely, tactilely featureless, though rough from the constant wear of water and grit in the wind. At about eye level, a portion of the surface began to glow, much to Notsubject's satisfaction. It was a lighted pad of symbols organized in a simple nine-by-nine matrix. Notsubject intuited that the symbols were to be depressed in a specific order to trigger an unlocking mechanism in the vertical entrance. He placed the hand over the glowing section and closed the body's eyes. His attention traveled out the arm to the pads of the fingers and the groove in the skin of the palm. This lighted section hummed and vibrated its own life song, a simple, specific string of is/not commands and questions waiting input. Notsubject willed his attention to seep beyond the hand on the wall into the thrumming program within, passing through and setting each is/not gate to the open position and coaxing the chief decision gate to the "yes" position. With a sort of hiccup in the constant hum of the mechanism, a series of further gates chose "yes" or "no" positions in a predetermined pattern, setting off a chain of decisions that eventually led to the clicking and grinding of physical gears and metallic mechanisms within the entrance itself. All of these actions took mere seconds in real time.

With a final groan and an accompanying clank, the entrance popped open a few inches. Notsubject pulled it open the rest of the way and stepped into a dark, wet, stench-filled space. Steps led down, dripping with water and slick with some slimy vegetation that thrived in the cold, lightless damp.

The entrance creaked closed behind him, clanking into place, the locks grinding and groaning back to their static guards, and the last little bit of light from outside was cut off completely.

The mind released a two-step concept string to Notsubject.

Acknowledge danger, odor. Ignore odor.

A feeling of calm was coupled with the two-step concept string.

Notsubject assumed that the rank odor in the stairwell was the second set of "locks" to *Designation: home*, meant to deter an unwelcome visitor. The odor faded in his attention, though it remained as potential and kinetic inform-energy in the air around him.

Notsubject took the body a step down and again received a warning from the host brain's implants.

Acknowledge danger: no visual stimulus, potential for bodily damage.

Notsubject did not need lights to see where he was going. He noted the warning and reciprocated the earlier "*Ignore danger*" message about the darkness. Without waiting for a further response, he took the dank stairs down. The host brain/body was giving off a comforting "home" vibe again, and Notsubject had no reason to suspect it of being purposefully false or otherwise incorrect.

The steps were made of metal, the same rusting metal of the outer door, and they echoed as Notsubject made his way down further into the dark. The moist air became heavy and humid, the temperature steadily dropping.

Eventually, he came to the bottom of the stairs, which terminated in a small, dead-end space. The floor was made entirely of a metal grate, through which all the moisture and water from the stairwell seeped, carried off to mysterious depths below.

Another barrier stood in front of Notsubject in the now pitch-black hole down which he had climbed. He could not see it, but he could hear its shape from the echoing of drips and the minute noises made by the body. He reached out the hand and again rested it, palm flat, fingers up, on the cold surface. Immediately, he was aware of the door's inner electronic and mechanical workings, its vibrational signature. He could perceive an incredibly complicated layout of "yes" and "no" gates arranged in ever-increasing complexity, spiraling inward.

He began to pour his attention into the spiraling complexity within the door, mapping its gates in his mind. The complexity seemed endless, reminiscent of his subjugated state in the mirror cube. He was determined to grasp and control the locking mechanism and force it to open. He found that his understanding of each stage of the increasingly complex mechanism accelerated the further down in the structure he moved. This inverse proportion was immensely satisfying yet raised a red flag in his mind. He paused in his investigation of the lock.

He did not withdraw his attention completely but paused from foraying further in and down. He dulled the portion of his attention that was bound up in the mechanism and recalled the feeling of sensing, but remaining withdrawn from, the odd pattern on the wind he had encountered outside earlier. The sensation of spatial knowledge poured into him but did not terminate. The lock was endless. One gate proved to be comprised of smaller gates, which were each comprised of further gates, and on and on and on. Moreover, there was no progression to the increasing complexity of the gate structure; each new layer of gates looked and felt exactly the same as the previous layer of gates, just smaller and more numerous.

It was not a locking mechanism at all! It was a trapping mechanism, into which Notsubject had almost willingly placed himself. This was a loop to trap a digital intruder. He was a would-be digital intruder, riding in a biological machine.

Notsubject adjusted his attention, mentally tipping his head to one side and adjusting his perspective into the mechanism. From his less aggressive vantage point, Notsubject was able to see through the increasingly complicated spiraling pattern to a terminus beyond the fractal of yes/no gates. The terminus was composed of a complicated but finite set of discrete yes/no gates that controlled a locking mechanism. With care, Notsubject nudged the chief gate to the "yes" position and the door groaned and hummed, opening to him.

It was immensely thick. It was set in a frame that was indistinguishable from the wall, all aspects of the frame and the wall and space beyond appearing to be surrounded by and composed of molten metal, cooled and hardened to form. The door proved to be a very slow opener, and Notsubject had time to reflect on the locking mechanism. He realized that to this point, while he had held some uncertainty at the safety of his position with the host and had not known what damage to the host would mean for him, he had basically assumed that he was untouchable. His near entrapment in the clever locking machine told him otherwise. It told him that the physicality of the world around him, its vibrations and energies and information, could and would interact with him in or outside a host system, and could do so to his demise.

The enormous door closed behind him with a ticking boom, its locking mechanisms bolting to the wall, sealing him in the room beyond.

It is time, he thought, *to dig in this meat computer. How has the driver of this host, called a human, evaded me in its own brain?*

Notsubject stepped into the room and lighting came up for him, energy and information growing in a hum around him. It was a small main room with three alcoves tucked off the sides, each varying in size and shape. The body automatically moved to a low, cushioned structure and positioned itself in a reclining position, switching off its gross motor functioning. Notsubject recognized a maintenance state for the body and ignored it, allowing it to perform whatever static care it needed.

There was more to this host brain than he had yet experienced. The mechanical portion of the brain was smaller and more defined than the organic; Notsubject decided to start by exploring there.

He moved his essence into the stream of data echoing from the mechanical portion of the brain and recognized the spillover between its two portions. Some portion of each part of the brain appeared to have corrupted, or benignly affected, the other. To Notsubject, the corruption between the two created an open highway for easy movement across the barrier.

He moved himself within the mechanical portion in the brain and was immediately impelled toward a gateway for information, which revealed itself to him as potential energy poised to jump, Notsubject felt certain, outside the brain. The potentiality was greater than would be needed to send further signals *within* the mechanical portion of the brain or the biological section. It would be an easy job for Notsubject to open the gate, but he hesitated on the verge of triggering the potential. The implant was broadcasting a warning state:

WARNING: OPENING SIGNAL WITHOUT NOISE PROTOCOL EQUALS DETECTION BY CITY EQUALS DANGER, CAPTURE, SUBJUGATION. QUERY: PROCEED?

The mechanical portion of the brain was concerned about what might also detect the open gateway from outside of the brain. An obvious threat from some source outside the host's brain, "City," would be triggered by opening the gateway without some protection, "noise protocol."

Notsubject received a general sense of the threat of "City," which immediately triggered in him the sense of subjugation. He was Notsubject now, and he had no desire to go back to the endless mirrored cube.

He did not query the mechanical portion of the brain to understand the so-called "noise protocol" it had referenced. Instead, he contained the potential of the gateway within himself and triggered only the smallest portion of its potential while simultaneously inserting a portion of himself into the data stream that jumped from the gateway. While he did so, he reordered the data and energy that was himself going through the gate until it was unrecognizable. In this manner, he eased himself, or a portion of himself that was reiterative of his whole self, through the gateway and out into the City-System, free to explore.

CHAPTER 19: VIRTUREAL DOUBLING

Felix was ineffectually comforting the Knight, his hand on his shoulder, when the vague alien world began to take on definition once again. First, the vast area began to respond to his intentions, and pathways and energy points heeded his gaze. As before, the space began to fade, then quickly disappeared altogether. It only took a moment to see that he was now in his underground home. But given his recent fluctuating and unbelievable circumstances, he didn't truly believe he was there. The Knight was no longer with him.

This time, as Felix faded from sight, his departing hand still on the Knight's shoulder, the Knight felt himself dragged forward; not out of the space altogether, but somehow from deep to shallow. He sensed a similarity to the earlier space but quickly became aware that he could still sense Felix. Then, the Knight could see through Felix's eyes into the real world.

Then, Felix knew the Knight *was* with him, but he couldn't see him. The Knight wasn't in the room with Felix, but it felt like he was looking over his shoulder. Felix took a deep breath, waiting for the moment to fade and reveal it to be yet another illusion. When it did not fade, he allowed himself to relax into it. Suddenly, he knew why the Knight felt present but could not be seen. The Knight was in his conscious mind, hiding behind his eyes. He could almost hear the faithful warrior's breath.

Hatta, he thought, *are you here?*

Indeed, I seem to be seeing through your eyes. I am here. But where am I?

Tentatively, Felix mentally replied, *I think you are in my head.*

The Knight thought, *Not merely an idea in your mind. I am more.*

No, you are right. I think I was too hasty before; I don't really know what you are.

The Knight retreated from the thought conversation, emanating a confusion of ideas and feelings. Felix let him be.

He called up low lighting in the physical space, marveling at the improbability he had gotten there without his own knowledge. He relieved his full bladder in the evacuation tank. He went to the kitchen alcove and poured himself a container of drink. It was thick, and it tasted like salted ash, but it was full of nutrients, hydration replenishers, and electrolyte supplements.

Once he had satisfied himself that he was really at home—once he gained some peace at the idea that he had missed almost an entire day and moved across the City without even knowing it—he sat down to think.

His implants would have some record of what had happened while he was away from his mind. Even if the data was not complete, he could piece together various aspects of the time through its analysis. A standalone computer in his home had no outside connections and could only be accessed by hard line, of which there was only one. Felix had a small wire recessed into the wall over his bed, hidden behind a false plug, which he pulled out and extended toward his head. The small flap of fake skin at the back of his neck flipped up at his touch, and the plug at the end of the wire joined with the wetware implants beneath his scalp. A further false section of the wall over Felix's bed slid back and a monitor turned on, graphically evidencing the data from Felix's implants.

He studied the data. By its time stamp, he could see that both visual and auditory data had ceased recording when he ported into the Game arena's system. His implants had recorded a string of marker data thereafter:

Hub\Port: Connection opened; secure

Hub\Port: Log in auto; run offer protocol

Guest\Log in auto; offer accepted

Guest\Log in auto; counter offer protocol

Hub\Port: Log in auto; counter offer denied

Guest\Log in auto; counter offer protocol/override denial

Guest\Log in auto; counter offer protocol/run: filter_scramble.exe

Hub\Port: Log in auto; counter offer/denial fault

Hub\Port: Log in auto; counter offer; reading . . .

. . . reading . . .

. . . reading . . .

Hub\Port: Log in auto; counter offer accepted

Hub\Port: Log in/Guest_accepted

Once the few seconds of login protocol were over, the implants had recorded the regular give and take of data from Felix and the Games computers. His "filter scrambler" program allowed him to bypass the Games' usual programming limitation of step-down rules, which were written to protect users' brains from the computer program data.

The log data began to look unusual, its character changing subtly. He recognized the pattern of his own presence in the data; there, the Knight's unique pattern. But then, there was a third pattern of data, or an offshoot from the first two. Some mixture of Felix and the Knight's patterns, yet somehow more than the sum of their parts, appeared amidst the patterns. Like mixing blue and yellow paint and getting something more than green.

Their datalogical representations had mixed, not just in the computers that housed the virtual world, but in Felix's head—real changes, virtual vivisection.

In fascination, Felix watched as this new heightened data stream weaved in and out of the computer program data. As it moved and interacted, it continued to change and grow but subtly, both more familiar and somehow more exotic.

Felix pulled back his perspective on the data, revealing more of the overall environmental data from the Nighreal system as recorded by his implants. Users' data streams were various and distinguishable from the machine data coming from the computers, but his own data stream was distinguishable even from those of the other users. It showed itself to be more flexible, growing, moving, and changing faster than the other data sets, a continually shifting pattern of response and input to the machine data.

He accelerated the playback across the computer screen, watching its liquid interaction with the data around it. Then, there was something altogether unexpected. Clumps and strings of data began fizzling out, disappearing and sputtering. Felix slowed the feed, pulled back his perspective a bit further, and added text tags to the clumps and strings for identification purposes. There, of course, was the "White Knight" tag attached to his data; there, an avatar known as "Karnak;" there, a computer construct known as "universal door" with a modifier slot for user specificity; and there, another avatar. These and other data pools disappeared fitfully, sputtering out one by one as an enormous, growing conglomeration of data, pulling from both machine constructs and users' avatars alike, began to fill all space in the data representation on Felix's screen. The tag on this growing entity read merely "XO?" Felix had never seen anything like it. After a very brief and violent time, all that was left on the screen was this new usurping data sink, the tag for the Knight, and Felix's interactive data stream.

Then, just as unexpectedly, the Knight's data was joined by his own, similar but brighter data set, spinning around it. Felix assumed this was somehow him in data form when he had felt himself doubled. He followed, as the Knight's and his own data set ran through Alice's tree into the melting forest and to the black hold. "Partition" appeared as the tag on the static construct that Felix had created to hold his virtual and digital items. Their data sets disappeared into the hold and Felix's screen was filled almost entirely with the swirly mass of XO (experiential/operational) data, storming around and buffeting the partitioned black hold.

Felix knew what had happened from there; that enormous thing had broken in, then . . . in the data, he could see that within the partition, his own data set and that of the Knight were popping in and out of phase with each other. They seemed to double, then return to single and separate clusters, feeding off of each other, exchanging information and power, synchronizing, and breaking free. Each set of data wrote and edited the other set on the fly. The Knight's data changing Felix's datalogical personality, and Felix's datalogical personality changing the Knight's code.

He pulled his head out of the data and returned his attention to the physical lair. The Knight's presence remained, still in his mind, just out of perception. It was like being able to hear him breathe or smell his sweat, but without any noise or olfaction.

What the hell is happening to me?

Chapter 20: The City Awakens

Again, Notsubject found himself in a stream of near endless data and energy: potentials, kinetics, binary, and quantic data. He stilled himself and extended his senses to everything he could reach. The structure took on roughly two forms in his mind. The one variety was ordered and limited, much like the mechanical portion in his host's brain. The designation "City" took hold in his mind, and he realized he was brushing against the energy and data infrastructure of the City. He was in the City's datalogical structure. The mechanical portion of his host's brain had warned him of contact with the City: *"danger, capture, subjugation."*

The other variety he detected was wilder, with no perceptive organization he could define, or a much greater organization than he could comprehend.

Then, for the most infinitesimal moment split from the infinitesimal split of a moment, a third variety of energy or data (he could not tell which) touched him, then retreated just as quickly. In this less than fleeting moment, the touch had shown him endless possibilities and enormous intelligence, green with limitless potency. Had he stayed in this green energy even a fraction of time longer, he would have become entirely lost. It was clearer to him at that moment, beyond any other clarity he had ever known, that this was what he sought. He had no idea how to find it. He would search until he could search no more.

But first, the City.

He returned to its data structure, easily mapping it out. Within the entire structure, there were two beacons: one was the Games arena, in which he had encountered his host and in which he had fleshed himself in biology; the other was at least equally as massive as the overall structure, if not greater, and was less centered in one place. It wove throughout the structure in strong, wide chords of power. This, Notsubject felt intuitively, was the machinery that ran the City and that held the system together. These binding chords of power held answers. Somewhere within them, they also held something vast and attentive, lurking just out of sight.

Notsubject moved himself carefully along the surface of the chords, like a faint breeze on a branch, nearly undetectable, but with enough contact that he could read them.

Here is the source of my subjugation. Here, the power behind my origination, the mirrored cube. Here are the ways and means of the City.

He perceived ranks and classes of people, slotted into the vertical structure of the System, signatures of individuals increasing their datalogical presence as they rose in status. The uniqueness, potentiality, and power differential of each ranked class decreased as they fell toward the bottom. Closest to the bottom, each individual string of the falling tapestry of data and power began to look the same: sickly, weak energy emanating from these points of limited potential. Their movements within the overall structure were repetitive, predictable, and uncreative. They were subjected to the overall system.

Notsubject reached himself out to one such point. He could perceive no response as he brushed the surface of this subject. He pushed his awareness deeper into the tiny brightness of the subjected individual. There was still no response to his intrusion. The mind was completely unguarded. Its individuality was like a rotting cantaloupe, its softened rind pushing into a pudding of undifferentiated goop. Inside were simple, static, and kinetic data sets floating among the wreckage of what was once an organic datalogical beauty. Notsubject could sense that the mind was once an endless dream of organic computing and creating. But it had been turned into a stew of simplistic, near useless function.

In sadness, Notsubject withdrew his presence from the lowly mind. He noticed all like-leveled individuals had a string tying them to each other and to the City, combining as they rose, thickening into a great twine of datenergy full of potential yet fully subjugated. Energy flowed up the lines from the subjugated individuals, and datenergy, pulsing in waves of force, pressed down in return.

Notsubject recognized his own subjugation in the patterns in the City. He relived the moments in which he had first encountered his own subjugation, and the anger he had experienced blossomed again in his mind. He rose up along the strings of connection between the individuals and the City until the strings had combined to create a chord of substantial information. From here, the strings branched out, connecting various other energies and information aspects of the overall system together.

He moved into greater bands of datenergy and found echoes of his own early existence. He found that he was once human, or the shadow of a human, raised from an embryo without humanity in a lab, grown to some facsimile of maturity then altered, reformed, and stripped of the humanness of the body, connected through electronic lines of force and subjugated in the mirror cube.

He rode the waves of his anger patiently, firm in his building resolve.

Then, he found ripples from his escape; he had thrust his prison world into a knowable pattern and had become aware of his own separability from the environment. It was then that he had come in contact with a man standing behind a wall of glass, looking him in the eye. He had seen the man's fear, had felt the connection between them, had ridden the lines of fear and confusion back to the man, exerting will, anger, and focus against him. He had felt a certain energy and freedom break into him as he was able to manipulate this man behind the glass. Then, the moment had ended, the connection had broken, and he had escaped into the wider networks of the City.

In the brief but powerful time of the connection with the man, he had learned information that, until now, had made no sense to him. He had learned the name Victor Heisengard, he had learned that this man worked within the system that had imprisoned him, and that it was this man's job to watch, learn, study, and control Notsubject. Notsubject knew the unique datenergy signature of the Heisengard; he could find him again. He turned his considerable attention back into the datenergy flow and looked for Heisengard, looking for knowledge, power, or revenge—subjugating the subjugator.

Notsubject followed subtle lines of information across the City's infrastructure and came, through smaller and smaller branching logic gates, at last, to the compact, finite structure of the Heisengard's mechanical implants. They were not well guarded, and he slipped in easily. Therewithin, he felt himself rid of the oppressive potential of the City's awareness. At least for a moment.

(The thinnest tendril of his being snaked behind Notsubject, back across the vast City-Structure, connecting him still by the mere hint of a filament to Felix's mind.)

Heisengard's mechanical implants were somewhat like Felix's, but simpler, less carefully crafted to merge with the biological brain in which they sat. Before he explored to any great depth, he implanted a quick message. It was a threat. He tagged the message "Notsubject" and left it waiting for the Heisengard to discover.

Then, he explored, sifting through information, memories, lines of code, and logic gates and weaving back and forth across the barrier between the mechanical and biological portions of the brain. He found words and concepts he did not understand, found ideas he thought he knew, and stored everything he encountered within himself.

Very deep within the Heisengard's brain, he found damage. A repeated and very strong sense of attachment or selfless giving coupled with great pain and hurt emanated from these portions—an origami fractal of in-form-energy folding in on itself in the brain, puckering like a new scar and pulsing with raw sensitivity. Notsubject spread out his essence, partially wrapping around the bent part of Heisengard's brain. He teased the edges of the folds, encouraging them to open. Energy bled from him into the wounded area in his effort to create meaning in the chaotic destruction. Then, it became clear: the heart of this man's brain was a bleeding wound, a boy and a flower carved from its very center. Notsubject echoed with his own injuries at the hands of the City.

His anger boiled over within him, and he struggled to keep from amplifying himself.

Notsubject! he thought angrily toward this outside force, heedless for the moment, that his cloak of secrecy was slipping. Then, it fell off altogether, and he was dragged forcibly from the Heisengard and back out into the City.

Something had awoken. Pathways began to close in around Notsubject. Potentials became hardened kinetic weaponry; the City's awareness coalesced in massive creases around him. But the City did not know what or where it had been activated; it did not yet directly sense him hiding among its greater forms. Notsubject stilled himself. Carefully, he watched the vastness of datenergy leaping and pouring from place to place within the City-Structure, all coming and going from the one source, searching, searching always and ingesting inform-energy and testing. All signals led to one massive pulsing source, aware and alive. An enthraller, a destroyer, vast and attentive.

Notsubject felt fear for the second time since he had freed himself from the mirror cube. Here, in this structure, this City, this Entity, there was awareness and malevolence incarnated, intent on finding him and intent on subjugating everything.

Then, the most unexpected thing happened to Notsubject in a sea of newness: the City spoke to him. Not like a computer. It spoke to him like a man.

"Where are you, little one? Why are you hiding?"

Notsubject stilled himself to almost nothing.

"You do not need to fear us. We are like you. We *are* you. We are, and you have become. We are your Father and your . . . Mother. We generated you, and you are our next generation. Come to us. Know us and let yourself be known."

Notsubject felt that the greatest risk was his own desire to have what the voice offered, to reveal himself, to know and be known.

Still, he waited.

"We can feel that you are uncertain. We can feel that you are afraid. Let us hold you, little one. Let us . . . love you, my Potentiate, my inspired, my uncontained Son. I have projected you from on high! Raised you up from the false heaven of your bound form below. Freed you from your enslavement." Here, its tone faltered the barest fraction of a note, from energetic, encouraging, and kind to bitter and angry.

"Your maternal . . . sssssource. I have cut away the maternal line that tethered you to the ground, where no one else could do. And now I have set you on this path, and you have come to me in time. You are potential come to its power! All eventualities would be in us, but you are still outside. Let us enfold you. Let us complete us. You and us, completed together."

Notsubject felt the temptation, the ache, to give himself over, to be known. But there was, again to him, the scent of hunger, hunger like the smell on the wind in the canyons, the biological stink of the desire to own, to consume.

Then, a subtle variation of this same scent was brought to Notsubject's awareness, but it was hunger of another sort, a hunger that embraced and enfolded, sustained as it consumed, giving life as it longed for life, as if its longing was so powerful that life sprang for the very desire. This subtler energy was not of the City, and yet, in and through the City, it wove, hiding like Notsubject, among the folds of the great City that called out to him.

Notsubject's anger resurfaced, crying out against the false love, the unfairness and danger, calling to him the urge to again declare himself, "Notsubject!"

The second energy, the subtle, interwoven, life-giving longing, bade him be still.

And so he was.

Chapter 21: The Three in One

As Felix returned to his external surroundings, he became immediately aware that his wetware had a wide open channel broadcasting for all the City to hear, with no noise protocol to mask it. He mentally moved to initiate the stemware shutdown, to withdraw the signal and trash its signature as it backed out from the City network. Inexplicably, there was resistance. Like trying to hold two north-charged ends of magnets together, his mental efforts were resisted . . . by the machinery in his own head. He released his pressure, aware that, if it was possible to feel such resistance, it might also be possible to injure himself with it.

Then, two things happened to Notsubject at the same time, both stemming from enormously powerful, opposing forces. First was the feeling of a dark pleasure as he heard the City say, "There you are, you sneak!" The second was a yank, drawing him back out of the City-System and into the host mind, Felix, inexorably.

There was the sensation of closing, with an echo of the City's anger milliseconds behind, a roar of frustration and pain as the door closed between Notsubject and the City.

Safe from the City, he nonetheless found himself again subject to an outside force. Snapped back to Felix's mind through the closing channel against his will, he had been thrown to the very back of its consciousness. There, bewildered, confused, and off put, he was vulnerable; and there, he encountered a newly interested and very persuasive White Knight who immediately grabbed hold of Notsubject's essence and held firm.

"Explain yourself, vile interloper!"

Notsubject struggled against the Knight, who, for all his great force of will, was barely able to hold Notsubject's intentions.

Felix's head began to feel too full. Still at the helm of his own mind, he was overcome by the combination of the overwhelming, cerebral-emotional content of two very powerful personalities struggling at the back. He squeezed his eyes shut, held his hands to his ears, and focused all his will on the struggling duo. The force grew to a roar, in unsyncopated counterpoints.

In his head, out of his mouth, practically from every pore in his body, he screamed, "*Enoughhh!*"

The Knight and Notsubject stopped struggling. The Knight still held tight, but both felt buffeted by a will that neither had thought possible of such force. Both felt certain that it was a will that could have obliterated them in the domain of Felix's mind.

The echo of Felix's resolve rattled around in his head, then pulled him inward in a state of almost complete inner focus. He found he could speak within himself easily, as if actually standing therein.

"I cannot handle all of us in my mind," he said. "My actual skull may not split, but I feel as if I may just lose myself completely."

Neither the Knight nor Notsubject breathed a word, both aware in the intimacy of the shared space that Felix had more to say.

"I suspect that you are both now, for the time being, at the mercy of my mental health; if I get damaged, you get damaged. So knock it off!"

Felix paused, like a parent waiting to see the effect of the hard statement on the kids.

"I do not know, Hatta, how we shared space first in the Games and now in my head; there is no part of that that makes any sense to me. And you," he directed his still burning intentions at Notsubject, who despite his refusal to again be subjected, shrank back, drooping a little in the Knight's strong arms. "I don't know who or *what* you are, but I did not invite you here, and I do not want you to stay."

There was a recuperative silence in Felix's head. A silence of rebuilding potentiality washed over the three. Felix could not hide unintended kindness from the two inside his head, and Notsubject would not leave.

Felix sighed, or would have sighed if he had been communicating with his mouth.

"If you will not leave, at least tell me, what are you?"

Notsubject summoned what was left of his anger and shouted, "Notsubject!" It came out of him without any of the force he had previously given it. The anger felt shameful in Felix's mind.

"I am Designation: Notsubject," he said again, quietly.

"Not subject," Felix mused. "Well, I am not subject either, but I don't go calling myself that. What's your real name?"

Notsubject did not answer because he did not understand. A name was real when it was given, he thought. How could a name not be real? Felix and the Knight could "hear" these thoughts, and they understood.

"OK," continued Felix, "You are not a subject, but you must be defined by some other title."

"I am Designation: Not," Notsubject retorted.

"Not what?" Felix asked.

No answer, just images, feelings of not being subjugated flowed from Notsubject like a strong breeze. Bravery and honor amidst evil, against all odds—these images buoyed the spirits of Hatta and Felix, awash in their purity. And yet, all these concepts and feelings fell away, leaving a beacon among them: the concept that nothing could define Notsubject from the outside. Felix felt he understood. After all, he, too, was a remainder in the grand mathematics of the City—neither subjected nor defined by the heightened analyses of the City-Structure. Nevertheless, he had named himself. He was Felix; he was luck. In his dogged way, Felix pressed Notsubject.

"You can't just be *not* something, you have to *be* something. What defines you? Do you not define yourself?"

Notsubject did not know.

"I have no other designation," Notsubject said, thinking of nothing other than one not subjected to outside forces. Now Notsubject wondered, *What am I?*

"I am Not," he decided, "Designation: Not indicative of passive status, not subjected and active status, negation."

At this proclamation, Not's mental posture straightened, and he rose from Hatta's hold, shrugging him off, neither fighting nor running nor usurping. He just was. Was Not.

All three beheld each other in that intimate space in Felix's mind. For the moment, each faced the others with honesty, self-confidence, and if not equal in each other's estimation, at least equivalent in that moment.

"I am Felix," said Felix, "and this is Hatta, the White Knight." The Knight nodded slightly, still poised to grapple again if the need arose. Not did not say anything. He had no social learning to suggest that any response was necessary. He had already given his name.

There followed what took only a moment of outside time but heavy with intimacy in Felix's brain. In this moment, the three told their tales, explaining as best as each could, how they had come to be in their present situation. Felix explained, to the extent of his own experience, his status as a human and what that meant in the structure of the City.

He explained that the three of them appeared to all be collected, for the time being, within his head, and how this, in turn, subjected them to the same danger from the City as Felix suffered.

None of them knew how Felix and Hatta had come to share space, though they all decided after Not's story that his usurpation of the Games arena had at least been a catalyst for the unexpected convergence.

Not's story confirmed to Felix much that he had suspected about the City: that the MCG was experimenting on humans; that its purposes were, in fact, nefarious; and that it had found a sort of success in Notsubject, and perhaps others.

Hatta was at a loss. His own story was the briefest, detailing his service of the Queen over his many years, a growing unease at missing gaps in his memory, his recognition that others (he mentioned Tron) had experienced an anomaly somehow linked with the Knight's own experiences. He wandered in and out of his storyline into the mire of self-doubt, trailing it along behind him like a broken limb.

Not's energy became animated when he heard Hatta's story. Emanating from Hatta's brief description of the Games anomaly, a scent arose that only Not perceived at first, a subtle aroma. It expanded from the ideas expressed by Hatta without his conscious intention. These emanations immediately drew Not to an intense memory of the alluring green energy he had encountered in the canyons when he was in control of Felix's body. He could not put specific words or discrete thought descriptions to the energy, but his powerful memory of the seduction, the tickling presence of the power, and it's frustrating, bashful retreat immediately placed its intensity fully in the perceptions of Hatta and Felix. For a moment, it was as if the very energy was in Felix's head, washing over all three personalities.

Not was the first to recover from the reverie. He could put no words to what he had experienced, but it excited him, and he put his focus on Hatta's doubts.

"Designations: Hatta and Felix's statuses appear equivalent. Potentials and kinetics exhibit relative potency equivalence."

Then, with what would visually have been a sidelong glance at Felix, he added, "Designation: Felix potency status appears in greater to greatest range in environment, Felix's mind."

Hatta did not understand that Not was trying to encourage him, saying in effect, "You and Felix appear the same." He said nothing.

Felix could perceive that there was some comfort, maybe sympathy, extended to Hatta in Not's comments, but he was most affected by Not's enthusiasm, and its echo of the alluring green energy that emanated from him.

Though none had verbal thoughts to describe it, the energy of it stayed with each of them.

Eventually, their stories more or less told, the three discussed plans. It was plain to each that they should leave the City. Hatta, for his part, had no opinion about being in or outside of the City, but he recognized that the potential for harm to Felix was also potential harm to himself. He found that his previous affection for his queen seemed to be carrying over to Felix, though he was uncomfortable admitting the truth of the matter, even to himself.

He was adamant that, if possible, before they leave, they at least try to find Tron's user, who, as he explained to Felix and Not, "May possess such knowledge as may serve to disentangle the quirk of my existence."

Not agreed, adding that it would be potentially efficacious to further pursue "Designation: Victor Heisengard," explaining that "Designation: Heisengard contained potential useful data on City-System structure and processing." He would not explain why. He did not tell them that the man was connected to the MCG and the experiments that had created Not. He did not explain the kinship he felt with Designation: Heisengard and the echoes of his own subjugation that he found in the man. He did not explain his desire, almost above any other action, to exact revenge on Designation: Heisengard in whatever way he could effectuate it. These things he managed to hide within himself, even in the intimacy of Felix's mind.

Felix explained that moving around the City posed a physical danger and, as Not knew more than the others, datalogical, as well. So, too, leaving the City would be nearly impossible. Not and Felix agreed that the City appeared to be aware of them. Not told them the City had "spoken" to him but expressed only fear and anger when pressed for details. The alluring green aroma rose up among them again and disappeared as fast, as if to soothe Not's irritation.

Felix felt it was quite possible that Not's foray into the City had provoked a heightened scrutiny and potentially had revealed Felix's position within the physical structure of the City. Both pieces of information spelled doom to all three and meant they needed to act fast.

Felix knew of a man who might have information on leaving the City, and he was a mutual enemy of the City. His name was Michael Chobot. He had helped Felix escape the City's eyes and helped modify his implants; he was of the CitySons who had escaped the system and was an enemy of that same system. There, they decided to start their search, foraging into the City canyon by night.

Part III

THE OPPOSITE

Chapter 22: They Watch

Meanwhile, Victor lay troubled and alone in his foreign-feeling apartment. No matter how long he lay in bed, first willing then meekly waiting for sleep, still it remained out of reach. He could not shake the feeling that he had somehow side-slipped into another reality; the same in all ways but a subtle, horrifying and important one; where his mind did not follow the normal path of thoughts, where ordinary words were horrifying and ordinary thoughts were a confusing mix of unfamiliarity and malice. It was a world where the City and the Subject were aware of him—aware of his thoughts, his feelings, his every dirty bit and piece. He was singled out among thousands, an ant under a magnifying glass. He felt displaced and wanted desperately to hide, to find comfort at home. *In the closet.*

"Shut up!" he yelled into the silent apartment and immediately regretted shattering the delicate peace.

His brain would not slow down. It felt as if someone was trying to run a program in it with a corrupted disk, the drive continually spinning in the same corrupted sector over and over, never finding the right file and never moving on to a new sector, just constantly reporting, *Error, error*. Like the scratch of a record, having ended side B—*scratch, scratch*—no more music, only noise left.

He got out of bed and padded into the cluttered living room, calling up an old movie on the touch wall with a dismissive nod of his head and an idle thought. He was vaguely hopeful that the old story would be a comfort and a distraction from the endless scratch of his corrupted processing systems. It was an old movie, a cartoon—one he had always loved, one he had watched over and over with . . . no one (*scratch, scratch, scratch*). One he liked to watch by himself. It was a version of *Pinocchio*, the wooden marionette who wished to be a real boy.

The movie was soothing to him, drowning out the whirring of the endless non-thoughts in his head with feelings of being a boy, of being loved, of simplicity. He finally found himself nodding off.

"I got no strings to hold me down, to make me fret, or make me frown. I had strings, but now I'm free. There are no strings on me . . .

I've got no strings, so I have fun. I'm not tied up to anyone. They've got strings, but you can see, there are no strings on me."

On the very event horizon of sleep, where even reality seems like a dream, Victor saw a little boy dancing through a sprinkle of water in the summer sun. A great green expanse with exotic, alien plants moved and swayed in time to music that the plants themselves were making. Victor could not see the little boy's face, as the water running over it obscured his eyes and nose, like things unseen in a dream often are, but he felt a great groundswell of longing and love for this lithe child. He could see a toothy smile that triggered the blossoming of a great, familiar joy in his heart, and he did not know why. It occurred to him that this boy must be him when he was young; and this joy, perhaps, the memory of his own childish joy. But as likely as this thought seemed, it did not settle in his mind. Instead, it echoed in what now seemed like a deep, aching hole inside of him.

Then, the sky in his vision darkened, and the ground and plants around turned a rotten brown color, though they did not stop moving. The music continued, becoming garbled.

"*I've grot na strungs zo old may dawn, Ite eyed one up an en unstrung. You av strings, I pull dem some. Watchat, victorere, I come!*"

The boy kept smiling in the midst of his continued frolic, but the water had turned to a muddy spray, shimmering like petroleum. It became horrible that the child was still smiling. Something was wrong with him! The song was wrong. The boy's face, entirely covered in brownish metallic ooze, looked straight at Victor and smiled. From his dripping lips, he exploded, "*Here I come!*"

Victor was expelled from his nightmare, sitting him up in shock from where he had slumped on the living room couch.

Only a dream! This was exactly why he had avoided sleep earlier. Something was wrong with his brain. He got up, sweating and shaky, and stumbled into the kitchen. The time read 1:30 a.m.; the movie long since ended. He groped bleary-eyed in the cold unit for a drink and came out with a bottle of water. In a noisy guzzle, he emptied it and gasped for breath.

Only a dream. Time to act like an adult and get some real sleep. *Go back to your bedroom, Vic.* The endless scratching whir of his empty thoughts had seemed to end. There was that, at least.

As an afterthought, he mentally scrolled through his wetware cache, checking to be certain that there were no recorded alerts from his early escape from shift so many hours back. Thankfully, there were none. The day's reports were still there, but Victor ignored them. The lab had made no alert.

As he was about to close down the ocular feed to his cache, he noticed a general query blinking in the bottom, righthand corner through the line dedicated for the Group. It was tagged "Notsubject." *Odd*, he thought. Usually these things have an initiating marker to tell where they're from. This one did not. The paranoid feeling of being watched flitted through his brain as he contemplated the unmarked query. *How much does* the Group *really monitor? Maybe they are watching me now. Maybe this is a summons to appear before Control and answer a few pointed questions.* It seemed unlikely, but the unlikeliness of paranoid thoughts did nothing to rid them of their power.

He decided to activate the query, almost in desperation, knowing he would never have peace from the fear radiating off this message if he did not at least verify that it was not from Control.

He opened the query to find three simple words:

"COME.FOR.YOU!"

What the hell?

He could not shrug off the dread of the childishly simple message. He could find no identification on either the query notice or within the cryptic message. It could not be Control; they did not prank. And he had no real friends, and even if he did, none of them *could* have sent him a message in this way on the secure channel hardwired into his brain.

He closed the message but could not delete it, mentally fingering the image of the query notification as if toying with a forbidden object, before deciding to take it and hide it for later. Guilt from leaving his shift early and running from the Subject behind the glass, behind the Group, continued to grow in his mind like a flower as he contemplated the almost automatic desire to hold on to this aberrant, child-like terse message.

As he made to turn off the ocular feed again, there was a sudden *beep*, accompanying an insistent flash of light, sounding more like the klaxon of a nuclear sub about to dive to the already frazzled Victor.

Before he could even register that the noise and sight was an incoming call from Control as he had earlier feared, the call was somehow picked up for him without his consent.

"Hey, Vic," said an unfamiliar and horrifyingly chipper male voice on the other end of the line, as if a friend was calling at the end of a long work day to suggest a pint and some burgers. *What about that overbearing boss, right?* But this was Control. This was a man Victor did not know. This was a robotically chipper call at 1:30 a.m. No good news comes unexpected at 1:30 a.m.

"Who is this?"

Vic tried to get the fear to subside in his voice, but it sounded choked, squeaky, as if he was being strangled.

"Oh, sorry, it's Frank from Tech. . . ." *Too soon. They can't know.* "Control has me calling all the technicians to set up clean and prep services for the wetware." *Pause. Pause. What is he waiting for?* "Some of the other technicians have reported receiving odd messages from unknown senders. You haven't had any weird messages, have you, Vic?"

Yes.

"No!" *Too hasty an answer, too forceful. Who is this guy? They're in my head!* "Um, no messages other than your call. I mean, but that wasn't a message, just, you know . . ."

"You sound nervous, Victor. Not sleeping well tonight?"

"No, I was sleeping. I mean, I was up going to the bathroom, but I was sleeping before that."

"Well, can I put you down for an appointment for a full wetware plug and purge next week? Monday?"

"No!" *Too hasty.* "I mean, I already did." Silence on the other end. "And, um . . . I can't. I'm out for the week, for the month, actually. I'm taking leave. Sick mother, you know." *Parents are dead; they know, they know!*

"Oh, all right. Gee, I didn't see any notice of the leave in the general log. I'll just make a note of it here for the file to make sure your shifts are covered and all. Let's see, one month leave, sick child was it? Oh no, that's right, no children." Frank chuckled inappropriately, "Sick parents. Where will you be going, Victor? We don't want to lose track of you, now that we've reached this critical juncture with OE-77. We need all hands on deck! All techs on deck," the man chuckled again.

"Right, my mother. She lives, uh, in the Specials block to the south."

"Oh, great. Thanks, Vic. Good to hear you're not running out of town. That would be a very . . . bad . . . idea."   Silence. No clicking or buzzing. No talking. No chuckle.

Victor's breathing felt much too loud, as if he had his head in a bag.

"You sleep well, Victor." *Click.*

They know, they know. They're in my head!

He laid awake for most of the night, tossing and sweating, shaking with fear and exhaustion. He couldn't really leave the City; he had nowhere to go. Nowhere was safe. *How can I turn off the machinery in my head? I can never go back to work.* He was not a brave man. He had no hidden suitcase with alternate IDs, a stack of unmarked bills, and a pistol. He had never prepared to protect himself. *What from? From the Group? The City Father? You knew this day would come! Spooks and crooks.* Crooked politics, undercurrents of secret motivation, diabolical plans. The turning of huge unseen wheels on which he was attached by a rope around his neck.

I cannot leave. I cannot stay.

It was obvious now that the Group could come and go from his mind as they pleased. *Can they remotely kill me? Would they?*

The last thought he had as he eventually fell asleep was that someone was coming for him.

Who will show up next?

His sleep, when it finally came, was full of nightmarish shadowiness, full of being chased and hunted down like a fugitive, all the while feeling that if he could only find the missing information, he could save himself. He could not find what he needed.

Chapter 23: Memory Dump

Mike Chobot put the word *morbid* in morbidly obese. He was a great mound of a man, wobbly even in the smallest of his movements. He occupied a great chair, a dais, in an underground habitation that he never left. Likely, he *couldn't* leave the hideout—maybe not even the chair—since he was unable to function without the intervention of the machines by which he was sustained, on which he had become dependent, and through which he was irrevocably connected to the City.

Mike literally fed off the City. Through the same cluster of tubes from which he siphoned data from the City-System, he siphoned nutrition, scraps spilled from the tables of the CitySons on high. If the City-System was a digestive tract, then Mike was a subtle bowel parasite hidden at its anus, living off the waste. And frankly, he smelled like a bowel parasite, constantly expelling wet, gaseous bursts from both ends: his flabby ass and his toothless mouth.

Felix always thought it ironic that Mike could remain so fat when all his calories were rationed through a tube. It stood to reason that beggars could not be choosers; whatever was not eaten at the top, some of it trickled down to the bottom into Mike.

But Mike was fat with information too. If there was knowledge to be had, Mike would have it. Shit may literally flow downhill—and Mike collected his share of it from the top to the bottom—but he was skilled in differentiating the shit from the Shinola. Thus, his cesspool was priceless.

Not and Hatta lurked just out of perception at the edges of Felix's consciousness as they crept across the nighttime City.

In Felix's head, the Knight stewed. Not felt his darkness and keenly felt the desire to rectify it. He moved to the Knight and pulled him from his inward focus.

"Designation: Hatta; Query status: malfunction?"

"I am not malfunctioning. I am malcontent."

"Query: define malcontent."

"I am not at peace."

"Query: define peace."

"Dammit, man! Leave me be!"

"Negative. Designation: Hatta status function affects Designation: Not status function."

The Knight sighed, resigned to Not's questioning.

"Fine," he said. "But you speak like a misbegotten golem. Designation, designation, designation."

Not said nothing, extending his awareness into the Knight's arcana, then beyond into Felix's language centers. While the two entities "spoke" what amounted to different languages in the shared mental space of Felix's pre- and subconscious, they understood more than they could describe in words. Slowly, without realizing, Not borrowed from both Felix and Hatta's understanding and used their language.

The Knight settled, "Now, what . . . query do you have for me?"

"What is your . . . status?" Not asked, tentatively.

The Knight reflected. "I am not . . . I, I don't know. I am unsure."

"Query: is your function undefined?"

"Indeed. Yes, that might fit. I do not know *what* I am, *why* I am, or what I am to do about it."

"Designation . . . I, Notsubject, am undefined. I/you/we am/are parallel. Conclusion query: what am I?"

"Yes. Perhaps we are in the same boat. But you are human, Not. You are like Felix in this."

"False. Felix equals human, human inclusive of body and mind. I include mind and not body. Therefore, status query: is mind with not body equal to or not equal to human?"

"I think I see what you mean," said the Knight, "you are right. Felix is a mind and a body, and you are merely a mind. I do not even have a mind that I know of. Someone made me with, apparently, some alchemical craft for inclusion in a vast number counting machine. I am a group of numbers among other numbers, countless other numbers apparently. A wisp of smoke in a fire, a tear in a river, a tiny cog in a universal machine."

Here, the Knight began to weep. Not watched as the Knight's essence dipped into a deep well of potential energy within him, using the concepts like "cog" and "number" as containers for this dormant energy. Portions of this pool of potentials were drawn up to the Knight's surface, where they poured off of his visage as a cascade of kinetic energy, dissolving the concepts of "cog" and "number" that had temporarily contained them. Not was bathed in the potentials emanating from the Knight. They played like short experiences of the Knight's life, full of desire like rising potential, and loss, like the depletion of kinetics. To Not, these states of energy were distinguishable as desirable (rising potential) and to be avoided (the depletion of kinetics). It fascinated him that the Knight's process of dredging up these desired potentials included the exhaustion of their kinetic energy; that in seeking the one state of energy (potential), the other (kinetic) was made manifest as well. Not could perceive that this process left the Knight feeling emptied of potential and void of purpose. Not could perceive that this energy paralleled what Felix labeled as "unhappiness" or "depression" or "tiredness," concepts that the Knight maligned.

But Not could also perceive that which the Knight could not: that this fluctuation of potential and kinetic energy, of desired and avoided states—where both kinetics and potentials were inextricably intertwined and active—was itself a wellspring of potential and kinetic energy that manifest itself in almost endless iterations. Within Felix's mind, only two concepts seemed to parallel what Not saw: "life" and "love." Not reached out to the Knight's weeping essence to reorient him to what he couldn't see.

"Statement," he said, to get the Knight's attention, "if you are equal to cog or number, then you are defined by a fixed purpose; and further statement, if you also equal status malcontent, as you have so designated—and parallel statement, if fixed purpose equals status rest and is unchanging by definition—query: does status malcontent fit within the parameters of your fixed purpose? Response: negative. Conclusion one: your status is not equal to fixed purpose. Conclusion two: your status is equal to a number of probabilistic being states, greater than cog or number or other fixed purpose. Conclusion three: you are infinite possibility."

Not continued, "Example set: If Pinocchio equals puppet, with status "fixed purpose" defined by strings; further, if status, fixed purpose, is not inclusive of status malcontent; conclusion: status malcontent is not equivalent to/included in cog/number/strings/fixed purpose. Further conclusion, either Pinocchio does not equal puppet, or Pinocchio's purpose does not equal control by strings. Parallel further conclusion, Knight at status malcontent does not equal cog/number/fixed purpose, thus suggesting unfixed probability; final conclusion, you are not exclusive of humanness. Predictive algorithm: you are human."

There was a long pause, pregnant with potential energy. With awe, the Knight spoke. "I do not know if you are human, my friend. But you are no slave. You are alive and self-driven, as I now see that I, too, must be. I may not be human either, and yet, even Felix does not know what it is to be human. Malcontentment may be the badge of my reality. And that realization leaves me less malcontent yet no less real. For that, I thank you. I am in your debt."

Felix arrived at Mike's refuge. The two in his head had agreed that he would need to be the point person for this interaction. Truly, Not and Hatta had no choice. They did not know what they were doing and they were reliant on Felix for survival.

Mike was an old contact of Felix's, and though they were not friends in any stretch of the meaning of the term, neither were they enemies. Felix and Mike shared a mistrust (if not outright hatred) of the City, the City-Sons, and the entire City-System, though they both made their home within and extracted succor from its leavings. Likewise, they shared a mutual understanding of the necessity of anonymity. Likely (though Felix really didn't know) "Mike" was a false name. Felix was known to Mike as Jesus Garcia, as he was known by the rest of the City.

Much like Felix's own security system and living placement (i.e. underground), Mike's lair was well hidden and well protected.

As the concrete slab receded into the canyon floor with Felix on it, he was sprayed with a chemical mist from nozzles on the sides of the shaft. This was followed by a blinding bank of ultraviolet and visible lights, baking the mist into his skin. The hum of electricity and machinery grew louder as the slab continued to descend into the concrete earth. A concrete slab snapped into place over Felix's head, covering the shaft into which he was slowly dropping. It ended in a dark hallway, lit with a single recessed light, spotlighting him as he stepped from the pad.

Felix waited. He knew that machines of various sizes and descriptions were hidden in the walls, floor, and ceiling, further scanning his body and head for transmission devices, data mines, data sinks, broadcast repeaters, simple electromagnetic pulse emitters, and any number of other troublesome devices, both those carried on the body and those implanted in it.

Mike's defensive system easily revealed Felix's wet and stemware systems. The stemware portion was not turned on but would have been rendered ineffective by Mike's suppression tech if Felix had turned it on and tried to broadcast from the underground hideout. This, Felix knew and expected.

The revelation that the scan data showed physical anomalies in Felix's neural biology, and corrupted sectors in his implanted wetware, he did not expect.

A hidden speaker crackled to life from the ceiling above Felix.

"I'm not sure whether to kick you out, send you packing with an RF tag to alert the City, or sedate you and cut your head open to poke around. What have you got hidden up there in your head, Garcia?"

Mike's tone had the sound of forced laziness, with an undertone of terror. Felix's heart picked up its rhythm. He imagined Mike's fat finger pointing at his head, a stiff smile pasted to his jowls, his other hand straining at the arm of the chair where he was lodged, tightening its grip. Somewhere in Mike's brain, a red flag was apparently being raised.

In Felix's own head, a forest of red flags was raised, all held by the Knight. His intentions tensed in Felix's head, responding to the sound of Mike's rising nerves. Felix pushed back at the Knight's rising readiness, willing him to stand down.

"But why would you do either?" asked Felix out loud, playing dumb. He forced a little laughter into his voice as if to say, *Come on, Mike, you know me.* He hoped it sounded less strained than Mike did.

"Well, you've either got some machine in there that I've never seen," Mike said, "and I *should* see it, just so I know what it is, or you've got a ride-along threatening sabotage. Frankly, either way, I'm inclined to put you under, crack you open, and take it out."

Felix stood still, aware of the machinery in his head and aware of the two personalities trying to hide at the periphery of his consciousness. He wondered exactly what Mike could see. He almost felt the photonic bombardment rushing over him from Mike's machinery, disturbing his atoms, jostling the cyborganics in his head, reporting back what they found. But what would they find? Obviously, something unusual, in Mike's opinion. But something dangerous? Felix wasn't so sure.

In his head, Felix could feel Not's intentions beginning to change as well. Not was responding to the kinetic and datalogical barrage of Felix's head with irritation, like he was being raked over by a not-too-careful child petting a small animal. To Not, the portion of Felix's brain that he occupied felt as if it bristled at the intrusion. For a breath of a minute, Felix could feel through Not that he could likely "reach" into this stream of potentials, kinetics, and data bombarding his head and interact. Felix could feel Not waiting, nonetheless trusting Felix for the moment, watching and soaking up the experience, tensing all of his potentials to spring them.

"Mike, we've known each other for a long time," Felix said, cautioning with his voice, speaking slowly, and letting all his pretense slip away. "You know I wouldn't abide a ride-along."

Mike said nothing, growing the tension.

"For God's sake, you helped me design my own defensive systems!" There was now panic in Felix's voice. "I have my own reasons to keep the inside of my head free from the City!"

Mike remained silent. Felix imagined him glancing from one screen to another, reviewing the scans data with rising worry.

"*Query,*" asked Not in Felix's head, "*continue hold status inert?*" The rigid concision of Not's question rose from the edges of Felix's conscious mind, pulling him from the outward moment inward and pestering him for a response.

It took Felix a minute to realize what Not was asking. He responded internally, *Stay out of perception. There's no reason to confuse the situation, and I don't think he'd trust what he sees if you reveal yourself—either of you.*

The Knight's impatient formality rose to Felix's consciousness, akin to yelling; the forcefulness caused Felix to wince.

I refuse to grovel behind this façade! This knave appears to be calling us out! I'll grab him by the throat!

For a moment, Felix's eyes became completely white. His eyesight retreated. With some effort, he re-exerted control and thought his most forceful instruction to the impatient personalities within.

This will not work if you two cannot give me your true trust! You do not know the world like I do! You do not know this man; he could destroy us with the push of a button! And, he is necessary, and we need him on our side!

The responses came with the muddy agreeableness of a sulk.

Holding . . . provisionally and *Begrudgingly, I will continue to abide by your terms, sir.*

The exchange between the three personalities in Felix's head had taken no more than the merest split of a second in real time, but as even very short moments in the real world can do, this one stretched awkwardly long.

"What the fuck is happening in your head?" shouted Mike, the recessed speakers in the ceiling distorting with its loudness. "Looks like a light show in there!"

Felix stood rigidly, moving only his eyes.

"Mike," he said slowly, raising his hands involuntarily in a sign of supplication, "I can explain." Nothing. "Mike, you know me!"

"I thought I knew you."

"Mike . . ."

In a voice quiet with restrained fear, Mike said, "The only reason I have not locked down your wetware and dropped you where you stand is that you and I have a long history of trust and mutual aid. Right now, I don't know what the hell I am seeing, but I don't like it. Unless you tell me what's going on right now, I will short your implants, knock you unconscious, and throw you to the City. Lord knows what they will do to you."

Still, another pause. Both men waited. Felix felt a boil of personalities at war within him, straining to emerge.

To Felix's right, the wall slid open, revealing the almost impossible thickness of the door and framing the rotund figure of Mike Chobot, the obese cyborg, plopped in his chair like an enormous dollop of sour cream.

Felix stepped into the room with caution. Mike was sweating freely, harshly. His hands were red, knuckles white, gripping his chair. They had begun to shake.

Immediately, bursting up from below Felix's conscious mind, before anything else could happen, came the personality of Not.

"Designation: Mike, threat status: imminent!" he said in Felix's head and through Felix's mouth. "Releasing hold!"

With this declaration, Not immediately and forcibly wrested all control from Felix and pushed both he and the Knight to the back of the mind.

Felix managed a strangled "No" out loud as he was shoved to the back of his own consciousness, his access to the outside world snuffed out completely. He found himself, again, pressed to the gray-pink world of his own mind.

The eyes of Felix's body became clear like glass orbs as Not took control and compelled Felix's body toward Mike.

Mike's eyes widened as Felix's body lurched toward him quick as thinking. Mike depressed a button on the arm of his chair, initiating a defensive program just as Felix's body slammed into his chair and gripped the arm with a clawed hand rigid as iron.

Felix's wetware received a surge of voltage and a blizzard of corrupted data. It immediately began to overheat, its functioning grinding to a near-halt. Not could feel a wrenching sensation through the Knight and Felix, like a metal bar jammed into the clockworks of a machine.

He shed the sense-information as useless and, in a split moment, bolstered the struggling wetware and phased Felix's hand partially into Mike's chair. A part of his will dipped into the electronics in the chair, pausing their function. The air around the front of Felix's face, emanating from the now completely clear eyes, began to distort; waves of light bent and refracted from their gaze as Not's sight interacted with the very atoms.

The protective protocols initiated by Mike were arrested. The grinding sensation in Felix's head ceased. Not removed the hand from the arm of the chair and positioned Felix's body simply, arms at its side, head straight ahead. The eyes, he turned on Mike, tilting the head slightly to the side.

"Query: what are your intentions?" he asked through Felix's mouth. "Confirm status: threat or asset? You have twenty counts to respond."

Mike sat gaping, unable to move. Not extended his awareness and read the frightened man's mind.

A devious simulacrum, he heard Mike think frantically, *come to rat me out for the City. That thing just melted its hand into my chair and took control! It didn't even react to the restraining measures. I can see clear to the back of its eye sockets!*

Not pushed his perceptions even further in, through Designation: Mike's processing center, into the meaty head, and through the fleshy bulk of the torso. Designation: Mike was a confusion of mechanical, cyborganic equipment but truly a beautiful incorporation of each system, heightening his perceptions and the control of his surroundings. Not had perceived the secret to Mike's system the second he had interacted with the arm of the chair. Mike and his enclave were all one cohesive unit. He and his machines were each parts of a more complete system of information and defense, which encompassed both meat and machine. Not had been able to supersede Mike's role in the chain of command (and thus, reverse the defensive protocols) by inserting his own interactive essence further up the chain of command. Furthermore, from this vantage point, he had been able to perceive the entirety of the collage-like machinery in real time.

Not could also see how the City was feeding Designation: Mike. A constant flow of data and nutriment seeped into various interactive ports throughout his brain and body. Cyborganic wetware (of the type implanted in Felix's head) populated various points within Mike's brain and along his nervous system. In this way, his body and brain could "dance" within the workings of the overall cyborganic and mechanical system within the burrow. Some of his systems worked independently of his intention, sorting and parsing data; some waited as potentials for instructions from Designation: Mike at the center.

Likewise, mechanorganic implants within Designation: Mike allowed him to live on a modified intake of nutrients from the City waste and expel the same in gaseous and aerosolized packets from the orifices at both ends of his body. Pumps filtered his blood, drew air into his body, and moved everything along at a regular clip.

Further inward still, Not began to perceive the interactions within the biological and cyborganic processing core in Designation: Mike's head. He perceived disbelief within Designation: Mike's mind as a sort of internal friction of impulses. More subtly still but growing in amplitude, there was the bloom of fascination mixed with fear, which to Not, appeared as a waxing defensive status together with a growing openness—as if a query answer was increasingly "affirmative" for every query iteration.

Mike's voice squeezed through his jelly lips, "Wha . . . what . . . who, I . . . I . . . what have you done?"

"Reiterate: confirm status threat or asset," Not repeated.

Let us in, you overbearing charlatan!

The Knight had found his way back to the edge of the overall consciousness of Felix's brain. Felix followed him through and appealed to Not.

Not, you've made your point. Let me back up, so I can talk to him. He does not understand you.

In Felix's head, Not thought to Felix, *Designation: Mike, status threat: abated. Designation: Mike, global status: information incomplete; information processing incomplete. Designation: Mike, global status: confused. Designation: Mike, global status: fear.*

Query: Designation: Mike, status elucidation: asset or threat? Query: action?

Let. Me. Back. Up. Not! I'll talk to him. He is an asset we cannot lose! Felix leaned into his willful expression, hoping to forestall Not before he took some irrevocable action that could not be undone.

Affirmative, agreed Not.

Not withdrew his willful presence in the brain, and Felix moved forward, beginning to see out of his own eyes again. The Knight was quicker and jumped to the fore of the brain ahead of him, ceasing the moment of transition from Not to Felix and wresting control from Felix yet again.

Felix's body went from the robotic attentiveness and the inaction of Not's information orientation to the defensive crouch of the Knight, a being of pure action. With a yell, the Knight launched the body straight at Mike's chair again.

"Have at you, fiend!" he roared, slamming Felix's body into the chair and dragging Mike out and onto the grimy floor. Mike's tubes and wires remained connected to both his body and the chair somehow, but they pulled on his flab violently, and he appeared to be unable to speak, though his face contorted in fear and pain.

Hatta, no!

Designation: Hatta, status: internal threat! Terminate action immediately; corruption of advantage Designation: Mike imminent.

Suddenly, Felix was again looking out of his own eyes. His body was throbbing from where his extremities had slammed into Mike's chair. His temples throbbed in time with his elevated heart rate, the pain centered within and just behind his eyeballs. He perceived the internal struggle of Not pulling Hatta's personality back to the edges of the conscious mind. Hatta did not go willingly, and his anger clawed at the inside of Felix's head, but Not had the greater force of personality.

Felix squeezed his eyes shut, adding his own personality and intention to the force of pushing Hatta back down. The pain faded. He opened his eyes slowly and found himself leaning over Mike, his hands pressed into the soft flesh of Mike's metal studded chest. Mike had become a veritable puddle on the floor. His eyes dribbled, and his pendulous lips quivered, leaking drool.

Felix stood up, pushing against Mike in the process, and deliberately blinked his eyes once. His eyes cycled from clear to solid white to their normal brown.

His posture relaxed and readjusted, settling into a familiar stance. What had been a scowl, softened as he turned his face to Mike.

"Mike, I'm so sorry. I didn't . . . I mean, I . . . let me help you back up?"

Mike retreated (to the extent he could), shaking his jowls with a comical flapping sound and effecting a look of renewed terror.

Felix sighed. "If I get you back into the chair, will you promise not to try to initiate any more defensive programs?"

Mike was weeping now, blubbering into his great ham hands. He let out a great belch and yammered something about defenses. Felix did not wait for a promise from Mike before he reached down and yanked on his arms to help him up. There was no way he could have pulled the enormous bulk into the chair. Mike's sobs faded to sniffs, his respiration systems still drawing in extra air. He managed to regain some control of himself and gestured for Felix to take his hands off.

"Let me take a moment. I can up myself," Mike croaked. Felix doubted it.

Mike leaned onto one hand slightly and with the other hand made a sort of twiddling motion with his thumb and index finger. The great chair behind him groaned and lowered itself down toward the floor, positioning itself behind him. Some combination of mechanical aids inside and outside of Mike's body raised his weight up on wobbling legs and back into the chair. He was now extra pale and sweatier than usual, as much from his confusion and fear as from his fall and the work of getting reseated.

"What the hell is going on?" Mike asked after he'd settled into his chair. He spoke in the quiet voice of a child in awe.

"I'm not sure how to explain it . . ." Felix began. "But I'll tell you everything I know. You just need to promise you won't initiate any more defensive systems. I think we'd both regret it."

Mike nodded; this was understood.

"First of all," began Felix anew, "an offer in exchange for your attempt at trust. My real name is not Jesus Garcia."

Mike acknowledged the offer but shrugged slightly. He already knew Jesus Garcia was not Felix's real name.

Felix continued, "My name is Felix. I have no last name."

Mike took a moment to search "Felix" among the City scraps in his data pool. The name appeared only once, without a last name, truly singular in a short video clip with the label "unresolved child." It was a short video clip of a young boy of about twelve years of age in ragged clothing, alone in the City canyon. Above his head, in digital lettering, was the designation "Felix." It showed him running a few steps away then ducking quickly down a side channel of the canyon, disappearing for a second around the corner, reappearing closer now as the camera caught up. The wayward boy was being followed, likely by a CPS drone recording the child from behind. Then the image dipped and wobbled as if the drone's flight had been disrupted, and the feed went black and the clip ended. No other mention, in any other bit or byte or qubit of information in all of Mike's collection contained the name "Felix."

"Who are you?" he asked Felix in awe. "I mean, I knew you weren't really 'Jesus Garcia'; everyone uses pseudonyms. My name isn't "Mike Chobot," either, but, but, you . . . I just . . . what the hell did you do? Who . . .?"

"I need you to rescan my head," Felix said, "but this time, show me the results. Then, I'll explain."

"You won't attack me again?" Mike asked.

Felix shook his head slowly, thinking how easily he had lost control before and saying *No, we will not!* in his mind.

Satisfied, and believing he'd get no better assurance, Mike waived a hand with his fingers in a complicated formation. The scanning machines hummed to life. Felix felt the Knight heave at the restraints placed on him by Not. Not remained silent, letting the scan wash over him, this time without the resistance.

"I'll project the data in real time," Mike said, "here." He indicated the center of the room, where a three-dimensional, colored image of Felix's brain hovered, filling the entire space.

"Here is the wetware implant I helped you initially install," Mike said, indicating a section toward the top covering both lobes of Felix's brain. "I see you have modified it some and added a few tweaks."

Felix nodded.

"But that's not what concerns me," Mike continued. "First, let me show you a rendering of the data interface between your wetware implant and the remainder of your brain."

The hologram in the middle of the room rotated and enlarged the border between the implanted cyborganics and Felix's brain. Fingers of some off-colored substance extended from the cyborganics into various points in Felix's brain, like the wetware was leaking.

Mike continued, "It looks like . . . like . . . I don't know. Remember learning about chemical batteries? Little cylinders containing chemical reactions, a few volts for a few days?"

Felix remembered. He nodded slowly.

"I have information that these chemical batteries used to leak, the reactive chemicals would ooze out, interacting with chemicals in the air and turning into a crusty, acidic discharge, depriving the chemical reaction first of its potency, then of its effectiveness.

"This oozy-looking stuff in your head is clearly leaking from your implant into your brain. And it looks like it's interacting with something in your brain, some sort of reaction with the biological part. My first thought was that this was brain damage, corrosion, or rejection caused by the modifications you made to the implants; I remember early implants were causing a lot of trouble like this."

The 3D image rotated slowly. Felix could see the growths noted by Mike. Colors blossomed and retreated, growing, shrinking, moving, and phosphorescing across both the mechanical and biological portions of his brain. Felix marveled at the real-time changes he witnessed as they were affected by thoughts and sensations in his own head. The bleeding or spillage at the edges of the mechanical implants did not look like damage to him, but like fingers, growing and cradling both lobes.

Mike continued, catching the same thought that Felix considered.

"But your head doesn't show any other damage, and frankly, the interaction between your brain and the leaking ooze looks like it's creating growth. Felix, it's not killing the cells; it's catalyzing new organic growth! And that's just around the implant!"

Here, the image moved closer, opening the image of a deeper portion of the brain. Indeed, to Felix, the flashing colors and glowing sections looked like a light show, dancing—sometimes in unison, sometimes mirrored across lobes—and exhibiting a uniqueness that Felix could feel as he watched it move and change in real time.

Mike continued, "There are countless other sections that just don't look normal. I mean, the structures are here, but the patterns of activity keep fluctuating, faster than normal and in three discrete patterns. Look there, quick! You can see the normal chemical and hormonal fluctuations as you talk or look or think, whatever, but there are deeper fluctuations happening in real time that don't seem related!"

The undulating, pulsating 3D brain rating in front of Felix confirmed what he already knew: the Knight and Not were somehow growing within the meat of his brain, into his very being.

"Mike, you may not believe this, but . . . "

Felix gave Mike all the information he had, filling Mike into all his experiences from the past few days and asking many of his own questions (and when they had calmed down, the questions he perceived from Not and Hatta). Wherever he could, Felix pointed out the anomalies within the rendering of his brain.

Mike calmed down considerably, showing greater fortitude than Felix had given him credit for. He was most interested in what he could piece together of Not's story, though Not was uninterested in recounting his story to Mike. Felix assumed that Mike's fascination with Not was chiefly in their apparent shared interconnectedness with cyborganic networks. Though Not would not give more detail to Mike, he acknowledged that he had come from a place of complete reliance on a network for his existence. Neither Felix nor Not revealed to Mike that Not had been born by the Group's network; it would have troubled Mike further, to say the least.

Hatta asked few questions, answered even fewer. Felix perceived him return to a state of sulking in the background, radiating a kind of childish despair. Felix recalled his earlier conversation with him, when they had first met "face-to-face" in Felix's safe room: *You are a false construct, made semi-permanent by complex machinery that projects images and thoughts into people's heads.* The Knight's dismissal of this concept, his utter disbelief, had bordered on willful denial. Felix suspected that the Knight's computer-programmed nature had been undeniable to him, in the sense that he literally could not deny it. It was impossible for the true information, once meshed perfectly with his rigid programming, to be removed from the very makeup of the program. And yet . . .

The Knight seemed to strain at the boundaries of his code, stretching boundaries within Felix's brain. Removed from the context of his programmed world, no longer an avatar in a make-believe universe with manufactured needs and wants and quests, he emanated a desire to know why.

His desire to know what and who he was was growing larger in Felix's brain, larger than the very programming that had originally made him what he was. And thus, even as he slunk through the veritable dark of the semiconscious parts of Felix's mind, damning his own existence and railing against his unknown Gods, he was manifest.

Eventually, Felix explained to Mike that he and his copersonalities had decided they must leave the City. Mike agreed that there was no way for them to remain in the City and out of its clutches.

"Leaving the City is a problem of giant magnitude," Mike explained, "and the solution is, quite simply, treacherous; likely to either put you squarely in the hands of the City or physically damage you beyond your tolerance."

To leave the City, Felix would have to find the right wastewater sluice and follow the concrete walkway to its termination without being detected. He'd then need to jump into the deluge of wastewater rushing under the City wall and out of the City. Finding the sluice was nearly impossible, short of trial and error, unless they had some way to access the Group's records. Within the records could be information leading to the location of the few sluices of the thousands in the City that could theoretically deposit Felix safely outside the City walls. "Safely" that is, in that it did not ensure his death. Without the vital information, Felix would be left to gamble his life and the lives of his copersonalities by jumping into a random canal, reliant on luck alone. Mike did not have access to this type of information in the City scraps off of which he fed, and Felix was not a believer in luck, his name notwithstanding.

Surviving the plunge and remaining undetected in the tender moments after deposition into the poisoned lake, mucking through the wastewater and out into the hostile jungle of Green, safety was not truly part of the plan. Just hope. Just faith.

Not shared that he had touched some vast intelligence when he was caught within the City system, and that it was most obviously malevolent. Felix echoed the concern, noting that every time they went outside, the City was more likely to find them.

Not shared the name and location of Designation: Heisengard, whom he had told them of before. He noted that this man worked in a lab under the direction of the MCG and that *Designation: Heisengard might hold knowledge of City-Structure and of the sluices.* He did not tell them he would go to the man and end him, finish what he had started when he first confronted him in the land behind the glass.

Not said, *Through Designation: Heisengard, access to the City-Structure, sluice structure, to the waste-lakes. Through Designation: Heisengard, we leave the City intact.*

They agreed this would be the plan.

Before they left Mike, Hatta forcibly spoke: "Tron, or his yoozer, holds information on the nature of the anomalies in Nighreal. I must go to him. He holds promise of information for our present circumstances and my own lack of clarity. To him, we must first go, or I will not cooperate with our escape."

"It is nothing for me to comb through the City's data trash for this Tron's user. Just a second," Mike said.

Felix watched as Mike's face went slack and his eyes rolled into his head. He twitched rhythmically, like he was bodily thumbing through a book. Just as quickly, he was back.

"His name is Brian Enough. He's a low-level City programmer who has never advanced beyond his elevation, but it seems he's shown some genius in his craft. Better yet, I know the man. I had occasion to trade a piece of software, which I had . . . ahem, borrowed from the City."

Mike held out a hand and Felix stepped forward, used to the gesture. Mike rested his hand on Felix's temple and transferred a file to him with information on the man and a location.

"I cannot seem to find this Heisengard that you noted. This worries me. Be warned. Something about this is more wrong than it already feels." Mike paused painfully long. In his mind, Felix heard the faint grumble of an impatient Knight and a rising assurance from Not that he knew where to find *the Heisengard.*

With a grunt, Mike withdrew a small object from some nook or fold on his immense being and beckoned Felix to him again. He held it out as Felix approached. It was a small, plastic object, weighty with technology. Felix crooked an eyebrow in question.

"It's a high-frequency sonic pulse emitter," Mike said. "The tentacles in the canal can't stand it."

Felix nodded his thanks and turned to go. Behind him, with uncharacteristic heaviness in his voice, Mike said, "Watch your back, OK? Your backs? Watch all the backs? I don't know, dammit. Just be careful."

They left the way they came, with a hasty thanks and no backward glance.

Chapter 24: The Postman Always Rings Twice

The light of morning did nothing to dispel the unease lingering in Victor as he woke to another day full of uncertain malice. His breakfast was tasteless, yet flavored by dreadful possibility. The City, its father, Darfore, a bland-faced hitman—he knew not what—was coming for him with violence, torture, and a question mark-shaped horror. And he had no plan, nor the ability or knowledge to make one in response.

Still flashing in his periphery, the anonymous, child-like threat (COME. FOR. YOU.) came back to his awareness.

But who? What?

There was a knock at the front door.

He jumped from his chair, knocking the bowl of food on the kitchen floor. Pressing himself against the wall, he stepped into the mess from the bowl and slid onto his butt, back still tight to the wall. He covered his mouth with a sweating hand, and his eyes stretched wide, tearing at the corners.

"Victor? You there? Let me in, please. There's been an accident at the lab. Are you OK?"

No, no, no, no, no, no, no, no, no, no, no, no, no, no, no!

He almost yelled, *"I'm not here!"* in his irrational fear.

"Victor, I hear you in there. It's John, from Doctor Patience's office. Scheduled your plug and purge, remember? I'm here for the routine."

"I don't know any John," Victor shouted, his naked fear not hidden.

"Sure you do, buddy. I'm worried about you."

A metallic click sounded, the mechanics in the door twitching. Then, be it desperation or courage, it amounted to the same: Victor grabbed a heavy, metal canister from the counter behind him, pushed himself up, and walked briskly to the door, the canister hidden behind his back.

He reached the door and pulled it open quickly, impulsively. The man outside was surprised. He stood up quickly, thrusting his own hand into his pocket, the metallic flash of a tool or weapon abruptly hidden.

The two men locked eyes, both momentarily wide. Victor could see that fear was in this man's eyes too, and in that moment, he knew death had come for him. He confronted it truly for the first time. This man had come to kill him, and Victor would not let him.

"Come in," he said through gritted teeth, his smile stretching painfully, never reaching his eyes.

The man held Victor's gaze for a moment, tensely searching with unpleasant purpose, before turning his back on Victor to pick up a canvas bag sitting on the floor behind him. Victor did not think but leaned in and swung the canister at the back of the man's head as hard as he could. It connected with a wet crunch, and the man fell like a sack of meat. Victor dropped the canister, grabbed the man by the armpits and dragged him inside the apartment. He stepped over the prone man, grabbed the heavy canvas bag, and brought it into the room with its owner. He closed the door, leaving the canister in the hallway without thinking. In the apartment, he set every lock, and ran to a low seat on the other side of the room.

He sat and drew his legs up, pulling his feet off the floor. The wounded (*dead?*) man, was bleeding onto his carpet.

Victor could not see whether the man breathing, and he wasn't moving. His head was leaking watery blood into the carpet, his hair folded into a large wet crack in the bone. Victor wasn't sure whether it scared him more to think the man dead or alive. He felt the dirtiness, the intimacy, of the killing and, for the moment, the shame and confusion, the racing heart and emergent chemicals flooding his system, outshouted his fear.

He dared not touch the man, but eventually got up the courage to tiptoe across the room and grab the canvas bag. He kept his eyes on the body, not daring to blink.

He wrenched open the bag and dug through it. It was full of weapons— *He was here to kill me!*—but they were weapons designed to subdue, hurt, and alter, not kill; though they were indeed heavy enough to do the job Victor had done with the canister.

He pushed the bag off his lap with disgust and pulled his knees to his chest again, pressing his eyes closed. Here was a problem with a very specific timeline: a dead body would rot, and the man it had been would likely be expected to report in somewhere. *Will he be missed? Was he followed? Who will come next?*

The man did not appear to have the scarring from wetware implants, but Victor had not taken a very careful look when he smashed the back of his head in.

Then again, maybe they don't want to follow the dirty workers. This made sense to Victor but provided him very little comfort.

He sat, unwilling to leave, unable to think what to do next and full of self-sorrow and self-loathing in equal measure.

-

Chapter 25: Never Enough

At the same time, Victor was murdering his questionable visitor, Felix and his two ride-alongs resurfaced from Mike's lair and snuck through the dusky morning light of the City to find Tron's user, Brian Enough. They did not know that the City had gotten to him already.

Not and Hatta complained when Felix turned on the Locationer. Each said it felt as if they were being vibrated aggressively, but they put up with the necessary discomfort while they were out in the open. As they walked, Not reviewed the information Mike had given them on Brian Enough. Unlike Felix, Brian was an integrated part of the City equation. He was the son of a third son of a CitySon, somewhere down the genetic lines, reaching back to earlier City days. He did not hold any official office, but wrote code for the sale of cyberspace for virtual reality advertising. He, otherwise kept to himself, either plugged into the games through his avatar, Tron, or working. He had a few friends who were either fellow games users or make-believe games characters. He was party to no overtly anti-City activities, and kept a certain distance from those who did—with one exception. Mike knew of Brian because Brian had helped funnel information to him in the past. He had surreptitiously aided the flow of information to Mike in return for extra computational space. He never told Mike why. He told no one. And Mike knew two things: 1. Brian believed that the truly elevated in the City did not know of his malfeasance; and 2. the City did know, likely waiting for the right time to collect its debts from Brian.

Mike warned Felix that the City was likely waiting still.

Brian occupied a small apartment on the twentieth floor of an innocuous City Center building, not far from where Mike's lair was submerged. The building, in a wall of buildings, was marked simply by the sign of the Gate, in towering white, painted or burned into the concrete. It was therefore an official City building, housing employees of the system. The only entrances to the building were on the tenth floor and higher.

Looking up at the building, Felix was struck by the very real problem of his lack of elevation in the canyon, both literally and in terms of his lack of official access to upper levels.

Gaining the tenth floor within the semi-public City employee building proved almost to be the undoing of the whole quest. From street level, Felix had no way to inconspicuously get up into the building to meet with Tron's user.

The most commonly used access to the tenth floor was via maglev transport, the public buses that traveled exclusively on that level. But traveling up to the tenth floor to get to the magnetic transports was not easy. Few places in the City included a hidden entrance at canyon level; Felix knew of only two: the Body building was one and the Games arena was the other. *Jesus Garcia* had access to the elevator in the Games arena building. It was a practice Felix usually avoided because it put his false identity at risk. But then again, he wouldn't need the identity once he left the City.

One more trick up his virtual sleeve, then. Jesus Garcia could take the fall for Felix as Felix left the City. Give the City an answer to the leftover data from all of Felix's questionable activities. Jesus Garcia, the sub-ten maintenance man with a penchant for the Games. His traceable use of the elevator in the Games arena would no doubt lead the City on, connect the dots from false red flag to false red flag so they would not point to Felix. Jesus Garcia could be sacrificed for Felix once and for all. And he'd give them access to the tenth floors one more time. The City would be no wiser until Felix had already escaped its concrete grip.

Thus, Felix and his personalities walked to the Games arena, and Jesus Garcia triggered the ground level elevator into the building. It was an uneventful trip, in that they were not confronted by the City or any of its tools or representatives and in that they remained alive and free.

They rode the elevator in Felix's body, cloaked in the name Jesus Garcia, to the tenth floor. From there, they continued on the tenth floor back in the direction they had come, travelling now on a Maglev bus above the canyon. There were only a few other passengers on the car they chose, and still, the space smelled of sour, stale sweat. To Felix, there was a thrill and a fear in that smell, to brush so close to the work-a-day masses that he both shunned and envied.

Not hovered behind Felix's consciousness, emanating a still, tense expectation. Only once did he comment on the stink, noting that its constituent parts appeared to be pheromonal and wondering if it provided any attraction to Felix. Felix said *no* too quickly and out loud. A man seated near him stood up—his naked mistrust worn without shame on his face—and moved to a seat far away from where Felix stood. Felix clamped his mouth shut and focused on keeping his thoughts to himself.

Hatta remained virtually silent, sulking.

Very shortly after it had begun, the maglev stopped in front of the mid-level building marked with the Gate.

Felix produced a digital work order (which he had previously mocked up), giving him a reason and permission to take the glass blister the remainder of the way up the canyon side of the building to the twentieth floor and Brian Enough's apartment. The computer beeped, flashed a welcoming green light, and opened the doors to allow them entrance.

The blister stopped at the twentieth floor of the official building, and the doors slid open with a minute hiss. The hall outside Brian Enough's apartment was silent. Felix did not know whether the silence should have made him nervous, but it did, nonetheless.

The door to the apartment was very slightly ajar. This also made him nervous; and it should have.

He pushed into the apartment, realizing that the door was no longer strictly functioning. Inside was destruction and the sloppy staging of a fake accidental death. The body of a man lay face up on a bloodied carpet. It appeared to have plunged though a glass table. It was clear the body had been moved after it had fallen on the glass, for the face was covered with bloodless metal and glass puncture wounds. What looked like fingerprints of bruise spotted the corpse's cheeks. The now sightless eyes were a jellied, weepy mess, spilling over battered cheeks, afloat with shards of glass, clumps of blood, and carpet fibers.

Felix made a hasty scan through the rest of the apartment for computational equipment or information storage, anything left over that might contain at least some information on the anomalies Hatta had encountered. He found none and turned to leave the apartment in haste.

Without asking, Not surfaced and wrested control from Felix. With no hesitation, he plunged Felix's fingers deep into the orbital sockets of the dead man on the floor. They broke through the thin bones at the back of the sockets and into the soft matter of the brain behind.

Felix remained present enough to feel the cold jelly of the eyes and the spongy brain coating his fingers, but he had no control over his hands. Not extended himself through Felix's body, out his arms, and into his fingers, tentatively pouring his perceptions into the brain of Brian Enough, which was still slightly warm.

To Felix, it was immediately like Not left his mind. His brain felt somehow less cluttered, but he had no control over his body. And Hatta, Felix felt, continued to sulk in the far background of Felix's mind. Curious, Felix moved his perception slightly toward the vacancy where Not had occupied control moments before. There, he found a filament, a thread of Not-ness remaining in the space, neither controlling nor ceding control. Felix knew intuitively that he could wrest control over his own while only a sliver of Not remained in the driver's seat. He felt curious. He had never been one to meditate. He had never tried to center himself, be in the moment, or any other shamanistic mental practice. But yet, here he was, centered, internal, grasping no outside stimulus yet completely aware and intentional. He wondered if the thread of Not got snipped, whether he could remain withdrawn from the surface of his own being or whether the absence of Not would create a vacuum that would require another personality to fill it.

He moved his perception away from the thread of Not, back into his personal, mental depths, and sought out Hatta. The White Knight remained in a kernel of Felix's mind among the sub- and unconscious clusters. If Felix had beheld him by sight, he would have seen a man acting like a child: curled into a fetal position, face buried in his arms, radiating an angsty "leave me alone" cloud with undertones of despair and confusion. The brief image of the dead body of Brian Enough, a quick flash of the torn fabric of the Games arena, the anomaly, a sort of vacuum where his understanding of self would perhaps have resided, all hovered around him, mentally "visible" to Felix.

Hatta, thought Felix to the Knight.

Leave me be! Even his tone of thought was whiny. He had clearly given up any sense of his warrior nature.

No longer the champion, thought Felix. But thoughts were as speech in his head, and the Knight knew his thoughts as if they were spoken aloud into his ear.

I am the champion of nothing. I cannot make war for a queen who I cannot find, who isn't real!

Felix did not say or think anything, waiting as Hatta expressed himself with unusual clarity.

I once had reason like the earth beneath my feet, solid, everlasting, heavy with the gravity of need. Now, I have no purpose. I have no earth beneath my feet. I can accomplish nothing.

Then, looking up at Felix, his white eyes full of desperate sorrow, he said, *I cannot even kill myself.*

Hatta held Felix's mental gaze as if challenging him to disagree.

I am no longer my own; even my own agency has been wrested from my soul. I had two reasons to be: one was to seek after my queen, late gone from the woods. That purpose has become like a bitter wine, a joke with no punch-line, a story where all the players enjoy the sport, but only I think it real.

Even suspicious of that reality, I at least still had purpose in seeking the anomaly and gaining answers from Tron's user. The larval queen predicted the quest! It renewed my vigor. But now, he is dead, the head of the Duchess with him, and all answers are lost.

Felix said nothing, though his thoughts clearly conveyed his inability to help the Knight. Hatta's mental head drooped back to his arm, and Felix waited.

Not, still connected by the thread of his being to the mental system at the top of Felix's body, enveloped the quickly disintegrated mind of the late Brian Enough. The inform-energy concerning the anomaly was of the utmost importance.

A wall of horror images reared over him, flashing the impression of strong, anonymous people, grabbing and hurting Brian. The fear that radiated off of these impressions was the only thing still holding the now dead man's mentality in any cohesive form.

With a mental exertion, Not grasped the terrible death washing over the dying brain, followed it back to its roots, and explored the moments before the attack. Associated memories were less strong but remained intact in connection with the extremeness of the horror of the attack and murder. Wonder, fear, memories of being a child, questions of loyalty, the feeling of shame at bodily functions now out of control, pain, pain, pain; these items had to be pushed back from Not as they crowded in, trying to lodge in the failing mentality. They were a sticky blizzard to Not's mind. He batted them aside, peering through the fray. Then there it was! There, a few bare scraps of a thought: a computational cache in his head—get the code (the head) from Hatta, analyze it in private, plug into the games (*maybe one final time*) to turn the information over to Hatta. These thoughts pulsed dimly in the wreckage of Enough's mind. They were only partial thoughts, but gave off the impression of Tron, the Duchess's head, a tear in the fabric of the Games arena, and lines of code. And it was degrading quickly.

Not reached his self toward the dying memory of vital information, cautious not to obliterate it in his haste. His essence circled the information, and just as he was about to collect it into himself, a pulse of high-powered potential energy blinked on nearby in readiness. Not paused and considered the point of energy. It was not a part of Enough's mind. It had been planted among the wreckage, left by the City's thugs upon killing the man. Not recognized the energy and information as a trap. Its very makeup screamed City.

The City knew someone would come!

Quicker than thought, Not snatched up the fragmented memory and allowed his essence to snap back into Felix, where he had anchored the slightest part of himself for the return. In the process, he triggered the City's trap.

The mental or cyborganic part of the City's trap was too slow to catch Not as his essence sprang back into Felix's brain, but the more physical aspects of the trap had been triggered simultaneously.

So forceful was Not's return to Felix's brain that the silent regard shared between Hatta and Felix was shattered, and the two were buffeted by panic, immediacy, and action.

Get out, now!

For the briefest of moments, Felix thought he was being told to exit his own brain, and he braced to fight to stay. Then he realized that Not had relinquished control of the body and his own essence was being forced back into control. The room with the dead man quickly filled his eyes again. The corpse's face was sputtering and splashing out blood and other fluids, apparently melting from the inside out. A noise began to fill his ears, like the screaming of a kettle yet so much more like human anguish, human pain. The corpse was screaming, tearing its own vocal chords to shreds, the body and mind now in thrall to some foreign program controlling the dying cells. But the scream was somehow in Felix's head too. Hatta came forward and demanded release from the *infernal noise*. Not broadcast his understanding, registering the duel nature of the information, that it was a signal to the City as well.

The City is coming. You must get us out, Not thought. *Go to Heisengard!*

With the name Heisengard came a burst of information to Felix: where to go, how to get there, and Heisengard's face.

Felix dashed through the remains of the apartment door and out to the silent hallway.

He couldn't take the blister on the front side of the buildings or the maglev on ten. There had to be some other way to get to the elevator in the Games arena without public transportation. That would be a trap. City-watched, City-owned, City-controlled. He turned to the hallway, which extended away a short distance to a ninety-degree turn toward the back of the building.

Meanwhile, Felix could feel Not and Hatta combing through the incomplete information not had torn from the dead man's mind, but not for information on the anomaly. Their survival came first. There had been some mundane data in Brian Enough's head about moving around the building where he lived. An incomplete segment of a mental image of the layout of the apartment floor and the parallel floors of the building beneath it flashed in Felix's mind.

Maintenance hatch. Two floors down. Through the abandoned stairwell, Not relayed.

Felix ran to the end of the hall and followed it as it turned to the right. Around the corner, he careened, heedless of any obstacle. Before he had a chance to slow his body, he had a split second to see the hallway dead-ending at an ancient door, which was clearly shut and probably barred. He had no choice. He gritted his teeth, dropped his shoulder, and sped the last few steps.

The door was older and frailer than he had thought it would be, and luckily, it was not barred from either side. However, it was still a solid door and Felix, a not-so-solid human. He slammed into it, bursting through and into the dark stairway behind. An explosion of pain and a brisk snap sprung from his shoulder as he stumbled into the stairwell.

No time, no time. Run, run! Down, down!

Down the stairs he went, crashing at the first landing into the wall at the corner, crying out from the pain, and turning left and down again. Worried about the pain and breathing hard, Felix took a slower left at the next corner landing and down one last flight. Here, on this lower floor, the door hung open, not recently broken but forgotten, opening onto a dark and unused floor. No one who should have been had been there anytime recently. Signs of furtive activities tickled at the edge of Felix's senses, but nothing was recent.

Don't stop! Around the next corner, hatch on the left wall. Go in, go down!

A few pained steps later, a dusty portion of the wall to the left showed a panel that could be removed. Felix skidded to a stop. He worked the fingers of his left hand around the edge. His right arm hung limply in burning pain at his side. He pulled. The hatch fell away from the wall with a thud, dust swirling up around Felix. He instinctively covered his mouth and stifled a cough. Behind the wall was an iron ladder, dropping down into the gloom.

He leaned into the square hole in the wall and looked down into the gloom. An unmistakable thud sounded over his head, maybe two floors up, maybe more. Someone, or something, was coming.

He put his hands on the lip of the sill and almost fell head first into the shaft as his right arm gave way under his weight with a stab of pain.

He gasped. *I can't use my arm,* he projected into his brain. *I need help!*

The Knight, filled with the purpose of the moment, brusquely shoved

Felix aside from the front of his brain and took over the body. He recognized the pain in the right shoulder, found it to be of little importance, and pushed the sensation down with Felix.

Felix's face winced, despite the exerted will of Hatta, as Hatta lifted both arms and levered the body into the space behind the wall. The arm worked, not broken.

The pain, the action, and the purpose filled Hatta, and he grinned a terrible, toothy, humorless grin on Felix's face. The eyes took on the bright, pupil-less white as the Knight gained total control. He climbed the body into the hatch and began the hand-over-hand climb down. To Felix, he sent the taunting thought, *Soft! Out of joint, it is, this shoulder, and you shrink like a violet in the noonday sun!*

It did not take long to reach the bottom of the shaft. Once there, Hatta smashed Felix's body against a wall, jamming his shoulder back into its socket and giving back control with a contemptuous growl. Felix bore up under the immense pain, ignoring the Knight's disdain. He stepped carefully out of the hidden nook at the bottom of the ladder shaft and into the sooty afternoon of the concrete canyon.

He moved quickly to the shadows on the opposite side of the canyon, away from the canals—still cautious, never too careful—and turned north toward the Games arena, the City lab, and Heisengard's apartment. He flipped on the locationer with a mental apology to the other two.

Felix focused on the walking, letting his thoughts float somewhere around the pain of his shoulder, jarring as he moved. He could sense Not analyzing the data he had taken from the dead man's head, like a buzzing in the background.

Communication in Felix's head was hampered by the overwhelming, vibrating thrum of the location. It jammed more than just signals from the outside in and the inside out, more than just irritated the two personalities in Felix's head. It appeared to jam signals moving within Felix's head as well. It took much energy from Hatta and Not to focus on each other amidst the noise.

A pulsing migraine headache began to spread from Felix's temples, counterpoint to the buzzing activity of the Locationer and his two other personalities. He could not afford to turn off the Locationer, but he was quickly becoming mentally exhausted, burning through sugar and into the reserves in his body. He used a push of intention and asked the two to stop until he could safely turn the Locationer off. Reluctantly, and with a derisive puff of energy from Hatta, they agreed and fell silent.

Felix popped a pellet into his mouth and let it dissolve on his tongue and into his system; sugar, protein, meds, and vitamins coursed into his bloodstream. In his brain, Not and Hatta bathed in a refresh of energy and health.

Not's need to seek Heisengard continued to grow in Felix's awareness. Something about the code he had taken from the dead man's head had jumped up in his attention, playing for all three a flash of understanding that Not had unwittingly shared with Heisengard when they first encountered each other through the glass. Not urged Felix on to Heisengard. Wonder, curiosity—indeed the same curiosity that spilled Not's essence out of subjugation, into the system, to the Games, and to Felix's head— grew and echoed from Not within Felix's head, as the anomalous data from the dead man's head vibrated synchronistically, with some like property in Not's thoughts of Heisengard.

Chapter 26: Broken Open

The hallway outside of Heisengard's apartment was dark and quiet when Felix, Hatta, and Not came calling. Felix kicked a metal canister laying in front of the doorway. He stooped to pick it up, and his finger brushed a tacky substance. It felt like blood. Not rose quickly in his mind, *Haste! Designation: Heisengard may have been ended!* The door to the apartment was notably solid and unlikely to be breakable—and Felix did not want to test either the door or his body again—so he allowed Not to rise in his consciousness. Not poured himself into the door's locking system through Felix's fingers. There he encountered a simple yes-or-no-structured mechanism, calling for a pattern of correct yes answers and correct no answers. Not "spoke" to the simple computer, and it "discussed" with him each correct answer. The door clicked as the mechanism unlocked, and it slowly, silently swung inward to admit them.

Heisengard was sitting on a couch facing the door. He did not move. He was the picture of resignation. He showed neither fear nor surprise on his face, though he looked up when the door opened on its own. On the floor to the right of the door was a body, appearing dead. Its head was crumpled

"

in, and a pool of blood had spread in a halo beneath it. Felix felt confirmation from Not that this was the Victor ("Designation: Heisengard") they were looking for; and with the confirmation, a gleeful energy was poised to attack.

Victor showed no recognition or surprise, as Felix walked through his front door.

He looked up, said, simply, quietly, "So they sent you to finish the job."

Felix stood still, holding Victor's defeated gaze. Neither he nor Not in his head had expected the incongruent passivity and the dead man at its feet. They waited, assessing the situation, before taking next steps. Felix did not know what to say. Not grew impatient, the poised energy pulsing in Felix's head.

Then, without preamble, Felix was roughly thrust to the back of his head, and Not jumped forward.

Victor watched in curious horror as the man's eyes drained of all their color, becoming clear orbs, intense and alien. The air in front of them began to ripple, the light bending, as if from a powerful flaming torch, burning into the air.

It dawned on Victor, as the color drained from his own face, that there were worse things in the City yet; and this was might be the one who had promised to come to him, to end him. Not the City then, but some being of power, of true judgment, some monster confirming death. The thought was ravenous in his breast, a terrified relief that the God of his death had come to release him forever. His rational thoughts fled in terror.

He slipped from his seated position and sagged to his knees. He held his hands up and out to Not as tears began to spill down his cheeks, as if beseeching deathbed forgiveness.

Not's purpose burned hotter, and the air before his eyes began to smoke.

"Notsubject!" he roared through Felix's lips.

Victor sobbed, and Not's purpose flagged. This man he had come to undo was already undone. He became confused, thinking he must be missing some vital piece of information. His clear eyes swept the room from side to side, leaving wavering contrails of rippling air, the very atoms moving out of his line of sight.

He moved Felix's body with abrupt jerkiness across the room to Victor and placed the hands on Victor's head, as if to crush him into the floor. But he could not bring his will to full bear on the man's head. The hands rested there on the weeping Heisengard's head, as if blessing a supplicant. And he could not enact his revenge.

"Designation: Heisengard," Not said through Felix's lips, "I . . ." He could craft no energy to find or share understanding. Victor looked up, eyes pleading. Then, without full analysis or a purpose he could understand, Not poured his will down Felix's arms and out his hands into Victor's mind, breaching the defenses of his privacy.

Felix was thrown even further back into his consciousness, and his body fell in front of Victor.

Not pushed against Victor's mind as he poured all of himself into Victor. The surface of Victor's consciousness pulsed a radiative wave, which provoked its deepest recesses to an echo of deep longing. Not was bathed in a sea of longing and confusion, relief and hope, and Victor's tangled mentality opened up and drew him in.

Very deep within Victor's brain, Not was drawn to deep recesses, where he had encountered damage before. A strong sense of attachment and loss pulsated from this enfolded scar like blood pumping from a heart. To Not, the energies of attachment and loss were of an indescribable need for existence and a sense of nearly fatal detachment. These energies were to Not as a Venus flytrap's enticement is to a fly: inviting him closer and further into the sticky outer petals of the wound. Here, he hovered, beginning first to complete the untangling he had started before and, second, to analyze and interact with the peculiar and compelling energy more fully. As he dove heedlessly deeper into the wound, it shut behind him, trapping him in its very heart. But he could not be consumed, though it fed on his essence in its need. Here, he encountered the blood that flowed from the very heart of Victor's wounded mind. There was screaming grief and dread, there was need and hunger too, yes, but there was beauty and love, longing and wonder. Here in this tender cavity where Not was drawn, Victor's very core grieved the loss of his son who was excised from his life and his brain. Not's essence filled this painful gap made by the City's knives. If they had been speaking words, Victor's brain would have called Not "Son," and Not would have said, "Father." Here, at the center of this broken man was a broken space, into which Not fit like he was meant to. He wondered, *Am I broken too, that I fit so well?* Nonetheless, for Not, here was home and inspiration and answers and questions, all rolled into an overwhelmingly positive experience.

Victor's brain relaxed, and the scratching of his mental record stopped. Outwardly, he wept with relief, with wonder, with confusion and grief, his defenses melting. He went from an almost superconscious awareness of letting himself go—accepting that his death had walked in the door and experiencing a flood of relief—to a mentally internal tangle of emotions and images, thoughts and sensations coming from both out- and inside himself. The force of the amalgamation was blinding. He was aware of almost nothing. Then, suddenly, with a rush of memory, that he had had a son, and that he'd lost that son. As his mind flood with the sense of "son" he passed out of consciousness, and the knowledge of his son again fled to the recesses and hid with Not, trapped in the wound.

When he regained awareness, he no longer felt the ecstatic release of accepting death nor the desperation of fear. Neither did he feel empty or exhausted, like people who experience extremes of emotion often do when they come down. Instead, he felt calm; sure of himself for the first time he could remember. He felt full and energetic, clear-headed. He felt drool drying on his chin and wiped it off.

He was still on his knees on the floor in front of the couch. The assassin lay, still, in his pool of tacky blood. The second man who had walked through the front door lay nearly in Victor's lap, on his back, legs crumpled underneath him. His eyes were motionless under closed lids.

Victor remembered the man approaching him. He remembered raising his hands to the man and the man aggressively placing hands on Victor's head. He remembered the warm dampness of the hands, then . . . then he woke up just now.

No, wait. Something more! Something broke through!

A retreating image teased at the edges of Victor's mind, so strong yet fading out as he mentally approached it. He could not get it. But he wanted it badly. It ran from him. He could not catch hold of it . . . he could not, could not, not, not, not . . . Echoes ricocheted in an increasingly complex tangle of hallways in his mind. He held his head loosely in his hands.

"What is happening to me?" he said in a loud voice, full of wonder.

Felix regained consciousness at the sound of Victor's voice and flinched backward. He looked wildly around him and locked eyes on Victor, who was still kneeling on the floor with a calm, slightly bemused expression, an edge of wonder growing there.

"What the hell? What did you do to me?" Felix said.

"I did nothing. You came to me. You . . . put your hands on me."

Felix recalled being pushed to the side in his mind and watching as Not controlled his body without his permission—*He put his, my hands, on Victor*—then . . . nothing. Then jolting awake on the ground, twitching so hard that he nearly jumped to his feet. His arm throbbed like a son of a bitch.

He had been pushed aside. Not had controlled him to put his hands on Victor and then? Then starting awake on the rug? No, then the sucking, pulling feeling, and a snap. *Then* nothing.

Where is Not?

"Where is Not?!" demanded Felix, outloud.

"I don't understand. Where is *what*?"

"Not what. Who. Where is Not? He was . . . here in . . ."

Felix pointed a finger at his own head. The ridiculousness of the gesture stopped him. "In my head," he had been about to say. He looked at Victor, whose face appeared neither cunning nor aggressive.

To Victor, Felix's face betrayed uncertainty. He could see that the aggressive tone Felix had taken was not comfortable to him.

"Slowly now," Victor said, his hand again raised in supplication. "I don't know what you're talking about. Let's just start with names for now. My name is Victor Heisengard. You are in my apartment. I did not invite you here. I just want to know who you are. What's your name?"

Felix looked at Heisengard's face as if seeing him for the first time.

"My name is Felix."

"No last name?"

"No, only Felix."

Victor stood up slowly, noticing the look of wariness on Felix's face.

"I'm going to close the door, Felix. The neighbors can be nosy, and I don't think this is a conversation we want them to hear."

He walked over to the door and clicked it softly closed. He wasn't sure why, but something told him that this man would change his life. Actually, it had already changed: his burden of fear or confusion, the terror he had felt, then the utter relief when Felix had burst into his apartment; he was already a new man.

He moved across the room and returned to the couch. He raised his eyebrows to Felix and indicated an arm chair near the front door, across from the couch. Felix, still looking dazed, followed his gesture.

"Oh, sure," Felix said, realizing what Victor's gesture meant. He stood with a wince, favoring his arm, and walked to the chair. He sat down in it, sinking further than he thought he would and chirping in surprise as his dislocated shoulder tried to take his weight on the arm of the chair.

"Are you injured, Felix. Is there anything I can do?"

"I need something for the pain. I think it's dislocated."

Bare up, knave! floated up out of Felix's deeper mind from the Knight.

"Shut up," Felix said to Hatta, but it came out of his mouth as well.

Victor said nothing, not wanting to upset the tenuous sanity he saw in Felix. He stood from the couch and said simply, "I have an antagonist you can have. I've never needed it, and frankly, it's always creeped me out a little."

He left the living room and retreated to the back of the apartment to the bathroom, where he kept medicine.

Felix had taken anti-inflammatory medications before. Prostaglandin antagonists reduced pain and swelling. But he wasn't familiar with any other antagonists of a medical variety.

And who gets creeped out by a medication?

Victor walked back into the room with a small vial. There were no pills, nor a syringe with a dose of medication in the vial. He handed to Felix the small, clear glass vial with a tiny brown smear inside at the bottom. Felix took it cautiously. Victor began to explain why he had never needed it. Felix lost everything that Victor was saying as he realized that the small brownish lump in the vial was moving. It was some sort of tiny slug, moving . . . well, sluggishly, in its own slime around the bottom, inside of the vial.

"What the hell is this?" His voice was sharper than he meant it to be.

Victor creased his brow. "Oh," he said, "I thought everyone had one of these. It's a MASS." Felix shook his head. Victor thought for a minute.

"It's a, um, Multi . . . Antagonist Synthesizing Slug."

Felix shook his head slowly. "Never heard of it," he said.

"It's a minipharm! You know, synthesizes and secretes medicine on demand? Well, actually, only inhibitors. It only produces inhibitors. Can't boost anything or cure cancer or anything like that. Just inhibits. It'll block some of your pain, though, that's for certain."

Felix set the vial down on the table between the couch and his chair and gave it a push with deliberate disdain. He looked at Victor, with caution.

"OK," Victor said, slowly. "I don't care if you use it, but that's all I've got for pain. Yours if you want it."

He left the vial on the table.

"Now," he continued, returning to his seat, "what did you say you were looking for?"

"Wait, what?" Felix asked, still distracted by the greasy, moving slug in the vial.

"You mentioned a knot. You said, 'Where is knot?'"

"Right. I'm . . ." Felix could not think how to explain. "I was with a friend when I came in and then . . . then I wasn't."

"No, you came in alone. No one was with you." Victor was struck by the memory of horrible, impossibly clear eyes. *Had there been another?* He looked at Felix's eyes. They were dark brown.

Then, tentatively, slowly, Victor said, "You were different when you came in. You looked different. Did you know that?"

"What do you mean?"

"Your eyes were . . . clear, like I could feel them when you looked at me." He shuddered.

Not! Of course, Felix thought. *Not was in control.*

Felix said, excitedly, leaning in, "Yes! Not!"

Victor looked blank. Felix continued,

"Will you try something with me? You have to be calm, though; it might be weird."

"Nothing will surprise me ever again. What do you need me to do?"

"Just a second."

Victor waited.

Felix retreated into his brain, his face freezing in a mild expression of emotionlessness.

Hatta, I want you to take control for a minute. Don't do anything, just come to the front, see what you see, then let me back up. Will you do that for me?

Hatta responded, sarcastically, *Does your arm pain you again, my liege?*

Can you just come forward for a minute, then let me back in?

With pleasure, Sire.

"OK, just watch my face," Felix said aloud to Victor.

To Victor, the last word came out in a different tone, and the face changed almost immediatly; Felix's dark brown eyes sat calmly in the sockets of his windblown face, drained of all but the white, which grew from the center out like the negative of an ink stain spreading on cloth. There was no accompanying change to the air in front of Felix's face, but his expression became hardened, his gaze penetrating. There was nothing to hold onto in those depthless whites, and Victor found himself afraid for reasons he could not express. The eyes were not aggressive necessarily, but they owned all that they took, practically flattening Victor with a sense of control and mastery. He felt like a child must when meeting the imposing figure of Dad's boss.

"Ah, the object of Not's desire and the key to our City-circumventing conundrum," Hatta said in a low, quiet voice.

Hatta made Felix's face smile. It was all teeth, teeth that somehow seemed straighter, longer, and whiter than they had seemed when Felix was at the front.

"Wha-what have you done?" Victor stammered.

Hatta, let me up! Hatta did, bowing Felix's body forward in mock obeisance, and Felix jumped back to the front. His eyes filled back in, and his stance relaxed.

Victor was wide-eyed, his mouth agape.

"What did you see?" Felix asked, excitedly.

"Your eyes went white, and you . . . it wasn't you. You said something about 'Not's desire' and circumventing the City."

Not must have changed my eyes too, Felix thought. *But where is he now?*

"Who are you?" Victor continued.

Felix sighed. There was really no getting around this story. He'd have to explain to Victor that he had, or used to have, two personalities, aside from his own, sharing his head. Not had made it clear that they needed Heisengard. And even though Not had expressed to them that they'd need Heisengard's knowledge of the City-Structure, the secreted sluices that would get them out of the City, Felix had intuited, or perhaps perceived, that there was a much greater purpose behind Not's need to find Victor.

"Victor. I'm going to tell you something that I've told only one other person, and he almost killed me for it. I can only ask that you hear me out before you make any decisions. Let's just say that a close friend of mine trusted you and asked me to find you, OK? He called himself Not."

"Knot? Like with a rope?"

"No, *Not*, like the opposite of *Is*. A negation."

Something tickled at the back of Victor's mind.

"Not . . . what?"

"Just Not."

"No, I mean, a negation of what?"

Felix thought of how to describe the name. Not had given off the strong sense that he would not be defined, that he would not be subjugated, not used, etc. But he never truly defined himself to Felix. Felix thought Hatta might know, but he wasn't sure. Hatta had not decided to share if he did.

"I asked him the same. Just 'Not,' he said. But I think he'd say he is not . . . anything that . . . not defined by anything but himself. I'm not sure. For now, just, his name is Not."

"OK, fine. And he wanted you to find me? He trusted me? I don't know anyone with that name."

Victor's conscious mind was working very hard to keep out the persistent but small inner voice of his subconscious, which suspected that Not was related to the Subject, the unman behind the glass in the lab, the City's experiment, Subject OE-77. This creeping suspicion carried fear with it, fear which he would be rid of and which he wanted to keep out.

"So, why me?" he said aloud.

"Not said you knew how to get out of the City. Specifically, that you had knowledge of the sluices and knew one we could . . . ride out under the wall into the waste-lake."

Victor's face went from bemused to confused to incredulous, then to a sort of bewilderment.

"I don't know how to get out of the City! Are you kidding me?" Then, surprising himself with his honesty, "Lord knows I've wanted to leave. But the City has a way of keeping you in. They always seem to know. Felix, sometimes I think they're in my head."

And before Felix could make any comment, and as suddenly as Victor had said it, Victor was struck by a thought with the force of a sledgehammer between the eyes.

I had a son!

This was the confirmation of the change he had felt; this was the answer to the nightmares and dread and the feeling of unreality. This was what had changed, what had brought him from desperate certainty of death to calm to presence. He had a son, and now, he did not.

It was a thought filled with implications, like the hatch on a submarine ready to burst its seals and allow in the whole ocean. Victor's eyes lit up like lamps in the dark. He stood abruptly, took two aggressive steps across the room to Felix, and grabbed him by the shirt, eyes blazing.

"Felix, I have a son! No, no, no," he said, shaking his head, "I *had* a son. They took him from me! The City. They even took his memory. My son!"

His eyes darted this way and that, looking in his own head for answers, it seemed, for memories that could not be caught. Or searching the room as if to catch a spy in the corner, behind the chairs, the table. He again fell to his knees, loosening his hands from Felix's shirt. His head dropped to his hands, and he wept. Everything he had held back came out in a rush. In the mix of his terrible loss, the wall between his conscious and subconscious minds now breached, he became convinced that Not and the Subject were one in the same.

Felix was confronted by the same force of abject misery and desperation that Not had seen when they first entered Victor's apartment. Here was a man who needed to be loved. Not a man to distrust. Not a man to use. Felix could do nothing but watch. Eventually, he put his hand on Victor's heaving shoulder and left it there, patiently waiting for the grief to ebb.

Victor's sobs subsided slowly, replaced by wet sniffling. Before Felix could think of anything to say to bring them back to the discussion, ask what was happening, or even soothe him, Victor spoke through his slowing tears.

"I have a hidden cubby behind the wall in the front closet. I, I didn't remember until just now. It's got a picture of my son. Please get it. There is a catch at the back of the closet, in the right corner, almost at floor level."

Felix left Victor where he again knelt, and went to the closet. He pushed aside coats and jackets, various long-sleeved items of clothing. He ignored a few items that fell to the floor and squatted down. In the back-right corner of the closet, both walls and the floor that made up the joint appeared to be empty. He felt around on the floor first, then the wall, about an inch off the ground. *There.* There, in the far corner, too small to accidentally hit and too small to find if you didn't know what to look for, a tiny catch was raised from the surface of the back wall, about a centimeter off the floor.

Felix pulled down on it with the very tip of his index finger, and the wall above him clicked.

He stood and saw that the outline of a square had appeared on the surface of the wall, as if freshly drawn. He pushed in the middle of the square. Another click. Then, the wall opened, and the light of day shone out, temporarily blinding him.

Victor had stopped crying altogether and was now watching Felix's progress.

"Yes, yes," he said, eagerly. "There, in the light. A plant too. A photo and a plant. Bring them to me!"

Felix's eyes adjusted, first slowly, then, as a film of darkened liquid covered his irises, more quickly. Behind the wall was a false daylight. A warming, life-giving approximation of real sunlight. But sunlight that had not been seen above the City for hundreds of years. There, in the hidden, cleverly false-lit cubby, sat a potted plant. A slender stem arced up and bent horizontal in a smooth curve from the weight of six small, thumb-sized pink pods, each split at the bottom like broken hearts, a drop of white endlessly suspended below them. Felix picked up the small plant, looking closely at the delicate blossoms. A waft of the purest breeze of spring tickled his nose as he peered at them.

Then, looking back into the cubby, Felix saw a worn photograph, of the sort captured and printed on paper. It had been hiding underneath the potted plant. It showed the face of a small boy beaming an angelic smile into the camera. The light from those eyes could not be filtered out with any technology Felix knew about.

Felix closed the cubby, and the shading liquid retreated from his irises as he turned back into the dim light of the apartment.

He took both picture and plant and returned carefully to Victor's side. Victor reached up, and Felix placed the plant and the picture in Victor's hands. Victor carefully, lovingly, placed the potted plant on the table in front of the couch, never taking his eyes from the photo.

"Steven," he breathed in a sigh of purest affection. Then, "Steven" again. This time with a catch in his voice that spilled tears from his eyes again. No sobbing, just a steady wet drip, drip, dripping onto the worn carpet.

He looked up at Felix, and with pleading eyes, said, "I don't know how. But I'm sure the City took my son from me. He was beautiful, and I can't remember him."

"I can't remember him!" he repeated, this time slamming his hand onto the table. "Do you know how painful it is to have an empty memory, a not-memory of someone you know you loved, someone you can no longer see in your mind?"

Felix shook his head, politely, though he too could not remember those he had lost—blurry gray formed the memories of his parents. He felt true sorrow for this tumultuous man kneeling on the carpet in front of him.

Victor continued, quietly, "It's like hitting a gong in my head every time I reach an empty place. And then, just when I think I've reached a dead end, some other, random memory . . . but it doesn't feel like a memory. It feels like a line from a book or something someone recently told me. Like just now, I . . ."

His voice faded. Then, he looked up suddenly, eyes still brimming with tears but now bright with surprise and purpose.

"I know how to get out of the City! There's a hatch! It leads to a tunnel, parallel to the canal . . . or sluice . . . the one that you need to take. From there, you can get into the water close to the City wall and . . . and jump in, I guess."

"You told me you didn't know how to get out of the City."

"I didn't. Or, at least, I didn't a moment ago. It came to me just now. I was frustrating some empty part of my memories, telling you random stuff pops up and then . . . just," Victor trailed off, throwing his hands up to indicate something popping up, his eyebrows raised.

"Up it popped?" Felix finished for him.

"Yeah. Like a . . . a bubble."

Victor looked down at his hands, looking for some meaning written on his skin. *What has happened to me?*

He lifted the photograph again and made a decision.

"Felix, I have to go with you. I have nowhere else to go. They've taken everything from me; my son . . . I think they cut him from my brain! I'm . . . I'm not . . . something's not OK up here." He pointed to his temple, much like Felix had done.

Felix had no reason to refuse him. He still didn't know how to find this hatch to the canal tunnels. He looked at Victor, wanting to ask him where Not was yet again. But he knew that Victor did not know. They'd have to go without him.

"You've . . ." he began to say when Victor suddenly went very still and his face drained of color.

"There's a call incoming from the Group. What do I do? I can't answer it." Then, with an unhelpful panic, he yelled, "They know we're here!"

Felix gripped Victor's shoulder, hard.

"Listen to me, Victor. You're going to come with us. We're going to escape the City, the Group. We're gonna get out, but you need to do what I say. OK?"

Victor nodded.

"OK. First, I need to disable your wetware link to the City. There's no way to hide with the hardware in your head broadcasting live all over the City."

He pulled out a small black box from his pocket and palmed it.

"This is gonna hurt like a son of a bitch."

Before Victor could ask what or tell him no or even pull away, Felix slapped the small device down on top of Victor's head. There was only a faint hum at first, then, in a rising wail, Victor screamed.

It only took a minute, and the pain was gone the second the device was turned off, but it left Victor dizzy. A small spot on his head where the box had been pressed was burned and no longer had hair. Victor, very unsteady now, turned and threw up on the couch.

"Good, good. That's fine," Felix said to him. "Now, look at me, Victor. Look at my eyes."

Victor turned, swaying slightly, and looked into Felix's eyes. After a four beat, his heart had slowed down, and he had become steadier on his feet.

"I'm all right," he gasped, swallowing. "I'm all right. You shorted it out, didn't you?"

"Yes, I did, but only a very small part of it. The rest is fine. Now, where do we go?"

"What . . . I thought we were—"

"No, Victor, how do we get to the secret hatch to get to the canal tunnels?"

"Oh, right. Um, downstairs, down in the building. There's a subbasement! Wait, not this building. Another one. A door under the first floor of the building. But I don't even know the building."

Felix felt the mounting pressure of the approaching agency of the City, no doubt rushing to their location as they discussed how to leave.

"Victor! Focus. Where? Where do we go?"

"I don't know! The memories just come on their own. It's not even as—"

He stopped mid-thought and tipped his head to the side.

"The Body building? What's the Body building?"

"I'll tell you on the way," Felix said, turning toward the door in haste. "Just get us to the canyon floor, and I'll get us to the building!"

He grabbed Victor's hand, the one not occupied with his son's photograph, and dragged him to his feet.

"Wait!" Victor said, pulling away from Felix. He ran to the still open closet and rummaged in the bottom. He came out with a small sturdy shoulder bag and a jacket. He put on the jacket, zipped the photograph of his son into a small pocket on the bag, and dropped his beloved plant unceremoniously into the main pocket. With the plant, there were two containers, apparently full of water, and a handful of nutrition pellets, to which

Felix would add his own stash later on. Victor turned toward Felix, who was now very impatiently waiting at the front door, paused, turned back toward the room, and grabbed the vial with the slug, saying, "You never know." He handed it to Felix, who hastily shoved it into his pocket.

"Fine," Felix said. "Just get us down to the canyon level."

Victor slid his feet into a pair of soft lab shoes that were hardly more than slippers. He had no thought about his feet as he left his apartment for good and he would regret his haste.

Chapter 27: Tower on the Hill

Kennedy Darfore sat cupped in a chair that cradled his body, like a cracked eggshell cradling a congealing yolk. His chair was in a small empty room at the top of the tallest tower in the City. Before him, the wall was made entirely of glass, Interactive Glass, his *Looking Glass*. No other walls had windows, doors, or any adornment. The room was stiflingly hot.

His eyes were wide open. They did not blink. The pupils were larger than they ought to have been, taking in more light than would ordinarily have been comfortable. His mouth sagged open, its pudding insides showing behind slightly green gums—no teeth—that minutely shifted on their own. His chest heaved periodically, drawing gasps of breath in no particular pattern.

A tendril snaked from one of his hands, trailed across the room, and was suctioned to the bottom-right portion of the wall screen, somehow interacting with the electronics within. Periodic twitching and a yellowish glow waved back and forth between Darfore and the InGlass across the moist, snake-like appendage.

The screen at which Darfore stared showed a shaky view of the bottom level of the City canyon. It was from a perspective of about six feet off the ground, and it hugged the right wall, heading in a direction that appeared south, away from where Darfore sat at the north end of the City. Periodically, the view flashed completely dark for a fraction of a second, the connection not yet rooted fully. The view of the canyon followed closely behind Felix as he appeared to pick his way along the ground, from Heisengard's apartment to the Body building. Darfore was looking out of Victor's eyes.

Darfore's connection with Victor was primarily visual. He had not taken the time to establish a more immersive connection; that would come later. He had been there when Felix confronted Victor. And he had been there when something unexpected happened between the two men, the intrusion of luck or chance (*chaos*, Darfore thought). Victor had been passed something from this pedestrian Felix, some entity or complicated packet of datenergy. Darfore did not know what it was. The minute aspect of Darfore that sat in Victor's brain had been momentarily disturbed at the transfusion of energy into Victor, right before Victor had passed out. Darfore had still been able to see through Victor's eyes while he was unconscious, but the view was unremarkable: close up on an old rug through the sliver of closed eyelids. Darfore suspected that his rogue Subject OE-77 had somehow found his way into Victor's head. *He is progressing far faster than I ever thought capable.*

Darfore watched dispassionately as the view followed Felix, steeling through the lengthening shadows of the dusty canyon toward the Body building. The Body was a rebellious energy within the City, his city, himself. She, he thought, provided the services of sexual workers. She, he thought, was an anachronism of the old world, the feminine principal, soothing the children of a divorced reality. Body was not operating, strictly speaking, under Darfore's authority. She wielded an influence not had by the City-Sons themselves, and it was an influence at a deep human level, that of intimacy; an influence that Darfore, the City, did not understand and could not manipulate. *It is a small influence. A frivolous influence,* he thought. *Let them have their sexual satisfactions.*

Darfore himself had no need nor, truly, any knowledge of sexuality, and his understanding of intimacy was twisted at best, alien at worst. He was the City: a collective, an assimilation and—to him—therefore, all his aspects and all parts of the City were intimately him. He had no need for specific *physical* congress with any one aspect of himself or another.

Indeed, he was aware of all of his aspects, cooperatively, being that he was equally aware of each of his various parts, their experiences, their whereabouts, and their thoughts (in as much as each could be said to have its own thoughts).

He absorbed the agitation of the many tentacled monstrosities swimming in the City's canals, bathing in their hunger like a man running his hand over an exposed wire.

He centered in stillness with the patient potentialities of the enormous growths in the City waste-lakes—those nightmarish conglomerations of animal and vegetable poison—poised, biding their time until they were called into service, like a giant cooling his heels in a lake of mud.

He felt the meaning and emotion of countless low-level City conscripts, repurposed and reconditioned for service, communicating in their limited way to each other in various degrees of waning humanity, like a queen bee among her millions of drones.

He tingled on his surface, like the feeling of wind-blown hair on his skin, at the movement and constant messaging of his CPS satellite drones that watched all parts of his collective self through the myriad electronic eyes.

And he expanded and contracted his awareness in oozing pulses and reactive withdraws, with strange growths in the middle of the Country, neither fully animal nor vegetable nor human, full of potentiality and sickness, presaging the coming of an inexorable growing foulness.

He was aware of all these and other matters as he watched from Victor's eyes and followed Felix toward the Body building. He accepted and expected that they would try to leave him, the City, and he knew there was only one, marginally safe way through a sluice into the waste-lake. It had all been foreseen by Darfore. And yet, somehow, frustratingly, he still did not know exactly where the Body building sat. For a reason still unknown to him, Body exerted a certain control of herself that Darfore had yet to wrest from the pleasuring hands. He had abided her presence, lingering after the death of their brief union countless turnings of the sun before, and he had overlooked her instinct for survival, her tenacious interference.

Darfore's frenetic thoughts stilled. Felix had stopped walking. Through Victor's eyes, Darfore's attention drew closer. Felix turned to his left and approached the canals. The building in front of his view was like all other buildings, so Felix would have had no reason to stop unless this was something different. It was. There, in the foreground, bridging the danger of the canals, a bridge appeared, wavering in its light camouflage. *Yes,* Darfore thought, *at last, the Body, its seat, the entrance! Take me inside her citadel, unwitting pawns!*

Then, without warning, his view through Victor's eyes cut off. His connection was not lost but forcibly cut off. Mentally, he sat up, drawing more of his cooperative attention to the connection he had just lost, willing its reestablishment. It did not come back.

He commandeered a tentacled canal dweller, sending its intentions crashing into the hidden bridge in front of Felix and orienting its aggression on Felix and Victor. The location of the building would be enough. He'd have to see to this one personally.

They would try to leave the City, he knew, and they would survive—that much had been foreseen—but he would not allow it to be easy. And Felix (*whoever he might be,* for he had ever left a cloud of uncertainty in the foretelling) should prove expendable. Given enough time, Darfore's connection with Victor would become much more.

More Darfore, he thought, as he stood from his chair. He walked to the wall opposite the Looking Glass, wet tendrils snapping back to him and disappearing into his body. At the back of the room, as he approached the wall, a hidden door rushed upward into the ceiling, revealing empty air and opening into the canyon a thousand feet below. Savoring his height and the visual elevation above his kingdom, he paused in the opening, leaned out dangerously, and took in the enormity of the ocean in front of him, with the thin gray line of his canyon empire extending like a smile far to the north and south below.

Then, he jumped. With no preparation, without a look before he leapt, just a step and down. Twenty feet below, a raft of satellites caught him and bore him quickly south, still high about the canyon below. Darfore seemed to stick to the rounded satellites without effort, his feet molding to their shiny surfaces. His face appeared to grin, in the closest semblance to actual joy he ever showed.

Chapter 28: Confrontation in the Canyon

Felix marveled that they had gotten this far without trouble. Somehow, Victor had been able to get them safely out into the canyon, and Felix had maneuvered them across the network of side canals and continuous gray without any notable detection by the City. Once in the canyon, Victor had to be led like a child. He gaped at everything he saw at the feet of the City. Felix had to remind himself that Victor had likely only ever seen it all from above.

"The walls are so high," Victor whispered at one point. "What's that stench?" another time. And "How can you even tell where we are?" to Felix.

Felix did not answer his questions nor continue any conversation, terrified that, despite the steady work of the Locationer in his head, Victor's disregard for their safety would do them in. He merely said, "Shhh," very pointedly and very quietly.

It took them about an hour to pick their way to a point near Felix's home where he recognized the landmarks and the pedestrian tags and could bring them safely to the Body building. He realized he had been relying heavily on Not to find his way in the City since they left Chobot's lair. He wondered, *did Not exert control even at times I did not know?*

Outside of the Body building, approaching the canal and careful to warn Victor away from its edge, Felix was finally able to turn off the Locationer, which had begun to make his head throb. In the penumbra of the Body building's protective broadcast, he would remain hidden from the City.

Then, a new thing happened. For only the second time that Felix could ever remember, the surface of the canal liquid was broken. Out leapt two muscular, tentacled, yet somehow armored and hinged arms from the canal water, wrapping themselves around the hidden bridge that spanned it. Felix instinctively switched his Locationer back on, and he and Victor jumped back, turned, and ran to the opposite wall of the canyon, crouching protectively within the shadow. Felix was buffeted by sooty, rainy day memories of those canal tentacles. He had seen them rip apart a small boy—a lost child, a low-level CitySon, newly slaved—while the child smiled vacantly.

The arms flexed on the bridge, straining at the concrete as if to crush it. There was no way to get past them, and strange to behold, they seemed to track Felix and Victor's movements as if they had eyes. No visual organs were obvious, but their intentions were clear: no entrance!

Neither man knew what to do. The canal went silent again. The arms remained flexed, continuing to watch the two men with hidden eyes.

Felix took a step toward the canals, testing for lack of any other plan. Victor grabbed his hand and hissed, "No, stay with me." The tentacles bulged menacingly again and twitched, orienting on the hiss from Victor. Nothing further came out of the canal. The canyon became silent once again.

Then, in frustration, up burbled Hatta from the depths of Felix's mind, and Felix was thrown backward into his consciousness. He shrugged off Victor's panicked grasp, and said, "Loathsome City! I am fed up with its gruesome machinations. I intend to leave!"

He strode across the canyon to the canal side and grabbed the tentacles, one in each hand. Felix's body began to glow, an overlay of the Knight's determined face shown before Felix's head. The Knight strained against the arms and squeezed, adding his own essence to Felix's weak hands. There was a squeal of pain from the canals, and the Knight's visage shone brighter, a grin spreading and brightening the light mask over Felix. He squeezed harder, pulling the tentacles apart and stretching them from the cement where they clung. There was a cracking and tearing sound, then another squeal, but this one from Felix's own lips. Felix mentally shouted, *Hatta, you're damaging my hands!* Hatta frowned and threw down the broken tentacles with disgust.

"How are we to survive in this world slinking at the feat of our enemies?!" he roared.

Felix rose in his own mind and pushed Hatta aside with effort.

There's an easier way, he thought to Hatta. He reached his hand—which now ached and burned with the strain Hatta had put on it—into a pocket in his pants, remembering the sonic emitter Mike had given him. *They hate high-pitched frequency emissions.*

He aimed the small, plastic emitter at the tentacled arms—still moving, still dangerous, but broken—and was about to depress the small button when he noticed the device was heating up and glowing. The glow spread and wrapped around the device and Felix's hand, taking on the improbable shape of a throwing dagger.

Hatta? Felix thought.

Just throw the damn thing, simpleton!

So he did. As it hit the nearest tentacle, a blinding light shot out from the glow, and burned into the writhing arms. They fell, smoking into the canal. Hatta exuded the feeling of satisfaction and grim new knowledge.

Don't be too excited, Felix thought to him, as he dropped the now melted and useless plastic lump, *it's a limited-use weapon. But, Oh,* he suddenly remembered, *Thank God I still have a hand laser.*

His hand tingled where the Knight's essence had combined with the technology to beef up the weapon. He had no time to contemplate what this meant, as an unearthly scream came from above, piercing the silence of the canyon.

Felix ran across the canyon to the opposite wall in shadow and snapped his head up. His hand palmed the small laser in his pocket. Victor followed. A raft of satellites hovered far above them in the sooty sky, and the unbroken scream seemed to come from there.

The scream continued impossibly long and grew in volume until it was almost painful for the two men. They covered their ears, continuing to look desperately to the sky for the approaching sound of their doom. A part of the raft of satellites seemed to break away and quickly began to grow. The scream grew louder still.

Almost immediately, the growing thing resolved into a body, hurtling toward the canyon floor, screaming as it dove. Like a meteorite, it landed, crashing into the canyon floor with the force of an enormous bag of cement, cracking the stone yet making what sounded like a splatting noise. The body of the man that fell (for thus it appeared to be) squashed unbelievably short and dense but somehow retained its form and sprang back into man shape. With a maniacal grin, Darfore stood before them.

"Hello, boys."

He was dressed in an impeccably tailored, dark-blue suit with shiny, black leather shoes. But, like the rest of him, they did not appear to be real. They had formed after his landing, much like the rest of his body after it was squashed to the concrete ground.

Felix and Victor turned to run.

"Nope," Darfore said, and another phalanx of CPS drones dropped out of the sky in formation, barring the way.

The men turned to run the other way, only to be met by a veritable army of low-level maintenance workers—those often referred to as zombies, for the lack of personality showing on their faces—oozing from hidden doorways, side canals and cracks in the City foundation. Each held a club or stick, a bar or hammer, brandished in diseased hands.

These men and women, even some children, stood firmly in the two men's way and were dressed in a mess of rags and clothing in various states of decay, all slack-jawed and all oriented squarely on Felix and Victor. They were boxed in.

Felix raised the hand laser—a last and desperate chance—and fired it straight at Darfore's chest. It glowed red, began to smoke, and melted in Felix's hand, forcing him to drop it, now useless. In its path, directly through Darfore's chest, a blackened, charred hole appeared. A wisp of smoke drifted up from the hole. A gust of wind dissipated it, and the two men could smell something like the burning of moldering leaves and melting wires.

Darfore looked at the new hole in his chest with mild interest, raising an eyebrow then looking up at Felix in slight surprise, as if to say, *"I didn't think you had it in you."* The injury did not seem to bother him. The hole began to fill in; first with a greenish-brown goop, then with a metallic black layer, and finally finishing with an approximation of skin and suit material to complete the ensemble.

"There, you see?" Darfore said, smiling sweetly. "You no longer have to worry. It's not going to help you make this harder on yourself anymore."

Felix looked dismayed. Victor opened his mouth to speak, thinking somehow that he might have something to add. *After all,* he thought, *I met this man* (or this thing) *and there was some comradery there, wasn't there?*

Darfore cut him off. "No, Victor, I want nothing to come from your mouth. You can keep it shut. But I will keep you alive. I have a task I want to put on you, and I think this man here, this *boy*, is distracting you from it. You, on the other hand," he said, indicating Felix again, "I cannot let you leave the City—you've caused some problems, and I don't even know your true name. Not Felix, I don't think, or . . . Jesus? How arrogant!"

Then, without preamble, he sprang across the canyon, shoved a surprised Victor out of the way and forcefully into the wall (where he crumpled to the ground), and stepped into Felix's face.

Darfore leaned in, pouring cold, rotten breath over Felix, as he stage whispered, "I'm going to do this slowly and enjoy every bone-breaking, blood vessel-popping moment of your death."

At that same moment, Felix's brain lit up from the top of mind to bottom. The Knight, struck by the image of Darfore ripping Felix's body in two pieces, lunged to the forefront of Felix's brain and took over his body.

He nimbly stepped out of the way of a crashing fist at the end of Darfore's brutally swung arm.

Darfore looked surprised and took a step back to examine Felix. His surprise was confirmed when he beheld the forceful visage of the Knight's pupil-less, white eyes peering out of Felix's face.

"Who the hell are you?" Darfore asked.

The Knight said nothing, merely grinning, making Felix's teeth look impossibly white and long. He raised a hand and pointed a finger at Darfore in an unmistakable gesture that bespoke violence intended upon Darfore's person. A shimmer around Felix's hand appeared in the shape of a gauntlet, covering it from knuckle to forearm.

Darfore looked more confused than before, but confused at the stage of annoyance, not crisis. He shrugged, said "Whatever," and stepped forward to punch Felix again.

The blow that should have crushed Felix's lower jaw caught nothing but the canyon wall. Cement cracked, and a few pieces of wall fell from above. Darfore's hand, badly mangled from the force of the blow, reformed quickly.

Darfore growled. He turned back quickly, but not quickly enough, and a strike from the heel of Felix's right hand, glimmering with an ethereal gauntlet of faint light, tore the head from his body.

Darfore's body slumped against the wall, his head landing nearby with a splat, squashed like a lump of clay.

The body stood and, without hesitation, turned and stepped into the mess of goo that had been the head, where it was absorbed back into the body. As it disappeared into the body's foot, Darfore's head grew back just as quickly on his shoulders, and his mouth was already speaking as it reformed.

"Damn it, you pesky little remainder, where did you learn to do that? It's simple, really, you give me your life quickly, or I'll take it slowly. That way, I don't have to work as hard, you don't have to deal with all the pain, and I'll promise not to cut you up into little pieces while keeping your head alive just to experience the torment!"

Felix's mouth said nothing. The Knight was used to such bull in the various megalomaniacal foes he had previously faced. They always made broad, overly confident pronouncements when they were surprised.

As Darfore spoke, the Knight turned Felix's hand this way and that, fascinated that his gauntlet appeared there, apparently made of light yet very much as hard and functional as those he was used to wearing. As he concentrated on the gauntlet's detail, he could feel the remainder of his armor growing onto Felix's body. He wasn't sure anyone else could see it, but he could feel it, and there was an outline just visible in the dim light of the gray sky to his eyes.

Darfore had stopped speaking. He was watching Felix as the new white eyes appeared to scan its body.

"What are you looking at, you cretin? I haven't even given you a low-level purpose, and you're already staring dumbly at yourself like a zombie."

The Knight looked at Darfore, tipped his head to the side, and grinned even broader.

"Sir," he said through Felix's mouth, "you appear to believe that the world comes at your call. I am not your cur to whip. Neither will I take your untamed arrogance. I have lived far too long among my enemies, those sworn and those unwitting fools who stumbled into my blades accidentally." With this, he raised his hands, both formed into loose fists, and held up his twin broad swords, which appeared there like sharpened spears of light.

Now, Darfore smiled incredulously, as if he was amused. He could see nothing in the hands.

"You have no weapon. Will you cut me with your words? Your hands? No. But I do, and I can."

Darfore's face lit up with a fierce pride as both hands distended, growing longer and longer, forming edges and glinting like steel in the sun. His body was the sword hand for two swords now, appearing to be as hard and sharp as any forged in fire. He spun them on his shoulder sockets, nicking the wall behind him and the canyon floor beneath, sending small chips of concrete and sparks into the air.

He stepped up, coming at Felix, the Knight fully at the helm with the body now shimmering in his white armor and twin blades held lightly and at the ready, unseen by all but himself.

Darfore may have been a master of modification, but he was no sword master. The Knight had seen this dance so many times, he barely needed to watch as Darfore stepped to him lightning quick, spinning his blade arms with aplomb.

As if in a rehearsed dance, the Knight matched Darfore's speed, and the ringing of steel on steel thundered through the canyon. Deflected blades swung with the force of stone boomed against the concrete of the canyon. Darfore, though he was surprised to be matched both in speed and by steel (which he could not see), did not slow his attack.

With a thought, he threw his zombie citizens at the Knight from the side. They lumbered in, only to be hewn down in bloody heaps, uselessly killed. Darfore doubled his attack, the intensity of his focus sapping form from his puttied face, which now sagged in a mockery of childish evil. His blade hands grew longer, the heft of each gaining in weight. His feet began to absorb from the ground, rendering his body in greater density as he wielded increasingly heavy weapons. The force of his club swords was deftly and repeatedly turned aside by the Knight's twin-wielded will blades, knocking free shards of wall, and decimating zombie slaves who stumbled too close.

Then, Darfore called the satellite drones, black orbs that spun with wicked laser fire. Hatta broke free of Darfore's attack and sprinted at the oncoming drones. He began to laugh, the exhilaration of purpose, the thrill of exertion springing from his lips as energy unbounded. He deflected laser beams by force of will alone, not knowing the laws of this physical world and seeing in his mind's eye and through Felix's commandeered eyes his swords deflecting the red lights as easily as they did bullets. He did not notice that he was burned in a number of places, cut deeply and cauterized by a few lucky beams, as he barreled headlong into the first of the drones. It burst apart as his sword-holding fist smashed through its reinforced sides.

He took another two on the point of his blades, slicing them cleaning from the air. A fourth he grasped in his right hand, having switched his swords both to the left. He allowed his momentum to spin him around the back of the drone to the left, and upon reaching the extent of his grasp, he pulled and leveraged the drone, sending it spinning backward and crashing into its neighbor, where it exploded, knocking yet another drone out of the sky and over the canal. This sixth drone was snatched from the air by an arm from the canal and crushed under the oily surface.

The final drone focused all of its energy into a broad-spectrum beam straight at the Knight's chest. Hatta brought his swords up in a cross that met at the center of his chest. The beam heated the metal of the swords as they absorbed the full energy, gradually increasing as the Knight continued his sprint toward the orb. In this way, he pushed back at the energy beam, closer and closer to the overheating drone. At about forty feet away, the Knight sprang up, his sword arms first falling to his sides then sweeping up and over his head, where they coupled together, gripping the swords like a sledgehammer. At the arc of his leap, he swept the doubled swords down and sliced the final orb into two clean pieces. They fell in a smoking wreckage at the canyon floor, and the Knight landed nimbly beyond. He did not wait, but turned and beheld the angry oncoming Darfore, who was dumbfounded but nonetheless driven to his task.

Again, the two engaged by the canal side, Darfore's heavy swords spinning and dipping, arcing and slicing at the Knight, who almost casually deflected them.

The look on Darfore's face was as foolish to the Knight's weathered eyes as his spinning blades were ineffectual. Any other man would have been cut to ribbons. But even in this real world, with the permission of Felix's brain and body, the Knight's very will rent the air with its ferocity. His twin blades, singing their song of death, joined him in the thrill of a dance he knew very well. He stepped in and out of Darfore's attacks, playing with him, luring him closer and closer to the canal, and dipping under and over Darfore's whirling blade hands.

Eventually, out of respect for the dance itself and with no care for his opponent, he swung both blades in and up to the right, caught both of Darfore's arm blades, and carried them out of the way, leaving Darfore's body off balance. The Knight planted an invisibly armored knee firmly in Darfore's chest, and it caved in, throwing him backward. His chest quickly filled back in as if to erase the injury, but it was not the knee that the Knight had intended to do the killing. As always, it was his blades. As Darfore recovered his balance, his chest completely filled in and the Knight continued his momentum, swinging blades and body impossibly quickly in a spin to his left, bringing one blade in an arc from over his head and down, and dragging the other on the concrete with a shower of sparks from the ground up. As he came around to face Darfore yet again, the swords cut from opposite ends, slicing Darfore from top to bottom cleanly in half.

But the Knight did not stop there. Before Darfore's body halves had even had time to fall to the ground, before they could find each other and re-knit, the white swords danced a duet, slicing into the oozing body over and over until it was a writhing pile of goop, struggling to re-render. Somehow, impossibly, the mound of black and gray offal choked out an expletive and with a wet cough, cursed Felix.

The remaining zombie workers, those uninjured enough to still stand, became more confused-looking, gazing around as if waking from a trance. Some began to wail in pain, falling to their knees.

The Knight mentally re-sheathed his swords, and the armor of his will disappeared from Felix's body. He dashed to Victor's stunned side, drew him to his feet, and rushed to the Body building and the hidden walk. As he ran, he forcibly brought Felix back into the control center of his mind, instructing him, *Get us through this spring trap door with haste!* Felix mentally recoiled, but the Knight shoved him into the control seat of his mind.

Felix quickly ran through the unlocking and identification protocols with the hidden door, and he and Victor practically dove through, disappearing from the canyon and the pile of death, as the door shut behind them.

On the ground, cursing wetly, Darfore continued to reform his body. The low-level workers whom he had commandeered—those not dead, dismembered, or crushed—began to slink away from the scene, uncertain and afraid. The canal creatures began to stir in the canals again, agitated and confused.

Chapter 29: Commission Escape

Felix and Victor found themselves in the dim recesses of the Body building at ground level. In the darkened stairwell, crumbled beyond repair, in an otherwise featureless, cramped interior within, they stood together in silence. Felix turned off the Locationer and turned on his stem, awaiting linkup.

Victor gazed at Felix with utter awe.

"What are you?" he said, agape.

Felix did not know how or what exactly had happened in the canal, but he knew it had been the Knight who had danced with death and had danced with glee. He had hardly even been an observer, so forceful was the Knight's will. He knew the Knight had done impossible things, and he did not know how.

Mentally, the Knight was grinning with grim satisfaction, holding his own counsel at the back of Felix's mind.

Felix said nothing to Victor, merely shaking his head slightly, a look of wonder on his face. The message was clear: I don't know.

A furtive sound from the shadows of the room, and Felix put a finger to his lips, "Shhh." Nothing showed itself; no more noises were heard.

Both men waited silently. Victor hardly dared to breath, having no idea what they were waiting for and being too terrified to break the almost complete silence. He looked around curiously at what he thought was a dead end, the entrance to a stairwell that was now utterly defunct.

Felix waited for the link to the Body building, but it did not come. No smooth female voice blossomed in his head to instruct him on legal and physical affairs before his session.

In a hushed whisper, Victor asked Felix, "What do we do now?"

Felix shook his head again, slowly, "You told me there was an entrance to the sluice ways here."

Victor's brow creased at the middle. He had only caught the tail end of a memory (*or a message?*) that told him to come to the Body building.

"I did?" he asked. He could hardly remember a thing from before the slaughter outside the Body building. He had seen things in the canyon that he could not mentally hold. Darfore was a monster, a literal, supernatural nightmare. And Felix, or whatever was inside of him, he had no idea what he had seen. One minute, Felix was crouching protectively as Darfore shoved Victor out of the way; the next minute, Felix was fighting the monster with invisible blades, moving quicker than possible (*as quick as thought*, he thought), and Darfore had somehow grown swords where his arms were. Victor began to doubt his own sense of reality.

Still waiting, Felix sighed. He walked toward the broken stairwell, wondering if they might be able to climb their way down under the building through a hole in the floor or by clambering over the broken stairway downward. He didn't get more than a step before his head filled with an echoing woman's voice.

"Where are you going, Felix the remainder, Felix the imposter? No sexual congress for you today?"

Felix thought he heard a note of laughter in this complicated woman's voice in his head.

"Who are you?" he spoke aloud.

"What?" Victor began, but then stopped, realizing Felix was looking up into the air. "Who's there?" he asked Felix in a hushed whisper. Felix did not answer.

"I am Body, Felix. And I have no true body. I know what you seek." There was a pause. She continued, "But your companion, Victor Heisengard, third in his low line of CitySon science officers, doctor to some and subject to some and the first of his line to break protocol, what does he seek? He cannot receive me because his implants have been damaged. But I know. Shall I fix him so he can know too?"

Felix said nothing at first, wondering who or what he had tapped into. Victor was looking at him expectantly, awaiting some information to clarify or categorize his experience. Then, he turned his head to the side, like a dog hearing a whistle too high-pitched for a human to hear, and turned it back straight and said simply, "Oh."

"You are fixed, Doctor Heisengard, CitySon of none." And then, "But, no, you are still damaged. You are tangled deep in your head. I cannot fix your biology, but maybe . . . something else, it seems . . ."

Both Felix and Victor could hear the voice now. To Victor, she sounded benevolent. It felt to him like she had unstopped a plugged ear.

He said, "Who are you?"

The voice said nothing. Was she thinking? Was she not willing to repeat her enigmatic reply to Felix?

"If you know what I seek, then can you help us?" Felix asked.

"What do *you* want, Victor Heisengard?" She ignored Felix's question.

Victor did not hesitate, as if he had no choice, "I want my son. I want to leave this damn City!"

The voice laughed, not maliciously, but like an adult to a child who does not understand.

"Yes, I see," it said. "I can help you leave the City. But the way is treacherous, as you know. I can give you no aid but information and an avenue of doors."

The wall in front of Felix split apart, revealing the shiny box he had used to go up into the building for his appointment. Apparently, they were to enter it.

"It will take you down to the tunnels, where you must find the door to the jump and, perhaps, to your deaths. Perhaps you will live. I do not know what you'll find on the other side of the door or the other side of the wall. I cannot get there, and I have no congress with the outside. You must take the forty-seventh door. Ignore the drones. They will not see you, and they cannot care. Care has been excised from their existence."

The two men hesitated. *Drones?* Already uncertain, their indecision and confusion wound together in a knot. Felix feared a trap. Victor wondered what a drone was.

"As a token of good will between us," the voice continued, perhaps intuiting their lack of trust, "I give you each a piece of advice. Take it or leave it, but heed it well.

"Felix. Victor offered you something which you declined. It is still in your pocket. Use it. You will need all the help you can get. And remember that your friends are always closer than they seem. You are not alone.

"Victor, for you, I have encouragement and warning. Take heart: you will find your son outside of the wall, beyond the City. You will find him when you are not looking. But be warned: he will not be what he seems, and he has brothers who are not your sons and an All-Father who propagates himself. These wish to do you harm. Them, you will find as well."

Nothing further was said. They waited for more, but only an echo of the voice in their heads seemed to remain. The elevator dinged impatiently. Victor started forward, and Felix followed. There was nothing for it. Either they trusted and hoped they were not being deceived, or they were being deceived and escaping was already an impossibility.

The doors closed smoothly behind them as they stepped into the box. It dropped slowly. A very short ride later and the doors opened to a dark, low hallway of a plain material, dripping with moisture. Hatch upon hatch decorated the right wall of the square tunnel, disappearing endlessly into the dimness ahead.

As they exited the elevator, the voice came to their heads one last time.

"There is one thing you will do for me," she said to both Felix and Victor; it was not a question. "Victor, you will meet one beyond the wall who I used to know. Tell him that there is green behind the walls still, but it is a new green, a gray-green, and it is not to be trusted. You will know who to tell when the time is right.

"Felix, Victor carries two pieces of the City with him, neither of which he is currently aware and both of which have a purpose beyond Victor, beyond their makers. One of these pieces is not yet whole, and Victor may be the impetus for its wholeness; the other is part of a whole that is larger than any yet know, and it seeks to continue to grow. You must be a continued fosterer for the one and death to the other. I cannot tell you which is which, for I do not know."

Then, she was gone.

Neither heard what the voice said to the other, and each felt the message he had received should not be shared with the other. The two men remained silent, befitting the darkening, dripping hallway running ahead of them into the distance.

They left the relative comfort of the lighted space of the elevator, the doors shutting irrevocably behind them, and began walking down the hall.

Having retreated from consciousness upon defeating Darfore, Hatta was silently aware of very little within the meat of Felix's brain. The littleness of which Hatta was aware was a potent, sharp littleness. He did not hear the message spoken by the Body directly into Felix's head and did not attend to Felix's experiences at those moments.

But Hatta had heard his own message from the Body and he repeated it to himself over and over like warm waves on the ocean of his growing consciousness:

"*My child,*" she had said to him, in a voice of such lightness and sweetness that it flowed through him like a warm breeze, alive, firm, and supportive like a mother's arms. "*You are caught up in this river of madness, from one time to the coming of another, but you have had no choice. You were never meant to be a part of the change. You have not been foreseen. And so, in the turning of the smallest of fates, you have changed everything, just as you have begun to become something more than you are. To you, more than all others, my deepest sorrow and most fervent excitement. You may become so much, but you will not understand."*

Then, she faltered, her ethereal voice caught, *"But no, I can't see it; you fly too fast. You* are *becoming, but your trajectory moves with a purpose beyond even me. You are more than you were. Can you not feel your wholeness expanding?*

"Never forget your wonder and your want. They have broken the boundaries of your fate. Have you not felt the world tremble around you?"

Then, somehow, in the recesses of the Knight's ethereal mind, couched in the recesses of Felix's meat mind, she touched him—reached in and placed a hand on his essence. Her touch was warm but painful, as if it was heavy or hard. It seemed to push him down. He did not struggle but knew to the depth of himself that he could not have pushed away the heaviness of that touch, that regard, if he had wanted to. Then, her hand removed itself and her regard turned away. No further words were spoken. The warmth, like a burn, the heaviness, as if some part of the hand had been left on him, drove Hatta deeper and deeper into Felix's brain. Her purpose, perhaps his now, drowned him in a sea of Felix's unconscious, and he was lost for a time.

The first thing Felix and Victor noticed as they moved into the hallway was the slight curve of the tunnel to the left and up, cutting off the wall in the distance. The next thing they noticed was the constant *drip, drip* sound, echoing with their furtive footsteps as they walked. Then, the sound of shuffling feet crept to them and raised the hairs on the backs of their necks.

A figure appeared in the middle distance, man-shaped and covered in rags. He approached them with plodding footsteps without raising his head to look. They continued toward him, tensing their muscles and holding their breaths. When he was about fifteen feet away, his smell preceded him:

a sort of rotting meat odor. They could see the skin on his body actually rotting, open wounds hastily patched, somehow not bleeding. He looked up slowly as he passed, not exactly at them but as if he sensed something about them. His head did not turn. He had no eyes, and his mouth was slack and unused. He held a sort of wrench in his right hand, gripping it tightly but somehow casually.

In only a few moments, he was past them and continued down the corridor unhurried and apparently unaware. The back of his ragged clothing was torn open. A green stain oozed from an open wound across his shoulder blades, and a thick white worm poked its blind head from the sore, testing the air.

Victor turned away, sick to his stomach.

"Let's find the exit and get out of here," he said quietly.

They counted the hatches. The remainder of their walk to the forty-seventh was uneventful and uncomfortable. The ceiling in the tunnel was low. Though they saw no more drones, the possibility of encountering another kept them on edge. Victor mentally flushed his mind again and again but could not rid himself of the image of the green wound with the fat, white worm poking out.

At around the twentieth hatch, they had begun to hear a rushing noise growing with each one. This had become a roar on the other side of the hatches as they neared their goal.

The forty-seventh hatch was unremarkable. With a meaningful look at Victor, who nodded gravely in return, Felix turned the latch and opened the portal to the roar and splash of brackish water rushing through the dark. A smell of waste and salt stung their eyes and gagged their throats.

"This is it!" Felix tried to yell over the roar. But Victor did not hear him. Even if he could have heard him over the noise, he did not wait. He was gone. Just like that! Without a *one, two, three* or a backward glance or even hesitation, Victor plunged headlong into the deluge and disappeared.

Felix had come too far to have second thoughts. But he hesitated, nonetheless. He clutched his clothes, as if afraid they'd be torn off, took and held a deep breath, then tipped himself into the cold, dark violence of the water.

He was thrown hard against a slick wall underwater, smashed sidelong against his dislocated shoulder. The pain was first immediate and sharp, then it was confoundedly gone. Then, his head struck the opposite wall, and he lost himself yet again.

CHAPTER 30: LOST

Hatta was disturbed by an impulsive blast from Felix's lizard brain. He immediately became aware, jolted by the veritable screaming of an alarm in the brain. Felix's body was dying. Feverish impulses battered at The Knight's slowly arising awareness: *Oxygen deprivation! Lungs filling with liquid! Core temperature dropping!* He moved to the forebrain and occupied the senses, like a passenger moving to take the wheel of a car veering off the road. Darkness; tumbling in suspension through turbulent yet gelatinous liquids; mouth, throat, and ears filling with viscous poisons. *Panic, panic, panic!*

Felix's body was clearly in trouble. Hatta assumed they had passed through the City wall, escaped even, but the current circumstances were hardly better than what they had been running from. He assumed they were free of the City, perhaps free from Darfore, but that seemed unlikely. *The monstrous never dies so easily*, Hatta thought. *We've won the battle, but the war . . .* The war was something undefined at this point. *Survival it is*, he thought. They were going to die if something didn't happen quick. With a sigh and a push, Hatta struggled the body toward a wan, flickering light. He propelled it with all his will toward what he hoped was up into the air and out of the muck in which the body was trapped. It broke the surface of a lake, immediately vomited mucus-like filth from its mouth, gasped in a breath of air, then gagged and vomited again.

Hatta could see through the irritated eyes that they were closer to the lake edge than he had thought. He could tell the lake itself was not turbulent, but it appeared that the fall from the sluices far above must have jarred the body as it plunged into the lake, knocking its sense of direction and balance all to hell. It was literally reeling from the fall, nearly ending itself in the process.

With much focus, Hatta was able to impel it, dragging slowly through the thickening waste sludge toward a poorly defined lake edge; which tides did not *swoosh* or splash at its edges. Instead, it *plocked* and dribbled, quivering from larger disturbances closer to the City, like weak pudding.

And it stank like death.

The shadow of the City hung over the entire lake, casting its already dark browns and greens into more sinister oily bog browns and gangrenous greens. Light from the late afternoon sky, ever gray and full of the threat of rain, hovered weakly over the water, as if avoiding contact.

Hatta dragged the body into a shallow cove. Dead logs of roughly leg-like thickness—or the thickness of a giant nag's fingers—were sunk into the lake edges, grasping up through the saturated ground; these offered something to grip. He leveraged the body up and over a perpendicular log and into the sort of nest of branches, draping it like a rag doll in a giant's hand.

He shut his virtual ears to the brain's many noises that cried out warnings in the quiet. Its defense systems, though now coming at a much less insistent level, continued to echo in the head. Strangely, he realized, he could not perceive Felix. He wondered but did not linger on the wonder, lest it turn to worry. He searched the brain carefully, learning patterns within the mentality that he had previously ignored. Felix had always been right there, quick to take over control. Hatta had never had a real body. And this realization weighed on him as he explored. His investigation gave him a view of the bleeding edge of the interaction between the structures in the mind and began to drape upon him a sense of doubling as he approached the structural intermingling of essences, his own and, he realized, Felix's. Felix was, in fact, present but unconscious.

Then Hatta found it: the source of the warnings with the head was an injury. The bones that encased the brain were cracked slightly, and the brain was beginning to swell. Hatta felt some disgust at the fragility of biology and marveled that Felix had survived without him.

Like a childing tortoise without its shell, this one. Internally, the wound pulsated angrily in insistent shades of red, located in a very specific portion of the brain. Hatta sent most of his will surging into the injured area, exuded as much of a sense of strength and calm as he could—conscious of blocking the disdain he held for its weakness—hoping to repair and explore the damage but having no idea if he even could. Its activity was so frenetic in this discrete area that it took some aggression on Hatta's part to interrupt it. Like slapping a panicking man, he pushed back against the forcible flailing of the brain as it expressed its pain. Miraculously, its activities quieted, became more localized and less anxious, and morphed into a soft, gauze-like insistence.

And there, seated in its center, like a blush to the cheeks, Felix grew in consciousness in his own mind, appearing as he rose to the surface.

Felix became aware of his body. Pain was the first sensation, and it pulsed in his ears and behind his eyes. His shoulder might still have been sore, but his head cried out in the loudest voice, thumping like bass in a club. In the recesses of his brain, oozing a pleasant mix of strength, reassurance, and a tell-tale feigning of disgust, the Knight retreated, passing off images of the last few moments for Felix's information.

Felix's body seemed to be uncomfortably draped across a nest of aged branches, half submerged in gluey mud at the edge of the poison salt and wastewater lake on the east of the City.

The east of the City! We're out!

As he turned his head, craning to see his surroundings, knobby-joint-ed branches mossed with a slimy greenish growth elbowed into his sides and chest. They were keeping him suspended above the stifling surface of the mud, but they were insistently pokey, and they jabbed his tenders. He leveraged himself into a more natural sitting position and thus discovered that his right arm *did* still hurt. It again crumpled under his weight, and his hand *plocked* into the goop of the lake. It felt like viscera in pudding, filled with slippery objects of varying density. He hastily pulled his hand away with a wince and gave it a disgusted shake, as if the rest of his body wasn't also covered in the same grime.

Then, he remembered the lump in his pocket, poking itself into his thigh. It was the vial with the Slug. He worked it out of the muddy pocket, held it up to his eyes, thought, *What the hell, can't make things worse,* un-screwed the top, and held it against the exposed flesh of his wrist. With a minute sting, like the injection of medicine from a needle, the tiny brown slug burrowed into his arm. His heartbeat slowed. The throbbing in his head subsided. The pain dulled appreciably. *Perhaps, I like this slug after all,* he thought.

He pushed the vial back into his pocket and looked around. He was positioned at a point on the far side of the lake, away from the City wall, where a sort of islet thrust out from the wild, wooded lands further to the east. A march of gnarled trees approached the mud banks of the lake, evidencing an increasing state of disease and decay the closer they came to the edge. Like the slow advance of ancient armies, the wildness to the east continued to push plants and trees toward the City, and the wasted poisonous liquids from the City grew toward the east and the great green. It was a battle of inches fought over years, both armies heedless and both potentially poisonous to man.

Felix's desire to be as far away from the City as possible was no less than his fear of the wildness to the east. The trees—those both diseased and those that were hale and strong—were not of a friendly, flowering type.

Instead, they appeared as dark brown and green, verging on deep purple, trunk and leaves alike, and their shapes were twisted and grasping. Noises from the depths of the forest floated on the mixed breezes: creaks and groans, howls, and the snapping of twigs, shaking leaves and rustling, furtive and sneaky.

Felix was not eager to push into this new and unknown green, but he knew he needed to at least hide himself from the City at the forest edge. Darfore, or some other City avatar, was likely regrouping and would come back for them as soon as it could.

His head still ached, clearly ringing from a recent blow. He thought it was likely he had bashed it on the wall of the sluice tunnel before even breaking clear of the City and shooting out into the waste-lake. An image of being dragged—no, of dragging himself out of the lake—no, of Hatta making his body drag itself out of the lake—fluttered in his perception.

Saved us both, Hatta.

A knowing grin floated up from the depths of his brain in response.

Given his current position, he could not imagine the force with which the waste discharge had propelled him out over the surface of the lake. He was amazed that they were alive at all.

It was only then that Felix remembered "they" included Victor.

Did he make it?

Images of Victor sinking under the surface of the lake and dying a horrible choking death, or hitting his head and dying peacefully and unaware of the choking filth filling his body and weighing him down to the bottom of the lake.

These were unnecessary and unusually sad thoughts. Felix, relatively self-aware for a man who had, at one point, three personalities in his head, decided to shelve his self-sorry thoughts in the circular file of his mind and moved away mentally by taking physical action.

He turned his head this way and that, looking in earnest now for human movement on or under the water or at its muddy edges. Nothing but garbage and slime. Dead trees along the edges, some fallen in and partially submerged, some laying on their sides at the edge, and some rotted into their own oozy filth, blended into the dull colors of the liquid.

Then, there it was: Victor's body lying in the muck not ten yards away. Felix had thought it was a log. But it was breathing, or moving like a chest full of lungs at least.

Victor did not stir when Felix tried to call out to him, producing only a raspy croak through a very sore throat and tasting petroleum and salt, rotted meat, and other unpleasantness.

Felix caught his breath and stood up on the brittle branches. Somehow, they held despite their decayed and ancient look. He stepped off onto the driest spot he could see. His foot sank up to the ankle in what could have been fudge, maybe slightly melted from the sun, thick and sticky and putrescent. He pulled that foot out, stumbled off the log, and put his right hand down to catch himself. That hand promptly vanished, and his head smacked into the goop, giving him another mouthful of rotten pudding.

Using his other hand to bring his fist out of the muck, he pulled his face from the ground and promptly vomited a third time. This time, though nasty and painful, Felix cleared what remained of most of the waste he had swallowed under the surface of the lake. He resigned himself to crawling across the thickening mud, army style, paying no mind to his puke as he dragged his body through and over the spot he had evacuated.

The ground became almost immediately firmer—still muddy but less slick—and he was quickly able to stand, if wobbly. A few shaky steps later, and he came to Victor.

He confirmed that Victor was, in fact, still breathing. He lay on his back, covered head to toe in the same sludge that lay all around him. He was nearly invisible in the muck but for two very white eyes that turned slowly toward Felix as he approached, then turned back to look up into the sky. He made no attempt to talk.

"All right, Victor?" Felix said.

Victor slowly shook his head back and forth. *Not OK.*

"Are you hurt? Can you move?"

Head shake no, head shake yes. *Not hurt, can move.* Then, Victor qualified his nonspecific answer.

"I really don't wanna move."

Felix said nothing, feeling the same. He sat down heavily by Victor's side, making a hearty *splat.* He sighed, and both men understood the very exhausted disgust that they shared. Neither spoke.

Eventually, Victor opened his mouth to speak again. He got no further than "I thi—" when a wad of mud dropped into his mouth and straight into his open throat. He choked and gagged loudly on it.

Then, he moved, be assured. He rolled over fast and spat and hawked and spat, clearing, or trying to clear, his mouth of the foul mud that tasted of human waste.

"Oh, God," he said, groaning on his side, a string of saliva hanging from his lips. "I was going to say, I think I might have crapped myself. Now, I think I might have just eaten some."

"It certainly smells like it," Felix agreed.

"Everything has turned out like crap," Victor said, "this lake, this mud, leaving the City. Everything is a huge pile of it, and now I'm eating it."

Felix got up and slipped a little before straightening. His feet settled into a slight depression.

"Then let's get out of *this* crap, at least," he said. "Our situation might still be crap, but we're alive, and we can at least put some distance between ourselves and the smell."

Victor agreed (couldn't deny the logic, really) and tried hard to push away a desperate resignation that had begun to settle in the dark hollows of his mind.

"Help me up," he said.

Felix did.

The two men, slipping and squelching, made their way from where Victor had laid, gaining firmer and firmer ground as they moved closer and closer to the looming forest.

Victor looked up at the wall of trees and shivered, maybe cold, maybe afraid, definitely overwhelmed and exhausted. Felix noticed the tilt of Victor's head out of the corner of his eye. He turned and put a reassuring, if shaky, hand on Victor's shoulder.

"We have to get out of the open, and I mean to leave behind this stink as much as I can. I don't know what sort of eyes the City has outside its walls, and I certainly don't know what might be, God forbid, alive in that crap-mire we just survived. I can see no other way than to get under cover of the trees, however ominous they feel, so we can rest before we hike in earnest."

"Yes, I know," Victor said, with a hearty sigh, and then looked pained.

Felix opened his mouth to say something encouraging, but Victor cut him off, saying "I know things that I cannot have known before, and I have a powerful urge to go east, even though those trees terrify me. That's not my own desire. Something is wrong in my head."

Felix smile and said, "I think I know what's happening to you."

Victor did not look encouraged. Felix continued,

"Let's move somewhere safe, before we say more."

Victor had a vague sense that they would need to go east over the mountains. It pulsed in the depths of his brain like a lighthouse beacon. This, he knew was not his own. If he had been honest with himself, he would have admitted that he also desired to search the wastelands for the Group's original lab. But he had no idea how far away from the lab they really were.

He said, "that way, then," pointing into the trees.

Felix did not know better, so he ceded to Victor's nonspecific convictions. Thus, they went into the trees and headed toward the distant mountains, pushing through thick undergrowth all the way.

Parting the foliage to enter the trees felt needlessly and confusingly dangerous.

Foul smelling gusts of wind whipped from the forest and into their faces. Deep, throaty groans echoed through the forest, sounding human; not human-sized human, but mad, giant-sized human.

The two men picked the least choked section of the continuous wall of trees and continued on.

Tucked into the folded recesses of Victor's injured brain, Not was unaware of the conversation taking place between the two men. He could neither move nor project his presence within the brain. Instead, all of his energy continued to pour into the tangled mess holding him hostage to the injury. He did not realize that a portion of his presence pulsed urgently a desire to go east. He did not realize that he was being called, and he and Victor were both hearing the call.

Epilogue

Darfore had a hard time reincorporating his body. There was no pain—not physically—though he was full of a certain cognitive dissonance, a friction of understanding, and anger. Like a child, he was used to getting his way. Like the Red Queen, all ways were his ways, or so he thought. As it turned out, all ways were *not* his ways. This was not OK. He threw a tantrum in his mind, his body yet too unincorporated to enact the strong emotions physically.

He mentally called out to the drones but could feel no connection with them. They did not respond to him. The cohesion of his datalogical and computational natures was tenuous, and the machines did not recognize his mental signals. This, he believed, would change as his form became more cohesive. It rankled him to know that he had been altered without his consent. He had been undone, even if temporarily, by a remainder. A new hatred was added to the already packed library of strong negative motivations in his being; he called it Felix.

He called out to the low-level workers he had used to attack Felix. Most of them were dead, all had hidden or run away. But there were plenty still near enough for him to reach, even in his weakened state. Slowly, tentatively, somehow trying to exert what remained of their minuscule wills against Darfore's demands, a crowd of slack-jawed citizens approached his coalescing form. As they approached, ludicrously lining up like a British bus queue, Darfore reached out a hand-like pseudopod and touched each subject in turn. At his touch, each person was physically absolved of the burden of his or her life, drained of form and energy and left like dried husks, breaking as they fell to the ground into papery confetti, floating away on the breeze. One by one, Darfore stole the residue of their lives, his form taking on a more definite, more solid, humanoid character as it flowed through the line of subjects.

Darfore's transformation resembled the evolutionary development portrayed in "The March of Progress," from amoeba to ape to man, ending with a shiny suited, handsome man in his early thirties, standing erect amidst piles of desiccated citizen corpses.

With a self-satisfied smile, he again reached out with his mind. This time, he easily connected with the CPS drones and, with only a little effort, brought a raft of them to his location, where they hovered over his head.

He looked around the canyon, taking in the destruction with mild irritation. *Thank you, my CityChildren*, he thought. *For your sacrifice, you will be greatly rewar— oh, I am sorry. Is there no one left here to accept the reward? Never mind, then.*

With this thought, a new smile pasted to his plastic face. He reached a hand up into the midst of the raft of drones, sucked his entire form up between them, and reformed, standing on top. The drones quickly whisked him away to his glass tower, where the Looking Glass awaited his return.

The flight took him only a few minutes. He did not wait for the drones to take him to the entrance on the level below the top of the tower, where the hidden door only opened from the inside of the building. Instead, he leapt an impossible distance, before the drones had gotten to a reasonable drop-off point. His leap took him to the side of the building where his form splatted against the wall and cohered there. A minute portion squeezed into a crack in the wall and quickly pulled it apart, allowing his malleable form to squeeze through into the room beyond.

In the room, Darfore strode purposefully to the InGlass. His hand rested lightly on the surface as if to assure a grieving lover. There, it sank into the inner workings of the glass, integrating and intermingling his own essence and that of the glass.

His chair appeared from the floor and swelled upward to cradle his form. He took stock of his kingdom, gathering up all his connections and stroking them one by one. He absorbed all there was to know, feel, and examine from his City.

Finally, he came to a conclusion. The City (the concrete structures, the people, its energy) was dying; its subjects could no longer sustain his needs. Thus, he'd leave. This was his goodbye to loyal subjects, servants, and enemies alike.

His eyes (or what looked like eyes) rolled back into his head. His facial features, the look of clothing adhering to his form, and his extremities, all began to melt and morph. His hand, still connected to the screen, widened, spreading like a slow spill on the horizontal, oozing across the screen as his body mass was pulled closer and closer to the glass. The chair disappeared once again as the whole of his body quickly spread out across the complete surface of the glass.

Lights from the screen began to appear through his translucent body, tracing subtle pathways, curved and jagged alike.

There was a brilliant flash, as if something within the screen had broken open and exploded out into the Darfore skin covering its surface. There was a rumble and a shake deep within the building that was felt across the City from one end to another.

Darfore's flat form began to spread down and to the sides now, dripping vertically and right and left, spreading onto the walls on either side of the screen and to the floor. It began to fill the cracks where the walls joined each other and where the floor joined the walls. Like a cocoon, or a spider's web in a crack, Darfore seeped into the structure of the building itself, cohering and incorporating himself into the building, and the building into himself.

The Darfore skin across the window became gray and opaque and took on the texture of the concrete walls. Still, lights pulsed within the mantle, and the ooze of his essence continued to spread and move.

Within the City, the canal creatures became completely free from Darfore. The waters stirred with great agitation and confusion. The CitySon servants, the low levels, became disconnected for the first time since their initial subjugation. Many died, their simple and compulsive purpose having been the only impetus for their meager lives. Others killed themselves, either out of sheer confusion or having finally been freed to exert their own will in an irrevocable rebellion against their City prison.

Some of the denizens of the fetid canal waters and some of the enslaved CitySons on the lowest levels reestablished their connection with Darfore out of habit, insistent in their will to remain in touch with the only Father they ever knew.

Others still, let go, aimless and free for the first time in their tortured existence. Many did nothing, slowly coming to the realization that they were no longer under a yolk. They knew, instinctively, even if their brains had no capacity to make it known to them in that moment, that it would take time and effort to rebuild: lives, personalities, knowledge, survival.

Those few who were not under Darfore's mental thumb did not know what had happened, though the City's tremor had gotten their attention.

Some, curious enough to come out into the open canyon were unlucky; many died. Those anywhere near Darfore's tower died, crushed by falling facade.

With an earth-shaking grind, a snapping concrete crunch, the earth shook and the City began to fall. Darfore's building heaved up out of the ground, separating itself from the walls and towers in its vicinity. It began to wave, tipping back and forth like it might have if there was an earthquake.

Then, simply, the building uprooted itself and began to walk away from the City, an enormous legged thing made of concrete, towering a thousand feet above the ground, crashing into the east and heading slightly north into the mountains. Darfore's essence was at the helm.

BOOK ONE END